D1431442

The Giants' Dance

Ane radhas a'leguim oicheamna;
ainsagimn deo teuiccimn

Also by Robert Carter

The Language of Stones

THE
GIANTS'
DANCE

BOOK TWO OF THE LANGUAGE OF STONES

ROBERT CARTER

HarperCollins*Publishers*

The names, characters and incidents portrayed in it are
the work of the author's imagination. Any resemblance to
actual persons, living or dead, events or localities is
entirely coincidental.

HarperCollins*Publishers*
77–85 Fulham Palace Road,
Hammersmith, London W6 8JB

www.harpercollins.co.uk

Published by HarperCollins*Publishers* 2005
1

A catalogue record for this book
is available from the British Library

ISBN 0 00 716924 8

Typeset in Plantin Light by Palimpsest Book Production Limited,
Polmont, Stirlingshire

Printed and bound in Great Britain by
Clays Limited, St Ives plc

For Gerald Wiley

CONTENTS

(N.B. In the novels of the 'Stones' cycle there is never a chapter thirteen.)

'First there were nine,
Then nine became seven,
And seven became five.
Now, as sure as the Ages decline,
Three are no more,
But one is alive.'

The Black Book of Tara

PROLOGUE

THE STORY SO FAR

*T*he *Giants' Dance* is the second book in the Language of Stones cycle. The first book, called *The Language of Stones*, recounted the story of Willand, a boy whose life was changed forever when the wizard, Gwydion, arrived at the village of Nether Norton in the Vale.

Gwydion, it is revealed, brought Will to the Vale when he was a baby, and has returned to reclaim him on his thirteenth birthday. Before Will leaves, Breona, the woman Will has always thought of as his mother, hangs about his neck a talisman of green stone which is carved in the likeness of a leaping salmon. She tells him how she found it inside his blanket when he first came into her arms, and says that it should go with him now he is entering the wide world.

No one from Nether Norton has ever been out of the Vale, and the wide world seems terrifying to Will. Gwydion explains that he must leave the Vale for his own good. Twice he tries to run away and go home, but each time he is prevented by Gwydion's magic, and eventually the wizard tells him they are being hunted by a fearsome enemy. At first, Will imagines it must be the Sightless Ones, the sinister fellowship of tax collectors who both squeeze the common people and engage in crooked politics with the lords of the Realm, but it soon becomes clear that a far more formidable foe is looking for them. Gwydion will drop only vague hints about this, but he says that Will is a 'Child of Destiny' – one whose coming has been foretold in the Black Book.

Soon they arrive at a gloomy tower in the depths of the Wychwoode, and there Will is lodged with the grotesque Lord Strange, a man who is afflicted by a vile spell and who wears the head of a boar. Gwydion leaves Will to live in the tower all summer long, and there he is taught to read and write. He also learns from the local Wise Woman something of the 'redes of magic' – these are curious rules that reveal the wisdom of the world and enable magic to be done. But Will's spirit rebels against Lord Strange. He secretly looks in a forbidden book and reads certain spells, which he then uses for the unworthy purpose of trying to impress a pretty girl. What he attracts instead is the marish hag, a dangerous supernatural creature that inhabits the ancient wood. He is almost drowned by the hag, and only saved by Gwydion's return.

But Will has also gained friends in the Wychwoode, among them the mysterious Green Man to whom he renders an unwitting service, and the girl, Willow, with whom he discovers Grendon Mill. This, it turns out, is Lord Strange's secret armoury, where men have cut down the great oaks of a sacred grove to roast into charcoal so that weapons of war may be forged.

When Gwydion returns, he shows his great displeasure at Lord Strange's activities. In turn, the hog-headed lord blames King Hal whose preparations for war are being fed by the mill. The wizard then leaves angrily, taking Will with him.

As they travel south Will is asked if he knows about King Arthur. He says he knows about him from old tales. Gwydion tells him that the tales about the sword in the stone speak about an Arthur who became king a thousand years ago, but that he was only the second incarnation of an original Arthur. That Arthur was an adventurer who lived in the time of the First Men in the far distant past, and travelled from the land of Albion into the Realm Below to bring out sacred objects known as 'the Hallows'. Moreover, there is a prophetic verse that speaks of a third and final incarnation of Arthur . . .

Will begins to feel uncomfortable because it seems that the wizard is convinced that Will himself is that third incarnation.

Unfortunately, the prophecy is confirmed at every turn. At Uff, Will recognizes the White Horse, and stands upon the Dragon's Mound where he experiences a vision of an army massing below. The earth yields up the gift of a horn to him, and in Severed Neck Woods Will is given the freedom of the wild-wood by the Green Man himself.

They come at last to the royal hunting lodge of Clarendon, where Gwydion warns the weakling monarch, and asks for aid in a vital magical mission that will prevent the Realm from sliding into war. But the royal court is already deeply under the influ-ence of the beautiful but greedy queen and her violent ally, Duke Edgar of Mells.

The queen is pregnant, and it seems to Will that Duke Edgar is the father. Will also suspects that the gentle king has been poisoned by them. And he notices a sinister figure lurking nearby, invisible to everyone but Will and the queen. Only later does he learn that this is the sorcerer, Maskull, Gwydion's arch-enemy, who, among other things, is trying to find Will and kill him. Fortunately, Maskull does not realize Will is present, but even so events are about to take a turn for the worse. Gwydion's request for royal aid is refused, and he is attacked by Duke Edgar, and forced to employ a powerful vanishing spell, which is accom-plished only just in the nick of time.

Where Will and Gwydion vanish to is a sacred place, even by the standards of the Blessed Isle. They appear on cliff tops high above the sea, standing on the westernmost point of land in the whole world. Here Gwydion renews his strength and explains to Will about 'the lorc'. This is a network of powerful earth streams that extend throughout the Isles. Long ago, he says, an array of standing stones was set up on these streams of power by an ancient race, the fae, who lived at the time of the First Men, but who long ago retired into the Realm Below. Each stone is filled with an immense quantity of harm.

According to the Black Book, these 'battlestones' were disposed across the Isles with the intention of repelling invasions. The fae believed that despotic sorcerers would one day arise in the Tortured Lands and begin to enslave men's minds with a powerful idea called the Great Lie. In time the Isles themselves would face conquest, and their people, the First Men, would be enslaved – unless the lorc was erected as a defence. After much debate, the battlestones were wrought and put in place, and the secrets of the lorc bequeathed to the First Men when the fae withdrew.

For many centuries, the Isles remained free from interference. The Age of Trees passed into a second, lesser Age. Then the First Men failed, and the Isles became the haunt of giants and fire-breathing wyrms. When a third Age dawned, the Age of Iron, the hero-king, Brea arose and set foot upon the shores of Albion. He vanquished the giants and proclaimed the Realm, settling the land once again. After that the Realm went unmolested for eighty and more generations, until the time when, as the fae had foreseen, the Slavers' power burgeoned in the east. By the time of King Caswalan, the sorcerers of the Tortured Lands had spread the Great Lie far and wide. They commanded huge armies, and made no secret of their desire to conquer the Isles. Their first coming, a thousand years after the landing of Brea, was repulsed. But soon afterwards the secret of the lorc was betrayed and its protective power undermined. The invading Slavers were then able to block the vital flows of earth power by building in stone. They shattered the Realm into many shards with their slave roads, and so the lorc was broken. But by Will's time the slave roads are more than a thousand years old. Many have begun to fall into ruin, and the lorc, so long inactive, has begun to awaken . . .

Gwydion tells Will that he urgently needs to find and uproot the battlestones or there will be a bloodbath. Each stone will mark a place of great slaughter, and the ensuing chaos will enable Maskull to gain control of the mechanisms of fate. If Maskull is allowed to steer the Realm it will slide towards a devastating future – a future wholly without magic, and one in which strife and terror will reign for five hundred years.

Will and the wizard sail back from the Blessed Isle, and soon afterwards encounter a skeleton inside a yew tree. It is the remains of a lad Will's age (and with a similar name) who has recently gone missing. He has been magically murdered. It is grisly evidence that Will is still being sought by Maskull. It cannot be long before he realizes that the wizard's young bag-carrier is his quarry, and so Gwydion decides that Will must once more be lodged in a place of comparative safety.

Meanwhile, Gwydion makes absolutely sure that Will is Arthur's third incarnation, by stirring up his latent magical talents and teaching him to 'scry'. And so, using Will's partly-fledged abilities and the wizard's command of ancient lore they manage to locate their first battlestone, the Dragon Stone. As they dig it up, Will experiences for the first time the frightening mental disturbances caused when such stones are threatened, but eventually Gwydion wraps it in binding spells and they take it to a place where Gwydion thinks it may be temporarily stored.

Once at Castle Foderingham, the stone is carefully mortared into a dungeon under the keep – Gwydion hopes it will remain dormant there while he searches for further fragments of the Black Book in order to discover how to drain the stone of its harm. But the owner of Castle Foderingham is Duke Richard who, with some justice, considers himself to be the rightful king of the Realm. He has just discovered that his claim to the throne has been fatally weakened because the queen has at last given birth to a son. He is also already aware that the boy is not the king's child, but fathered by Duke Edgar, who happens to be Richard's political rival. Richard must do something about this, and soon. And Gwydion realizes that he must accompany Duke Richard on his urgent mission to the great city of Trinovant, or affairs will certainly take a turn for the worse. Thus, Will is abandoned once more. Now he must live with the duke's family and the captive battlestone. He is told that *under no circumstances* must the Dragon Stone be interfered with.

As the weeks become months at Castle Foderingham, Will turns from boy to man. He begins to learn lordly ways alongside Duke Richard's sons. But while he learns how to ride and hunt and fight as they do, he also starts to understand more about his own developing magical talents. He is befriended by the old herbalist, Wortmaster Gort, and battles with the duke's fierce heir, Edward. One night, despite Will's warnings, Edward acquires a set of keys and leads his many brothers and sisters down to visit the Dragon Stone. There, though they do not understand it at the time, they are stricken by the stone, and none more so than Edward's brother, Edmund.

Life at Foderingham settles down again, but soon a wagon train of new weapons bound for the king's armoury is captured by Duke Richard's men, and Will is unexpectedly reunited with Willow, the girl he met in the Wychwoode. As vassals of Lord Strange, she and her father had been set to drive one of the ox-wagons from Grendon Mill to Trinovant, but they were intercepted by one of Duke Richard's allies. When Will sees how scared they are of returning home to face Lord Strange's wrath, he begs the duchess that they be attached to Duke Richard's household, and she agrees.

Willow says that Will is turning into a young lord. Will thinks there might be more to Willow's unlikely arrival than meets the eye – perhaps the Dragon Stone is warping the fate of everyone around it, as Gwydion has hinted it may do. Perhaps they are all riding for a fall.

As winter closes in, the news from Trinovant is sketchy, but Will learns that Gwydion's patient diplomacy has so far failed to settle peace upon the factions. Despite having extracted the Dragon Stone the influence of the reawakening array of battle-stones continues to increase. The harm contained within them begins to corrupt the political atmosphere. Greed, vengeance and malice begin to get the better of the spirit of compromise within the opposing parties, and the Realm slips ever closer to war.

Will's fears grow when Duke Richard gathers his armies and moves his household to Ludford. This is a great castle, deep in the hills of the west. As soon as he arrives, Will's sensitivity to the stones' influence begins to grow beyond his control. A bout of suspicion overtakes him. He feels that Edward is becoming his rival for Willow's affections, and so acute does his jealousy become that he begins to fear for his sanity. When Gwydion appears Will says he believes the duke has fetched the Dragon Stone to Ludford and is trying to use it to his own advantage. Gwydion settles his fears and then gives Will a choice: he can either stay at Ludford and fight with Edward for Willow's favour, or he can venture out upon the land as Gwydion now must, and help in the tracking down of the other battlestones – and especially the crucial Doomstone, which appears to control the others. Will reluctantly chooses to follow the wizard, and Gwydion says that this brave decision is yet another proof that he is indeed the Child of Destiny that was foretold.

Gwydion now explains Maskull's intentions. The two magicians are the last remaining members of an ancient wizardly council of nine whose task it was to direct the progress of the world along the true path. As Age succeeded Age their numbers have shrunk, until there are now only two, but one of the nine was always destined to become 'the Betrayer'. When three wizards remained there was still room for doubt, but as soon as the phantarch, Semias, failed it became clear that Gwydion's long-held suspicions about Maskull must have been right. Maskull has now thrown aside all pretences of guardianship and is working openly upon a plan of immense selfishness. As a sorcerer – one who misuses magic to his own benefit – he is seeking to direct the future along a path of his own choosing. It is one that will concentrate power in his own hands, but will also entail a new Age of Slavery and War far more dreadful than any that has gone before.

Maskull must be defeated, but the battlestones are the immediate problem. Fortunately, they can be made to reveal verses that predict events and describe in maddening riddles where the next stone in the sequence lies. Will manages to track down two more battlestones, and though neither of them is the Doomstone, they seem to be making progress at last.

But Maskull lays a clever trap at the stone circle known as the Giant's Ring. Will is caught, and Gwydion is lured in to save him. Wizard and sorcerer fight and the wizard is defeated. His body is burned and his spirit banished into an elder tree. But he is saved by Will who braves his fears to restore his mentor to human form. Gwydion then sets to work on the perilous task of draining the nearby battlestone.

After several quantities of harm have been drained from it a verse is forced from the stone:

> *The Queen of the East shall spill Blood,*
> *On the Slave Road, by Werlame's Flood.*
> *The King, in his Kingdom, a Martyr shall lie,*
> *And never shall gain the Victory.*

which, in the language of stones, has an alternative reading:

> *When a Queen shall Enslave a King,*
> *Travel at Sunrise a Realm to gain,*
> *Werlame's Martyr shall lose the Victory,*
> *And lie where Blood never Flows.*

Gwydion is elated, but as soon as he has read the verse disaster strikes. An entrapping spell that Maskull has set on the stone causes the remaining harm to escape all in a rush. Will and the wizard must flee through the night on the back of the White Horse of Uff which Will summons using the magical silver-bound horn that was given to him one Lammas night. They are pursued through the darkness by the manifest harm that has emerged from the battlestone. It almost catches them, but is then forced to fight with the earth giant, Alba, whom it devours. The harm is dispersed at last by Will as the red light of dawn glints from his raised sword above the forgotten battlefield of Badon Hill.

They turn again to face two great armies marching, ready to give battle in the east. The shrine town of Verlamion is dominated by the great chapter house of the Fellowship of the Sightless Ones, and it is here that the Doomstone lies. Gwydion tries once again to avert disaster. He uses all his persuasion on Duke Richard, but the Doomstone has too strong a grip on the minds of those who have been drawn here to fight.

The duke's army closes on Verlamion, which is strongly garrisoned by King Hal. As the two hosts come together, thousands of men clash in a terrifying death-struggle. Showers of deadly arrows darken the skies, and as soldier battles soldier in the market square, wizard battles sorcerer in a flame-fight that blasts across the rooftops in a blaze of fiery magic and counter magic.

Will is trapped among the savagery and bloodshed below. He knows he must reach the Doomstone and try to stop the battle, but the stone is somewhere inside the chapter house. Will claims the 'sanctuary of the Fellowship' and so gains entry. He fights his way through hundreds of blind, kneeling, enraptured Fellows before he locates the deadly stone under the Founder's shrine. The power of the Doomstone is very strong, but Will remembers everything that Gwydion has taught him. He digs deep and finds the courage to do what he must – go down into the tomb to attack the battlestone directly.

As his spells are spoken out, the Doomstone fights back, but Will hangs on grimly. Appalling visions are cast into his mind, and it is only when he uses the leaping salmon talisman which Breona gave him that the stone submits. There is a blinding flash, and when the smoke clears he sees that the monstrous slab has been cracked in two!

Will emerges from the tomb, his head ringing. Outside, the roar of battle has ceased, brother has stopped killing brother, and war seems to have been averted. But there has been bloodshed – Duke Edgar, Baron Clifton and several of the other corrupt lords who have been controlling the king now lie dead. Others, including Queen Mag, have fled. As for Maskull, Will finds him atop the fire-blackened curfew tower where he has been conducting his own magical duel against Gwydion. When Will confronts him, Maskull recognizes him as the Child of Destiny, and prepares to kill him, saying, 'I made you, I can just as easily unmake you.' But as Maskull readies the killing stroke he is vanished away by a spell that Gwydion manages to land on him while his back is turned.

Now the battle is truly over. The king and Duke Richard jointly announce that they will ride to Trinovant together and put in place the foundations of good government.

Will is rewarded and says he wants nothing more than to return to his home village of Nether Norton with Willow, whose father has been killed in the fighting.

As they part, Gwydion gives Will a magic book, and bids him read from it often.

Will and Willow arrive home to general delight. Will tells his friends in the Vale that the king has freed them from the tithe and so they will never again have to hand over their livestock and grain to the sinister Sightless Ones. Then Will is reunited with his happy parents – after all they have not lost a son but gained a daughter – even so, there is a sense that things are not over quite yet.

★   ★   ★

The Giants' Dance

More than four years have now passed since the fighting at Verlamion. We meet Will and Willow again in Nether Norton in the Vale at the Lammastide festival. It is the time of the first fruits and of harvest blessing and the joining of man and woman . . .

PART ONE

JEOPARDY'S DILEMMA

▫ ▫ ▫

CHAPTER ONE

THE BLAZING

Flames leapt up from the fire, throwing long shadows across the green and dappling the cottages of Nether Norton with a mellow light. This year's Blazing was a fine one. Tonight was what the wizard, Gwydion, called in the true tongue 'Lughnasad', the feast of Lugh, Lord of Light, the first day of autumn, when the first-cut sheaves of wheat were gathered in to the village and threshed with great ceremony. On Loaf Day, grain was ground, and loaves of Lammas bread toasted on long forks and eaten with fresh butter. On Loaf Day, Valesfolk thought of the good earth and what it gave them.

Today the weather had almost been as good as Lammas two years ago when Will had taken Willow's hand and they had circled the fire together three times sunwise, and so given notice that henceforth they were to be regarded as husband and wife.

He put his arm around Willow's shoulders as she cradled their sleeping daughter in her arms. It was a delight to see Bethe's small head nestled in the crook of her mother's elbow, her small hand resting on the blanket that covered her, and despite the dullness in the pit of his stomach, it felt good to be a husband and a father tonight. Life's good here, he thought, so good it's hard to see how it could be much better. If only that dull feeling would go away, tonight would be just about perfect.

But it would not go away – he knew that something was going to happen, that it was going to happen soon, and that it was not going to be anything pleasant. The foreboding had echoed in the marrow of his bones all day but, unlike a real echo, it had refused to die away. Which meant that it was a warning.

He brushed back the two thick braids of hair that hung at his left cheek and stared into the depths of the bonfire. Slowly he let his thoughts drift away from Nether Norton and slip into the fire-pictures that the flames made for him. He opened his mind and a dozen memories rushed upon him, memories of great days, terrible days, and worse nights. But the most insistent image was still of the moment when the sorcerer, Maskull, had raised him up in a blaze of fire above the stone circle called the Giant's Ring. That night he had seen Gwydion blasted by Maskull's magic, and afterwards, as Gwydion had tried to drain the harm from a battlestone, the future of the Realm had balanced on the edge of a knife . . .

It had been more than four years ago, but the dread he had felt on that night and the redeeming day that had followed remained alive in him. It always would.

'Will?' Willow asked, searching his face. 'What are you thinking?'

He broached a smile. 'Maybe I've taken a little too much to drink,' he said and touched his wife's hair. It was gold in the firelight and about as long as his own. He looked at her, then down at the child whose small hand had first clasped his finger just over a year ago. How she had begun to look like her mother.

'Ah, but she's a beautiful child!' said old Baldgood the Brewster, his red face glowing from the day's sunshine. He had begun to clear up and was carrying one end of a table back into the parlour of the Green Man. The other end of the table was carried by Baldram, one of Baldgood's grown sons.

'Seems like Bethe was born only yesterday,' Will told the older man.

'She'll be a year and a quarter old tomorrow, won't you, my lovely?' Willow said dreamily.

'Aye, and she'll be grown up before you can say "Jack o' Lantern". Look at this big lumpkin of mine! Get a move on, Baldram my son, or we'll be out here all night!'

'My, but he's a bossy old dad, ain't he?' Baldram said, grinning.

Will smiled back at the alehouse-keeper's son as they disappeared into the Green Man. It was hard to imagine Baldram as a babe-in-arms – nowadays he could carry a barrel of ale under each arm all the way down to Pannage and still not break into a sweat.

'Hey-ho, Will,' one of the lads from Overmast said as he went by.

'Hathra. How goes it?'

'Very well. The hay's in from Suckener's Field and all's ready for the morrow. Did you settle with Gunwold for them weaners?'

'He offered me a dozen chickens each, but I beat him down to ten in the end. Seemed fairer.'

Hathra laughed. 'Quite right, too!'

'Show us a magic trick, Willand!' one of the youngsters cried. It was Leomar, Leoftan the Smith's boy, with three of his friends. He had eyes of piercing blue like his father and just as direct a manner.

Will asked for the ring from Leomar's finger, but when the boy looked for it, it was not there. Then Will took a plum from the pouch at his own belt and offered it.

'Go on. Bite into it. But be careful of the stone.'

The boy did as he was told and found his ring tight around the plumstone. He gasped. His friends wrinkled their noses and then laughed uncertainly.

'How'dya do that?' they asked.

'It's magic.'

'No t'aint. It's just conjuring!'

'Away with you, now, and enjoy the Blazing!' he said, ruffling the lad's hair. 'And you're right – that was only conjuring. Real magic is not to be trifled with!'

Two more passers-by nodded their heads at Will, and he nodded back. The Vale was a place where everybody knew everybody else, and all were glad of that. Nobody from the outside ever came in, and nobody from the inside ever went out. Months and years passed by without anything out of the ordinary happening, and that was how everybody liked it. Everybody except Will.

Though the Valesmen did not know it, it was Gwydion who had made their lives run so quietly. Long ago he had cast a spell of concealment so that those passing by the Vale could not find it – and those living inside would never want to leave. The wizard had made it so that any man who wandered the path down from Nether Norton towards Great Norton would only get as far as Middle Norton before he found himself walking back into Nether Norton again. Only Tilwin the Tinker, knife-grinder and seller of necessaries, had ever come into the Vale from outside, but now even his visits had stopped. Apart from Tilwin, only the Sightless Ones, the 'red hands', with their withered eyes and love of gold, had ever had the knack of seeing through the cloak. But the Fellows were only interested in payment, and so long as the tithe carts were sent down to Middle Norton for collection they had always let the Valesmen be. Four years ago, Will's service to King Hal in ending the battle at Verlamion had won him a secret royal warrant that paid Nether Norton's tithe out of the king's own coffers, so now the Vale was truly cut off.

And I'm the reason Gwydion's kept us all hidden, Will thought uncomfortably as he stared again into the depths of the fire. He must believe the danger's not yet fully passed. But with Maskull sent into exile and the Doomstone broken, is there still a need to hide us away?

Maskull's defeat had given Gwydion the upper hand, but he had shown scant joy at his victory. He and Maskull had once been part of the Ogdoad, the council of nine earth guardians whose job it had been to steer the fate of the world along the true path. But then Maskull had given himself over to selfishness, and though a great betrayal had been prophesied all along, that had not made it any easier for Gwydion to accept.

Will sighed, roused himself from his thoughts and looked around at the familiar surroundings. It was strange – in all his months of wandering he had thought there was nothing better than home. And now he had a family of his own there was even more reason to love the way life was in the Vale. And yet . . . when a man had extraordinary adventures they changed him . . .

It's easy for a man to go to war, he thought. But having seen it, can he so easily settle down behind a plough once more?

It hardly seemed so. Occasionally, a yearning would steal over Will's heart. At such times he would go alone into the woods and practise with his quarterstaff until his body shone with sweat and his muscles ached. There was wanderlust in him, and at the root of it was a mess of unanswered questions.

He stirred himself and kissed Willow on the cheek. 'Happy Lammas,' he said.

'And a happy Lammas to you too,' she said and kissed him back. 'I guess we're just about finished with the Blazing. Looks like everyone's had a good time.'

'As usual.'

'What about you?'

'Me?' he asked, his eyebrows lifting. 'I enjoyed it.'

'It looks like you did,' she said, a strange little half-smile on her lips.

'And what's that supposed to mean?'

She fingered the manly braid that hung beside his ear. 'I saw you looking into the bonfire just then. What were you thinking?'

'I was thinking that only a fool would want to be anywhere else today.'

She smiled. 'Truly?'

'Truly.'

It *was* good to see everyone so happy. They had watched the lads and lasses circling the fire. They had listened to the vows that had brought the night's celebration to a fitting close. Some had plighted their troths, and others had made final handfasting vows. Now couples were slipping off into the shadows, heading for home.

There was no doubt about it, since the ending of the tithe the Vale had prospered as never before. They had put up three new cottages in the summer. They had filled the new granary too, and all this from the working of less land. Now the surpluses were not being taken away to make others rich, the plenty was such that Valesmen's families had already forgotten what it was to feel the pinch of hunger.

'About time this little one was abed,' Willow said.

'Yes, it's been a long day.'

They walked up the dark path to their cottage, his arm about her in the warm, calm night. In the paddock, Avon, the white warhorse that Duke Richard of Ebor had given him, moved like a ghost in the darkness. Away from the fire the stars glittered brightly – Brigita's star, sinking now in the west; Arondiel rising in the east; and to the south Iolirn Fireunha, the Golden Eagle.

An owl called. Will remembered the Lammastide he had spent six years ago sitting with a wizard atop Dumhacan Nadir, the Dragon's Mound, close by the turf-cut figure of an ancient white horse. Together they had watched a thousand stars and a hundred bonfires dying red across the Plains of Barklea.

He sighed again.

'What's that for?' Willow asked.

He scrubbed fingers through his hair. 'Oh . . . I was just thinking. You know – about old times. About Gwydion.'

It seemed a long time since Will and the wizard had last set eyes on one another. How good it would be to wander the ways as they had once done. To walk abroad again among summer hedgerows, enjoying the sun and the rain, or feeling the bite of an icy wind on their cheeks.

'I wonder what he's doing right now?' Will muttered.

'Unless I miss my guess, he'll be striding the green hills of the Blessed Isle,' Willow said. 'Or sitting in a high tower somewhere out in the wilds of Albanay.'

Will's eyes wandered the dark gulfs between the stars. 'Hmmm. Probably.'

'Wilds?' he could almost hear Gwydion chuckle. 'It is not wild here. See! These trees in a line show where a hedge once grew. And what of those ancient furrow marks? The Realm has been loved and tended for a hundred generations of men. It is almost, you might say, a garden.'

While Willow went indoors to put Bethe into her cradle, Will lingered in the yard at the back of their cottage. He could smell the herbs, all the green leaf he had grown in the good soil – plants ripe and ready to offer the sweetness of the earth's bounty. The scents of the orchard were keen on the still air. He heard Avon whinny again, and tried to recall when he had noticed the elusive feeling in his belly before, but when he looked inside himself he was shocked.

'A premonition about a premonition,' he told himself wryly. 'Now that would be something . . .'

Willow came out and said, 'I'm glad we chose to call her Bethe. There's strong magic in naming, for I can't think now what else we could have called her.'

'Bethe is the birch tree,' he said. '"Beth", first letter of the druid's alphabet, and Bethe our firstborn.'

'I like that.'

'You know, the birch was the first tree to clothe these isles when the ice drew back into the north. Her white bark remembers the White Lady, she who was wise and first taught about births and beginnings, the one who some call the Lady Cerridwen. Our May Pole is always a birch, and Bethe was born on May Day, which is my birthday too. In the old tongue of the west "bith" means "being". And "beitharn" in the true tongue means "the world". Maybe that's the reason I suggested the name and why you agreed – because our daughter means the world to us.'

Willow squeezed him close and laid her head against his breast. 'There's such a power of learning in that book of yours.'

She meant the magic book that Gwydion had given him that sad day at Verlamion. He said, 'There's much to read and more to know. It's said that a country swain comes of age at thirteen years, that the son of a fighting lord may carry arms in battle at fifteen, and that a king must reach eighteen years to rule by his word alone – but one who would learn magic may not be properly called wise until he has come to full manhood.'

Willow looked at him. 'And how old's that?'

He shook his head. 'I don't know. But as the saying has it: "The willow wand is slow to become an oaken staff." And so it must be, for if I know anything at all it's that there's much more to be understood in the world than can ever be learned in one man's lifetime.'

Now it was Willow's turn to sigh. 'Then tell me true: do you read that book every day in the hope that one day you'll become a wizard too? Like Gwydion?'

He laughed. 'No. That I can never be.'

'Then why?'

'Because Gwydion gave it to me and bade me read it. And I gave him my word that I would.'

She squeezed him again, but this time it was to stress her words. 'Well, now, you're going to promise me something, Willand Bookreader: that you won't be burning any candle stubs over hard words tonight!'

He grinned. 'Now *that* I'll gladly promise!'

They held one another in the starlight for a moment. A shooting star flared brilliantly and briefly in the west, and then a coolness stirred among the leaves of the nearest apple trees. She looked up, and he felt her stiffen.

'What is it?'

But there was no need for an answer, for there, high up over the Tops, an eerie purple glow had begun to bruise the sky.

'Don't look at it,' she told him, turning away suddenly.

He felt his foreboding intensify. 'It's . . . it's only the northern lights.'

'I don't care what it is . . .' Her voice faded.

He stared at the flickering as it grew. 'Gwydion once told me about the northern lights,' he whispered, 'but I've never seen them.'

As he looked into the darkness he felt the earth power crackling in his toes. The apple trees felt it too. His eyes narrowed as he realized that this flaring glow was not – could not be – the northern lights. This was brighter, more focused, and it spoke to him.

'Will, come inside!' she said, pulling at his arm.

'I . . .' The light pulsed irregularly like distant lightning, though there was not a cloud in the sky. It was livid. It seemed to reach out from a source that was hidden by the dark hills surrounding the Vale. When he recalled what he knew of sky lore, his unease grew, for this was no natural light.

His thoughts went immediately to the lorc, that web of lines in the earth that fed the battlestones. They had glowed with an eerie light. At certain phases of the moon they had stood out in the darkness, clothed with a pale and otherworldly sheen.

'Look!' he said, pointing. 'That halo. It seems to be coming from near the Giant's Ring.'

The ancient stone circle could not be seen from the Vale. It was in Gwydion's words *Bethen feilli Imbliungh*, the Navel of the World, a place of tremendous influence, and the fount through which earth power erupted into the lorc. That, Will had always supposed, was the reason the fae had set up one of their terrible battlestones there, the one that had fought Gwydion's magic and won.

'It can't be the battlestone, can it?' Willow asked as she peered into the inconstant light. 'You said Gwydion had drawn all the harm out of it.'

'So he did. But tonight is Lammas when the power of the earth waxes highest.'

'We didn't see lights there last year. Nor any year before.'

Willow's words ceased as a low rumbling passed through the ground. It was so low that it could not be heard, only felt in the bones. Will heard Avon whinny, then came the sound of ripe apples dropping in the orchard. The ground itself was trembling. As he stared into the night he was aware of Willow's frightened eyes upon him. Then two flower pots fell from the window ledge at the back of the cottage. He heard them crack one after the other on the stone kerb below. Willow jumped.

'What's happening?'

'I don't know.'

'I'm going to see if Bethe's all right.' She vanished into the cottage.

Will let her go, listening only to the night as the rumble passed away beneath his feet and stillness returned to the Vale. Gwydion had once spoken of mountains of fire that rose up in remote parts of the world, mountains that spewed forth flames and hot cinders. But there were none of those in the Realm. He had spoken too of tremblings that shook the land from time to time. They came sometimes as workings that had been delved deep under the earth long ago shifted or fell in on themselves.

Could that have caused the rumblings?

And if so, what about the light?

There was something about that light that caused a shiver to run up Will's spine. This rippling, eye-deceiving glow was the same colour as the flames that had once trapped and burned him within the compass of the Giant's Ring. It was purple fire that had lifted him up high over the stones and had begun to consume his flesh. Purple fire that would have killed him in dreadful agony had not Gwydion's magic saved him. And such a flame as that came only from Maskull's hands.

'By the moon and stars, he's found me . . .'

A great terror seized him. He recalled the time when he had sat alongside Gwydion in a cart and the wizard had told him what could happen if someone tried to tamper magically with a

battlestone. *'If all the harm were to be released in a single hand clap
. . . it would be enough to torment the land beyond endurance.'*

And who else but Maskull would dare to tamper with a battlestone?

Fears stirred, wormlike, in Will's guts as he looked up at the Tops
now. There was no doubt what he must do. He went inside and lit
a fresh candle. The damp wick crackled as it caught from a flame
that already glowed in its niche. Dust still sifted down from the
rafters in the gloom. Willow stood by the cradle, her daughter in
her arms. Bethe had been woken up by the quake and was mewling.

'Where're you going?' Willow asked, seeing him climb the
ladder into the loft.

'To call on an old friend.'

He went to his oak chest and brought out the book that grew
bigger the more it was read. He brought it down the ladder, took
a soft cloth and wiped clean the great covers of tooled brown
leather. There was not much time. Soon the other Valesmen would
notice the glow and they would come for his advice.

He placed the treasured book on the wooden lectern by the
fire, a piece of furniture he had made himself specially for it.
Then he composed himself for the ritual that should always attend
the opening of any book of magic.

He placed his left hand flat on the book's front cover and
repeated the words of the true tongue that were written there:

'Ane radhas a'leguim oicheamna;
ainsagimn deo teuiccimn.'

And then he voiced the spell again in plain speech.

'Speak these words to read the secrets within;
learn and so come to a true understanding.'

There were no iron clasps on this book as there were on most
others, for this book was locked by magic. As he muttered the

charm the bindings were released and he was able to open it. Inside were words for his eyes alone. He turned to a special page with Gwydion's parting words in mind.

> '. . . *should you find yourself in dire need, you must*
> *find the page where flies the swiftest bird. Call*
> *it by name and that will be enough.*'

His fingers trembled as the page before him began to fill with the picture of a bird, black and white with a russet throat and long tail streamers. He hesitated. Is this truly a moment of 'dire need'? he asked himself. Am I doing the right thing?

He looked inside himself, then across to where Willow nursed their daughter, and suddenly he feared to invoke the spell. But then he saw the livid light flare and heard Bethe begin to cry, and he knew he must pronounce the trigger-word without delay.

'*Fannala!*'

He spoke the true name of the swallow. Immediately, his thoughts were knocked sideways as if by a great blow to his head. A bird flew up out of the book and into the candlelight. There was a flash of white breast feathers and it was gone, so that when Will's bedazzled eyes tried to follow it he lost it in the shadows. When he looked again not knowing what to expect, a grey shape had appeared in the corner.

'Who's there?' Willow shouted, clutching Bethe close to her and snatching up a fire iron.

Will was overwhelmed. It seemed that a great bear or tiger cat had appeared in the room and was making ready to attack. Yet the shape gave off a pale blue light that faded, and then the figure of an old man walked out of the darkness.

The wizard was tall and grave, swathed in his long wayfarer's cloak of mouse-brown. His head was closely clad in a dark skullcap, and his hand clasped an oaken staff. Bare toes peeped out from under the long skirts of his belted robe, and he wore a long beard that was divided now into two forks.

'A swift, I told you! Not a *swallow*! Fool!'

Will stared as the wizard stroked the two stiff prongs of his beard together and made them into one.

'Master Gwydion . . .'

The wizard looked around the homely room with heavy-lidded eyes, his brow knotted. He footed his staff with a bang against the fireplace. 'I hope you have good reason to summon me thus!'

Will felt the wizard's displeasure like a knife. Their parting had been more than four years ago, and Will expected warmer words.

'Good reason?' Willow said, putting down the fire iron but still unwilling to have her husband roughly spoken to beside his own hearth. 'I should say there's good reason. And less of the "fool", if you please, Master Gwydion. Those who don't mind their manners in this house gets shown off these premises right quick, and that's whoever they may be.'

Gwydion turned to her sharply, but then seeming to bethink himself he swept out a low bow. 'I have offended you. Please, accept my apologies. If I was rude, it was because I was upon an important errand and I did not expect to be disturbed from it.'

Will stepped towards the door without hesitation. 'I can't be sure, Gwydion, but I think this is something you ought to see.'

Once they were outside Gwydion shielded his eyes from the purple glare, then took Will's arm. 'You were right to summon me. Of course you were.'

Will's heart sank. 'What is it?'

'Something I have feared daily these four years.'

'Hey!' Will called, but Gwydion had already taken himself halfway down the path. 'Hey, where are you going?'

'To the Giant's Ring, of course!'

'Alone?'

'That,' the wizard called over his shoulder, 'is entirely up to you.'

Will watched the wizard stride away into the darkness. He looked helplessly towards the cottage door. 'But . . . what about Willow? What about Bethe?'

'Oh, they must not come! There is likely to be great danger on the Tops.'

Will ran to the doorway and put his head inside. 'Gwydion needs my help,' he said. 'I have to go with him.'

Willow dandled their daughter. 'Go? Go where?'

'Up onto the Tops.'

Her pretty eyes quizzed him, then she sighed. 'Oh, Will . . .'

'Don't worry. I won't be long. I promise.' He held her for a moment, then kissed her hurriedly, unhooked his cloak and left.

'What do you think it is?' he asked as he caught up with the wizard.

Gwydion tasted the air. He made hissing noises and held out his arm, but no barn owl came to his call. 'Do you see how the night creatures hereabouts have all gone to ground? No bird can fly in this glare.'

They climbed up the stony path that no one but Gwydion could ever find. It led up through the woods of Nethershaw, yet it wound past trees and the phantasms of trees and passed through impenetrable thickets of brambles that parted to let Gwydion through but then closed behind Will. He scrambled smartly up a mossy bank after the wizard and felt the earth crumbling away under his toes. But then the trees gave out and a dark land opened before them, stark under the purple glow.

They walked onward across tussocky grass, over pools of shadow and a maze of spirals that Will sensed patterning the earth. Soon five great standing stones loomed out of the night, huddled closely one upon another like a group of conspirators. They were, Will knew, vastly ancient, all that remained of the tomb of Orba, Queen of the Summer Moon, who had lived in the Age of the First Men.

She it was who had ruled the land here long ago, and close by was the dragon-ravaged tomb of her husband, Finglas, now no more than a bump in the flow-tattooed earth. The wizard swung his staff before him, his eyes penetrating the dark like lamps.

Will's heart was hammering as the wizard paused and shaded his eyes against the sky's sickly violet sheen. 'It's not coming from the Giant's Ring after all,' he said. 'It's coming from somewhere in the west!'

The wizard drew Will to a sudden halt beside him. 'Behold! Liarix Finglas!'

The awesome flickerings rose up in the sky behind the King's Stone like a monstrous lightning storm. Will saw the great, crooked fang cut out in black against the glare. Beside it stood the twisted elder tree where Gwydion had once been trapped by sorcerer's magic. Four years ago he had crossed blackened grass; now it had regrown and was lush and dew-cool underfoot.

A clear view to the west opened up. There the sky was smudged by cloud, and far away a great plume had risen up through the layers, its top blown sideways by high winds, its underside lit amethyst and white.

'Look,' Will cried. 'It's a lightning storm on the Wolds!'

'Did you ever see such lightning as that?' When Gwydion turned a silent play of light smote the distant Wolds, making crags of his face. 'And the rumble that shook down your pretty flower pots? Was that thunder?'

'It seemed to come from far away.'

Gwydion gave a short, humourless laugh. 'You want to think the danger is far away and so none of your concern. But remember that the earth is one. Magic connects all who walk upon it. Faraway trouble is trouble all the same. Do not try to find comfort in what you see now, for the further away it is the bigger it must be.'

Will felt the wizard's words cut him. They accused him of a way of thinking that ran powerfully against the redes and laws of magic.

'I'm sorry,' he said humbly. 'That was selfish.'

'Liarix Finglas,' Gwydion muttered, moving on. He slid fingers over the stone, savouring the name in the true tongue. 'In the lesser words of latter days, "the King's Stone". And nowadays the herding men who come by here call it "the Shepherd's

Delight". How quaint! For to them it is no more than a lump from which lucky charms may be chipped. Oh, how the Ages have declined! What a sorry inheritance the mighty days of yore have bequeathed! We are living in the old age of the world, Willand. And things are determined to turn against us!'

He heard the bitterness in the wizard's words. 'Surely you don't believe that.'

The wizard's face was difficult to read as he turned to Will again. 'I believe that at this moment, you and your fellow villagers are very lucky to be alive.'

A chill ran through him. 'Why do you say that?'

The wizard offered only a dismissive gesture, and Will took his arm in a firmer grip. 'Gwydion, I asked you a question!'

The wizard scowled and pulled his arm away. 'And, as you see, I am avoiding answering you.'

'But why? This isn't how it was with us.'

'Why?' Gwydion put back his head and stared at the sky. 'Because I am *afraid.*'

A fresh pang of fear swam through Will's belly and surfaced in his mind. This was worse than anything he could have expected. Yet the fear freshened his thinking, awakened him further to the danger. He felt intensely alert as he looked around. Up on the Tops the sky was large. It stretched all the way from east to west, from north to south. He felt suddenly very vulnerable.

With a sinking heart he looked around for the place where they had unearthed the battlestone and found its grave, a shallow depression now partly filled and overgrown, but the burned-out stone was nowhere to be seen.

'You're not as kindly as I remembered you,' he told Gwydion.

'Memories are seldom accurate. And you too have changed. Do not forget that.'

'Even so, you're less amiable. Sharper tongued.'

'If you find me so, that is because you see more these days. You are no longer the trusting innocent.'

'I was never that.'

The wizard gazed up and down an avenue of earthlight that stretched, spear-straight across the land. To Will's eye it was greenish, elfin and fey. But it was a light that he knew well, though very bright for lign-light, brighter than he had ever seen it. It passed close by the circle of standing stones.

'That shimmering path is called Eburos,' Gwydion told him. 'It is the lign of the yew tree. Look upon it, Willand, and remember what you see, for according to the Black Book this is the greatest of the nine ligns that make up the lorc. Its brightness surprises you, I see. But perhaps it should not, for tonight is Lughnasad, and very close after the new moon. All crossquarter days are magical but now is the start of Iucer, the time when the edges of this world blur with those of the Realm Below – Lughnasad upon a new moon is a time when even lowland swine rooting in the forest floor may see the lign glowing strongly in the earth. *"Trea lathan iucer sean vailan . . ."* Three days of magic in the earth, as the old saying goes. Even I can see it tonight.'

Will nodded. 'The lorc is once more growing in power.'

Gwydion met his eye. 'I feared you would say that.'

Frustration erupted sourly inside Will. 'But how can that be? I destroyed the Doomstone at Verlamion. The heart of the lorc was broken!'

'But *was* the Doomstone destroyed?'

'Do you doubt that I told you the truth?'

There was silence.

'The battle stopped, didn't it?' Will said.

The wizard inclined his head a fraction. 'The battle did not continue.'

'I only know what I saw, Gwydion. The Doomstone was cracked clean across. It must have been destroyed, for it fell silent and all the Sightless Ones in the chapter house lost their minds.'

To that the wizard made no reply other than to give a doubtful grunt. Then he raised his staff towards the livid glow. They walked the lign together across the crest of the Tops. Earth power tingled in Will's fingers and toes as he walked. They soon came to what looked from a distance like a ring of silent, unmoving figures. He looked at the perfect circle of eighty or so stones, the ring that was forty paces across. The shadows cast by each stone groped out across the uneven land. He felt as if he was intruding and said so.

'You know,' Gwydion said in a distant voice, 'the druida used to come here unfailingly at the spring equinox – and then again in the autumn of each year. Ah, what processions we had when the world was young! They brought their white horses, all marked red upon the forehead like so many unhorned unicorns. Here they made their signs two days before the new moon and sat down to drink milk and mead and witness the waxing of the power of the lorc. They were great days, Willand. Great days . . .'

They entered the Ring respectfully, going in by the proper entrance, bowing to the four directions before approaching the centre and sitting down. The stones of the Ring were small, no taller than children, hunched, misshapen, brooding. The greatest of them stood to the north. When Will had come here four years ago he had made no obeisance, asked no formal permission, but when he had touched the chief stone there had been a welcome all the same. He had been privileged to feel the rich and undiminished power that lay dormant here. Before Maskull's sorcery had ambushed him he had felt an enormous store of power, something as vast as a mountain buried deep in the earth, and its summit was the Ring. That sense was still here, a muted but deeply comfortable emanation, a power that spilled endlessly from the Navel of the World. Will understood very well why the stonewise druida had come here twice a year without fail.

He waited for Gwydion to decide what to do, and meanwhile he watched the distant glow in the west until it guttered low and they were bathed in darkness. Breaths of wind ruffled the lush grass. Overhead high veils of cloud were sweeping in. They were not thick enough to hide the stars, but they made them twinkle violently, and that seemed to Will a sign of ill omen.

He pulled his cloak tighter about him and was about to speak when he felt a presence lurking nearby. As he turned, a wild-haired figure broke from cover. Then a blood-freezing scream split the silence. The figure dashed towards them, and came to within a pace of Gwydion's back. An arm jerked upward, and Will saw a blade flash against the sky.

'Gwydion!' he cried.

But the wizard did not move.

Will was aware only of soft words being uttered as he dived low at the figure and carried it to the ground, pinning it. Will's strength slowly forced the blade from the fist that had wielded it. He was hit, then hit again, in the face, but the blows lacked power and he held his grip long enough to apply an immobilizing spell, which put the attacker's limbs in struggle against one another.

'Take care not to hurt her, Will. She cannot help herself.'

He shook the pain from his head and staggered to his feet. The furiously writhing body repulsed him. Strangled gasps came from the assailant as he picked up the blade.

'Who is she?' He wiped his mouth where one of the woman's blows had drawn a little blood. 'It's lucky you heard her coming. I had no idea.'

'I did not hear her so much as feel the approach of her magic.'

'That's a trick I wish you'd teach me.'

Gwydion grunted. 'It was never easy to kill an Ogdoad wizard. And quite hard to take one by surprise.'

Will shook his head again and brushed back his braids. Then he turned the blade over in his fingers. It was broad and double-edged and had a heavy, black handle. 'This knife is an evil weapon,' he said, passing the blade to Gwydion.

The wizard would not take it. 'It is not evil.'

'No?'

'Nor is it a weapon. Or even a knife. Did I teach you to think that way?'

'It looks like a dagger to me,' he muttered. 'And it would've made a mess of you.'

'Look again. It is made of obsidian, the same black glass which the Sightless Ones use in the windows of their chapter houses. It is a sacred object, one used in ritual and not to be lightly profaned with blood.'

'Well, the blood it was intended to spill was yours.'

'It has more in common with this.' Gwydion drew the blade of star-iron from the sheath that always hung on a cord about his neck. He held it up. 'An "iscian", called by some "athame", though strictly speaking athamen may be used only by women. It is not a dagger but a compass used to scribe the circle that becomes the border between two worlds. It is the season of Iucer, and tonight this Sister has travelled here by magic. I do not know why she has chosen to meddle far above her knowledge, but look what it has done to her.'

Will turned to where the woman still kicked and struggled as arm fought arm and leg fought leg.

'Release her, now. But be mindful of the powers that flow here.'

Will rebuckled his belt over his shirt and straightened his pouch. He felt his heart hammering as he danced out the counterspell. At length the woman's body collapsed into the grass, as if her bones had been turned to blood. Though slender, she was of middle age, with long hair, silvered in streaks now. Twenty years ago it would have been dark and she would have been a handsome woman.

'Speak to me now!' Gwydion commanded, and made a sign above her head.

The Sister shrieked and writhed, but then her voice became one of malice.

> *'Slaughter great,*
> *Slaughter small!*
> *All slaughter now,*
> *No Slaughter at all!'*

'Peace!' Gwydion said, and made a second sign over her. Instantly she fell quiet, and seemed to sleep comfortably.

'Who is she?' Will asked.

'She comes from one of the hamlets near . . . that.' Gwydion gestured towards the last glimmerings of lilac fire in the west. 'She invoked a spell of great magic to bring herself here. She should not have done that, nor would she have unless her life had been threatened. By rights she should not even have known how to use such magic, but curiosity is a powerful urge in some of the Sisters of the Wise. This time it has saved her life, though we shall soon see if it was worth the saving.'

'What do you mean?'

'The spell was ill-wrought. It has touched her mind with madness. That is, I hope, the only reason she tried to fall upon me as she did.'

Will examined the blade critically. 'I didn't know it was the practice of Sisters to go abroad with their athamen upon them.'

'Ordinarily, they do not. Take care to keep that one from her, Will. I recognize it for what it is, and I believe that unless you keep it away from her she will try to kill herself with it when she wakes.'

CHAPTER TWO

LITTLE SLAUGHTER

Gwydion slowly unwound the strands of magic that had afflicted the woman. Will marvelled at the wizard's calm composure as he laid her down inside the circle and danced the harm from her. He laid charms upon her head, made signs above her body with his staff, and finally he drew a glistening adder from her mouth. He laid it down to vanish into the night.

Afterwards Will found himself drawn to watch the simmering lights. The corner of his lip tingled, and a lump had started to come up where the witch's flailing fist had marked him.

'What are you going to do?' he asked.

'Do?' Gwydion stirred. 'Perhaps you should decide what's best.'

'You're the wizard.'

'But it was *you* who summoned *me*.'

'Yes, well I thought you ought to know about . . . *that*. It seemed to me to be Maskull's doing.'

'You are right. It is.'

Will was about to ask the wizard how he could be so sure, but then he remembered how seldom Gwydion was wholly open with the truth, and how closely he shepherded his wisdom. Of course a wizard needed to, for he was a guardian and therefore must be adept at manipulation. It was the entire purpose of the Ogdoad to steer fate in order to keep the world going along on the true path, and so many times during the long history of the Realm members of the wizardly council had intervened at crucial moments. Gwydion knew about cause and effect and the motivation of folk, and he had lived for such a time that long consequences were plain to his eyes. Will understood very well that there were some things Gwydion could afford to divulge and others that he must certainly not, but it did not hurt any the less to think that certain of the wizard's secrets probably concerned his own origins.

He felt discomfort run through him while the Wise Woman twitched and muttered in dream at their backs and all three waited for the dawn to come. At last, the east grew grey with filtered light.

'She'll be worried,' he said, meaning Willow. 'I'll bet she hasn't slept a wink.'

Gwydion stared at him for a moment and then broke off the look. 'Why not wait until the sun is truly up?' he said. 'You will find it easier to decide by the full light of day. The spell that cloaks the Vale is of necessity a powerful one. It is unlikely that even you would succeed in finding your way home in this half light.'

'Decide? About what?'

'About what you should do.'

Will sighed. He had heard Gwydion speak this way before, and he wondered where it was leading.

In the grey of that cold hour before sunrise the dew was penetrating. Thin mists rolled in the valleys that clefted the Tops, and as the stars went out one by one, he went over to the elder tree. He would not approach it too closely for fear that it might swallow him up again. Instead, he kicked his toes at the edge of the hole from which the battlestone had been taken. It was like the gap from which a rotten tooth had been pulled, but the pain and the stench had almost been washed from the ground.

'Gwydion, where's the stump gone?'

'Stump?'

'The big piece of battlestone that was left.'

'I took it away.'

He inclined his head, surprised. 'Why would you do that?'

'I wanted to give it to my friend Cormac.'

'It's a strange gift for a friend.'

'Strange, perhaps, but useful certainly. Cormac is Lord of the Clan MacCarthach. He is a lord of the Blessed Isle, and a great builder of castles. Once drained, the battlestones are changed from deadly to mildly benign. Once the harm is gone there remains a small residue of kindness that works much as a charm does. I believe the stone will sit well once it is mortared into the ramparts of Cormac's castle of An Blarna.'

'What power will it confer, there? Invulnerability?'

'Ha! Not that. Cormac will have to look to his own security as ever he did. But now he will be able to defend himself with the gift of diplomacy, for it seems that this particular stump gives those who touch it a fine way with words.'

'Then you yourself must have slept seven nights upon it, I'd say.'

Gwydion laughed. 'Did I never tell you that mockery is a very childish skill? I will have you know that many is the night since last we met when I have wished myself upon a bed that was as soft as a castle parapet.'

'I'm wishing myself abed at this very moment.' Will stretched again and yawned. 'As sorry as I am for your poor old spine, it's time I rested mine. I really should be going home.'

At this Gwydion looked silently away, and Will knew the wizard had more to say for himself. They sat until the skylarks began singing, until the eastern sky had turned a fragile blue above the pale mists of a summer dawn. Long, low streamers of cloud hovered close by the eastern horizon, as pink as the boiled flesh of a salmon. They turned slowly to fiery gold as the sun rose to burn off night mists that still clung to the land.

'Did you ever find the Black Book?' Will asked, meaning the

ancient scroll that Gwydion had often spoken about, the one that told of the history of the battlestones.

The wizard stiffened. 'I did not, and perhaps I never will. But I have not been idle. I have learned something of what the Black Book might once have contained. There are here and there snippets to be found, lines taken from fragments, copies of copies, translations made from memory long after the Black Book was lost. My gleanings have been meagre; still they have given me some much-needed clues regarding how best to set about the perilous task of draining a battlestone.'

'Surely you don't think—'

'My first attempt was foolhardy. I am aware of that now. But if I had been wiser sooner, then I should not have done as I did. And where would that have left us?'

Will grunted. 'All decisions must be made on the basis of imperfect knowledge, I suppose.'

The wizard's chin jutted. 'I will say that now I believe I have almost learned enough to try again.'

There was a noise then, and Will turned. 'Look! The Sister. She stirs.'

They went to attend the Wise Woman as she came out of sleep. First her eyes opened and rolled in her head, then she struggled weakly and spoke like one in a fever. Gwydion lifted her head and made her drink from a small leather bottle. Then he said firmly, 'Where are you from, Sister?'

'My home is at Fossewyke, Master,' she said in the voice of a young girl.

'That is by Little Slaughter, is it not?'

Her eyes roamed, but then she said, 'Yes, Master. It is in the vale of the Eyne Brook.'

'Well, get you home now without delay. Do not eat or drink again until night falls. By which time you will be wholly yourself again. Do you promise to do as I bid you?'

'Yes, Master.'

Will hid the sheathed blade away from her as Gwydion pointed a warning finger in her face. 'To thine own self be true – now promise me that also.'

'I promise, Master.'

'Go now! Prosper under the sky, and do not be tempted to meddle again with crafts that lie beyond your scope.'

And with that the Sister rose to her feet and skipped away as briskly as a lamb, leaving Will in awe of the power that lay in Gwydion's words.

'Is she in her right mind again?' he asked doubtfully.

'Not yet. But by sundown she will be, save for a strong cider headache. And that might teach her to go more slowly in high matters. I did not chastise her further, for she must have acted in fear to save her life. By rights great magic such as she used should have killed her, but it did not, and that is a discrepancy which troubles me.'

'Discrepancy?' Will asked, his heart sinking. 'What do you mean?'

'Come, Willand, I have a favour to ask of you.'

He followed, going towards the lign and out along it to the west until Gwydion said:

> *'Slaughter great,*
> *Slaughter small!*
> *All slaughter now,*
> *No Slaughter at all!*

Do you know what that means?'

Will shook his head. 'Should I?'

'It is the answer to the lights that burned last night over the Wolds.'

'How could that be an answer?'

Gwydion sat down on the ground. 'I will tell you, but first you must tell me again what happened to the Doomstone of Verlamion, the same which you think you destroyed – but cannot say how.'

Will sat down too. He thought back to the desperate moment

when he had struggled against the Doomstone. He told all he could remember of what had taken place in the cellar under the great chapter house of the Sightless Ones. The Doomstone had been none other than the slab that covered the Founder's sarcophagus.

'In the end I used this to break it,' he said, hooking a finger inside the neck of his shirt.

He had meant to draw out his fish talisman and show it to Gwydion, but it was not there. He patted his chest in puzzlement, then remembered how the day before he had washed his hair and replaited his braids ready for the Lammas celebrations. He had hung the fish on a nail and had forgotten to put it back on. It was only the figure of a fish, no bigger than his thumb, carved in green and with a red eye, but he missed it.

'No matter,' he said regretfully. 'It's probably not important.'

Gwydion's grey eyes watched him. 'The power of magic is often made greater by tokens. Much strength may be drawn upon in time of peril if a true belief lies within your heart. You knew what to do without being taught. I have said it many times, Willand, you are the Child of Destiny. The Black Book has said so.'

He chewed his lip, a heavy weight burdening him. 'I don't know where I come from, and that scares me, Gwydion.'

The wizard touched him with a kindly hand. 'Willand, I must interfere as lightly as possible where you are concerned. I know little enough about the part you are to play, except a pitiful portion revealed by the seers of old. Believe me when I say that I am hiding nothing from you that it would serve you to know.'

He sighed and hugged his knees. 'I've been having the same nightmare over and over lately. An idea comes to me in shallow sleep – that Maskull is my father.'

Gwydion shook his head. 'The Doomstone traded in fear and lies. The planting of deceits in men's minds is the way all such stones make a defence of themselves.'

'Then how do you explain what Maskull himself said when

I faced him on top of the curfew tower? That was something else I can't forget. He said, "I made you, I can just as easily unmake you." I've wondered too many times what he meant by it.'

Gwydion said gently, 'Maskull is not your father. Be assured of that.'

'Then why did he say what he did?'

'Try to forget about it.'

The wizard got up and walked away. Will wanted to leap up, to go after him and badger him on the matter, but Gwydion's certainty made him pause, made him remember that a wizard's secrets must be respected.

'If you say so.'

As he watched his long morning shadow stretching before him, a keen hunger gnawed at his spirit. After a while, he shivered and got up. A cool westerly breeze had sprung up and he felt an ache in his bones that he thought must be coming from the damp-ness of the grass. The power flowing from the Giant's Ring was subsiding as the sun rose higher, but still he could feel the echoes coursing in darkness beneath his bare feet. He looked inside himself for an answer, then went to talk with Gwydion about the power that moved in the earth.

'Can't you find a way to stop the empowering of the lorc?' he asked. 'Why not halt the flow right here at its source? That way the battlestones would never awaken.'

Gwydion shook his head. 'What you suggest is impossible.'

'But why? You said the Giant's Ring controls the earth flow like a sluice controls a millstream. I can feel the influence surging under here. It's huge.'

'So it is, but I could not control it any more than I could dam a raging river torrent with my bare hands. And in any case, it would do no good. Any attempt to block the flow would wreak havoc – blocking the millrace would surely stop the mill-wheel turning, but it would also raise the millpond to over-flowing and eventually it would burst the dam. To interfere with the lorc directly would risk disrupting all the earth flows that sustain us. In the end it would turn the Realm into a wasteland.'

'If the power of this lign is anything to go by, I'd say the lorc is about to do that anyway. It's definitely waking up. Can't you feel it, Gwydion? Have your powers declined that much?'

The wizard's glance was sharp. 'Declined? You know very well that I could never feel the lorc directly. In that respect, your abilities are unmatched.'

Will's mind tuned to a sound high in the air. The untiring warbling of the skylark. Could they hear that song in the Vale too? Could Willow hear it? He stopped and turned.

'What's the favour you wanted to ask me?'

Gwydion leaned on his staff. 'I now know what must be done. No matter what the dangers, I must find the battlestones one at a time. I must either drain them or bind them, for I dare not confront them as you did the Doomstone.'

'How many more have you found?'

'In the past four years? None.'

'None?' The news was shocking.

'Without your talent to guide me I have been blind.' Gwydion opened his hands in a gesture that showed there was no other answer to the problem.

'You should have called on me,' Will told him. Then he saw the trap the wizard had set for him, and added, 'Before Bethe was born I would gladly have come with you.'

Gwydion met his gaze knowingly. 'Would you?'

He stared sullenly into the western haze, noting the starlings and how they flew. Their movements said there was something wrong with the air, something nasty blowing in from the Wolds.

'You know I would have done anything to help you, Gwydion.'

'But would you have *wanted* to?' The wizard pulled up his staff and gestured westward. 'I see you can taste the bitterness that lies upon the west wind. Do you smell that ghastly taint of burning? It is human flesh. We must go now. Straight away. To the hamlet of Little Slaughter to see what a fatal weakness in the spirit of a powerful man has done.'

Will's heart sickened to hear the words that he had known were coming since before sunrise. 'I'm a husband and a father now. I can't just leave without a word. It's harvest time, Gwydion, and I promised Willow I wouldn't be long.'

His words were reasonable, sane by any standard. But they already sounded hollow in his ears.

As the morning wore on, the August sun rose hot on their backs. Will saw its golden beams glittering on the head-waters of the Evenlode stream, and by midday they were across it and turning south, so that the sun began to fill the ups and downs of their path with shimmering patches and pools.

They went a league or two out of their way to the south and passed many folk on the road. Gwydion made a sign to them and warned Will to silence. Some people seemed to see Will but not the wizard. Some seemed to see neither. Others turned about as if alarmed, or at least puzzled by some unaccountable pres-ence. Occasionally there were those who embraced Gwydion as if they had been met by a long-dead kinsman, and to these Gwydion gave a word in friendship and sometimes a token of reward.

They came down to a little river and saw a bridge-keeper's shack. Here two men in red livery guarded the bridge. Arms had once been painted on a board but they had faded and peeled away.

Neither the keeper of the Windrush crossing nor the two men-at-arms seemed to notice them, though a witless beggar put his hands out for a blessing and Gwydion clasped his hand briefly as he passed.

'Welcome, Master Jack-in-a-box!' the beggar said.

'Keep up!' Gwydion warned as Will looked pitifully at the beggar's sores.

'Has he no friends to take care of him?' Will asked angrily. 'Is he a man or a dog? And why is he clad in such filthy rags? Is there no Sister here? What sort of place is this?'

'We are at the village of Lowe, and shall soon be through it,' Gwydion said.

'Can nothing be done for the people here?'

'This village belongs to an ill-starred fellow whose company is best avoided. This lord has driven the local Wise Woman away, and for that his people will one day murder him, for it is a true rede that "by the least of men shall the best of men always be judged".'

There were cottages clustered here, with folk sitting at their doors. Half a dozen dirty children played in the way, and the people seemed odd. They made no acknowledgment of Will's greetings as he passed. One old woman, however, received Gwydion as a subject would receive a king. She gave him a bundle which was put into the wizard's crane bag which was instantly passed to Will to carry. As they left the village and rose up the hill high above the mossy thatches Will looked back down into the valley to where the brimming waters of the Windrush shone in brash daylight. There was a large manor some way to the right of the bridge.

'Do not look at it,' Gwydion said, and pulled him onward.

'But how did the village get that way?'

'It is a place of poor aspect. Land-blighted. Not every village in the Realm is as well set as Nether Norton. Many do not have a kindly lord. You should think yourself fortunate that the Vale is a place without any ruler, for some delight in making themselves overmighty while they may.'

Their journey, Gwydion had said, would not take them far, but they had already walked many a long league and Will's feet ached. They were going to the place where the violet light had burned, but it was ever the wizard's way not to go anywhere very directly. He took account of the flows in the land, choosing ancient paths, or striding along great arcs that swirled from hill to saddle and then swept on along the spring-lines of an upland or plunged down into the cool heart of a wood. Always the wizard's staff would swing out in a striding rhythm, seeking narrow deer paths, and more often than not Will found himself following in his guide's footsteps instead of walking at his shoulder as he preferred. Seldom did they follow the ways used by men, though sometimes they found dusty tracks, or a line of gnarled trees, or a trackway that meandered among planted fields. By now Will had begun to worry about Willow and his regret at their not having said a proper farewell was eating at him. He went through what he would have liked to have said, then he pictured his daughter crawling across the grass while her mother gathered windfall apples, and that image brought him back to the events of the night and to the matter in hand.

There were dangers. There was no denying that, for Maskull was implicated. And no denying the bubbling excitement in Will's belly that others might have feared to call fear.

When he paused to take stock he saw people in the distance, working in the fields or making their way to market. As soon as Gwydion saw them he turned away and passed into the dark shade of a wood. He whispered to himself, nor was he whispering blessings. From time to time he would put his hands flat on the smooth grey trunk of a tall beech tree to mutter an incantation or to ask the air for directions. He stooped to crumble soil between his fingers, then to drink a handful of cool water which he found bubbling fresh from the earth. Will thought of old Wortmaster Gort, whose own skills upon the land were a delight. But he had once said that a true wizard such as Gwydion knew all parts of the Realm, from having walked every step of it a dozen and one times. He said that Gwydion could tell from the taste of a handful of water, or the feel of a pinch of dust, where he stood to the nearest league, just as carriers upon the Great North Road might know how far they had gone just by listening to the way people said certain words.

'How far is it now?' Will asked.

'Not far.'

When Will began to feel hungry, Gwydion plunged into a wood and brought out a great armful of morels. They had a delicious taste. And again, down beside a stream where willows grew he found several white fleshy growths on the tree trunks that looked like giant ears and tasted like they looked but which filled the belly well.

Here there were many dry-stone walls and sheep meadows, and ahead a country of windy heath on which the bracken was slowly turning russet. Gwydion halted as they approached one of the ancient roads that he detested so much. Will looked up and down it, finding that his eye could follow it a long way to north and south. It was dead straight and did not yield to the earth in any way. Though old and broken in places now, still it scarred the land like a knife wound.

'Slave road!' Gwydion said with disgust as he hurried to the far side. 'The straightest of them, built here fifty generations ago, when the Slaver empire took the Isle by force. Its name now is the Fosse. Do you see how it still works its dividing influence upon the land?'

After so long following Gwydion, Will's feet had learned how to tread a true path through the land. When he planted his feet and felt for the earth streams, he could sense the way the power was turned and pent up as if into brackish pools by the ancient highway. He could see what Gwydion meant about the village of Lowe being a place that was land-blighted. He wondered at how his talent had sharpened and matured during the past few years. What could that mean?

After crossing the Fosse their own path trended more southerly. The land began to open out and there was more rising than falling. They began to cross a wide sweep of planted country that rose up into the higher Wolds. At length, Gwydion stopped and danced magic, calling out in the true tongue that there might now be an opening. In moments a path between the briars appeared where no path had been before. They went along it, and Will felt a tingle in his bones, the same he had felt when entering the Vale. At that time there had been joy in his heart, but not now, for the smell of burning had been rising on the wind and he began to taste something unpleasant at the back of his throat. Fine grit stuck to his lips and gathered in the corners of his eyes. The track before them and the leaves on the trees and bushes were dusty. Now they gave way to leaves that were rain spotted and again to leaves washed clean by a recent downpour.

Will thought of the great towering cloud that had risen high into the sky last night. It was as if a column of rain had been sent deliberately to damp the fires down. The stream that came from the higher land was running milky-grey with dust, carrying black flecks on its surface. Gwydion stooped to look at it, but this time he did not dip his hand in or try to drink.

'This is the valley of the Eyne Brook,' he said at last. 'Yonder lies Fossewyke. We are nearing our goal.'

Will looked at the scum of ash that floated on the brook's surface. He soon found the reason for it – the water had bubbled across a great heath that had been turned black by fire. When they ventured into the valley the soil was warm underfoot and smoking in places even though there had been rain heavy enough to douse it.

'Steam,' Gwydion said, nodding at the wisps. 'Nothing could have survived here last night.'

As they journeyed to the heart of the devastation, Will found himself gagging at the acrid smell. All the trees nearby had been smashed down, their trunks charred black on one side. Everything was layered in thin ash. In places it had drifted into banks that looked like so many grey snowdrifts. The woods seemed to have been brushed flat by a tremendous wind. Nothing green remained. Nothing stood properly upright. All around was a steamy haze, heaps of roasted dust and twisted rock rubble.

Will gouged at his eyes to clear them as they came to what had been a fish pond. Its bed was still too warm to walk on. It had been dried so suddenly that the fish had been boiled alive and lay simmered on the cracked clay. Will stretched out his hands and felt the remains of oven-like heat. Now he could see why Gwydion had not striven to get here sooner.

Everything around them was strange and terrifying. He walked into a stinking ruin, staggered on after Gwydion over the hot ground until they came to a rise. A great bank of loose, smouldering earth reared up before them, and beyond stretched a curtain of smoke. Ash and cinders were raw and sharp underfoot. They scraped and crunched under Will's feet as he climbed, sending up dust and a vile smell. He tried not to breathe but then as he reached the top of the bank he gasped, for beyond was a sight that he had not expected – a huge, smoking crater.

'What could have done this?' he whispered, looking across the shimmering waste.

'Welcome,' Gwydion said emptily, 'to the village of Little Slaughter.'

The whole village had been obliterated. But how? Ten thousand lightning strokes would not have been enough to cause such destruction. Nothing was left of cottage, granary, alehouse, mill. Everything had been smashed to powder and the powder scattered for half a league.

'There was a battlestone here,' Will said slowly. 'A battlestone that someone tried to break. Is that it?'

Gwydion looked at him for a moment but said nothing.

Will went as close to the hole as he dared. It was still red hot, and fuming. He could not see how deep it was, but it was so big around that all of Nether Norton could have fitted inside. He felt numbed, drained of all feeling. His mind raced as he tried to understand what could have happened. When he knelt to touch the dust at the crater's edge he saw there the brightness of what had been molten iron; now it shone like a solidified pool of the Wortmaster's most precious quicksilver. He could not speak or tear his gaze away for a long time.

Gwydion laid a hand on his shoulder. 'I am sorry you had to see this.'

All around were ashes, but here and there away from the crater they saw small signs that this place had been home to many dozens of folk – a horseshoe, a burned chair, a child's rag doll.

A fist of fear clutched at Will's stomach, and he suddenly looked up into the wizard's face. 'I remember Preston Mantles and the lad, Waylan, who Maskull mistook for me. This ruin was meant for Nether Norton, wasn't it?'

'It might have been.' Gwydion closed his eyes and drew a deep breath. 'And it may still happen.'

Will stood up and walked away. He wanted to run, to run from the wizard, to run far away. And when his thoughts touched Willow and Bethe the blood in his heart froze solid. He was scared to open his mind in case too many terrors rushed in on him at once. Instead he wandered wherever his feet might lead him and cried for the people of the lost village, and his tears fell upon the wounded earth.

In return the earth threw up an unlooked-for gift. He bent to look at a reaping hook that was lying on the ground nearby. It was rusted as red as hearth iron and the handle was black, turned wholly to charcoal. It flaked away as he tried to pick it up. But then a blood redness caught at his tear-blurred eyes. Something was down there in the dust at his feet. It was a little figure, carved in some material that was not harmed by fire. When he picked it up it was warm in his hand. It was a stone fish.

He looked around, suspecting sorcery. This little fish was so very like his own in size and shape. But whereas his own had an eye of red set in green, this one had an eye of green set in red. On its side were marks he could not read, but they were just like those on his own talisman, and it bore the same sigil of three triple-sided figures set one within another. Hardly knowing why, he closed his hand over it as Gwydion came to stand beside him. The wizard signalled that they should leave, for there was nothing else to be done here.

Will said, 'You knew last night that something as terrible as this was happening, didn't you?'

Gwydion fixed his eyes on Will's own. 'As soon as you showed me the light in the sky I knew that a vicious revenge had been taken. I did not know precisely how, but it was clear that we were already too late to stop it.'

'Then it *was* a battlestone?'

'You are wrong.'

'But what else could have done this?'

'This was the work of a fireball.' The wizard took his little knife from its sheath and showed it to Will. 'I have spoken of this before. It is made from star-iron, the only thing of metal I carry, for it was neither wrested from the earth nor roasted from the rocks by men. This iron came down from above, just like the fireball that destroyed Little Slaughter. Have I not told you about the great, turning dome of the sky? How it is pierced in many places by holes through which we can see the brilliance that lies in the Beyond? Those holes are what we call the stars. It is said that nothing lives on the far side of the dome of the sky. There is only a great furnace that goes on forever, a parched realm of heat, of blinding light and searing fireballs.'

Will nodded, seeing what the wizard was driving at. 'And sometimes it happens that a fireball falls through a star hole and it's then what we call a shooting star.'

'Correct. Mostly these lumps burn away in the upper airs. But sometimes they are big enough to fall to earth as pieces of star-iron. Such iron was once rarer than gold. And in the days before men learned how to burn iron from the bones of the earth the finest magical tools were made from it.'

'Is that what happened here?' Will coughed and rubbed at his eyes as he looked around again. 'A shooting star landed on the village? A lump of star-iron? But it must have been as big as a house to have done this. How could a thing so big fall through something so tiny as a star?'

'Stars are not tiny. They are far away – nearly seventeen hundred leagues, which is half a world away. Each star is a hole, a great round window like the pupil of your eye. It opens as it rises and

51

closes as it sets. And the biggest stars at their largest are large indeed – as many as twenty paces across when fully open. I know, for I have sailed to the very rim of the Western Deeps and stood upon the cataract at the end of the world. There the stars seem as big as the sun does here, and they move at great speed.'

Will listened as Gwydion spoke. He shook the dust from his scalp as he tried to make sense of what he was being told. Stars that were giant eyes twenty or more paces across. Great holes through which fiery lumps of iron flew down to kill whole villages of people . . . It made no sense. It made no sense at all.

He said, 'It's strange to me that Little Slaughter should have been hit so exactly.'

'Do not imagine this was a chance misfortune.'

'Then the fireball was *directed* here? By . . . *Maskull?*'

The wizard nodded. 'And the purpose of the thunderstorm we watched afterwards was to put out these fires. The storm was whipped up so that folk in other villages of the Wolds would believe as you tried to believe – that the noise and light were no more than a particularly violent summer storm, that what happened here was none of their concern.'

Will thought again of Willow and Bethe. He said, 'Gwydion, I must go home right away.'

But the wizard took his arm. 'That,' he said, 'is the very last thing you should do.'

'But . . . if Maskull's free again and in the world . . .'

Gwydion took himself a few paces apart and conjured a small bird from one of his sleeves. He gentled its head with his finger, kissed it or perhaps murmured to it, then threw it up into the sky where it took wing and quickly flew away to the east.

'Recall, if you will, the battle of Verlamion, and the moment when Maskull vanished. Do you know where I sent him? It was into the Realm Below. He has remained for years lost there, trapped in that great maze that was made by the fae when they withdrew from the light. My hope and belief was that Maskull would take far longer to find his way clear of those myriad chambers. I thought that in that time I would be able to solve the problem of the battlestones, but my hopes have proved groundless. Late last year I began to notice an uneasy presence at Trinovant and elsewhere. It warned me that Maskull had made good his escape. "By his magic, so shall ye know him!" The rede says that spells betray their makers to others who are skilled in the same arts. You see, I have known for some time about Maskull's return. I have read his signature in much, and I have expected his power to be unleashed again. But not like this. Not like this.'

Will's anger surfaced. 'Why didn't you warn me?'

'Warn you?' There was recrimination in Gwydion's eyes. 'To what end? You were already in what I believed to be the safest place there was. Living where you do, Willand, it would not have been clear to you that the spirit of the Realm has been growing steadily darker since this year's beginning. Mistrust is burgeoning, confidence slackening. A great turbulence and greed is increasing among the lords in Trinovant. As Lord Protector, Richard of Ebor is the centre about which all now revolves, but that centre cannot hold for long. An attempt will soon be made to arrest him. His enemies are ready to move again. You see, I have had much to contend with.'

Will followed Gwydion's words with difficulty. The shock of seeing Little Slaughter filled his mind, and his fears about Willow and Bethe and the Vale came once again to the fore. If Maskull was now at large and the lorc drawing power again, then nothing but misery could be foreseen.

Gwydion turned to survey the fuming waste they had left behind. He spent a moment deep in thought, and then measured his words carefully. 'You may rest a little easier in your mind, my friend, for I do not believe Maskull will have quite the opportunity to do again what he has done here. Nor do I believe you were the reason he destroyed Little Slaughter.'

CHAPTER THREE

WHAT LIES WITHIN

Gwydion led Will some way back eastward, heading towards the Four-shire Stone before the light died. This was no battlestone, but a benign landmark that showed the place where four earldoms met. On the way they spoke of the strife that was growing among the lords at Trinovant. The trouble, Gwydion explained, had not come solely out of the queen's viciousness. Richard of Ebor had also played his part.

'That is not what I required of the man whom I chose to be Lord Protector,' Gwydion said ruefully. 'He is by nature a ruler, and usually dedicated to good governance, but as long as a year ago I began to look for reasons why his nature might have been turned. I now ask myself whether leakage of harm from the Dragon Stone might not be to blame, for when I told him I wished to visit Foderingham Castle to inspect the Dragon Stone, he denied me out of hand. "No one," said he, "is to go near that stone."'

Will listened with mounting alarm, and also a pang of guilt. He already knew, from having lived among the duke's family, that Richard of Ebor was a man who treated his duties seriously. He was not a crudely ambitious man. He did regard himself as the rightful king of the Realm, but that was more out of respect for the laws of blood than any personal desire for power. Following the battle at Verlamion he had been prepared to agree to Gwydion's compromise, which was to content himself with the modest title of Lord Protector and to take on the day-to-day running of the Realm. For the sake of peace, he had allowed the weak usurper-king, Hal, to continue on the throne as figurehead despite his having fallen twice into further bouts of incapacity and madness.

But things must have soured a great deal, Will told himself, if Duke Richard won't allow Gwydion to see the Dragon Stone.

As for Will's uncomfortable pang of guilt, that came because he had never admitted an incident when one night he and Edward, the duke's eldest son, had led the other Ebor children down to look at what Edward had called 'the magic stone'.

'Duke Richard has not been quite himself lately,' Gwydion said.

'Do you think he's hiding something? About the Dragon Stone, I mean.'

'It may be nothing more than Friend Richard's woebegotten attempt to haggle with me. He is inclined to treat everything as if it might become part of a political bargain. He often says: "I will do something for you, Master Gwydion, if you will do something for me." Though he must know well enough by now that magic cannot be traded that way.'

'That would be a hard lesson for any lord to learn,' Will said. 'It seems to me that Duke Richard is not a man who'll ever understand magic.'

Gwydion grunted. 'You are right, for the trading of favours is how men of power try to gain advantage over one another. What self-seeking fools they are, when trust and selflessness are what is truly needed. So little magic is left in the world that men have lost their taste for it. Even the greatest exercise of magic does not stick for long in the memory. It fades from men's minds – speak today with anyone who fought at Verlamion and they will keenly remember arrow and sword, but they will have little recollection of the beams of fire that burst so scorchingly over their heads as the fighting raged below.'

Will thought about that, hearing a note of regret in the wizard's voice, and realizing that his own memories were vivid enough. A sudden suspicion prickled him. 'Were you by any chance on your way to Foderingham when I conjured you?'

'In truth I was already there – passing through the inner bailey and about to reclaim my wayward charge.'

Will blinked. 'You were going to take the Dragon Stone away without the duke's permission?'

The wizard made a dismissive gesture. 'I had not yet made my decision.'

Will wondered at what Gwydion knew and what he needed to know concerning the Dragon Stone. He had always said there was no such thing as coincidence, that every weft thread in the great tapestry of fate touched every warp thread and vice-versa, and from all those touches was made the great picture of existence.

Will's thoughts returned to what had happened that night at Foderingham when he had last clapped eyes on the Dragon Stone. 'Gwydion, I think there's something I ought to tell you . . .'

He explained how he and Edward, and all the Ebor children, had got more than their curiosities had bargained for. The stone's writhing surface had terrified them. It had begun by posing a morbid riddle for Edward, and had finished by attacking Edmund, the duke's second son, sending him into a swoon from which he had never fully recovered. He told of how he had wrestled with the stone and how it had almost overcome him, before cringing back at the mention of its true name.

When Will had finished explaining, the wizard leaned heavily on his staff and said, 'Let us overnight here. We shall talk more on this after supper, though it would have been better for all concerned if you had told me about this sooner.'

'I couldn't break a confidence,' Will said lamely.

'You are breaking it now.'

'That's because Edward is boastful and very close to his father. He may have told tales about the powers that dwell in the stone. That might be the reason the duke is behaving this way.'

Gwydion turned sharply. 'You think Friend Richard seeks to use the battlestone's power for himself?'

Will knit his brows over the suggestion. 'I don't think he would ever be *that* foolhardy.'

'Hmmm. It would depend on how desperate he became.'

Here, east of the Slaver road, the air was cleaner and the grass greener. At their backs a slim crescent moon was following the sun down over the western horizon. Their camp was made on a rise close by the manor of Swell. Once again Gwydion had avoided the villages and farms that nestled nearby. He chose the best ground and then carefully cut away the turf to make a fire pit and piled up enough dry sticks to give them good cheer until they should fall asleep. Will was very hungry, and glad of old dry bread and a delicious soup of dried roots and morels that Gwydion cooked up from ingredients he took from his crane bag.

Will's eyes drooped as, with a full belly, he listened to the crackle of burning wood and the calls of night creatures. The ground was hard under his elbow and hip bone. He smelled the drowsy perfume of cow parsley and meadowsweet and bruised grass, and felt pleased to be back in the wider world.

'My First in the West shall Marry . . .' he said, stirring himself to recite the riddle that had appeared in the skin of the Dragon Stone.

> *'My first in the West shall marry,*
> *My second a king shall be.*
> *My third upon a bridge lies dead.*
> *My fourth far in the East shall wed.*
> *My fifth over the seas shall send.*
> *My sixth in wine shall meet his end.*
> *My seventh, whom none now fears,*
> *Shall be reviled five hundred years.'*

'What are we to make of that?' Gwydion asked.

Will looked into the night. 'If the Black Book said there were many battlestones, maybe it's the Dragon Stone's way of giving clues about its brothers. Maybe one of the stones is fated to be reunited with its sister-stone in the West – that might fit with the piece you sailed over to your friend Cormac in the Blessed Isle. Or maybe that's the second stone mentioned, because it stood in the shadow of the King's Stone. It could be that the third will be found, or drained, on a bridge. Or maybe it lies near a place called Deadbridge – oh, you know better than I how riddles go.'

Gwydion settled back, watching the last rosy blink of moonset. He said distantly, 'It may be that the Dragon Stone is more important than we have so far supposed.'

'Why did you choose to lodge it with Duke Richard?' Will asked, unable to keep the criticism from his voice.

'You think that was a mistake. In truth, it was no choice of mine, but a course forced on me by events. There was nowhere better to lodge a battlestone at the time. Do you know that time itself has a most curious character? I have discussed it much with the loremaster who lives at the Castle of Sundials. Though he speaks of "time's arrow", its nature, he says, is not straight so much as turning ever and again upon itself – wheels within wheels, like the cogs that turn within his confounded engines. As the rede of time says, "History repeateth." Thus, if we are wise, we may learn from the past—'

'Gwydion,' Will knew when he was being distracted, 'what are we going to *do*?'

The wizard stirred restlessly. 'Rather than return to Foderingham, let us find out first if it has been put back in its original resting place. That is my greatest fear. And in any case we must go by Nadderstone if we would go to Foderingham by the shortest way.'

'Who would want to re-bury the stone at Nadderstone?'

'Who do you think? If it has come to Maskull's notice, and if he is making it his business to tamper with the lorc, then we should know about that.'

'What if we find it's been put back?'

'Then the time will have come for me to drain it. For, whatever the other merits of your midnight visit to the Dragon Stone, you have certainly given us a great advantage by discovering its true name.'

'Oh, no, Gwydion,' Will said, feeling dismay blow through him. 'Please promise me you won't try another draining.'

'I must do what I must do,' Gwydion said, then added with a note of finality, 'Do not worry about it yet. It may never come to that.'

Will blew out a long breath. He watched the flames of their little camp fire and wished himself back at the Blazing, but the coils of intrigue seemed to have wound themselves more tightly about him than any serpent. He said doggedly, 'Gwydion, before I set off anywhere else, I must get a message to Willow.'

'As a matter of fact, Willand,' the wizard said archly, 'I have already sent word to her explaining your absence. Good night.'

After three days' walk along highways and byways they came at last to the village of Eiton. There were many harvest carts about the lanes and straw was blowing everywhere along the dusty road that led to the Plough Inn. Gwydion looked for signs that the Sightless Ones were out overseeing the tithe, but he saw nothing.

The Plough was a much-praised alehouse and inn, and one that Will knew well. It was a long, low building set to the side of the road, with a walled yard, a great spreading thatch and a big square sign swinging between two stout posts. It glowed now in the mellow golden light of an August evening. A straw cockerel stood guard on the rooftree and seemed to tell the world that all were welcome, except troublemakers.

The inn was frequented by travellers and local folk alike. It was far bigger and busier than the Green Man, and had not changed at all since Will had come here last. A dozen churlish folk were slaking harvest thirsts in the homely, rush-scattered room.

The man who kept house was called Dimmet. He was a big man, very busy and jolly, the sort who folk took care not to upset. When he looked up his welcome could not have been warmer. 'Now then, if it ain't my lucky day! Master Gwydion! How nice! How nice!' He roared with delight as he came to greet them. 'Duffred! Come down here and see who's paid us the honour of yet another visit!'

The innkeeper's grown son poked his curly, ginger head in at the door and grinned broadly. 'Hey-ho, Master Gwydion! How goes it with you?'

'He looks like a man what's footsore and road-weary to me. And properly in need of a drop of my best ale – if you'll take the hint, my son.'

'That is very kind,' Gwydion said.

'And a jar of ale for the young feller too, I'd guess?'

The Plough's big, black mastiff dog came out to see what the excitement was. Being fond of dogs, Will put out an open palm to help it decide he was more friend than foe. It sniffed at his feet, then began to lick his toes.

'It's a big, old dog you have here,' Will said. 'Maybe you should put some water out for him.'

'Pack that up, Bolt!' Duffred called, pulling on the dog's iron collar. 'Out in the yard with you. Go on, now.'

Will grinned and shook Dimmet's huge, freckled hand.

'Glad to meet you.'

'They call me Will.'

'Do they now? Then, we shall have to do the same.'

'He don't recall you,' Duffred said impishly from the taps. 'Cider still more to your taste than ale, is it?'

Will nodded vigorously, pleased to be recognized after so long.

'I never forgets a face!' Dimmet touched a finger to his chin. 'Wait a bit! Are you not the young lad who came here that time Master Gwydion led our horse, Bessie, off on some business or another up by Nadderstone?'

'That's it.'

'You see! I never do forget a face. Though you was a mere lad then, and not so filled out. Must have been all of five or six year ago.'

'I hope Bessie got back safe to you.'

'That she did.' Duffred set down two tankards. 'She was fetched back by a man in my Lord of Ebor's livery as I recall.'

'Always happy to render Master Gwydion a service if I can.' Dimmet glanced shrewdly at the wizard. 'And in return he'll often put a good word on my vats, or he makes sure my thatch don't catch fire.'

Duffred tugged at his father's sleeve and said, lowering his voice, 'You might think to tell them about the odd one who's been sat in the snug all day.'

Will looked sharply to Gwydion, knowing it was not usually possible to get into the snug.

'Easy, Will,' Gwydion said, as if reading his mind. 'The Sightless Ones do not agree with the drinking of wine or ale. Nor would Dimmet here take kindly to one of them poking his nose in at the Plough, much less getting into his snug.'

'Oh, yes,' Dimmet said. 'He's a shifty one. Got wilted primroses on his hat, though I don't know where he got them. Said he wanted "privacy", if you please!'

Dimmet's eyes rolled as he made the last remark. The last reason anyone would come to the Plough, Will thought, was to be alone. He looked to Gwydion again in puzzlement, but then followed the wizard into the passageway and along a swept stone floor that was so footworn it shone.

They passed a great oaken table that was stacked with platters and bowls as if a celebration had only just been cleared away. In the middle was a trencher decked with flowers and a large pig's head with a red apple in its mouth. The head seemed to be grinning. It reminded Will of Lord Strange.

When they came to the great empty hearth with its stone chimney and inglenooks on either side, Gwydion paused and raised his arms. Then he muttered words and laid a spell on the little room that lay behind the chimney breast.

'What are you doing?' Will mouthed, suddenly anxious about what might be lying in wait for them inside.

The wizard looked around, then whispered, 'Calling down a defence against eavesdroppers.' Then he ushered Will through the hidden entrance.

The snug was cool and dark, for it was summer and the little grate was empty. The only light came from a small window and the polished oak boards that made it seem like a ship's cabin gave the room a rare cosiness. At the table sat a man Will was delighted to recognize.

'Tilwin!'

The dark-haired travelling man rose with a heartening greeting and gave him a bear hug. His eyes were as blue as chips of summer sky. 'How are you now, Willand?' he said. 'And Master Gwydion, well met, my old friend!'

Then Will heard Tilwin utter words half under his breath to the wizard, and something made him think that a formula had been spoken in the true tongue, words of recognition, a greeting between men who stood tall in one another's esteem. He watched them embrace briefly, then all three sat down together.

'You're the last person I expected to meet here,' Will said.

'Whereas I've been waiting for you to turn up like a bad penny all this fine afternoon!' Tilwin grinned, and there was laughter in his eyes, but also, Will thought, a deeper gleam that spoke of troubles.

In all the years of Will's childhood Tilwin the Tinker was the only outsider who had ever come up the Vale as far as Nether Norton. He was a knife-grinder and a trader who travelled far across the Realm. He had always helped take the tithe down to Middle Norton, and he had brought many necessaries to the Vale – tools, medicines, bolts of cloth, pretty gems and love tokens too, for he knew all the different kinds of precious stone and what could be done with them. One day he had given Will a black stone to put under his pillow to ward off nightmares. Another time he had cracked a glassy pebble for Breona, cutting it with a series of skilled blows, and so had made a false diamond for her to wear as a brooch on high days.

Some of the Valesmen swore it was Tilwin who had thought up the game of cards, and as if to prove them right he always carried a faded card stuck in the band of his hat. He usually put wayside flowers there too, to lift the spirits of those he met. Today, as Dimmet had said, there were primroses but, like Tilwin, they seemed a little worse for wear.

'Tell us why you've stopped coming to the Vale,' Will said. 'We've all missed you, you know.'

Tilwin glanced at Gwydion, and some more of his smile faded. 'I've had a deal to do lately, and little time to do it.' Then his smile came bravely again, and he poked Will's shoulder. 'Besides, there's less need for me to come to the Vale these days. Now the tithe has stopped and Nether Norton can afford its own grinding wheel. That was hero's work you did for your folk, Willand. I hope they appreciate you.'

Will reddened, embarrassed.

'I sent word for . . . Tilwin . . . to meet us here,' Gwydion said. 'But a word of warning to you: do you recall my saying that Tilwin the Tinker is not necessarily what he seems?'

Will looked uncertainly from the wizard to Tilwin and back. 'I've long known there was something rare about him, but I never knew quite what.'

'My name is not Tilwin – it is Morann.'

Gwydion smiled. 'He is, among other things, a lord of the Blessed Isle.'

'I can see that now you mention it,' Will said. And it was true, there had always been an assured manner about the man. Will jumped up and took his tankard in both hands. 'Allow me to greet you properly in your own name: here's to you, Morann, Lord Knife-grinder, as keen a blade as ever there was!'

'And here's to the meadows and mists of the Blessed Isle, where strange tales begin!' said Gwydion, rising and lifting his tankard also.

Then up got Morann. 'And here's to you, Willand of the Vale. And to you, Master Gwydion Pathfinder. You're both of you no better than you should be!'

They clashed tankards and supped, then all laughed together and sat down again as one.

'You're a loremaster like Wortmaster Gort,' Will said. 'Isn't that it?'

Morann made a modest gesture. 'Where old Gort's learning concerns all the forests and all the herbs of the field, mine only touches bits of pebbles and such like.'

Gwydion laughed. 'He gives himself no credit. He's a "magical lapidary" – the greatest jewelmaster of latter days.'

Like Wortmaster Gort, Morann was another of the ageless druida who had wandered abroad, collecting magical knowledge for a hundred generations and more. They had no homes, but attached themselves here and there as circumstances arose. They were not quite wizards, but their magical skills were great, and they had lived long.

Will thought immediately of the strange red fish he had found at Little Slaughter. How could it be that a thing so exactly like his own talisman had been there for the finding down in the dust? Surely a jewelmaster as knowledgeable as Morann would be able to cast light upon its origin.

But as Will put a hand down towards his pouch a powerful feeling came over him that he should not tell Morann about the talisman any more than he had told Gwydion, which was nothing at all. He examined the feeling suspiciously, and had almost decided to put his doubts aside and draw out the red fish, when Duffred arrived with cheese and bread and apple jam.

Then Morann unsheathed his favourite long, thin knife and in deference to Gwydion laid it handle inwards on the table before him. He said to Will, 'Be it hidden or carried openly, in former days it was thought a deadly crime to wear a blade in the presence of a druid, much less a person of Master Gwydion's standing.'

'I'm thinking you'll be cutting no flesh, nor even bread with that knife, Morann,' Gwydion said, his eyes twinkling.

'Indeed not, Master Gwydion. However I like to respect the Old Ways when I can.'

Will saw that a wonderful pattern like knotted cord was worked into the old steel. He wondered what was so special about the knife, but he could not ask after it for the two old friends were already busy with one another's memories.

They munched and drank as they talked about former times. Will listened more than he spoke and the three wore away most of the golden light of evening in remaking their friendship and gilding old memories. Morann told of recent travels, and of his adventures in the land of his fathers. Gwydion spoke of his wanderings in the wilds of Albanay, and of voyages he had made in frail coracles far out into the Western Deeps. Then they asked Will to tell of his wedding, and to speak of his life with Willow and the joy he had felt at his daughter's birth.

He told them as well as he could, but when a pause came in their talk the fears that had been banished for a while began to crowd in on him. Again he began to reach for the red fish, but then he told himself that he did not want to be the first to speak of troubles, and so once more he chose to lay the matter aside.

Instead, his eye caught the ring on Morann's finger. A ring of gold, it was, and the stone in it one of emerald green. Will had seen it many times before, but now its colour seemed to capture his attention and he felt prompted to ask about it.

'It's the ring of Turloch of Connat,' Morann said. 'It bears the great *smaragd* emerald of my ancestors. The tale says that Turloch used to wear it when trying suspected traitors. He would strike in the face any follower who was accused of treachery against him. If the man got up and kissed the ring then he was innocent. But if he could not bring himself to kiss the ring then he was guilty.'

65

Will wanted to hear more, but Gwydion cleared his throat and said, 'We could listen all night with great pleasure to the deeds of your forebears, Morann, but I fear that darkness is pressing. Let us not forget that we are met for a more solemn purpose.'

They pushed their empty trenchers away and sat back. Then Gwydion laid out matters concerning the battlestones, and as the sun set he began to make a summary of what was presently known.

'According to ancient writings, there were nine channels of earth power made by the fae long ago. These channels are called "ligns" – and collectively "the lorc". The battlestones are planted on the lorc. There are two kinds of battlestone – the greater and the lesser. The greater sort come to life one at a time. Each of them has the power to raise bloodlust in the hearts of men and draw them to battle. We have tracked down five battlestones so far—' Gwydion raised a stark finger, '—the first was the Dragon Stone, which we found just a few leagues to the east of here.'

'Gwydion put it into Castle Foderingham for safekeeping,' Will added. 'It's one of the greater sort.'

'And you hope it's still entombed there,' Morann added dubiously. 'Hope, but do not know? Is that it?'

'Quite so.' Gwydion unfolded his thumb. 'The second of the stones was the Plaguestone, which was left by us in the cave of Anstin the Hermit.'

A cloud passed fleetingly across Morann's face. 'Surely stones such as these will not be safe in castles and hermits' caves.'

Gwydion said, 'Indeed. But I judged they would do better when placed in fresh lodgings than when left to rot in the ground. Foderingham's walls are thick and I counted its master to be a stalwart friend. As for Anstin's cave, no man dares go there for fear of leprosy. It is hardly spoken of locally, and not at all elsewhere, therefore it is one of the most secret places in the Realm.'

Morann shook his head. 'Would the Plaguestone not have been better mortared into Foderingham's foundations alongside the Dragon Stone?'

'Yes, Gwydion,' Will agreed. 'Surely Maskull, with all his arts, would not fear the leper's touch. If to get at a stone, even one of the lesser sort, is his aim—'

Gwydion held up a hand at mention of the sorcerer's name. 'Hear me out. Of the Plaguestone I shall say more presently. Meanwhile, let me speak of the third stone.' He unfolded another finger. 'This is the Stone of Aston Oddingley, whose malignant power Willand first felt in his bones as we combed the land in search of the lign of the rowan. That stone, which he says is probably of the greater sort, remains undisturbed, for when we found it we had another quarry in mind, and my advice was that we should leave it be for the moment.'

Will turned to Morann. 'That's because the Aston Oddingley stone was planted on lands controlled by mad Lord Clifton, who Gwydion said would never bid us welcome. It was true. He was killed at Verlamion.'

Gwydion looked to Morann and the many charms hanging at the wizard's chest rattled together. 'I wanted to show Will here that according to the redes of magic some problems, though they are insoluble in themselves, in time often turn into different problems which may be solved.' He raised another finger. 'Fourthly came the stone we found near the Giant's Ring. Our triumph over it was accomplished at great risk, for it was a stone of the greater sort, though its nearness to the King's Stone had muted it. Its downfall was complete, and now its stump has been returned whence it came. Henceforth it will do good service for a mutual friend.'

Gwydion now unfolded his little finger and tapped it significantly. 'And that brings us to the final stone of which we have sure knowledge, the Doomstone of Verlamion, the same one that Will may have destroyed.'

'*May* have . . .' Will repeated.

The wizard took a deep breath. 'That stone, I believe to be the controlling stone, and without it the power of the others will be so diminished that they cannot complete their tasks. But when

Will made his brave attack he was young and untried, so it is possible that the Doomstone was not destroyed after all. Perhaps it only suffered a disabling shock, one which temporarily shattered its power into many parts. But perhaps those parts have been growing together again like drops of lead in the bottom of a fiery crucible.'

'And when enough drops are gathered into one?' Will asked.

'Then we shall know if I am right.'

Gwydion's mouse-brown robes had merged with the shadows of the snug. Will had been aware of a bumble bee buzzing at the trellis, but now even this tireless labourer had gone to its burrow and the climbing flowers that had listened in all around the window had closed their trumpets for the night.

Morann, whose chin rested on his hand, said, 'So, of the stones you know about, one has been drained, two are stored, one lies yet undisturbed, and the master of them all, the Doomstone, has been attacked but may be repairing itself. The sites of the other battlestones – if there are others – you have not yet learned.'

'We do know something.' Gwydion clasped his hands before him. 'When Willand was at Ludford Castle he felt himself affected by a strange melancholy. He thought it may have been caused by the emanations of a powerful stone, but in such a fortified place it was hard to tell exactly where they were coming from.'

Will thought back to the morbid feelings he had endured while staying at Ludford. 'I was certain it was a battlestone, Morann. At first I believed it to be the Dragon Stone, and I suspected Duke Richard of having carried it there for his own purposes. But then Gwydion explained to me that my thinking was out of kilter. The Dragon Stone was still at Foderingham, and my state of mind must have been roused up by another stone.'

'But you couldn't find it?' Morann asked.

Will shook his head. 'Though it seemed very strong. Ludford Castle and the town itself is a maze of walls and towers. There is too much dressed stone there. My feelings were confused. It was like listening for a sound inside a cave full of echoes.'

'Yet you were able to find the Doomstone, even though it lay under a great stone-built chapter house,' Morann said.

Gwydion spread his hands. 'That is because the Doomstone was by then awake, in the full flood of its power and actively calling men to the fight. It is possible that some powerful hiding magic is at work at Ludford. That may be a good reason to let the battlestone lie for the meanwhile, just as we have let the Aston Oddingley stone lie.'

'The trouble is,' Will muttered, glancing at Gwydion, 'we can't keep deciding to let sleeping dogs lie.'

Gwydion nodded at the hidden accusation. 'What Willand wants to know is why I seem to have done nothing to unearth the battlestones in the intervening years. I will tell him, for what youthful impatience sees as idleness may now appear otherwise. When the battle at Verlamion was halted I believed that the breaking of the Doomstone had likely solved the problem of the lorc. The Black Book predicts that Arthur's third coming signals the end of the fifth Age – therefore we know that it must end within Will's lifetime. When he cracked the Doomstone and I banished Maskull into the Realm Below there seemed little like-lihood of trouble arising again before the current Age drew to a close, and so I went about on other errands, in Albanay and else-where. It has turned out that my optimism was misplaced. I might have known it would be, for the end of each Age is a strange time and in the last days odd things do happen. But if optimism is one of my failings, I have at least learned not to put all my eggs in the same basket. It could be that neither Maskull nor the lorc were wholly settled – and so I kept Will safe in the Vale against the possibility of rainier days.'

Morann nodded. 'He dared not risk squandering you, for you are the only way he has of finding the stones.'

Will compressed his lips. 'You make it seem as if my life is hardly my own.'

Gwydion's face was never more serious. 'It has never been that, Willand.'

They lapsed into a gloomy silence, but then the wizard strove to lift their spirits. 'My friends, let me speak rather of what lies within the hearts of brave men. I should tell you that the true tally of stones is more encouraging than you presently imagine, for my efforts during the past four years have not been entirely without fruit. I returned to the cave of Anstin the Hermit, and now a second stone is undone.'

'You mean you succeeded in draining the Plaguestone?' Will said, sitting up in amazement.

The wizard set a taper to a candle and brought a rich golden light to the gloom. 'It was a far from simple task. My plan was to take the Plaguestone across to the Blessed Isle, but I could find no safe way to sail an undrained battlestone, even one of the lesser sort, over the seas. I could not hazard the lives of a ship's crew. Nor could I allow the stone to sink itself into the Deeps, for even the lesser stones will blight whatever they can, and many a ship would be wrecked by such a hazard forever afterwards.'

'So what did you do?' Will asked.

'Anstin the Hermit agreed to aid me, and in the end he paid dearly for his decision.' Gwydion's face set in sadness once more. 'I was much troubled, for when I reached Anstin's cave he told me the battlestone had been struggling against the bondage into which I had placed it. He said he feared that soon the harm would succeed against the spells that contained it. Every month it would writhe and spit at the eye of the full moon. Anstin was a man of true worth who came to know the nature of the stone very well. Great valour lived in his heart. In his younger days he was a lad with a good head for heights and for this one reason he was sent into a trade that did not sit well with his spirit. Even so, his hands proved to be talented. They were taught to work stone, and he decorated many of the high spires that sit atop the chapter houses and cloisters of the Sightless Ones. But in time his spirit cried against such work, and the feeling withdrew from his fingers. When the Sightless Ones learned of his plight they pressed upon him admission to their Fellowship, and when he refused them they said he had deliberately dropped a hammer, meaning for it to fall onto the head of an Elder. He repeatedly swore his innocence until they saw that he would not be moved. Then they drove him off, saying they would have nothing more to do with a man who was touched by obstinate evil. When I came upon him in Trinovant he was a lonely leper whose flesh was rotting on the living bone. I took him to dwell in a cave, away from all others, and there he was cared for by a Sister who brought him bread, but whom he would not suffer to see him, so ugly did he imagine he had become.'

Will said, 'I remember a rede you once told me: "Delicious fruit most often has a spotted rind."'

'And so it does. Anstin the Hermit was never ugly to my eye, but he yearned only for death when I first came upon him. I could not heal his flesh, for the damage had come of a deep contention within his heart, but I could and did reveal to him the true length of his lifespan. This he asked of me, for he said he wanted to know how much more suffering he must endure.'

'You actually told him the day on which he would die?' Will asked.

'That is not something to be undertaken lightly,' Morann said.

Gwydion's face betrayed no regret. 'I told him he was fated to die a hero. Only when he knew the true date of his death was I able to arrest his illness and thereby win for him a space of time to make a proper peace with the world. For this he was grateful, and when I brought the Plaguestone to him he was quite pleased to take it.'

Will thought back to the time when they had delivered the Plaguestone. He had waited outside Anstin's cave, imagining what was going on inside. He wondered if Gwydion had also foretold the manner of Anstin's death.

The wizard went on. 'Anstin understood very well the dangers the Plaguestone posed, but as ever he had a wry answer at the ready. "There can be no danger to a man who is already composed for the grave," said he. And I replied that, in truth, there was no gainsaying him. Therefore, this man whose fingers once knew stone so well kept the Plaguestone for thirteen seasons of the year under close watch and ward. At all times he lived in its presence. Fearlessly and with great strength he repulsed its struggles to ensnare him. When I returned to him just before the end he told me movingly of the continuing misery of his life, how he wished to pledge his last day to my cause if I should choose to attempt a draining of the Plaguestone. Hearing this bravery, how could I have done other than agree?'

Gwydion stirred and the living flame of the candle shivered. 'I will not tell in detail what happened that night in the cave of Anstin the Hermit. Suffice to say that there are few horrors that were not visited against his mind and body as the black breath of the stone was slowly drawn. I had learned much from my earlier mistakes, but even so the drawing out of the Plaguestone did not go well. The Black Book said the Plaguestone was far less powerful than the Doomstone, yet it was all I could do to drain it. Poor Anstin died when a cloud that had issued from the stone enveloped his body. He alone soaked up the harm, yet until the moment he was burst asunder he laughed at death and showed more courage than all the knights of this Realm might hope to muster. Such is the power of what lies within.'

Will clasped his hands in respect. He tried to dispel the images that swarmed in his mind, but it was difficult, for he himself had been under attack from a battlestone and his memory of the agony was sharp. Never before had he heard Gwydion speak with such a power of sadness in his voice. But the wizard was not yet done, and strength gathered in his words again. 'Friends, my decision to try to drain the Plaguestone was not taken lightly. There is a very deep rede of magic that says: "There is no good and no evil in the world, except that which is made by the wilful action of people." Yet all things are but vessels in which two contrary kinds of spirit are equally mixed. Some call these spirits "bliss" and "bale", the one having the power to drive kindness and the other the power to drive harm. Men, by their choices, liberate both into the world just by moving through it. We upset the balance whatever we do, unwittingly and without malice, sometimes through our failings, sometimes even when we strive to do what is best. But those imbalances are mostly small, and it is only when malice aforethought is involved that the balance is more widely upset, for then the malicious man acts as a sieve. He strains out the bliss from all that he touches, and so he gathers harm about him in ever greater concentration.'

'But how are kindness and harm different from what the Sightless Ones preach about good and evil?' Will asked. 'Aren't you just using different names for the same things?'

'Do not think that! Words are important. Dogs are not cats, which is why we trouble to call them by different names.'

'But surely good and kindness are the same, aren't they?'

'If you mean kindness, then you must say kindness. Good and evil are notions invented by the Fellowship for their own purposes, and the difference is this: the Sightless Ones say there are conscious sources of good and evil. They say that both good and evil are active in the world, driven by intent; one is sent to scourge us, and the other to save us. The Sightless Ones would have us believe that invisible monsters of great power use us as their play-things. This is quite different from the magical understanding of the spirits of kindness and harm which lie latent and in balance and scattered throughout all things.'

Will shook his head. 'I still don't understand.'

'The idea of good fighting to survive evil is a very dangerous one. It represents the second greatest tool of the Fellowship, and is something that softens and warps the minds of any who allow themselves to see the world in those terms.'

'The second greatest?' Will raised his eyebrows. 'You mean there's a worse one?'

'Much worse. Long ago the Sightless Ones harnessed an even more dangerous idea, one that came from the Tortured Lands of the east. It is an idea that makes folk into willing slaves once it is planted in their heads.'

73

'A simple *idea* can do that?'

'Do you doubt it?'

'But what can it be?'

'I dare not tell you for, though it is lethal, it also has great appeal. It might seize you and destroy you, and do so seemingly within the bounds of your own free will.'

'Gwydion, I am no longer a child. I have a child of my own.'

'Then I will tell you, but . . . are you sure you are ready to hear it?'

He thought about that for a moment then shook his head. 'No, I'm not sure. How could I be? Maybe I'm just letting idle curiosity get the better of me.'

'Ah, now that is a mature response. Then I can at least refresh your memory on the matter: the idea is called the Great Lie. The Sightless Ones have used it ruthlessly to bend the common people to their will, for once brought to a false belief they are easily persuaded into other lies. They become obedient and willingly swap their lives for no more than the promise of a better one to come. Thus may a man's true fate be twisted out of his own control. Thus is a real, living person sent walking into a glittering maze of deceptions.'

Will sat back, unsure about what Gwydion was saying. He knew little enough about the Sightless Ones, except that thinking about their red, scaly hands made him itch. He wanted to ask how an idea could make a man give up his life, and what reward could possibly be offered to make him do it, but then he thought about what he had seen inside the great chapter house at Verlamion and he knew that whatever this idea was, it certainly did drive men insane.

He held up his hand, suddenly fearful. 'I don't think I'm ready to know what the Great Lie is.'

Gwydion smiled and then said, 'Perhaps we are straying from the true path, for the kindness and harm that exist in the battle-stones are another thing entirely. What is known is this: the fae of old readied two similar stones and worked high magic upon them. They drew all the kindness they could from the first and put it into the second, while at the same time they drew almost all the harm from the second and put it into the first. Thus the sister-stone was filled twice over with unbalanced kindness, whereas the battlestone contained a double measure of almost pure harm. The draining in which Anstin offered himself as bait was attempted to prevent a battle in which thousands would have died, but there was a second reason. We must not permit the battlestones to fall into Maskull's hands, for he will certainly misuse them if he can. My belief is that, at present, he knows less than we do about them, but he learns speedily and is ever ready to experiment in matters which he would not touch if he were wiser. I fear he may have taken the Dragon Stone. Perhaps he has even put it back into the lorc. That is why tomorrow we must go to Nadderstone and see for ourselves.'

In the silence that followed, Will heard the muted sound of merry revels coming from the rest of the inn. Voices were raised in laughter, a round of song and the scraping of a long-handled fiddle. Perhaps Gwydion's spell of defence against eavesdroppers had spent itself. Duffred came in to collect the trenchers and to flap the crumbs from the table. He brought a measure of brisk good cheer with him that dispelled their thoughtfulness, and when he asked if they needed their tankards refilling, they agreed that that was a very good idea.

They spoke more lightly for a while, reminiscing about this and that until at last Morann rose up. 'I think it's time I was away to my bed.'

'In that case, may you remember to forget only what you forget to remember,' Will told him in parting toast.

Gwydion drained his tankard. 'Black swan, white crow, take good care, wheresoever you go!'

Morann picked up his knife and sheathed it. 'And I have a parting toast for the both of you: may misfortune follow you all the days of your life . . .' he smiled a warm smile, '. . . but never catch up with you.'

75

And with that Morann was walking with uneven steps towards the passageway, and soon the stairs were creaking under his heels. When Gwydion also took his leave, Will sat alone in the snug for a few moments, his thoughts darkening as he wondered about Willow and their baby daughter and the peril that still seemed to him to hang over the Vale like a dark cloud.

CHAPTER FOUR

THE LIGN OF THE ASH TREE

W ill was surprised to find the sun high in the sky by the time he awoke. Bright shafts of sunlight pierced the shutters, and he sprang up from the mattress and got dressed as quickly as he could, fearing that Gwydion and Morann might have left without him.

But he soon found them outside in the yard, talking with the inn's people.

'Morning, Gwydion. Morning, Morann.'

'And a fine morning it is,' Morann said.

'Ah, Willand,' Gwydion said. 'I hope you are feeling able today. There may be tough work ahead.'

Dimmet sniffed at a side of beef that was hanging in his outhouse. 'Not too high for the pie, nor yet too low for the crow,' he said with satisfaction. 'Now, Master Gwydion, shall I expect you back by noon?'

'You may expect us, Dimmet, when next you see us.'

'Right you are,' Dimmet said affably. 'I'll take that to mean I should mind my own business.'

He went off to take delivery of the milk jugs, but soon Duffred had hitched Bessie, the bay cob, to the tithe wagon. Will got up onto the cart to sit alongside Morann and Gwydion, and then

77

they were off, heading east along a road that Will had travelled before.

A rolling land of good, brown clay met them as they drove steadily onward. The going was easy past Hemmel and Hencoop. The wagon ruts that had been made in the road during a wet spring had been baked into hard ridges by the summer sun and worn to dust. Hills to their left threw out low green rises that sloped across their path, and the sun shone on the part-harvested wheatfields to their right. But soon, tended fields gave way to wilder country.

Gwydion told of the times he had visited Caer Lugdunum, an ancient fortress that had once stood on a hill a little way to the north, and how graciously he had been received in poem and song by the druida who had lived there. Then Morann sang 'The Lay of the Lady' in a rich, clear voice that knew the true tongue well. His song was about the brave Queen of the East and the stand she had made long ago against the armies of the Slaver empire. It was so sad a song that Will felt shivers pass through him, and it was a long while before he returned to himself and felt the hot sun on his face again. When he did, he found that Bessie had already covered half the road to Nadderstone.

Hereabouts the land was scrubby and unkempt, and Will looked to a cluster of bushes on his left that he knew hid a pond. Gwydion had once said there was probably star-iron in the bottom of it, and now Will realized how the pond had been made, by a shooting star landing hard on the earth, though one much smaller than the one that had smashed Little Slaughter. The thought made him shiver.

'There's power flowing here,' Morann said, his blue eyes on the far horizon. 'We may expect miracles, or worse, I'm thinking, before the day is done.'

'Remember, the road follows the path of a lign,' Gwydion said, 'whether we can see it or not. Willand, do you feel anything yet?'

'Not yet, Master Gwydion. You can be sure I'll speak up soon enough when I do.'

A short shower of rain came to refresh the land and went away again as soon as it had come. They continued across the valley and soon Will noticed a tall tower of mottled brown stone. It was the same one he had seen before, standing sentinel on a ridge, above lands that had once been tilled by the Sightless Ones, or those who laboured for them. But those fields were now neglected and overgrown, and that caused Will to wonder, for the Fellowship was notorious for never allowing its lands to lie fallow if gold could be mined in them.

As they drew near Will was shocked to realize that the tower was now in ruins, as was the cloister and chapter house it had served.

'What happened to the Fellows?' he asked in amazement.

'Gone,' Gwydion said.

They passed by two large fishponds. Once this place had made Will feel very uneasy. And now, as their road climbed up past the tall, iron-brown walls and vacant windows of the chapter house, Will suppressed a shudder. He turned to Gwydion and saw the wizard's keen, grey eyes examining the battlements. The wizard called Bessie to a halt.

'What are we stopping for?' Will asked.

Gwydion handed him the reins. 'We must look into what has happened.'

Will shielded his eyes against the sun and studied the tower, but he saw nothing more noteworthy than a lone gargoyle that stuck out from the corner of the parapet high above them. Morann jumped down from the cart and they both followed Gwydion through a yard of tumbled graves beside the chapter house.

The garden that had once held neat rows of green plants was now overgrown and its bee skeps smashed. The iron weather vane that had once shown the sign of a white heart and had stretched its four arms out above the roofs, had been cast into a corner of the yard. The roofs themselves were broken and pulled down too. Ahead the great gates were unhinged, and where, to Will's recollection, the arch of the doorway had been incised with the curious motto:

EROBALENISLIN

Now the stonework was defaced so that only the letters R, A, N, S and I remained. Gwydion stood before the doors, deep in thought.

'Strange,' Will said, looking at the damage. 'Do you think it means something?'

'Everything means something.' Gwydion made no further answer but continued to stare at the arch and then to run his fingers over the letters.

Morann spoke in a low voice. 'Isnar is the name of the late Grand High Warden of the Sightless Ones. It seems the letters of his name were spared from the Fellowship's motto when the rest were stricken out.'

Gwydion stirred. 'This has meaning, for it surely was Isnar who ordered the roof of this chapter house to be broken in.'

'How do you know that?' Will asked.

'Because no one else has the power to order it.'

Will heard the scurry and squeak of rats as they moved inside. Black glass had been shattered from windows. It crunched under-foot in the dampness. Two or three winters had ruined the fabric of the building, yet a greasy odour still clung to the place. They came back out into the open, entered the walled tithe yards and saw hurdles of woven willow sticks scattered about the cobbles. They were all that remained of stock pens and stalls. There was rotting gear here, tools for hauling animal carcasses: blocks, hooks, red rusted chains . . .

Will picked his way through the ghastly ruins and saw the slaughter sheds and the stone basins that had once caught the hot blood of terrified animals. The slaughter knives and poleaxes were all gone from their racks, but the grim channels and lead pipes put down to feed a line of barrels were still there. In the next shed was what remained of the fat-rendering cauldrons – the vats and moulds where the Sightless Ones had once mixed up wood-ash and fat to make their ritual washing blocks. The stone floor was still waxy from old spills, and slippery.

Will's skin tingled as he looked around, but he could not be sure if it was the lign that was causing it. The pillars of the cloister stood like broken teeth now and the space of the great hall was open to the sky, though half of the roof beams remained over-head like the ribs of a great whale. Will saw ear-like growths on the timbers, and many of them were nibbled, as if by rats, though how rats had got up so high he could not imagine. Fragments of gilding and painting remained on the walls. Everything was defaced, rain-washed and sun-faded, and the gravestone floor was scattered with thousands of broken candles and spoiled washing blocks. The place seemed to have been ransacked and then abandoned quite suddenly many months ago. There had been much violence done here.

'Now you see the horrible truth about what happens when the Sightless Ones gather the tithe,' Morann said. 'It's not just carts full of grain they take to hoard and sell. Horses, cattle, sheep, fowl – all go into their slaughterhouses.'

Will saw the place where sheep and calves had been strung up to have their throats cut. Anything that walked on two legs or four was bled into ritual jars, then soap and wax made from their fat.

'A sickly smoke always hangs over the houses of the Fellowship at tithing time,' Gwydion said. 'Many trees are hewn and much wood burned for ash to make soap. Flesh is boiled up and rendered of its fat, and the meat buried or left to rot, for the Fellows partake only of the blood.'

Will knew that the soap was used in ritual washing, which was why townspeople nicknamed the Fellows 'red hands', though never in public for that was punishable and could end in a person's lips being cut off.

'And why do they make so many candles?' Gwydion asked, and when Will made no answer he added, 'The Fellowship make candles to light their sacred pictures.'

Will looked to the wizard and then up at the faded remnants of paint and gold leaf. 'But . . . why? When the Fellows have no eyes to see them? And why would a Grand High Warden want to visit destruction upon one of his own chapter houses?'

'The Fellows call such a thing a "Decree of the Night Fogs",' Gwydion told him distantly. 'It is ordered only rarely. It is their punishment for *deviation.*'

'Deviation?'

'That is, if a house strays from their creed so far that they cannot whip it back into line. Then they cut it off and trample it into dust. This is done partly lest the disease spreads to other chapter houses, and partly by way of example. They erase all reference to the broken house from their records. They destroy its chronicle, take away its adherents. Such a house becomes to them a house that has never stood, and the Fellows who failed become men who have never lived.'

'Is that what happened here?' Will said, looking around. He could feel the prickling in his skin growing stronger and wanted now only to get away from the place.

'I do not know what happened here, for the doings of the Fellowship are kept a tightly bound secret. But did I not tell you how the houses of the Sightless Ones are most often built upon ligns and other streams of earth power?'

'How could this house have failed?' Will asked, stepping over piles of broken wood and fallen slates.

'This may be the explanation,' Gwydion said. 'You know that the Doomstone was the slab that capped the tomb of their Founder. When it was broken that source of power which is habitually tapped and abused by the Sightless Ones must have shifted. Did you not tell me of the madness that beat through the chapter house of Verlamion when the lorc came alive?'

Will remembered. 'It was hardly to be imagined. As if the one idea filling all their heads had suddenly gone out like a candle and left a darkness which they could not bear.'

Gwydion turned to him. 'In like wise, Willand, the troubles of this house may have started as soon as we plucked up the Dragon Stone. For the power of the lorc certainly shifts when a battle-stone is taken from the earth, and this house also stands upon the lign of the ash.'

Will looked around the stone-cold walls, aware of the perpetual shadows that lurked in the corners.

'You must beware the Sightless Ones,' Gwydion told him earnestly, 'for they do not love you. They will not easily forgive the intruder who defiled their most revered shrine.'

Will felt the walls close in around him. 'I've wondered more than once why the Fellowship has not come into the Vale to get me. They were the only ones, apart from yourself and Morann, who ever came near.'

Morann shook his head. 'They cannot find the Vale. They've never come into it, nor will they ever. I was always at Nether Norton when the tithe fell due. It was I who took the carts through the quag and down to Middle Norton. The red hands from Great Norton never approached further than that. They don't know of the Vale's cloaking. They're interested only in amassing wealth. It's gold that gives them influence.'

Gwydion said, 'The Fellowship does not connect the Vale and what they call the pollution of their chapter house at Verlamion. Still, at their annual public self-mutilations in Trinovant Isnar has sworn to destroy the one who broke the Doomstone. You must not underestimate him, for he never underestimates his enemies. And the threat you pose them is very great.'

'With all their wealth and power?' Will said, looking about. 'What threat could I be to them?'

'That is easy to answer. I have already said that you are the Child of Destiny, third incarnation of Great Arthur of old. What you will do if the prophecies of the Black Book are brought to full fruit, will cause their spires to topple. And not before time!'

'But I don't see how—'

Morann made an open-handed gesture at what lay around them. 'It's been their habit for at least a thousand years to build where the men of olden times set up cairns and groves, and so supplant the Old Ways.'

Gwydion grasped his staff tighter. 'Many of their chapter houses must be built upon ligns. They do not know it, but they feed on the power of the lorc as greenfly feed upon sap that rises in a flower stem. With every battlestone we discover and root out, Willand, another of their houses will fall as this one has.'

Will folded his arms. 'Then let us hope we find all the battlestones. Whatever it was that made the Sightless Ones leave here, I'm glad.'

'Bravely said.' Morann clapped him on the back. 'The red hands tell all who will listen that they bring freedom, life and peace, but they trade in slavery, death and war.'

Now Gwydion hastened forward like one who has suddenly found what he was looking for: a steep stone stair that led down into the cellars. They followed him into the stinking darkness, until he struck up a pale blue light for them to see by. The place was vacant now, the treasury emptied of its gold and all the strong-room doors thrown open. The blue glow that lit the palm of the wizard's hand seemed reluctant to penetrate the gloom. He walked alone in the magelight shadows, and unguessable thoughts troubled him. 'Behold!' he said, raising his staff. 'It is as I suspected. This is more than a thieves' hoard-room.'

As Will's eyes adjusted there appeared in the cellar wall a low gate of iron bars. It was meant to stop off the way, but it was wrecked. A hole had been rent in it as if by some powerful beast.

'What is it?' Will asked. The magelight did not penetrate far beyond the bars.

Morann clasped his arm tightly, hushing him. Gwydion's voice was rising: 'I can smell it! Truly these are dungeons of despair!'

'What could have done this to iron bars?' Will asked, looking to Morann and putting his finger on the place where brute strength had torn the barrier.

Morann whispered, 'Do you know what this is? It's a passageway into the Realm Below. Can you feel the air moving up, and with it the salt of the Desolate Sea?'

And Will could feel it. On his face, a dank draught that issued up from a hidden place below the earth. Air that bespoke tremendous depths, great caverns, ceaseless tunnels, dark rivers that had never seen the light of the sun. This was truly the air of another world.

And something in Will wanted to go beyond the bars and venture into that darkness. He wanted to see for himself what lay below, but Morann drew his knife and said he thought the cellar unwholesome and that the fissure had the whiff of sorcery about it and needed to be blocked up. He wanted to leave the vile place for the sake of his lungs.

Will, and then Gwydion, followed him up the stone stair and out into the light. They stepped back across the rubble-strewn yard, and Will blew out a great breath. 'Let's go. Just being here makes my flesh crawl.'

Gwydion set a bleak eye on him. 'The Sightless Ones are involved in a bigger way than I thought.'

The wizard quickly turned away and Will said, 'So big that you daren't speak of it?'

He was not sure Gwydion had heard, and the wizard offered no reply, saying only, 'Have you forgotten why we set out?'

'What's bothering him?' Will whispered to Morann as they followed on.

'I think he's found what he came here for. And whatever it is, he doesn't like it.'

Out in the open again the wizard climbed quickly aboard the cart and clicked his tongue at the horse. Will looked up at the dismal tower and his eyes sought the lone gargoyle that he had seen on his arrival, but it was nowhere to be seen.

They rode on in silence, their spirits overcome by the stagnant earth streams that ran sluggishly now under the cloister. But Will's low mood stemmed more from the gloom that Gwydion showed. Their walk in the ruins had put the wizard in a mighty sulk.

When the road rose and Bessie laboured in her pulling, Morann and Will jumped down and walked the meadows for a while. Morann renewed the flowers in his hat with bright yellow dandelions and purple knapweed. Will cooled his toes in the lush grass. He said, 'What are the Sightless Ones involved in? Finding the stones? Did Gwydion mean that?'

Morann looked back towards the cart. 'You must ask him that yourself, but if I had to hazard a guess I'd say he's most worried about those broken bars and what must have come through them.'

'I can feel the lign right here,' Will said. He stopped suddenly.

Morann took his hazel wand and began to scry, but unsuccessfully. 'I feel nothing unusual.'

'It's dispelled the bad taste left by the ruins. It's running strongly under my heels.'

'Where?'

Will ignored the question. 'Oh, how can I explain it? It's like a fiddle string, and once the chapter house was a finger pressing down on it in the wrong place, making a discordant note. And now the string is open the note is more pure again.'

'We'll tell Master Gwydion that. Maybe it'll cheer him up.'

It was not long before they arrived in Nadderstone. Will hardly recognized the place. Flow along the lign was swift and joyous, like water in a new-dredged channel. Where once there had been abandoned buildings now there were new, white cottages. Lime-washed walls were bright in the noonday sun and new thatch shone neat and golden. Much of the land round about was under cultivation or had been fenced to keep cattle in. Men, women and children were busy in a barn threshing grain with flails. When they saw the cart approaching they came out. The place was clean and prosperous and the four or five young families who lived here now were courteous and welcoming.

Gwydion approached the foremost. 'Where have you come from?' he asked. 'And who is your lord?'

For a moment it was as if a shadow had passed over them. The man fell under the spell of Gwydion's voice. He shifted his feet and said, 'We are poor, landless folk. We came here from a faraway place on the strength of a rumour that there was good land here that might be had.'

Gwydion smiled. 'Have no fear – that rumour was mine. Enjoy Nadderstone and make it your own, for your hard work and care have already won me as your protector. I offer you a blessing of words upon your new homes, so that all will be well and when the time comes your sons and daughters will find good husbands and wives in the villages round about.'

While the wizard talked, Will and Morann went up into the meadows north of the hamlet. As soon as Will began to feel the lign running strongly underfoot again he took back his hazel wand and began to pace out the limits of it, scrying just as Gwydion had first taught him in this very same place.

Either the flow had increased several fold since then, or his own talents had developed greatly. 'All the pain's been cleaned out,' he said. 'It's the difference between dirty ditchwater and a mountain stream.'

They came to the spot where the Dragon Stone had once lain. Its hole was filled in and there was a bed of pretty yellow flowers growing there. 'I'm sure the Dragon Stone hasn't been returned to the place where we found it. Let's go and tell Gwydion the good news.'

Morann laughed. 'I think he already knows. It doesn't take a talent such as yours to see that this place is flourishing as never before.'

Will scrubbed at his head. 'You know what I think? I think Nadderstone's now taking its fair share of earth power – flows that were for too long pent up by that chapter house.'

Morann looked eastward. 'This is the lign of the ash, you say?'

'Yes. Its taste is unmistakably Indonen.' Will shaded his eyes and looked east also.

'Taste?' Morann said, turning to look back the way they had come. 'That seems a curious way to speak of it. Did you not just tell me that the tower and chapter house were like the finger that stops a fiddle string?'

'I could just as easily have said it's like the grip that pinches off a vein in a man's arm and so holds back the flow of blood to his hand, bringing numbness and robbing his grasp of strength. I said "tasted", but it's not really a flavour I'm talking about.' He shrugged, finding his talent impossible to describe.

Morann let out a piercing whistle and beckoned to Gwydion. 'Let me see now. There are supposed to be nine ligns that make up the lorc. The one that runs by the Giant's Ring is "Eburos", the lign of the yew. The battlestone that you say is planted at Aston Oddingley lies upon the lign of the rowan, and the true name of that lign is "Caorthan". While this lign is "Indonen" of the ash. What of the others?'

'I've felt other ligns sometimes as we crossed them. There's the one named "Mulart" for the elder tree, and "Tanne" for the oak. The rest are named in honour of the hazel, the holly, the willow and the birch. I've not felt them at all, or if I have I can't easily call to mind their particular qualities.'

The wizard came up to join them. He leaned on his staff, seeming troubled still.

'A fair old morning's work,' Morann said.

Gwydion wiped his brow and resettled his hat. 'But as is so often the case, work begets more work, for now I must go urgently to the place that I was called away from.'

'Foderingham?' Will said.

'Plainly, the Dragon Stone is not here, so I must go there.'

'Now?'

'As the rede says: "No time is as useful as the present." Nor, in this case, is there any reason to delay. I shall leave at once.'

'What are you going to do?' Will murmured, sure that Gwydion had set his heart on a perilous path.

'In what I must now do you cannot help me. I mean to gain entry to the dungeon of Foderingham. I will do it with or without Richard of Ebor's consent. Once there, if the Dragon Stone is present, I shall lay hands upon it. Recall the rede: "By his magic, so shall ye know him!" I shall search for Maskull's signature, and if I find he has not meddled with the stone, then I shall renew the holding spells in which I first wrapped it, and perhaps add a few more for good measure.'

'You won't try to drain it?' Will said, only half convinced by the wizard's assurances.

But Gwydion smiled an indulgent smile. 'I promise, I will not try to do that.'

'And if you find that Maskull *has* been there?' Morann asked.

'Then I shall have to undo that which he has done, before renewing my own spells.'

Will brightened. 'Surely we can help you, if only in keeping the jacks who guard the walls of Foderingham occupied for a while.'

'I have greater need of stealth than assistance.' The wizard regarded him thoughtfully for a moment. 'But, Willand, if you would help me then make a promise.'

'Anything.'

'Go to the Plough and wait quietly for my return. Do not stray far from that place. Dimmet will begrudge you neither board nor lodging if you tell him of my request. If you will heed my advice, you'll lay low. Speak to no one, and do not advertise yourself widely abroad. This is most important.'

'I'll do my best.'

The wizard took his hand briefly and nodded as if sealing a bargain. Then he clasped Morann to him and words passed between them in a language that seemed ancient to Will, though it was not of his ken.

He watched Gwydion go down into the hamlet, speak to one of the farmers and then he was up on a piebald horse and riding away east out of the village, while Bessie was being led towards the farmer's stable.

'Well, I like that!' Will said as he realized their ride back to Eiton had just been bargained away.

'That's wizards for you,' Morann said. 'For a man who cannot be in two places at once he's powerful good at being in one place not very much at all.'

Will put his hands on his hips. 'I suppose we'd better start walking. It'll be thirsty work in this warmth. I guess Gwydion'll be right about Dimmet's charity. I just hope it lasts when he finds out that Bessie's been handed to a farmer in Nadderstone to ease a wizard's emergency!'

The walk back to the Plough was indeed hot work and much was talked over as they wended their way towards Eiton. When they were about halfway there Will cut and whittled for himself a staff. It was fit for a quarterstaff, though he wanted to use it as a walking stick. Morann would have nothing of it, and was not content until Will had whittled a second staff and given him the choice of which to use.

Gwydion had once said that the quarterstaff was the diamond among weapons, striking like a sword and thrusting like a spear, it was able to disable and dispirit without inflicting undue damage. 'The skilled wielder of a staff has the advantage against even two swordsmen, for a staff has two ends, and if one opponent should break his distance against a skilled staff he will suffer a hit. Against the single sword, a staff always has four paces in hand. Such is its dignity it metes out humiliating reminders while barely drawing blood.'

Will had never forgotten that lesson, and had practised the staff until he could easily beat the best who lived in the Vale. But there were many more whacks that Morann was able to teach him, and their journey back to Eiton became in part a running fight.

They got back aching and bruised and laughing. Once they were in the Plough's yard Will found Dimmet among his flitches of bacon. They told him what had happened to his horse.

'No matter,' Dimmet said, wiping his hands on his apron. 'One good turn deserves another, or so they say. And all things have a way of coming full circle in the end. If Master Gwydion's gone off all of a sudden, there's bound to be something needful at the root of it. I know he'll return her to me some time. Now, what's it to be for you?'

Morann grinned broadly. 'A quart of your finest nut-brown ale. And we'll take it to the snug, if we may.'

'That you may, and with pleasure. Stew and leftovers all right for you?'

'Enough is as good as a feast, as my friend the Maceugh always used to say.'

'The Maceugh?' Will said, his brow rutting. 'Have I heard of him before?'

'Maybe you have not,' Morann said lightly, then added, 'But maybe you will come to know him one day.'

Will took a tallow dip, passed behind the inglenook and the snug door opened at Morann's touch. The space inside was soon golden with candlelight. They slaked their throats with first-mash ale, and then set to work on a supper of spoon-meat, barley bread and cold roast goose before they pushed their bowls and trenchers away from them and sat back content.

'Old Dimmet's right about something needful being at the root of Gwydion's going,' Morann said. Once more he took out his knife and laid it on the table before him. 'There's talk of Commissioners riding abroad all up and down the Realm. Folk are worried. They're talking about war everywhere you care to go.'

Will knew that Morann meant Commissioners of Array, the officers that were sent out in the king's name to raise an army.

'It must be serious if they're coming for men in the middle of harvest,' he said. 'Who'll gather in the crop if all the able-bodied men are marched off the land?'

Morann lowered his voice. 'Gathered in or not, the Commissioners will have their men in the end. Have you ever known a lord starve because of a bad harvest? Likewise, it's the churl, the common man, and those who depend on him, who come most to grief when a war begins.'

'That's right enough.'

'It's said that in Trinovant the Sightless Ones are offering large loans. They lend only to lords, so what does that tell you?' Morann's eyes twinkled. 'If lords are borrowing gold, it's for only one purpose.'

Will laced his fingers together, stretched and yawned. 'They'll spend gold enough on the feeding and equipping of soldiers, but it's a risk they care to take. They go to war in hope to gain the lands held by their enemies.'

The large green stone in Morann's ring seemed to glow with crystal fire, and his voice became passionate. 'I tell you, Willand, the queen has spent most of the past four years trying every way to undermine Duke Richard's rule as Lord Protector. If he's stopped taking Master Gwydion's good advice there'll be a clash soon. That's why I must be on my way tomorrow.'

'Not you too?' Will's spirit rebelled at the idea. 'Am I to wait here all alone and do nothing?'

'It can't be helped. Master Gwydion asked me to go to Trinovant. I'm to do what I can to steady events. I could hardly refuse him, so I've agreed to speak to some friends I know there. They are people of influence who owe me a small debt of gratitude and are willing to pay it – which is the best kind of friend a man can have.'

'What will these friends do?'

'Tell me how things truly stand at court. It's rumoured that the king's latest insanity is ended. Perhaps it was a natural brain fever, but poison cannot be ruled out, and Master Gwydion suspects that the queen has arranged for spells to be cast upon his mind to make him appear well again.'

'She's done that kind of thing before, and that was at Maskull's prompting.'

'These days Master Gwydion sees the sorcerer's hand in everything.'

Will took the remark without comment and thought to console himself with a slice of cheese. He reached out for Morann's knife, which was handy, but when he came to cut the cheese the blade would not enter.

'Either this cheese is a lot older than I thought,' Will said, frowning at the knife, 'or your steel has lost its edge.'

Morann laughed. 'Do not worry yourself. Being a knife-grinder I'm never far from a whetstone.'

Will tried again, but looked up, seeing the cheese rind was untouched. 'What's wrong with it?'

'Nothing's wrong with it. What you have in your hand is the second most precious item that I have ever clapped eyes upon.'

'This old knife?'

'It's an old knife, surely, but not any old knife. This knife has been sharpened on the Whetstone of Tudwal, which is one of the spoils that was brought forth from Annuin by Great Arthur of old.'

Will's interest deepened. 'Master Gwydion has spoken many times of prophecies that concern Great Arthur, but he's never told me much.'

Morann sat back in his chair and began to sing,

> *'Where is the man who is mightier?*
> *The four winds tell it not!*
> *When greater the treasures that were taken?*
> *Won in war and fair fight.*
> *How bright was the blessing*
> *Brought upon Albion?*
> *Whose land now shall be the Wasteland?*

Before Great Arthur led,
the Cauldron swirled . . .
Before Great Arthur sailed,
the Sword smote . . .
Before Great Arthur entered,
the Staff upheld . . .
Before Great Arthur's coming,
the Star shone . . .

'Aye, Willand. In those early days the Hallows were bound, blind and in darkness all, down in Annuin, in the Realm Below.

'The spoils were brought out by Arthur, upon his ship,' he said as if half remembering. 'Out from a sea cave in the north. The Cave of Finglas, which was then a mouth into the Realm Below . . .

'Many adventurers sailed with Great Arthur aboard the ship *Prydwen*. Bards, warriors and harpers – great men of old, they were! Among them, the famous Wordmaster Taliesin, who was one of seven who survived to tell the tale. He wrought a great poem about it called "The Breaking of the Dark". Much went missing from the Black Book in the days when giants ruled the land of Albion, yet there was enough of it remaining for it to speak of a promise to be redeemed – a king shall come, a king whose forewarning sign shall be the drawing forth of a sword from a stone.' And Morann sang again,

'Child of magical union,
Hidden among hunters, weaned upon warriors.
Brave son of a poisoned father,
Sent to the city, tried at the tourney.
A king of tender years,
Sired by a sovereign, but made by Merlyn,
Drew he forth Branstock,
Great Arthur, the once and future king . . .'

The loremaster's eyes softened, and he smiled. 'So you see, Willand, you are not the only one to have been named in the Black Book. Master Gwydion is there too, when Master Merlyn was his name.'

Will tried to smile back. 'It's an uncomfortable feeling sometimes knowing that whatever path you choose, the outcome has long been decided.'

'Don't think that! Master Gwydion did not mean that when he said your life was hardly your own, only that you were mantled with duties and responsibilities that are heavier than those of most men. But your choices have always been free. It's not the fulfilment of prophecies that matters, so much as the manner in which they are fulfilled. That's where final outcomes are decided. Consider the next fragment of the Black Book in which we hear of Great Arthur's passing, there by the lakeshore of Llyn Llydaw. He made another promise without fear or faltering, one that was to last a thousand years. The verses tell it thus:

> *'The worth of my life, such that it be,*
> *Has chained the future to a fateful turn.*
> *When comes the final catastrophe,*
> *Then, only then, shall I return!'*

'When rises the greatest need I shall come again . . .' Will whispered in the true tongue.

'Those were your words. And what turbulent times have we seen since the overrunning of the Realm by the Easterlings. Though none have been worse than those that are upon us now. I will say it straightly, this is the final catastrophe.'

'The once and future king did not come to save us from the Conquest.'

'Perhaps the arrival of Gillan might have seemed to warrant it, but in the end the Phantarch, Semias, reached an understanding with the Conqueror and we saw that his invasion was not the ending of the world such as we had feared. That was near four hundred years ago.'

'How long is it since Arthur fought his last fight at Camlan?'

'I think you already know the answer to that – near a thousand. So we come to you, Will, and the last pitiful fragments of the Black Book that Master Gwydion has cherished in a secret place down so many generations. This also seems to speak of a king, though no one can be certain. One who is ". . . a True King, born of Strife, born of Calamity, born at Beltane in the Twentieth Year, when the beams of Eluned are strongest at the ending of the world".'

'The ending of the world?' Will felt the shock of the idea. 'I was born in a twentieth year . . .'

'Aye, in the twentieth year of the reign of King Hal. And on the night of the full moon. And it was said that you would deny yourself thrice, and so you did.'

'And "One being made two"?' Will said, looking up suddenly from the strange knife that lay upon the table. 'What does that mean?'

'It too seems to be a part of the prophecy.' Morann looked away. 'As also is the suggestion that "two shall be made one".'

Will straightened. 'Then it was written all along that the Doomstone would mend itself!'

'That could be one interpretation.'

Morann reached out to take his blade but Will stayed his hand. 'You said this had been sharpened on the Whetstone of Tudwal. So what if it was?'

'Ah, well, you see, a blade so sharpened will deal only a lethal blow, or no blow at all.'

Will quickly put the knife down.

'Morann, if you're leaving tomorrow, may I ask a favour of you tonight? Could you go to Trinovant by way of Nether Norton? I don't know of another messenger who could find his way into the Vale.'

'You may consider it done.'

CHAPTER FIVE

MAGICIAN, HEAL THYSELF!

When Will woke the next day at first light, he found that Morann had already left. He sat down at a small oak table and, while he waited for breakfast, took out the little red fish from his pouch. It was so like his own green fish that there could be no doubt that it had come from the same place. And as Gwydion always reminded him, a famous rede said there was no such thing as a coincidence. But what the meaning might be in the fish was far from clear. As he turned it over in his fingers he wondered why he had not shown it to Gwydion, or to Morann, who was surely the best person to give an opinion. He had just put it in his pouch and forgotten about it. *Or had he?*

Delicious smells wafted in from the kitchens and soon the Plough began to fill with Eiton's harvesters. Will, who was sitting alone in the corner, saw how they first noticed him then touched their foreheads and shook him by the hand as they filed in.

'Morning. Morning . . .'

Will breathed deep. He seemed to have lost his appetite, and took a little oatmeal. When he had finished it he took up the red fish and studied it again, while its beady little green eye studied him. It was so like his own talisman, yet the comfort he had always got from the green fish did not come from this one.

Now, as he looked up, he saw the harvesters holding out their sickles towards him.

'Thank you, Master,' the nearest of them said.

'What?'

'For your blessings upon our trade tools.'

He looked back at the man blankly, then he saw that his quarterstaff was propped up behind him and he realized with a bump what the men had taken him for.

They think I'm a wizard, he thought, smiling. A wizard! Would you believe it?

The men would not leave until he had touched each of their sickles in turn and muttered the name of it in the true tongue.

As the last of the harvesters left, a young mother came to him and asked to have a blessing laid on her child.

'A blessing? Well, I don't think I—'

'Please. Just a good word for the babe, Master,' she said. 'To keep the horse flies off her while I ties up the corn stooks. See?'

'You want *me* to put a good word on the baby?' Will asked doubtfully. He looked across the room and saw Dimmet watching with folded arms. Will inclined his head, then shrugged. 'Here. Give him to me. What's his name?'

'Rosy,' said the child's mother.

'Oh, yes. Yes . . . of course.'

Will made a sign on the babe's forehead, while muttering a spell of general protection against insects. He realized he couldn't remember the true name for horse flies, so he protected her from wasps and creepy-crafties of all kinds, then he handed the child back.

'She'll be fine in the fields, but make sure she stays out of the sun, won't you?'

'Thank you, Master,' the woman said and went away.

But no sooner had she gone than a toothless old woman appeared. She had with her a girl of five or six. When Will looked up the old woman said nothing, but the child smiled the most astonishing smile. She had no more teeth than the old woman, and was also cross-eyed.

'Can I . . . help?' Will said at last.

'Begging your pardon, Master,' the old woman said. 'I brung the daughter's daughter when I heard you was here.'

Will waited, but when nothing more came from the old woman except an expectant look, he said, 'What I mean is . . . is there something I can do for you?'

He watched as the old woman shuffled and then said something to the child, pointing to Will's staff. Straight away the child put her hands to her mouth and grinned shyly, then she darted forward to touch the staff.

'Hoy! What's this?' Will asked. 'What did you just tell her? That's no wizard's staff.'

The old woman looked suddenly cast down and began to beg piteously. 'Is there nothing can be done for the poor little one, Master?'

'What's your name?' Will asked the girl.

'Thithwin.'

'Thithwin. What a very nice name.'

'It's Siswin,' said the old woman. 'I'm africkened she'll never get a husband looking like she do, Master.'

'Surely it's a mite early to be thinking of husbands for . . . ah, Siswin,' Will said frowning. He was uncomfortable discussing the child's looks in her hearing.

'Ain't there nothing at all can be done against plug ugliness, Master?'

'Just . . . wait a moment.'

He thought back to his studies and knew there was something that could be done, if only it was to make the child believe that she was beautiful. According to the magic book Gwydion had given him that usually did the trick, for children had a way of growing into what they thought they wanted to be most of the time.

He took the girl's shoulders in both hands, steadying her before him. Then he brushed back the hair from her face with his thumbs and put a pinch of salt on top of her head, after which he muttered a spell that was used to untangle knots.

'Look at this finger with this eye, and that finger with that eye,' he said holding up two fingers before her. Then he slowly moved his two fingers apart and muttered a 'let it be' spell.

'You are a very pretty girl, do you know that?' he said solemnly, and the girl nodded.

'Now will you make my teeth grow, pleeth?' she said.

'Don't worry about them. They'll grow out in their own good time. They always do.'

Will waited for them to leave and allow him to finish his breakfast in peace, but they did not move.

'And what about grandmammy? Will her teeth grow out ath well?'

Will spread his hands in regret. 'Now that I can't promise.'

'Say "thank you" to the Master,' the old woman said.

'Thank you, Mathter.'

When they had gone Will finished his meal then, alerted by a buzz of voices, he got up to look along the passageway. There was a knot of people at the door of the inn, and all of them were marvelling at the improvement in the girl's eyes. Dimmet was foremost among them, his voice booming.

Will spoke to Dimmet the moment he came in. 'What did you tell them?'

'Oh, 'twern't me. Word has just got about.'

'What *word*?'

'Why, that there's a wizard in the district.'

Will tried to lower his voice. 'But I'm *not* a wizard.'

'You could have fooled me about that. That was as pretty a piece of healing as what ever I've seen. And I've seen a fair few healers in my time, genuine as well as the other sort.'

'But that was just a little helper magic.'

'Well, that's it! Folks'll walk for days to have a touch of magic. Don't you know that? Many a time when Master Gwydion's come here there's been a crowd of folk started to gather outside. One time there was a line stretched halfway up to Lawn Hill. That's why he don't never stop in a place for too long.' Dimmet grinned. 'I expect he asked you to look after business for him for a day or two, did he? Save him the bother?'

'What?' Will said, aghast.

'You're welcome to stay here as long as you like, Willand, you know that!' Dimmet winked. 'I expect I can handle all the extra customers. And there's generally a powerful thirst on folk who've walked a half dozen leagues or more on a summer's day in search of a cure.'

Just then Duffred put his head in. 'There's a man out here says can he bring his cow in to see the wizard?'

'No, he cannot!' Dimmet said and marched off down the passageway.

'Where're you going?' Will called after him. 'Duffred, where's your father gone?'

But Duffred only grinned and said, 'He's found a mare's nest and he's gone to laugh at the eggs. What do you think? You'd better come out here before they start breaking the door down.'

Will groaned, and resigned himself to a long day.

A clamour began as he came to the alehouse door.

'One at a time!' he said. 'Please!'

Duffred and two of his father's serving men came out and marshalled the folk into a line, saying that if they did not stand quietly and in good order the wizard would not see anybody.

'What did you say that for?' Will hissed as Duffred went back inside.

'Eh?'

'What did you call me a wizard for?'

'Oh, they don't know no different. Besides, you are a wizard to us.' And Duffred went off whistling.

When noon came, Will hardly stopped to eat. He had not bothered to count but he supposed that over a hundred folk had gone away happier than when they had arrived. He helped them over everything from bunions and hens that refused to lay to pig-bitten fingers and a troublesome toothache. But no matter how hard he listened, or how many signs he placed on heads, still more folk presented themselves.

Throughout the afternoon it seemed that two hopefuls arrived for every one who went away, and as the heat of the day began to mount, Will began to wonder how many folk there were left in this part of the Realm. The promise he had made to Gwydion to lie low had somehow failed without any intention on his part, and that was worrying. If I keep on like this, he thought, someone nasty is bound to hear of me and be drawn here – if only to have a cure for their boils.

'I don't want to disappoint anyone,' he told Dimmet at last as the innkeeper brought him out another tankard of cider. 'They come here with such faith in me. But there's got to be a limit. I'll have to call it a day when the sun does the same.'

'You'll never get through this lot by sundown!'

'I'll have to. It's necessary to transpose spells when they're cast at night. And of that art I know very little.'

The end of the line was still a long way down the road, and only when Will refused to see another person did Dimmet send Duffred along to guard the end so that newly arriving folk could be sent away.

The crescent moon was setting when Will finally escaped to take his supper. Dimmet, who was counting a stack of silver pennies, said Will deserved the best room in the inn, which was up a set of stairs jealously guarded by Bolt, the Plough's big black dog.

'That's it!' Will announced. 'No more! You'd better tell them to go away, Dimmet. Because I am not seeing anyone else.'

'There's always tomorrow.'

'Not tomorrow. Not ever!'

He went to bed very tired, but he could not rest easy, for though none of the casts had been great in power or extent, the exercise of so many spells still sparked in all the channels of his body.

As he lay restlessly, a thousand faces appeared to him – all the poor folk who had passed under his hands, all the wounds and worries, all the ailments and afflictions.

Surely, he thought as he turned onto his side, I couldn't have advertised myself more widely if I'd shouted my name out from the rooftops.

The next day he woke early. He was still tired, and quite ravenous, but when he opened the shutters he saw a swelling crowd was already gathered below. They waited in hope, though they had been told that there would be no more healing. Those who had arrived since dawn were reluctant to believe what those who had waited all night were telling them. And so the crowd had continued to grow.

As Will sat at breakfast he debated what he would say. When he peeped through a crack in the shutters he saw that several hawkers had come hoping to profit from the crowd. There was even a juggler in red and yellow walking up and down with a chair balanced on his chin.

'You'll have to be strong with them today,' Dimmet said, a gleam in his eye.

'I'm not going out there. Tell them I've gone.'

'Tell them yourself.'

Will's fists clenched. 'Dimmet!'

Dimmet was about to go out to make the announcement that Will was shortly to address them all when there came the drumming of a horse's hooves.

'Master! Master!' someone cried at the back door. 'Come quick!'

That sounded too urgent to ignore, and Will decided to go into the yard. He pushed his way through the onlookers and was met by a man sitting astride a dun pony who begged him to come along the Nadderstone road with him.

'What is it?' he asked anxiously. 'Is someone injured?'

'It's up on the tower!' he cried. 'Come quick!'

'What's on the tower? What tower?'

'They caught a goggly in a trap up by the old chapter house!'
'A goggly?'

A great gust of surprise swept through those who were listening at the gate as they all caught their breath at once.

'They wants to kill it! You got to come quick!'

That sounded sinister, though Will had no idea what a goggly was. Still, it was his opportunity to escape and he seized it. 'Stand back!' he said, waving an uncompromising arm at the crowd.

There were groans for fear that he would leave them. Some gave tongue to angry shouts and began to press in around him, but he leapt up behind the rider and thrust out his oak staff. He cried out as he had once heard Gwydion cry out, 'Give way, there! Hinder me who dares!'

The crowd was struck dumb by that. Dimmet and Duffred and their helpers began to push people back from the gate. A way parted and allowed the pony to canter away. A moment later they had left Eiton village far behind, and Will clung on as they passed into open country.

They followed the road that Will had taken the day before along the broad valley and past the ruined chapter house. But when they came up the ridge where the tower stood he saw that it was abandoned no more. A knot of folk were gathered at its foot, and they were looking up at the mottled brown stone. Many had armed themselves with sticks and were shouting angry oaths at the tower. They broke off when they saw their messenger had returned with the wizard.

As Will got down from the horse he saw one of the young men begin throwing stones up at the tower.

'Hoy!' he shouted, and made the lad turn. 'What do you think you're doing?'

'Trying to wallop that there goggly.'

When Will shaded his eyes and looked up he saw they were trying to dislodge the gargoyle.

'It's naught but a carven image!'

'Nooo! 'tis a goggly! Look, it moves!'

Will stared at their red faces and began to suspect they had been put under an enchantment. But then the creature actually did move.

'See, Master! Now then! What kind of a carving is that?'

Will's eyes narrowed. It was a live animal trapped high up in a corner of the wall. One of the ugliest creatures he had ever seen. Its every movement lifted the hairs in Will's flesh, as the sight of a spider did in some. The creature was brown-grey and mottled, batlike yet baby-faced at the same time, and there was something elfin about it. It had wings and a tail and four thin limbs, and was about the size of a three-year-old child, though it was built much slighter and in strange proportions. Whenever it moved the folk below gasped and hooted. And when the bold lad made to pitch another stone up at it Will stayed him with a question.

'Who found it?'

One of the men spoke up. 'My brother seen it up there around dawn when we come up from Morton Ashley to check on the snares.'

'Snares?' Will asked sharply. 'Shame on you. There's a deal of suffering in snares, you know that.'

'Well, fetch it down then so's we can kill it!' the man said.

'Is that what you brought me out here for?' Will demanded.

'Look!'

The thing moved again, crouched in a corner, then scuttled at speed across a sheer wall, clinging to the vertical surface and the overhang of the parapet with long, claw-like nails. Will saw that something was clamped to its ankle and it trailed a long, rusty chain that seemed to be attached to the masonry of the tower.

Stones were let fly at it and fists shaken.

'Naaw! Naaaw!' it cried, and a shower of grit flaked down into their eyes from its struggles.

'Stop that!' Will cried with all the authority he could muster. 'You must try to calm yourselves!'

'At night them gogglies fly out from caverns and drink the

milk of our animals,' a woman said, hate shining in her eyes. 'And they steal babies from out their cradles!'

'And they shuns the light,' another told him. 'But 'tis said they can sit out even in the noonday sun and not budge once they've tasted of the flesh of a child!'

'Nonsense.'

''Tis true! That's why they hide out on towers and the like. Pose as gargles in the daytime, they do. Until folk discovers them and drives them away. Pitch a rock at it, Erngar!'

'I said no throwing!' Will pointed his staff at the man and he dropped the rock. 'Or I shall not help you.'

A memory stirred as he caught the latest movement. He was reminded of a candle-blackened roof and hideous faces and winged creatures just like this one. What he had at first taken for carvings had clustered high up among the roof beams of the great chapter house of Verlamion, looking down on him with hungry eyes.

'Goggly child-stealer!' a fat woman shouted up at it, wrathfully shaking her fist.

Just then, Duffred came up on a horse. 'What's to do here?' he asked.

Once he had dismounted Will drew him aside out of earshot of the others. 'What is that thing?' he asked shading his eyes.

'Don't rightly know. But you want to be careful, the folk at Morton Ashley and right down as far as Helmsgrave say these creatures steal newborn babes,' Duffred murmured.

'So I've discovered.'

The Nadderstone man who had brought Will here joined them, and so did his wife. 'Gogglies come from a land under the ground.'

'How do you know that?' Will asked, a sudden anxiety seizing him.

The man looked back challengingly. 'Every seven years them gogglies must pay a tithe to the infernal king who lives down below. But it's a living tithe. They must give over one of their own young – unless they can find a man-child to offer instead.'

'That's why they're always prowling for our young ones,' the woman said, picking up a stone.

Duffred said quietly, 'I don't know if it's the truth, but it's what they believe. They all do. When this chapter house was still lived in, the folk hereabouts would bring their children here to have a mark put on their heads – the Rite of Unction they called it. It was supposed to be a protection against these . . . things.'

Will folded his arms. 'And was it paid for?'

'Aye. A gold piece taken from the village coffer.'

He snorted. 'Gwydion says the Sightless Ones love gold above all else. And that the Elders of the Fellowship delight most in taking it piecemeal from the needy and the credulous.'

'But is that not a fair exchange?' Duffred asked. 'A piece of gold for a charm against evil?'

'Evil!' Will gave Duffred a hard look. 'That is a meaningless word, an idea invented by power-hungry men to enslave folk's minds. And how many times must it be said: true magic is never to be bought or sold. Don't you see? The red hands were just squeezing these folk, frightening them into bringing their babes here. Doubtless so they could be registered with a magical mark, one that helps to make recruits of them in later life. Gwydion says the Sightless Ones believe in something very dangerous.'

'And what's that?'

'It's called the Great Lie.'

Duffred looked unsure and gave the cloister a thoughtful glance. 'So you're saying the goggly ain't a child-stealer after all?'

'I hardly think so. Look at it, Duff. It's terrified!' Will thought of the vent in the cellar under the chapter house and smelled again the strange air that had issued from below.

As he walked towards the tower, one of the skin-like wings flapped pathetically and he knew the creature was in pain.

'I'm going up there,' he said, rolling up his sleeves.

'You can't do that!'

'Why not?'

'It's said they got a poison bite on them!'

'I'll bet that's a lot of nonsense too!'

Inside the tower a few floorboards were still clinging to the beams and three broken and rotting staircases led precariously from one level to the next. Will had to be helped up to the first floor, but then he climbed alone, walking with arms outstretched along the beams, testing his footing with care as he went. Birds had nested here and the rain of several winters had made the walls mossy. When he reached the top he saw marks that showed how the roof of the tower had been deliberately broken with axes and hammers. He looked down from what seemed now to be a dizzying height, and began to edge out along the bare parapet. At last he came to the place where the iron chain was wedged tight in a crevice of the stonework. One of the creature's ankles was shut in an iron trap, and the ring on the chain that dangled from the trap was fixed through a staple in the masonry.

He wiped the sweat from his eyes and tried not to look down. The sooner he did what he had come to do the better it would be. But when the creature found that he had come close to it, it began to screech. It had big eyes, a broad muzzle and a wide mouth with many needlelike teeth. Its grey fur was threadbare, and its lips were bloodied, which gave it an even more monstrous appearance.

'Naaw! Naaaw!' it cried, and tried again to escape, but it could not bite through the chain, nor was it strong enough to pull the ring free, no matter how it tugged.

'Stop flapping, you foolish beast. There, now,' he murmured, trying to gentle it. 'Can't you see you're only hurting yourself?'

'Naaw! Naaaw!' the thing cried back.

Balancing on top of the parapet was difficult. The masons who had built the tower had made castellations on top, perhaps so that princely armies marching by would believe it was part of a great fortification and so leave it alone. Will sat astride the battlement and inched along the wall. His left leg overhung a sheer drop every bit as far down as the ground beneath the curfew tower at Verlamion. When he came to the iron ring he found it was made fast, and was too strong to break.

He thought about using a spell, but he had no knowledge of the creature's true name, nor could he say how magic would work upon it. There's no alternative but to speak calmly to it, he thought, and to try, bit by bit, to tempt it in.

'Naaaw!' it screamed when he put his hand on the chain.

There was no trust in the fragile creature. It pulled against his efforts, obstinately hurting itself, and he worried that he might break its leg if he were to pull too hard. It was already in pain, for the rusty teeth of the trap had bitten deep.

'How long have you been here?' he asked, leaning out as far as he could. 'You poor little thing. Are you hungry? I wish I'd brought a sausage or two for you. That might have tempted you down, eh? And by the looks of you you're parched too. I've never seen such a depth of mistrust in any beast. Where did you learn that? Now, if I can only reach out and . . .'

But when he stretched out his hand towards the trap the creature flapped in a renewed frenzy. It flew at him, and scratched him with its slender claws.

'Steady . . . I'm not going to hurt you,' he muttered, drawing away.

His outstretched fingers trembled as he tried to reach the trap, and perhaps turn it over a little to see how the mechanism worked and how the iron teeth might be parted, but the creature took fright once more. Terror flashed in its eyes. It hissed and lunged, and then sank its teeth into his hand.

A sharp pain shot through him. He stifled a yell, but then the creature pulled back, jerking furiously on the chain in another vain effort to pull itself free. Its claws began to scrabble horribly against the stone, and then it flattened itself on the wall. It shut its eyes and made a horrible face, freezing in an outstretched pose in a last senseless effort to deceive the hunter by playing the gargoyle.

'Come on! Let's be sensible now,' Will said. 'We both know you're not a stone carving.'

He hung on to the chain even though he felt the fingers of his other hand sliding. Fear of falling froze him, put a rod of steel in his arm. He summoned the power to ignore pain and the strength of three men to slowly drag himself back. His braids brushed his cheek, and as he came upright he found he was shaking.

'I'm only here to help you, you stupid creature,' he said. There was blood on his fingers where the ingrate had bitten him. Drops of blood pooled at the wound and began to run in red lines down his arm as he watched. Blood dripped from his elbow into the void below.

He was dimly aware of upturned faces as Duffred and the other folk watched him. He hoped Duffred's claim about a poison bite was empty.

'Those folks down there think I'm either very brave,' he told the frozen creature, 'or very foolish. I'm not sure myself which it is. What do you think?'

But the beast was not listening.

'Magician, heal thyself!' he said, and laughed at the irony. So much healing had come from his hands just lately, yet he could do nothing for himself.

'That's how magic works, I'm afraid,' he said, looking hard at the beast. Then he realized that nothing his magic could do was likely to be worse than the injuries he would end up with by fighting the creature's stubbornness head-on.

There was nothing for it but to use a spell of great magic. He resettled himself on the wall like a man astride a horse. He put his hands together and summoned up his inner calm. After all the practice of yesterday a magical state of mind came to him easily and he felt the tingling in his skin begin to rise in waves. Then he fixed his attention on the chain.

He began to blow on it. Hot breath, hotter as it left his lips, hotter still as it played on the iron chain link. Soon the rusted iron began to glow a deep cherry red. The red intensified until it was glowing yellow and then white. Will put two fingers through the link and opened it easily.

The Giants' Dance

When magic snaps, best beware the afterclap!

Will recalled the rede only just in time as the effort of the spell broke back against him. It was like a fall from a great height. Darkness closed in on him very suddenly. For a moment he was in a faint, then his thoughts seemed to move outside his head, and he was looking down at an unconscious fool who sat astride a battlement with two pieces of chain clasped in unfeeling hands.

But as the chain swung free the creature's eyes opened. It sensed freedom and came to life, scuttling first halfway across the wall. Then it launched itself into the air.

It fell for a moment in a great flat-bellied curve, weighed down by the trap and chain that dangled from its leg. But the rush of air under its wings bore it upward, and it flapped in a desperate arc over the trees and disappeared.

Will saw everything haloed in blue light. He battled to bring his mind once more into focus. Stupidly he looked at the patterns of the ground far below but could make no sense of them. But then he felt a trickle of spittle run wetly from the side of his mouth. He felt his teeth grating on the stone and a great sickness welled up in his belly.

A moment passed before he understood his precariousness. Another moment before he began to wonder just how long he had been slumped on the wall. He heard Duffred calling to him. Then the life started to flow back into his limbs again, and he breathed a deep draught of air that made him realize just how close a fool had come to killing himself.

□ □ □

CHAPTER SIX

AN UNWELCOME GUEST

B right sunshine was shafting through an open window and sparrows were chasing one another noisily through the eaves when Will came to again. He found himself stiff in every joint, and his left hand was tied up tightly in a cloth strip.

Bolt began to bark and came up to him with a wagging tail when he tried to turn over. Then Duffred appeared and said, 'How are you feeling this fine morning? – what's left of it, anyway.'

'Sore.' He smiled. 'And hungry.'

'Soon fix that. Does bacon and eggs sound good enough?'

'Hmmm.' He glanced up at the window. 'What about the folk outside?'

'Oh, they've all gone.'

'But I can hear voices.'

'Market day. And a busy one too. I should lay low if I was you, in case folk start to put the word out you've come back again.'

He gave Duffred a nod of agreement. 'Good idea.'

Will replaited his braids, dressed and slipped down to the snug. Dimmet appeared from one of the pantries. He planted his hands on his hips when he saw Will was awake and laughed his great laugh. 'Oh, so you've come back to us, have you? You was as mad as a March hare when we put you to bed. Rattling on about this and that.' He turned to Duffred. 'How is he now?'

'Says he's hungry.'

Duffred raised his eyebrows. 'And how's the hand?'

Will flexed it testingly. 'Stiff. And I still feel tired, despite sleeping a full night on your softest mattress.'

'Two nights and the day in between if you really want to know. We was getting a mite concerned about you.'

Will was astonished. '*That* long?'

'I suppose doing magic takes it out of a body.' Dimmet's voice hardened. 'Duffred here says them folks from Morton Ashley weren't best pleased you let their goggly get away, mind.'

'It didn't get away. I let it go.'

Dimmet blinked. 'What? A-purpose?'

'Yes.'

'Well, then. No wonder they was upset with you. Gogglies ain't the easiest of things to catch ahold of by all accounts.'

'I thought I'd been called there to save a life. But they'd caught the creature in an iron snare. They wanted me to kill it for them. What do they think I am?'

Dimmet put a pewter platter down in front of him and withdrew. Will make short work of the breakfast, then he went back upstairs, having remembered the red fish that was still in his pouch. He took it out. A stunning idea had come to him.

Maybe, just maybe, it *was* his own green fish. Maybe something or someone had stolen it away from Nether Norton, and had taken it to Little Slaughter where it had been altered by the heat of the fireball.

He looked at it with new eyes. If it had been altered, then it was a change for the worse. There was something secretive about it now, something that did not sit very comfortably with his magical sense. Even so, he felt prompted to put it on a thread and wear it inside his shirt, just as he had before. But after a while sitting alone he began to feel so restless that he decided to go out.

He tied a bundle to his staff, stuck his hazel wand in his belt and put up the hood of his cloak. Then he crept downstairs again and stepped out by the back way.

He felt drained, like a man who wakes in the thin hours of the night and cannot get back to sleep. The wound in his hand had begun to throb. He knew he should rest, but what he wanted most was to get away from Eiton and its throngs of people for the rest of the day. He needed to plant his feet in the good earth, drink his fill of pure spring water and feast on fresh air. He would walk the lign, and soon he would feel more like his old self again. The sun would burn the tiredness out of him, and he might even be able to think a few things through at last.

He slipped back into the Plough's yard unnoticed a little after sunset. He was tired and displeased with what now seemed to have been a fruitless and ill-spent day. The night was clear and warm. Many stars were twinkling overhead, but he had no time for them. He came in past the stables, and felt the presence of a big animal shifting its weight from foot to foot. His magical sense flared vividly, and he got the impression that the beast in the stall was thirsty, but he was too tired to pull the thought fully up into his conscious mind or to do anything practical about it.

The inn was warm and welcoming and busy with village folk making merry, but it seemed to Will both close and stuffy. There was a man sawing on a fiddle and another beating on a tabor. Duffred was washing a bucket of greasy wooden spoons over by the ale taps, and he hailed Will.

'It's too busy in there,' Will said, preparing to slip upstairs.

'My old dad says that "too" and "busy" are words that never go well together in an innkeeper's hearing. Mind you, after all the tumults of this week I confess I'd be happier if it was a little quieter just now. Where've you been all the day?'

'I . . . think it's best if I make myself scarce.' He glanced at the many customers, disliking their raucous laughter and the merry singing that had begun.

Duffred looked up and handed him a full tankard. 'Here. This'll wet your whistle. You get yourself down the far corner. Nobody much'll bother you down there.'

He took the cider. 'Thank you. I don't think I'll need to whet my appetite though. I'm ravenous.'

He watched Duffred break off half a loaf and then ladle out a bowl of pauper's pea soup for him. Will carried it off down the passageway and found the quietest corner, but no sooner had he broken bread than a bent-backed old man shambled over. He was wrapped in a dark cloak, and there was a dusting of sparkles about his hair and upon the wool of his mantle, as if he had just come through fine rain.

'Hey-ho, Master!' the old man said in a jocular voice, and sat himself down.

Will resettled himself. 'How do,' he said more than a little gruffly and fearing that more was about to be asked of him. The old man edged his stool closer to the table and leaned forward and Will felt a pair of faded eyes boring into him as he ate.

He looked up at last and saw the old man nod at him. 'Looks right tasty, does that, Master.'

'I'm nobody's master.' He frowned. There was something about the old man's appearance that made Will feel mightily uneasy. He wished the singers would quieten down. 'I dare say Duffred'll give you a splash of good pauper's soup and the rest of this loaf if you ask him.'

'Oh, I ain't much hungry for soup.'

'That's all right then,' Will said with his mouth full.

'But see, I heard there was a crow visiting hereabouts.'

Will stopped chewing and put his hunk of bread down. 'Crow' was the word some used to mean a wizard. 'I wouldn't know about that.'

'And I heard there was a lot of healing going on here. A regular hero of a healer at work they told me – a friend of the crow's, a young feller not unlike yourself.'

'I'm no hero,' Will said lightly, and started eating again.

'Maybe you're not,' the old man said, but his eyes strayed to Will's staff, and then to a meat knife that was on the uncleared table, and finally back to Will's face. 'But what if I said I'd been looking for *you*?'

Will saw the old man's eyes fasten upon his own. His hand went unconsciously to the place where the red fish was concealed. 'Looking for me, you say?'

The old man smiled a yellow smile. 'Oh, I've known about you for a very long time, Willand. As a matter of fact, we've met before.'

The singing stopped and the sudden silence was blemished by the sounds of a big horse snorting and big hooves clopping out in the yard. Will looked to the tiny window, then to the door and irresistibly back to the old man. 'Who are you?' he said, his blood running cold. 'How do you know me?'

'You know very well, I think.' The old man's arm moved as fast as lightning. He suddenly plucked out the hazel wand that Will had in his belt. 'I see you've a talent!'

As the old man snapped the wand in two a surge of fear ran through Will's belly. He found he could not look away from the other's binding stare. Not even towards the knife that was within easy reach on the table top.

'Who are you?' Will demanded.

'One who wishes to know if you are a born fool who has learned nothing since.' Suddenly the old man's voice was gone and another that was deeper and wholly compelling filled the air.

Will's mind whirled in terror. His hand moved towards the knife, knocking his soup bowl from the table. But the bowl and its contents froze in mid air and never reached the floor. Nor would his hand move further towards the knife no matter how hard he tried to make it.

'Who are you?' he asked for the third time, though he had already decided he knew the answer. He heard his voice rise in panic, betraying him as complete powerlessness overtook him. He tried to get to his feet but he could not move. You fool! his mind screamed. You broke a promise and look what it's brought you to!

'You know who I am. And I command you – speak my name if you dare!'

A blade of ice slipped into Will's heart. All the hairs on his head stood up, and against his will his lips formed the word, 'Maskull!'

No sooner was the word spoken than the face of the old man began to change. It shimmered like ripples on a pond. Will watched motionless as a new face began to form. Nor did much relief come to him when the face that appeared was Gwydion's.

'Easy now, Will. There is no danger. Fortunately you are with a friend.'

But Will still could not speak. He blinked and looked again, still unsure if the apparition was real. Then the shock that gripped him began slowly to ebb away. The soup bowl clattered to the floor, splashing his feet.

Anger overtook him.

'You scared me half to death!' he cried, and sprang to his feet.

'I am sorry to have frightened you, Willand, but the lesson was an essential one. I told you to remain here but you did not remain here. I told you to lie low, but you did not lie low.'

'I only did what I had to!'

'Is that what you call it?'

'What was I supposed to do? It all seemed like the right thing to do at the time.'

But the wizard's grey eyes were on him, relentlessly accusing and shaming him. 'Listen to me, Willand. You are not taking the task that lies before you seriously enough. In future you must be more guarded. You must make an effort to recognize and pierce magical disguises. You act as if you have forgotten the dangers that you face.'

'I'm sorry,' he said. 'But it's not my way to mistrust everyone I meet.'

'That must become second nature to you.'

'No!' Will shook his head. 'That will never be. I can't live like that, Gwydion.'

'Then you will not live long!'

'At least I'll stay myself.'

'Fool. If that really had been Maskull, you would have become his unwilling slave, and our world would have been lost!'

The wizard sat back and allowed Will's anger to fully subside, then he said in a more composed voice, 'Too much depends on you. You must listen more closely to your inner warnings.'

'What inner warnings?' he asked, still shaking. 'If I'd felt anything then I would have listened to it.'

'Is that the truth?'

'Yes!'

But when Will looked inside himself he saw that a part of him *had* noted the spangling that had covered the hair and shoulders of the old man. It had made him think of fine rain, but how could it have been rain when the sky outside had not a cloud in sight? And, to add to that, he had ignored the sounds of Bessie moving about in the stable yard. He had selfishly ignored the horse's thirst. If he had been more alert – or perhaps if he had been a little kinder – he would have noticed Bessie and straight away he would have been warned of Gwydion's return.

He said, chastened, 'I was wrong to disobey you. But what am I to do when I have the power to cure ailments and ailments come to me to be cured? I didn't plan to spread the word of my being here, it just happened.'

Gwydion muttered and Will's stomach turned over as he watched the pea soup slowly return to the bowl and the bowl settle itself back on the table. 'You must learn to understand a very basic rule, Willand. The Sightless Ones say that life presents endless choices between good and evil. They are wrong. In their terms, life's endless choices are all about choosing between two "evils" or comparing two "goods". Now weigh the many small mercies you have given to the local people against the vastly greater mercy that you alone can give to the world. Keep a sense of proportion. Be mindful of your true duty.'

'You speak as if I was pursuing gratitude, or fame, or that I did it for gain.'

The wizard put a hand on Will's shoulder. 'I know that your motives were not ignoble or unfitting. Nor is it my wish to lay blame on you. I am concerned for your safety. Now let me see that hand.'

Will unwrapped the strip of linen from his hand and the wizard looked at the angry redness of the wound.

'Teeth,' Gwydion said.

Will told him what had passed. The wizard spoke healing words and treated the wound with a kind touch and a pinch of aromatic powder whose sting made Will flinch.

'It wasn't the prettiest or best-tempered of beasts I've ever met with,' he said. 'But it seemed to me more pitiful than malicious.'

'It seems that your kindness may have rebounded on you, Willand.'

'That's an odd sort of remark to come from you. Did you not once tell me that the Rede of Friendship lies at the very heart of magic? And is there not a common rede that says: "One good turn deserveth another"?'

'In the natural world, but perhaps not so when matters have been twisted into their opposites by sorcery.' Gwydion slapped his hand hard then held it tight.

'Ouch!' He recoiled from the sharp pain as Gwydion let go, but when he looked down the wound had almost gone. Only two purplish pits remained where the deepest punctures had been.

Suddenly, Will heard the sound of hooves. He wheeled about and made for the door.

'Come on, Gwydion,' he cried. 'You told me to take notice of my inner feelings. That's just what I'm doing!'

They headed for the back door and reached the yard at the same time. Two shapes loomed at the end of the yard. The lead horseman drew his mount up sharp and Will felt his right hand grasped in friendship.

'Tilwin!'

'Tilwin if you must, though I prefer my own name.'

As Will caught hold of the horse's bridle his eyes fixed on a pale horse that walked through a pool of moonlight. It was Avon, and on his back was Willow.

CHAPTER SEVEN

A GOOD NIGHT'S REST

Despite his surprise, Will embraced Willow as soon as she got down from the horse. Then his surprise turned to alarm.

'What's happened?' he asked her, taking his daughter in his arms.

'As you see, we're as well as we've always been.'

'I was worried about you—' he turned a questioning eye on Morann, '—but I didn't expect you to be brought here.'

'Well, here we are,' Willow said.

He cuddled the child. 'She looks well.'

'She's fine! I was more worried about you.'

He looked to the wizard as he hugged Willow again. Gwydion's silent sternness said much. When they all went inside the inn, Will hissed at Morann, 'I only asked you to give her my message.'

'That may be so, but you have a wife who is not so easily put off.'

'I don't want to sound ungrateful, but—'

Morann was blithely unconcerned. 'I'm sorry we've arrived so late. It's hard travelling on horseback along a dark road when there's a babe-in-arms to cope with. And our journey was not without peril.'

'Peril?'

'Don't *worry.*'

'What about that important errand in Trinovant you said you were going on?'

'Things have already gone too far for that – as you shall soon learn.'

Fiddle music met them as they opened the door. There were better than two dozen folk in the Plough. Some were singing, others talking in huddles. One or two turned to look as the new arrivals came by, but Will led them along the passageway and down to the far end, where they squeezed one at a time into the inglenook, and so into the snug. It was only when food and drink had been brought to them, and after Dimmet had left, that Gwydion called down a fresh spell of privacy upon the room and the sounds of merriment faded away.

'We were almost caught out as we tried to cross the Charrel south of Baneburgh,' Morann said. 'I spied a column of five hundred men or more.'

'Five hundred?' Will said in alarm.

'At the very least. They were marching south and east under the Duke of Mells' banner. From the way they carried themselves I judged them to be farmers only lately raised to arms, but there were veteran horsemen with them, hard men who had been set to chase down any of the column who might decide to stray. I thought it likely these riders would ask unwelcome questions if they spied us, so we went a longer way round.'

'There's no doubt that war is coming again,' Willow said. 'If a while ago they were taking men off the land by the dozen, now they're taking them by the score, and even by the hundred.'

'That's right enough.' Morann nodded. 'I'd guess the Commissioners will be here in Eiton by the week's end.'

Will took Willow's hand, thinking about the harvesters who would be swept from the fields like so much chaff. Many of them would never return if the spectre of war was allowed to escape into the world. Willow asked what the wizard foresaw, and

Gwydion told her about the battlestones and the significance of what had happened at Little Slaughter. She shook her head in concern at the news that Maskull was once more abroad.

'Did you find the Dragon Stone?' Will asked.

'I entered Castle Foderingham and saw that the stone remained entombed there. I enmeshed it in fresh holding spells, and did all that I dared short of attempting to drain it. It now slumbers as deeply as ever it did.'

Will wondered what more there was to the wizard's story. In particular, whether the Duke of Ebor had in the end given his consent.

He leaned across to check on his sleeping daughter. 'Why did you bring her?'

She searched his face. 'What else was I going to do?'

'You could have left her with Breona.'

'Will, she's our child, and her place is with us.'

'The work we're about is perilous.' He shook his head at her lack of understanding, still feeling the shock of the lesson that Gwydion had taught him. 'I don't want her to be put in danger.'

She gave him a hard look that stifled further comment. He glanced at Gwydion anticipating what the wizard would have to say on the matter. He did not have to wait long.

'Tomorrow our fight against the battlestones must resume in earnest,' Gwydion said. 'Willow, you must stay here tonight, of course. But at first light tomorrow you should set off for home.'

'As you can see, Master Gwydion,' Willow said, unmoved by the wizard's persuasion, 'I'm well, and Bethe is well also. Far better than either of us would have been if a shooting star had landed flat on our village like it did on Little Slaughter.'

The wizard glanced at Morann with displeasure. 'Be that as it may—'

'So the Vale is no safer for us than anywhere else, I'd say.'

Will jumped in. 'Gwydion's right. It's more dangerous for you to be here.'

'Well, maybe there's another thing that you should know,' she said stubbornly. 'You can thank Master Gwydion for his advice. But I'd say it's my duty to go with my man and help him in whatever business he's upon. That's what I undertook to do at our handfasting, and that's what I'm going to do. And as for Bethe, babies are a lot tougher than folk generally give them credit for. She'll want for nothing on the road.'

At that there was silence. Then Gwydion laid both hands flat on the table. 'It is right and proper that we have all been able to say our say tonight, but it is getting late now. Let us go to our beds and settle the matter tomorrow.'

When they emerged from the snug the dancing and music and eating and drinking were all finished. The inn's big room was quiet and half in darkness. Will took Willow and Bethe upstairs and saw they were comfortable, then he went out through the darkened yard, down the lane, over a stile and into a grassy field in which an old oak grew. Overhead the stars of late summer twinkled. He asked them to tell him what to do for the best, but they only gazed down in pitiless silence.

The stars don't know what to do, he told himself sternly. They're just holes in the sky, holes seventeen hundred leagues away. You'll have to answer questions like that yourself, Willand, as hard as they are.

Whatever happened tomorrow, it was going to be an eventful day. It would be wise to meet it fully prepared. He did not know why, but he took the red fish from around his neck and put it back into his pouch. Then he found a place that felt right, stood straight, his feet a little apart and his arms loose at his sides. When he felt the time had come to begin, he closed his eyes and breathed three deep draughts of air, drawing them in through his nose and blowing them out each time from his mouth. Then he planted his feet hard in the good earth and invited the power to fill him.

First it trembled in the soles of his feet, an irresistible force rising through his legs, then up through his body. He felt the tingling rush over his ribs and all the way up his spine. It surrounded his heart, and there split into three streams. Slowly, he raised his arms until they were as far apart as they would go. The power kept rising inside him until it reached his hands and it seemed to Will that a pale blue light that only he could see had begun shooting out from the tips of his splayed fingers. But it was when the power reached his head that he was hit by an overwhelming feeling of joy and peace.

He felt he was inside a great cold flame, and even though his eyes were closed he could sense a brilliant light filling him. As he accepted it, it grew brighter and stronger, blotting out everything, so that in that ultimate timeless moment he forgot who and what he was.

But then, gradually, the light began to draw back inside him. He did not mind that it was dimming for he knew that, although he could no longer see it, the power had not forsaken him. It was wonderful how that moment seemed to last forever and yet to take no longer than a brief moment. Wholly refreshed in spirit, he went back inside, feeling content and happy to be with his family despite everything.

Will did not know what woke him. At first he thought it was Bethe's crying, but as he lay still in the darkness the echoes died in his mind and he heard only Willow's breathing and what he thought must be the furtive rustling of mice in the thatch.

But then, as he came fully awake, he felt pins and needles tingling in the nape of his neck, and he sat up when a scratching and scrabbling came at the shutters.

That's no mouse, he thought. It's far too big. Someone's trying to get in!

He was about to shout out, but he stopped himself. A shout would wake everyone, but it would also drive away whoever was outside.

Silently, he pulled his clothes on, wrapped himself in his cloak to cover his shirt's whiteness, and crept along the passageway. He moved carefully down the stair, pausing only to take up the balk of wood that barred the door, and went out into the slanting moonlight. No sooner had he stepped outside, than he heard a scream. It was Willow. Then Bethe began to cry.

'Hoy!' he shouted as he reached the place below the window. There, up on the thatch and scraping at the shutter, was a goggly.

So they *are* child-stealers after all, Will thought. It's after Bethe! But it hasn't reckoned on the spells of protection that Gwydion's put on the Plough! That must have been what woke me up.

'You! Get away from there!'

The thing was fighting to open the shutters, and now it was hissing and scratching like a mad thing, then it slid down a little among the hard moonlight shadows and began to tear at the thatch.

Will flung the balk of wood at it, but missed. Then he picked up a piece of broken floor tile. It was sharp and three-cornered and he aimed it well. The creature twisted away, but this time it was hit on the back. It screwed up its face at him and shrieked, before flapping up into the air.

As soon as it settled again, the shutter was flung open. That knocked the creature away, but it was the last thing Will saw of it, for, without warning, a dark shape loomed out of the shadows and slammed heavily into him. The weight of it knocked him down and forced the breath out of his lungs. He was pinned down as a muscular body landed on top of him. A rough rope was neatly looped around his neck and pulled tight. The attacker was trying to choke him, but the rope snagged on Will's wrist and dragged his hand across his throat. It prevented him from using his arm, but it saved him, because as the rope was drawn tighter his hand was pulled up inside the loop. The attacker pulled harder, but he soon saw that no matter how tight the rope was pulled it would not do what he wanted, and so he let go.

Instead he tried to beat Will unconscious. Blow after blow rained on his head, but Will fended them off. He matched the attacker punch for punch, and eventually managed to thrust him back and get on top of him.

But no sooner was he up than a new threat came at him from above.

'Naaw! Naaaw!'

The creature flapped and squealed in the darkness, diving and jerking and raking his head with its claws. Will threw up his arm and swatted it away, but that unbalanced him and he lost his grip on his attacker's arm.

As he fought it became plain to him that the man who was trying to kill him was exactly as strong and skilled as himself. He had determination too, and seeing that gave Will a vital strength of his own. He fought back, countering every move with one of his own. They rolled over and over, gripped in deadlock. He grunted and snorted, felt a hand close on his windpipe; another knocked his head back hard against the ground. By bucking upward and twisting, he threw his attacker off. Then shouts came.

As Will grappled, he drew his arm back and a shaft of moonlight fell across the other's face. He gasped, and recoiled from it.

By now, lantern beams were piercing the gloom. Patches of light swam drunkenly. Heels scraped against cobblestones and a dark figure fled. Bolt growled and there was the tearing of cloth, then a yelp. Will struggled to his feet to find Willow rushing out with his oak staff in her hand. She swung and hit something hard. Then the mastiff leapt at the stranger again, but the man was already scrambling away into the night.

Duffred ran out of the yard with a fire-iron in his hand, shouting, 'Bolt! Bolt!'

Then Dimmet was holding the lantern up in Will's face and saying, 'Is he all right?'

In the aftermath, Will could make little sense of what had happened.

'Who was he?' Willow asked, cuddling Bethe close to her now.

Morann strode about the yard. 'I wish you'd hung on to him a moment longer.'

'I'm sorry I didn't,' Will said, rubbing his jaw.

Dimmet growled. 'But you're all right, and that's the main thing.'

'Whoever he was, he was strong,' Will said, picking up the door bar and taking it inside. 'It was all I could do to hold him off. There was one of the flying creatures helping him.'

'A goggly?' Dimmet said. 'I told you they was wicked vermin!'

They all followed Will indoors. Willow sat him down and began to dab at his hurts with a dampened rag.

'I'm all right,' he said. 'A few cuts and bruises and – *ouch!* – a twisted finger.'

'Looks like he's tried to throttle you,' Morann said, looking at the rope burn on Will's neck. He stared watchfully into the darkness and started as he saw movement.

It was only Duffred and the dog. Duffred was breathless and empty-handed. 'Got away. I called Bolt off. Didn't want him hurt on no thief's account.'

'What happened, Will?' Dimmet asked. 'What do you think he was after in my yard?'

'He was after me.' Will touched a tender spot on his head, still shocked by what had happened. 'Just when I thought I'd got the better of him, the strangest thing happened. I saw his face clear as day in the moonlight.'

'And?' Willow asked.

'It terrified me.' He shook his head. 'He had no face. I just . . . let go of him.'

Morann exchanged a mystified glance with Willow. 'Had no face, you say?'

The big mastiff paced round them, still excited. Will said, 'It was like something from a bad dream.'

Gwydion stepped into the lantern light. 'Whatever else it was, it was not a bad dream.'

'What I want to know,' Willow said, rubbing her arms, 'is what that *thing* was! The one that tried to get in at our window.'

'It was a goggly,' Will said.

'A what?'

Morann explained. 'Here the country lore calls such creatures "gogglies" or bat-elves. They're supposed to come out of burrows in the ground. It's said they steal babies away.'

Willow put down the bloodied rag and clutched her daughter tighter. 'Was it after Bethe, then?'

Gwydion sat down at the table and made the candle flare. He said sternly, 'I have already warned that you and your child are in danger here.'

Will shook his head. 'I don't think it was after Bethe. It was trying to lure me outside.'

Morann said, 'In the Blessed Isle it's said these creatures come up from the Realm Below. They prowl the places where there are vents leading up to our world.'

He looked meaningfully to Will, who straight away thought of the strongroom that lay under the abandoned chapter house and of the cleft that led down into the measureless depths below.

'It was surely the same kind of creature that bit my hand,' he said. 'And I've seen things like it before. They were clustering in the roof vaults of the great chapter house of Verlamion.'

Morann put his hat on the table and raked his fingers through his long hair. 'Then my guess is that your attacker was an agent of the red hands.'

'The Sightless Ones?' Willow said, looking around, worried. 'Do you think so?'

Will grunted. 'Rather the Sightless Ones than Maskull.'

He looked from Morann to Gwydion, who said flatly, 'We must go from here at first light. Until then, you should all try to sleep. I shall keep watch.'

When Willow had finished cleaning the blood from Will's face and looking over his bruises they took to their beds. Gwydion went out into the darkness, insisting that Dimmet bar the doors behind him. 'Let no one in or out for any reason while night reigns. I will knock three times when dawn comes.'

As Will laid his head down for the second time that night he ached and smarted in a dozen places, but he was pleased to have taken no serious hurt. He took the red fish from his pouch and decided to put it under his pillow, just as he had once put Morann's protection against nightmares under his pillow at home. Yet the fish seemed oddly cold to the touch, and in the muted moonlight its green eye looked at him with a baleful stare. He wondered again about what had happened that night.

Where had Gwydion been while the attack was going on? And if he had webbed the Plough about with magic to counter harm, then how come the flying creature had almost got in through the window? Nor had Gwydion cast any magic to help capture the attacker. Why?

He yawned but could find no rest. More disjointed doubts bubbled up from the mud at the bottom of his mind. Maybe Morann was right – maybe the would-be killer was an agent of the Sightless Ones. What if the sorcery the Fellowship employed was stronger than Gwydion's magic?

As sleeplessness gripped him, Will's thoughts began to riot, turning ever darker. What if Gwydion had left him alone at the Plough deliberately, knowing that he would make himself known to the whole district? Maybe he had been used as bait to draw Maskull here! Gwydion never told all that he knew; wasn't his mysteriousness no more than deceit and manipulation?

The more he thought about it the more reasonable it seemed. But, whatever Gwydion's game was, he was right about one thing – Willow must be persuaded to go home. And soon.

Eventually, the first faint glimmerings of daybreak began to creep in around the edges of the shutters. He heard Dimmet and Duffred moving about, and so he got up and went down to help them prepare the farewell breakfast. He found Morann was already dressed for the road.

'I couldn't sleep either,' he said. 'And since Master Gwydion has stood sentinel over us through the darkest hours, I thought I'd set another pair of eyes to watch over him while the light came up.'

Three knocks came at the door. Gwydion appeared. He nodded at Morann who spoke a brief word in the true tongue, then let him in. 'Old friend, you have a stout heart. There are few like you remaining in the world, which is a great sadness to me. And as for you, Willand, we must be gone from here as soon as the sun is risen.'

Will waited for Gwydion to sit down, then he leaned forward and lowered his voice. 'Listen – I want to help prevent the war if I can, but after what happened last night I can hardly believe that Willow and Bethe will be safe anywhere. You told me the Vale was in danger of ending up like Little Slaughter. How can I ask Willow to go back there?'

'The Vale may recently have been in as much danger as Little Slaughter,' Gwydion said, seeming to choose his words with care. 'But it is not in danger now.'

'How can you be so sure?'

'Because the Vale would only be in danger if Maskull had found it.'

'But maybe he has.'

'Maybe. But you are no longer there. And Maskull knows that now.'

Will sat back, unsettled. 'How do you know he knows?'

Gwydion's eyes were steady on him. 'Because last night's assailant was sent by him.'

'Why do you say that?'

'Remember the rede, "By his magic, so shall ye know him." Last night I went to see if I could smell him out.'

'And did you?'

'It is surprising what the weak of character will do when they believe they are not being watched. Maskull's reek was faint but clear.'

Will rubbed at his chin, night doubts still swirling in his head. 'I'm scared for Willow and my daughter – I can't deny it.'

'Then persuade her to return home.'

He nodded at last. 'I'll try.'

When Willow appeared she cuddled her daughter and sat down. 'Morning,' she said, looking at them in turn.

Will took her hands. 'Will you do something to help me?'

'If I think it *will* help you.'

'Do you remember my talisman? The green fish?'

She searched his face and he saw she had not been expecting the question. 'You mean the one you usually wear around your neck? What about it?'

'I don't have it with me.'

'I know. You left it on a nail by the back door. Don't worry, I put it safe.'

He shook his head. 'But I need it.'

She gauged him suspiciously. 'Will, if this is your way of getting me to go home—'

He pressed her hands earnestly. 'I wouldn't lie to you, Willow – this is important to me. The fish was with me when Gwydion first carried me into the Vale as a baby. It was in my hand when I cracked the Verlamion Doomstone. I've always been comforted by its touch. I need it with me.'

She met his look squarely, part of her still thinking she was being pushed around, but then she sat back and sighed. 'Well, if you're sure you need it, then I suppose I'll have to go and fetch it.'

'Thank you,' he said, truly relieved. 'I knew you would.'

But she did not seem pleased to have been thwarted. 'There's a couple of questions I have for you, Willand. Just how do you expect me to find my way home? And how am I to find you again once you've moved on from here?'

'That is easy,' Gwydion said. 'Morann brought you here. He will guide you home again. Is that not so, Morann?'

And Morann sighed and nodded. 'It looks that way.'

PART TWO

A LOSING BATTLE

CHAPTER EIGHT

THIS BLIGHTED LAND

W ill waved farewell as Avon followed Morann's horse from
        the Plough.

'Mind how you go,' he told Willow as she left the yard.

'And you.'

'Look after her,' he told Morann.

'I surely will.'

Gwydion lingered for a while, talking with Dimmet, then he
gathered up his staff and called Will after him and they also went
on their way. Will chose the south road out of Eiton. They followed
it for a little while, then, as soon as they reached the place where
the road and the lign of the ash tree crossed, they set off across
the meadows. After a short while they came to a brook.

'This is the north fork of the Charrel Brook,' Gwydion said.
'The stream wanders many leagues southward, through lands
owned by the Sightless Ones. These waters join up with a greater
river in the domain of the Earl of Ockhamsforth. That river, called
Iesis, flows on to the great city of Trinovant. Do you see what
example in the fundaments of magic this little stream holds for
us?'

'I would say the lesson it shows is that all things are connected
– all places and all times, as all flowing waters are,' Will answered.

'Well said, indeed!'

Will waded across, confidently following the lign. By now the phase of the unrisen moon was almost at full, and so the lign was hard to lose. Even so, the influence would ebb and flow as the day progressed, and Will knew they would almost certainly wander off the true line. He hunted along the bank of the Charrel for a little way among the osiers then found what he was looking for. A hazel tree. He cut himself a nice fresh wand, and split it ready for scrying. As they walked, Will thought about Willow and her leaving.

'You take care now, Willand,' was all she had said as they parted, but a moment before she had squeezed him tight and hung on to him as if she might never see him again. Now he wondered what Gwydion had told Morann to do once Willow and Bethe were back in the Vale. Would he just leave her there, no matter what she wanted?

He looked at Gwydion, wondering at the fears that had plagued his sleepless night. They had faded away as soon as he had got up, and now Gwydion seemed once more to have his best interests at heart. The morning sun was bright. They were two again, two against a tide of troubles, and a dangerous journey stretched ahead of them through a land filled with endless possibilities.

'It's strange,' he said, 'how a man remembers what's passed in his life while he's walking the land.'

'A man journeys through life much as he journeys upon the road,' Gwydion said. 'What memories have you come across?'

'Oh, fond memories mostly. I was thinking about Wortmaster Gort. A picture of him came to me when I passed that field of meadowsweet back there. How I'd like to see him again!'

Gwydion looked at the meadows with their verges of nettle and dock leaf. 'And who are you reminded of in this place?'

'The beast that bit my hand.'

'And what have you decided?'

'I know it's never a good plan to question a wholesome cure, but I was wondering if you could have closed up my wound quite so easily without knowledge of the creature's true name.'

'So you suppose I have that knowledge.'

'Yes.' He glanced across at the wizard. 'What is it?'

The wizard inclined his head as if he had decided he had no choice but to vouchsafe a secret. He said, 'It is called a ked.'

'A ked,' Will said, weighing the word.

'All that was said about them by loose tongues is true – except the part about child-stealing. That is just a tale encouraged by the Sightless Ones.'

'I knew the beast wasn't malicious,' he said triumphantly.

'Of course you knew, because you have unusual fellow feeling –"affinity" as Gort calls it. Keds come from the upper regions of the Realm Below. You saw them in the chapter house at Verlamion. Many of the Fellowship's cloisters, including the Verlamion chapter house, are built over old vents. The creatures are encouraged up to the surface by the Fellows who make promise of mushrooms to them.'

Will looked askance. 'Mushrooms?'

'And earth-tongues. The creatures like them very much, especially when spread with honey. They are tempted and so come up. But then the red hands trap them and make them roost among their roof beams.'

'But why would they want to do that?'

'They keep them for food.'

Will's brow furrowed. 'Who would think it right to eat such a creature? And, anyway, I thought the red hands lived only on blood.'

'Quite so, but they regard ked blood as the sweetest. Anstin the Hermit told me long ago, it is the practice of the Fellows to shoot the captive creatures down with crossbow and line so there may be plenty of the "best wine" on the most sacred days of the Fellows' calendar.'

'That's disgusting!'

'The Sightless Ones must keep control over the minds of those they enslave. How could they do that if they allowed their own people to live in the ordinary way? They have rituals that take the place of every activity of life, rituals that are meant to dissolve away the individual spirit of a man until he feels he is no more than a mote floating rudderless in a powerful current. That way he is forced to *belong*.'

'You think this ked escaped when Isnar had the chapter house pulled down?'

'It is possible.'

'No wonder it bit me. I'd have done the same in its place.'

'It is a sad day when one of the creatures is tempted to the surface for any reason, but thankfully such days are rare. Most are lured up by the Fellowship, but occasionally they do come up into this world of light of their own accord, for they are by nature as curious as young cats. Those that escape into the open are unjustly persecuted as villains.'

'What can be done about that?'

'It is the task of all people to make life less unfair if they can.'

Will fell silent. Despite the hot sun on his back, the cool green grass under his feet and the sweet smell of wildflowers that was on the air, he was troubled by what Gwydion had told him. He tried to turn his mind to something else, and found a ready subject at hand.

'I've been meaning to ask if Duke Richard gave you permission to enter Foderingham in the end.'

Gwydion thought for a moment then struck the ground ahead with his staff. 'It is well that you be told how things stand among the lords, for it has a bearing on how we must proceed. When I went to Foderingham I found the castle infested with soldiers and everyone alert for war. The queen has been plotting again, this time with Henry de Bowforde, son of the late Edgar de Bowforde, Duke of Mells, the same that was slain at Verlamion.'

'How could I forget him?' Will said, recalling the stripped and bloodied body he had seen. It was said that Duke Edgar had secretly fathered Queen Mag's son, and that child, now a five-year-old boy, had been officially named as heir to the throne by King Hal.

Will said, 'Now Henry is Duke of Mells, and I imagine he's as committed to Queen Mag as his father was. After all, she's the mother of Henry's half-brother.'

'Correct.' Gwydion stroked his beard. 'The queen is considered by those who look no further than skin-deep to be a blemishless beauty. She has always used her looks to ensnare those whom she would use. I have no doubt she encourages Henry. And I have no doubt that is done at the behest of Maskull.'

'I've heard she's used to treating courtiers as her playthings. It's surprising how easily she's become a pawn herself.'

'Maskull is hard to resist.' Gwydion sighed. 'He does not believe in restraint and so many have become his tools down the years. The queen and Henry de Bowforde make a formidable pair. Ever since Henry put on his father's ducal robes he has burned to revenge himself against Richard of Ebor. Four years ago he swore to humble the man he blames for his father's death. He is, at twenty-two years of age, the most lawless blade in Trinovant.'

Will brought down his wand and planted his feet in the grass. 'There seems to be little enough law for noblemen to obey.'

Gwydion stood clear a pace. 'Little enough now that King Hal has been found to be well again. That was announced by a committee of eminent leeches who were, I happen to know, paid very handsomely by the queen herself for their convenient decision.'

'So the Protectorship has fallen?'

'And worse. Once again there is a plan to call a Great Council of Lords. That does not bode well for Richard of Ebor. He fears that he will be impeached and sentenced to death all at a single stroke. Friend Richard is politicking furiously in Trinovant in an effort to save the peace, but his position is fast crumbling.'

'What will happen?'

'He will be forced out. My bet is that he will retreat into his heartland, go once more to his castle of Ludford. There, in the

Western Marches, he will begin drawing to him forces and friends, calling Lord Sarum down from the north, and the Earl Warrewyk to come to his aid from across the Narrow Seas. I think he may be forced into a glorious last stand.'

Will scratched his head, realizing that he had lost the lign. He looked out across the patchwork of greens and yellows, a land that seemed so peaceful and well-ordered, yet was on the brink of terrible bloodshed. 'You must ask Duke Richard to give us men and horses so we can go more swiftly about the country to find what must be found! With horses to ride and to draw and men to dig and to guard we'd root out the infection all the quicker!'

Gwydion bent down to look at the ground at his feet. 'Alas, Friend Richard will afford us no such help. Perhaps he is already falling under the spell of the lorc.'

'Then he must give us enough strength to move against the Sightless Ones at Verlamion! We must pull out the Doomstone and see if it has truly healed itself!'

'No lord dare move in strength against the Sightless Ones.'

Will scried a little, picked up a pebble and threw it ahead of him to where the grass sprouted in unruly fashion. The bleakness of Gwydion's words gnawed at him. 'Then what shall we do?'

'Work patiently,' the wizard said. 'And keep putting one foot in front of the other – though you presently seem to be leading us into ever more boggy ground.'

It was true. The grass was wet underfoot now, and soon Will found his feet being sucked down. He tried to press on where the hazel wand showed, but then it was as if the sun had gone behind a cloud, and he felt a sudden chill eating at his flesh. When he lifted his wand again he thought he felt a faint hint tingling in his hands, but the feeling was indistinct, as if the power had for the moment retreated deeper underground.

The flavour of it was wrong – like Indonen, yet not quite. He shivered, looking about. There were no birds flying here. It was damp underfoot, a shadowy mire where none of the trees had grown tall but had become gnarled like those that grew on a windswept moor. A ball of midges danced above a pool of fetid water. He thought it a dismal place, and felt his heart squeeze tight. More than anything he wanted to see Willow. It suddenly felt as if he would never see her again.

He began to feel his feet slowly sinking into the boggy ground. He warned Gwydion of the unpleasantness in the place, saying it would be better if they tracked around to the south. But Gwydion stood back on firm ground and leaned heavily on his staff. He began to question Will closely about his thoughts and feelings.

'It's like . . . like treading through a field of open graves with my eyes shut,' he said, feeling a new ripple of horror pass through him. 'No birds or animals come here. See those midges dancing madly? Look at them! Do you see how insane they are? They're trapped. I can feel my heart faltering and my courage with it, Gwydion. It's a cold, deadly feeling. I don't like it here.'

When he tried to move his legs again he found that his feet had sunk under the surface. The suction was hard to break. First he tried to pull one foot free, then the other, but he only trod himself deeper. He felt coldness clutching at his calves, then black water closing over the backs of his knees.

Panic tore through him. 'Gwydion! I can't get out!'

'Tread softly, Willand.'

He tried, but it was no use. 'Gwydion, help me! I'm sinking!'

'Are you truly unable to free yourself?' Gwydion asked, watching him calmly, doing nothing.

'Gwydion, please! Look at me! I'm stuck fast and it's pulling me down!'

But the wizard only watched dispassionately as Will struggled. It was as if the meadow bog itself did not want to let him go. As his legs churned the ground a stink rose up from the filth. It was vile, like rotten eggs. And now the mud had reached almost to his waist.

'Gwydion!' He felt panic rising as easily as his body sank.

And then the wizard danced. He came forward lightly and laid his staff towards Will, then muttered words until the head of the staff glowed with a blue incandescence. Only then did Will find that he could begin to fight free. He staggered to firm ground and lay down.

'Thank you, friend!' he said accusingly as Gwydion came up.

He pulled his spare shirt out of his bundle, marched a hundred paces away to sit alone on a tussock of grass. Still angry, he wiped his legs clean then went down to the stream and washed himself and his spoiled clothes, wrung out the grey sodden mass of his shirt and laid it out to dry. His anger flashed, but then he felt the sun warm on his back once more, and his mood lifted. He knew that he had been in a place of unquiet horrors.

'I thought you were going to leave me to go under. Why didn't you act sooner?'

Gwydion waved his staff vaguely at the bog. 'I wanted to see exactly where the battlestone lies.'

Will shook his head ruefully. 'This is no work for a grown man. We've found a battlestone, though we've come barely two leagues from Eiton. At this rate we'll have stopped the war before it's begun!'

'It is the way of young men to fall prey to optimism. To prevent the battle we must first uproot the stone. And that will prove difficult here. Alas, this blighted land!'

Will looked at the black, boggy ground near the Charrel Brook and saw that Gwydion's words were undeniable. The ground Will had churned up was already glassy with water. He wondered how two men could ever hope to dig a battlestone free.

'I fear the Charrel must have altered its course since the battle-stone was buried.'

'Maybe it was the stone that caused its course to change.'

The wizard nodded. 'Maybe.'

Will frowned. 'What do you think we should do?'

'Nothing for the moment.'

'Nothing? Not even wrap it in holding spells?'

The wizard cast him a disappointed glance. 'With the stone still in the ground and able to draw readily on the power of the lorc? I think that would be very dangerous. My spells would not be hidden out here in the open. They would attract the wrong sort of magician.'

'Then what?'

'That depends on whether you think this is a stone of the greater or lesser kind.'

Will gestured uncertainly. 'In this case I can't be sure. The moon and sun are not making the right angle with the stone for me to tell.'

The most potent time for the earth power to peak was at what Gwydion called 'syzygy' – when the moon was full or new – or to a less extent at the time of 'quadrature', when its disc was exactly half lit.

'We can do nothing to alter the phase of the moon,' Gwydion said, sighing. 'It will be best if we continue on along Indonen. Do you think you will be able to keep to its path as you have?'

'I think so – at least for a few hours.'

'Then point out your best guess as to where this battlestone might be. I shall fix the place in my mind.' Gwydion looked around then and his eyes fixed on the woods beyond the meadow. 'The nearest village to this place is called Arebury. You should remember that name, for one day you shall have to return here.'

CHAPTER NINE

STONEHUNTERS

They halted on a rise soon after Will lost the lign. Gwydion took them to higher ground to read the land for signs, looking for notched ridges, hidden wells and sacred groves, but also for the towers and spires of the Sightless Ones which he expected to see desecrating the ligns. He suggested Will turn his attention this way and then that, and so he did. Then Will picked up a faint clue and once more it had the sense of Indonen about it.

By now the afternoon had worn through and the evening sun was sinking red in the western skies behind a great veil of mist. The Middle Shires stretched out before them – fat, productive, comfortable. The land seemed empty of men now, through the spells that Gwydion laid to fend off inquisitive eyes, but Will saw the work of their many hands upon it. Long centuries of careful keeping had made the Realm what it was, and its form was beautiful in Will's estimation. The recent years of Duke Richard's Protectorship had allowed the land and the people to recover, and it broke his heart to think that all their gains must soon be despoiled by war.

To the south he could see a distant dark grey smudge: the town of Baneburgh. He led the wizard on during the long twilight, vaguely following the lign, avoiding hill and hamlet, crop and cowfield. Interested sheep came to them as they passed, animals innocent of eye, friendly and more than usually expectant. They knew something was amiss with the strange power that ran under their meadow. Sheep often came to Gwydion when he appeared among them, and they did so now perhaps because the wizard carried an aura about him that seemed to them benign. It looked like love, but perhaps they had been made anxious too.

Will stared now into the reddening west, wondering at how much the lign had strengthened in so short a space of time. When they came to a hill that overlooked the village of Tysoe, they paused, then climbed it in vanishing daylight. Will went ahead up the slope. He found that two rough wooden stakes had been hammered into the ground. Each was almost as tall as he was and set twice as far apart. One was limed by the droppings of a sparrowhawk. Gwydion took an unusual interest in that, and as Will sat cross-legged and gazed into the sunset the wizard did not come to join him as Will had expected, but instead danced quiet spells around the hilltop.

The long dusk died slowly, bloodily, and with an accompaniment of complex birdsong to which Gwydion listened with care. Will drank in the full beauty of a sunset seen with an open horizon. It was a kind of beauty the Vale did not afford. Red and gold and pink and violet made the sky a vast, fiery furnace. It made him wonder about the Beyond, the realm of bright, burning nothingness that lay on the far side of the sky.

As night deepened the brighter stars began to peep out and a profound peace came over the land. Will took up the scrier's stance to prepare his mind. From small beginnings, almost unfelt and unseen, a powerful tension was revealed. In a little while the Indonen lign began to glisten in the earth like a silvery blade picked out by moonlight. It reminded Will of that first night he had followed a stranger out of the Vale, and the stranger had touched his eyes and lit the night all around with the silver-green glow of elflight.

'Tell me what you see now,' Gwydion said.

'I see glimmerings very clearly,' he whispered, his voice awe-filled. 'Indonen runs from a point on the skyline near that elm tree: I judge it to be about halfway between east and north-east. It passes below the small hill over there to the south of where the moon is rising.'

Gwydion's eyes narrowed as he committed the track to memory. 'What else?'

Will gasped, hardly able to believe what he was seeing. 'Yes! There's another lign. I can see it crosses Indonen. Down there!'

'Describe it to me.'

'It seems much fainter. A darker, more turbulent flow. Perhaps . . . greener.' He put his right arm out from his shoulder and sighted along it, though his eyes were now closed. 'It comes from a place between west and north-west and runs over there to the south of Baneburgh.'

'Is it Eburos?' That was the lign on which the Giant's Ring stood.

'No.'

'Are you sure?'

'Very sure. Can't you sense how different it is, Gwydion?'

But the wizard just peered into the darkness near Tysoe like a look-out peering into a dense fog. A nightjar's churring call came to them from far away. Gwydion had once taught him that hearing that sound meant the sun had been down for an hour. It was as good a clock as any. By now the moon was rising harvest gold.

'It will set at the full at the moment of sunrise,' Gwydion said. 'I guess that is the reason the ligns are so visible to you.'

'They're very active,' Will said, feeling the flow strongly now. 'The power's surging down below.'

'I believe the second lign must be Caorthan – the lign of the rowan,' Gwydion said.

Will stared hard at the lign. It seemed to brighten even as he did so, spilling power into the swirling and spiralling earth streams that bordered it. Then Will said in wonderment, 'Oh, Gwydion! There's a richness to it!'

The wizard came to him. 'Then tell me what you feel.'

'Two flows. Both rising. Both swelling with power. But something's wrong. It should be beautiful. It should make me think of moonlight and waterfalls and great forests, but it doesn't.'

Suddenly there were colours swarming everywhere in Will's mind, and a music that seemed to fill the sky. Then fire swept across the stars, a golden flame, licking and swirling and finally dying until all that was left was a depthless blue pricked by countless jewels of scattered light. And now above all rode the pain-bright whiteness of the moon, a perfect disc that blotted out the stars. His face upturned, Will bathed in the mystic shine. He lay down as the radiance pierced him, was transfixed by silver beams that nailed his flesh to the earth. And as he lay on his back he listened to the music that rose and thundered like the ocean, and filled everything under the sky. The hollows of his bones hummed, reverberating with the one great chord that connected him to everything and to everyone, so that he cried out in gladness to have so sudden and complete an understanding come to him.

Then it was as if he had come awake from a good night's sleep. He looked around and felt Gwydion's hands firm on his shoulders, shaking him gently. He was sitting cross-legged, facing east, with his back to the setting moon, waiting for the dawn. By the look of the sky, sunrise was no more than an hour away. It looked dull and grey compared to the vivid visions that had filled his mind's eye moments ago.

'What happened to me?' he asked, touching the dew on his arms and legs.

'You have been inside yourself all night long. You were lulled.'

'Lulled?'

Gwydion chuckled. 'By the music of the lorc. What a harper you would have made, Will, had you been born in the old days. Are you feeling well? I would say you have been well and truly moonstruck.'

Will got up and walked around, but there was no need to

loosen his limbs. He felt neither cold nor stiff, as he should have been after a night on the damp ground.

'I feel . . .' he brushed back his braids and said dreamily, '. . . very, very well.'

'But can you feel the *battlestone*?'

He heard patience being sorely tried, and knew Gwydion was waiting for him to regiment his thoughts. 'Is there a stone near here?'

'I would say so.'

'Let me see.'

He stumbled around for a while, then they went down and approached the lign and immediately Will's feeling of wellbeing dropped away. A sick feeling of despair seized him.

Gwydion demanded, 'Is this one a greater or a lesser stone?'

Will, wary now and fully awake, steeled himself to address the question. Finally he clenched a fist and put it to his forehead in an effort to make the answer come. 'I think it might be weaker than the Arebury stone.'

'Willand . . .' Gwydion was shaking him gently. 'We have work to do.'

He made another effort to dispel the sickness. 'Without getting closer I can't say for sure. I daren't go closer. Not yet.'

'Why not?'

'Maybe if the moon were to set, or the sun to rise. Just now it's like trying to see into the distance on a rainy day. One day a man can look out and see a faraway hill as clear as clear, another day he won't see a thing. Maybe if we went just a little bit closer.'

Gwydion looked around carefully, then nodded. 'If you think so.'

They skirted the place where the two earth streams crossed and, as they came abreast of it, a sudden nausea rose in the pit of Will's stomach. He was reminded very strongly of the sludgy, sucking bog into which he had stumbled the day before. He caught again the same unbearable whiff of corruption, though there was nothing here to make the air unsweet. He retched drily, staggering as he waited for Gwydion to come to him.

'It's right here,' he said shortly. 'Do you want to make a start?'

But Gwydion continued to look back at the hill from which they had come. He was unhappy at something. 'We should not unearth it.'

'You want to leave *another* one alone?' Will felt the blade of annoyance flash inside him. 'What's the excuse this time, Gwydion?'

The wizard's gesture seemed to dismiss his anger. 'It is perhaps too deeply buried.'

'Gwydion, surely we must dig it up. What's the purpose of finding these monsters if we don't slay them?'

'I think we must not slay this one until we have slayed another.'

'What *other*? What are you talking about? You mean the one back there? The one near Arebury that we did nothing about either?' Will waited for Gwydion to answer, but the wizard added nothing, and so Will came back at him. 'I've been thinking about Maskull. I don't understand why he wants so much to kill me. And I don't understand why you won't tell me about him.'

The wizard circled the site of the battlestone warily, then began to dance. 'This is not a good time or place to speak of this.'

'Gwydion, when will you ever say it is a good time to speak of it? I want to know what's going on!'

'You will not understand. His motives are complex.'

'Is he evil?'

'Not in the way that you still insist on misusing the word.'

'Then what?'

'He has come to believe in unkind solutions.'

'Why did you banish him when you could have killed him?'

The wizard broke off his movements and looked at Will sharply. 'I banished him because it is beyond me to kill him.'

'Are you saying his power's greater than yours?'

'That, Willand, remains to be seen.'

Will folded his arms, irked by the wizard's magical dance

around the site. It seemed faintly ridiculous. 'Surely it would have been better to imprison Maskull in plain sight rather than to exile him. For too long, you didn't know he had escaped. And now you don't know where he is at all.'

Gwydion's half-glance scorned him. 'You speak as if I had had all the time in the world at Verlamion to have Maskull whipped and shipped to the Isle of Gulls! I have already told you, I was fortunate to be able to land any spell at all upon his person as he battled me from the curfew tower. I did not plan my action as a lasting solution. It was an emergency. You already know that such a vanishing spell always brings with it a jump in time for the one who is vanished away. I therefore knew we would be free of him for thirteen months, at the least. And there are other considerations.'

'There always are.' Will walked away, but as soon as he had gone two paces from the lign he saw that he was goading the wizard and could not help himself. 'You seem to me far too cautious for this kind of work.'

'Caution is one of the prerogatives of having lived so long, and perhaps also a reason for it.'

'And cowardice? Is that one of your old man's vices too?'

Gwydion's eyebrow curved like the black blade of an eastern sword. 'Now that is a failing that I will not allow.'

He continued to work his way sun-wise around the burial site as the golden disc of the morning sun sent its shadows long into the west. The wizard's gestures seemed to Will like those of some strange insect sensing the world then halting to make up its mind about what to do next. But, as suddenly as the wizard had begun, he stopped and said, 'As for rushing madly into the draining of battlestones, Willand, it may be more dangerous than we yet know.'

'Who understands battlestones better than I?'

Gwydion came and looked at him closely. 'And you know *this* much!' He snapped his fingers in front of Will's face. 'Show me the true path, Willand! Show it to me, and I will agree that you know better than I how to deal with the problem!'

'True path? I have no knowledge of any such thing.'

'It is, at least, something to the good that you can admit your ignorance.'

'How can I learn when you choose to tell me so little?'

The wizard marched away from the unhallowed ground. 'It is a rede of magic that a little knowledge is more dangerous than no knowledge at all – as you so amply prove.'

'An old man's excuses! You've done next to nothing in four years! Or so you claim! What are you hiding from me, Gwydion?'

'You can be very tiresome when you are in the vicinity of a battlestone, Willand. At least your rudeness allows me to gauge the strength of what lies in the ground, but you should try harder to guard your mouth, for it is most irritating to listen to an uncontrolled flow of nonsense.'

'We ought to be doing something about this evil. Quickly! Before it's too late!'

'And I do strongly advise you that patience is a very great virtue indeed.' Gwydion made Will stand back, then he danced final magic and cast general calming spells over the earth all around the stone, but never once did he approach it.

'What are you doing?'

'This is a light cosmetic. So that for a year and a day any innocent who strays here will change his mind about staying, and he will do so without ever knowing why.'

'Coward!'

'Do you remember the stakes that are up on the hill?' Gwydion said evenly. 'Do you know what they are?'

'What?' he said, interested despite himself.

'They are sighting stakes. Posts driven into the ground so that their alignment points to this place. They sight where the ligns cross.'

'*What?*'

'Oh, indeed! So the stone may be found at a later time, whatever the phase of the moon might be.'

Will's arms stiffened, his face was colouring with an unreasoning anger. 'You mean you've been here before? Then you've lied to me! You *knew* about this battlestone already, and you were *testing* me!'

'Willand, it was not me who put the stakes up there.'

'Then who?'

'You were not listening very closely when I asked patient questions of the place. Come! We must be moving on.'

'First tell me who put the stakes there!'

'Oh, who do you think?' The wizard rolled his eyes.

'Maskull?'

'The whole hill reeks of him.'

Soon after the full of the moon, the ligns quickly faded, and though Will cut several supple wands, he could scry the flow no more. There was only a sense of fast-receding depth, masked by the mystic swirls and criss-crossing lines that showed enduring ancient streams. These, Will knew, were the natural surface flows that always patterned the land, the shapes the folk of old had learned to feel in their bones and which had given them so fine a talent for planting the right crop in the right place and building without offence to the land. It was a talent not shared by lordly builders with their city walls and their great stone keeps, a talent the Sightless Ones had all but snuffed from the minds of men.

They left the site of the Tysoe stone and, as the wizard went onward at half his customary pace, Will recovered his courtesy and began to review what had happened. While it deepened Will's understanding to feel each stone attack his mind in its own fashion, the experience was vastly tiring. He wondered if Gwydion was wholly immune from the stones' suffocating embrace, for if that was the lorc's way to protect itself from disturbance, then it seemed to be succeeding.

That day and the next they continued westward, but progress was painfully slow. Gwydion's vigour had deserted him. He instructed Will in geomancy – the proper reading of the land. He spoke of the rude way in which the bones of the earth had been rooted up. He pointed out quarries, calling them open wounds upon the land. He denounced distant towers and spires, saying they had got above themselves. 'See how the villains pile stone upon stone to such a height that they humble the hearts of men! The only true house is one built of stones that the earth gives up freely. Of flints or red clay baked to a good hardness, or better, houses built of wood and well thatched with reeds. The best dwellings are those that nestle in the land, Willand. Those that respect the Tenets of Amergin, who was a great architect of old. Those that do not seek to dominate men or the earth around them! No building should be made to glorify its builder or its owner, for that makes it a boastful monument, and boastful monuments are best left to the dead!'

Will listened, hearing frustration and bitterness in the wizard's words. It was worrying that the discovery of the sighting stakes had upset him so much. Perhaps they spelled some kind of disaster for Gwydion's great master plan. As for buildings, Will knew very well what style of house his own heart yearned to see again. It was a modest place, oak-framed, with whitened walls of wattle and daub and a neat thatch. It was home.

The wizard was talking about the balance now, how it must always be kept, and of how the powers of recovery of the earth were being sorely tested by the demons of greed and selfishness that seemed every day to be growing stronger in men's hearts.

'Oh, men are mostly wilful blunderers. They disturb the balance in whatever they touch – kings more so than shepherds.'

'And sorcerers more than kings, I suppose,' Will ventured, hoping to steer the wizard towards the subject of Maskull.

'Sorcerers far more than kings. What better poacher will you find than the one who has been a keeper of game?'

'Have there been many sorcerers?'

'There have been many dangerous men in the history of the world. They have arisen mostly in the kingdoms that lie across the Narrow Seas, in the Tortured Lands far away, but also here from time to time in the Realm. The worst of these dangerous men possess a clear vision of a particular future they wish to bring about. They have certainty about what must be and why. So certain are they that they easily convince others that their way is best. Maskull is such a man as this.'

Shortly after they crossed the River Stoore Gwydion halted next to the raised bed of another ancient stone highway. He threw out his arms to north and south, announcing to the sky in a resounding voice, 'Behold, this work of sorcerers, Willand! It is the Fosse, the same we have seen before, yet called hereabouts "Trench Strete", or "the Ditch Way". It was made fifty generations of men ago, but see what ruin has befallen it in the present season.'

Gwydion shook his staff angrily at the crooked slabs that marked an arrow-straight highway. 'See with what cunning the Slavers ravaged the common treasury of this Isle! A peaceful folk were enslaved in great numbers to rip up stone to build these vile paths. And we shall soon see armies moving along them once again.'

'Then we must make greater haste,' Will urged, trying to stoke up further the fires that had sprung up in the wizard's belly. 'We must find the next battlestone before it's too late.'

'We cannot make more haste, for we must wait until the equinox.' Gwydion looked at him, his features seeming again careworn and haggard. 'In magic, remember, there is always a powerful link between time and place. Oh, I wish I knew the answer!'

And then Will saw clearly the root of the wizard's fears, for Gwydion was the last phantarch. It was his task to steer the world along the track of fate that yielded up the best of all possible worlds, yet he had lost his way.

No wonder he's angry, Will thought. He's afraid. He can no longer see what the true path is. He's almost convinced that we're lost!

He looked out across the land and saw how for the most part the Slaver road was mounded up high above the meadows and how a ditch followed it along the side, though in places both road and ditch were in ruin.

'Where does it go?' he asked, shading his eyes.

'To the north it cuts in two the once-sacred precincts of Elder Tree Copse, a glade of leafy boughs, where green rings on the summer lawn show where the fae once danced. Then it runs onward across Dunn's Moor and beyond to the city called now Leycaster that was founded by King Leir in ancient days. It goes further north still, eventually to the city of Linton, which is in the earldom of Lindsay. But were we to follow it southward we would come first to the Four-shire Stone, go past what was once Little Slaughter, and thence to Cirne. But we will follow it in neither direction.'

Gwydion levelled his staff at a great gap in the raised roadbed. There were large, flat stones scattered all about, as if some great burrowing animal had come this way and had scraped and pawed until the stuff of the road was scattered. The gap, Will saw, ran for hundreds of paces, and there were others in the distance.

'See how lordly ambitions imperil us all! The one who claims the land about the Four-shire Stone as his own, and who calls himself lord of that place, has done this. In recent times he sent his men to plunder the stone from these Slaver works. His plan is to increase his power by the building of a great house and fortress for himself three leagues to the south of here. These new disturbances he has made in the earth have freed the flows in the lorc and helped bring it to life all the sooner. Though he knows it not, this lord will in time be the loser, for by this mischief his bloodline shall now fail, even as that of Lord Strange has failed. He cannot see how all things come round in a great circle.'

Will raked fingers through his hair and looked up and down the old Slaver road. 'I don't see how—'

'Because the contract that Semias struck with Gillan the Conqueror was ever that the lords were to be stewards – servants of the land more than masters of the people! They were to hold the Realm in trust for future generations. But that contract was soon broken. The lign of the rowan, Will. It passes through that gap there. Where once its flow was dammed, now it is dammed no longer. And the same, I believe, is true of Eburos and Indonen to the south. Too many breaches in the Slaver roads have been made.' Gwydion's finger traced lines of coloured fire in the air, showing how the lorc was once again getting in touch with its extremities. 'A great error has been committed here, and a terrible consequence set in motion. Thus it is, and always will be, when the works of man are heaped upon the earth too quickly, with selfishness and greed as their motives!'

They passed through the gap in the old road and went on, still hoping to follow the lign of the rowan into the west. To Will's surprise, as the afternoon wore on and the heat of the day mounted, Gwydion began to speak more freely of Maskull and his journeys into the realms of forbidden knowledge:

'"Much have I travelled, much have I tried, and much have I tested the powers of this world." Those were his words to me when last we spoke. And it is true. He has ventured through fantastical places – east across the Narrow Seas, down through forgotten empires beneath the earth. Maskull has taken ship to the very Edge of the World. He has walked in the Drowned Lands, that once were lit by the sun but now lie deep beneath the ocean. He even claims to have bathed in the Spring of Celamon, to have touched the moon and to have found a doorway set in the star-punctured dome of the sky – one that leads out into the furnace of starlight beyond. That doorway can only be reached by voyaging to the Baerberg, Willand. The Baerberg, which lies at the top of the world. He has been there, and so have I. That is how I know what is in his mind. He has seen another world, one not unlike our own, yet quite separated from it. He is steering the fates of that world and ours ever closer, setting us on a collision course. He means for the destinies of our two worlds to merge, to become one, so that afterwards there will be only one future, and he the undisputed master of it!'

◙ ◙ ◙

CHAPTER TEN

THE MAD BARON

There was a chill in the air and a faint mist lay over the early morning. For the first time autumn seemed to be on its way and with that change came another – their success reached an abrupt end. For several days progress had been slow, and now the equinox had come and gone and Will was having an even harder time scrying the western path of the Caorthan lign. When they came into the increasingly hilly country around Flyefforde, their trend was a little north of west. Then Will began to suspect that he already knew where his wand was leading him.

'I get the feeling we've been here before,' he said.

'From here we must tread softly,' Gwydion told him as they came to a wooded rise, 'for yonder lie the lands of the mad lord.'

Will nodded at Gwydion's words. He understood the danger that lay in wait for them, for they were near the hamlet of Aston Oddingley.

Years ago they had found a battlestone here, but Gwydion had chosen to leave it be. Partly that was because it was not the Doomstone, but another reason had been that it was buried on land owned by Baron Clifton, a man famously cruel, quick to take offence and easily roused to anger.

Thomas, Lord Clifton had allied himself with the queen. He

had ridden with his knights and three hundred men-at-arms to Verlamion under the banner of the red wyvern. There he had been more affected than most by the fell emanations of the Doomstone, and his heedless bloodlust had proved his undoing. He had fallen under hideous wounds and, after the battle, his broken body had been reclaimed by his son, John, in whose heart lay no shred of forgiveness.

'The son is mad too,' Gwydion said.

'Is that so?' Will said.

'He is sworn to avenge his father. When Morann was last in Trinovant he noted Friend John's closeness to the queen's cause. After learning of his vows of revenge, she has cultivated him, and now keeps him continually about her at court. He is always ready to do her bidding. His mind is three parts rotted by the battle-stone, and all the while the queen inflames him further against Duke Richard. He wants only to set upon his enemy and tear him limb from limb.'

'Then you're right,' Will said, looking at the hill beyond which the Baron's manor house stood. 'We shouldn't look for a welcome here, even though the master of the house has changed, for it seems to me you are thought of amongst the queen's friends as little more than Duke Richard of Ebor's magician.'

Gwydion sighed. 'Alas! That is their oft-repeated complaint. To such a low esteem have I lately fallen. Come! For we must now draw nigh.'

They went by quiet ways, fringing woods and following hedge lines that covered their movements. They soon reached the crest of the hill where they had camped in the rain long ago, and a great house came into view.

Though Clifton Grange was not a castle, it was a strongly built house, surrounded by a ditch and walls that were twice the height of a man. It possessed stout gates and two towers from which arrows might be shot. Will thought back to the lessons about fortification that he had learned during his days at Foderingham. He decided the baron's house might be expected to stand for days – maybe even weeks – against a hostile force of consider-able size, and that a great cost in lives would be paid by anyone attempting to enter it uninvited.

That thought also caused Will to wonder what cost might be paid by someone seeking to leave the house against the owner's wishes. But before he could think the matter through, Gwydion danced and clothed them both in magic. A bright blue light shone suddenly about them, and when Will looked again he saw the same old man that he had seen at the Plough Inn. He felt a momentary pang of disquiet at the sight of a white heart carved in bone upon his breast, and at the broad-brimmed hat and patched grey cloak on which the mark of the Fellowship was also pinned. But then he gasped, for when he looked down at himself he saw that he was similarly clad, in the dark grey travelling gear of a novice mendicant of the Sightless Ones, and girt with the thick leather belt with its knuckle-shaped clasp that was famously used as a weapon. Will also wore the bone-white heart as his badge, and a soap bag slung across his back and chest like a foot-soldier's blanket. To add the finishing touches to their beggary, Gwydion produced two wooden bowls and then, perhaps remem-bering the sombre weather that had attended their last visit, he called down a shower of rain upon them.

'Well! That was quite painless.'

'Of course.' Gwydion looked askance at him. 'What did you think? I've done it *before*, you know.'

And then there came to Will some recollection that long ago there had been a king whose name was Uther, whose passions had been roused over another man's wife, and that he too had been changed in form . . . 'You did it to Uther Pendragon,' he said, hardly knowing where these strange thoughts came from. 'You did it shamelessly, to deceive a lady. So she would become pregnant by a king. So Arthur would be born.'

'Was that me?'

'You know it was!'

Again the wizard's eyes alighted on him, and in his new guise of Fellow his smile was frightening. 'It may have been me. And if it was, then you may suppose that what was done was done out of *necessity*.'

Will drew apart, wiped the rain from his face. He was uncomfortable. He felt suddenly wretched and caught up in things that were far too big for him. But he had agreed to this insane adventure, and there seemed to be no alternative.

'What are we waiting for?' he asked, as Gwydion lingered in the trees, watching the rain fall.

'What do you think?'

Will licked his lips at the question, keen now to get the deed over with. Then he saw Gwydion's eyes scour the skies briefly.

As always the wizard looked slightingly on his impatience. 'We're waiting for noon.'

'Why?'

'We must gather all the advantage we can to help your talent.'

'I'm sure there's no need to wait on my account,' he said sharply.

Gwydion rolled his eyes. 'Willand, do not take my words amiss.'

'Forgive me,' he said with hardly less edge, 'if I'm not *quite* myself.'

'Never fear. I'll change you back.'

'Yes, you will!'

They started off down the hill towards the manor, letting the rain soak them thoroughly.

'Gwydion, what about these?' Will said, pointing at his eyes. 'Just a little detail, I know, but won't they tend to give us away?'

'Sarcasm is a very low form of wit, Willand.'

'It's not irony. It's a straight question.'

'Many mendicants are sent abroad by the Fellowship,' Gwydion said, kicking through the puddles to muddy himself. 'In that way, you understand, the influence of the Sightless Ones is not confined to the chapter houses. The Fellows come out at harvest time to claim the tithe, of course. They are seen sometimes upon the roads, going from cloister to cloister, but the red hands have collected about them many sighted followers who do their bidding in the wider world – messengers, agents, spies, sneaks of one kind or another – men and women who have unwisely accepted the charity of the Fellowship, accepted the Great Lie even, but who have not yet repaid their debt with surrender.'

Will felt the weight of the soap bag that girdled him, and looked at his hands in horror. Had he been a genuine Fellow, ritual washing many times a day would have made his hands raw. He saw they were red and scaly and his nails hard and yellow, as were Gwydion's. The sight took him back momentarily to the dangerous enterprise he had so thoughtlessly undertaken at Verlamion.

'How many folk do you think live down there?' he asked.

'Upon the lands that Friend John boasts to own? Some thousands.'

'I meant in the manor house itself.'

'There? Perhaps two dozen. No more while the baron is with his retinue in Trinovant – though I think he will not remain there much longer with war so near.'

'Is he married?'

'Married? When his mind is bent solely on avenging his father? There is no mistress of any kind at Clifton Grange. The baron's mother is already gone into one of the cloisters which the Fellowship maintains for ladies of rank who have wearied of the world.'

Will shivered at the choice she must have had to make. 'I don't know what I would've decided if I'd stood in her shoes – join the Sightless Ones or stay in a house built over a battlestone.'

'I would not be surprised to find that the people hereabouts think of this as a house of ill omen. That should make our task a little easier.'

They came to the gate and found it unguarded and the yard within quiet, apart from the hissing of rain. Gwydion went to the back door and knocked three times with his staff. It was now a banded rod, hung about with coloured ribbons and the pewter medals of pilgrimage that rattled like a jester's wand. When the door opened, an anxious serving woman looked them up and down and enquired suspiciously what purpose they had in coming to the Grange.

Gwydion bowed low and said in a wheedling, pitiful voice, 'You may say it is a pilgrimage that we are upon, woman. You may say that we seek the Shrine of the Siren Sisters.'

'Then you've missed your road,' the servant said, not opening the door any wider. 'You must go back the way you've come and take the Crowle road.'

'Precipitation . . .' Gwydion said with a yellow-grey smile. Big drops fell from the brim of his hat. 'If you were a friend, you would afford us shelter while this downpour continues.'

The woman looked unhappy. She hesitated, then said, 'Wait here.'

Soon a manservant appeared. He was a big man with a bald head, and he seemed to carry some authority. He wore the colours of the baron, and on his chest six gold rings upon red with a badge showing a red wyvern on his arm. 'You cannot stay here, rain or shine,' he said.

'You may suppose it invites adverse fortune to refuse a pilgrim his right and due,' Will said as slyly as he could.

The man advanced across the threshold threateningly. 'Right and due, you say? On your way, beggars!'

'We may retire,' Gwydion said, drawing back. His fingers went to his bone badge and lifted it menacingly. 'But common beggars we are not. See! We are mendicants of the Fellowship. What if we should petition the Elders at Cirne regarding your treatment of us?'

'I care nothing for your Elders.'

'Oh, but it may be that you should care.'

The man's anger seemed fit to burst, but he controlled himself for Gwydion's weaselly words had put him in a quandary. The serving woman touched his arm fearfully.

'Give him what he wants, Gryth.'

'Not this side of the grave!'

'But what'll the baron say if he returns home to a *letter*?'

'What letter?'

She lowered her voice and half turned away. 'The one that would come back from the Warden of the chapter house at Cirne.'

'Which lord's wicked servants would refuse a mendicant of the Fellowship food and drink and asylum from the heavenly flux?' Gwydion muttered mournfully. 'You may already know how it is with the red hands.'

The words that were commonly used to speak slightingly of the Sightless Ones made the woman gasp.

'Now, I didn't say that!' Gryth objected. 'They were your words, not mine!'

'He said it!' Will found himself blurting out. 'He spoke the execrable phrase!'

'I never did!'

'The words came from his own lips! Defiler!' Will called out.

Gryth began to argue, but now there was fear in his voice.

'May it be "come taste of our food and drink" was all that this man said after all . . .' Gwydion put in, and though the bald man scowled and blustered, still he bade them follow him to the bakehouse.

Will forced his mind to shut tight as he walked. He could feel the battlestone affecting him. The onset was sudden and sickening, and the magical disguise in which Gwydion had enwrapped him did not react well to its presence. When he looked down he counted six fingers on his left hand. He looked away, feeling suddenly panicky. His mind swam as his eyes fixed upon a large brown and white mare. She waited steadily enough in the rain, hitched to a large victual cart, but it seemed that she was vastly uncomfortable about something.

Will blinked and swallowed hard, following on after Gwydion, feeling every bit as fearful as he looked. He took himself in hand.

'Here!' Gryth said, giving Will a hard loaf and a lump of cheese. 'Put this betwixt you. You may sit here on this bench until you have eaten and until the rain has eased, but then you must go on your way, do you hear? I warn you: neither stray from this passage nor poke your noses into anything that does not concern you. Begone quickly! The master of this house is due home soon, and he is a man of short temper and fiery ways. You will rue it if he finds you here, protected beggars or no.'

'Then the baron must have a sour character indeed,' Will muttered as the man left. The piece of cheese he was holding was cracked and as hard as rind. 'I have little love for the Sightless Ones, but we did not ask for much by way of hospitality. What does he call this?'

'Never mind the cheese,' Gwydion said sharply. 'What about the stone? The equinox is now some days past. Tonight the waning crescent of the moon will lie midway between last quarter and new. We must not miss our chance!'

Will began to look around. They had been left in a small, draughty passageway that joined the yard and the back of the stables. Two cool storage rooms led off and Will saw sacks and barrels and sides of meat hanging in the first. In the second there were wooden shelves stocked with big, round cheeses and more dry goods.

Will drew out the split hazel wand from under his cloak. But no sooner had he taken up the scrier's stance than he began to tremble and then to shudder.

'Oh, it's powerful, Gwydion! We're right on the lign. And the flow's moving that way very strongly.'

'How far away is the stone?'

'No more than fifty paces. Augh! What's that rank smell?'

Gwydion ignored him. 'What is the nature of the stone?'

Will shook his head. 'A big one. I feel its attack on my spirits. It feels *cunning*, as if it's undermining me in a way that I can't even grasp.'

'I detect no great change in you.'

Will cocked an eyebrow at that. He turned in the direction of the flow, looked into the blank wall for a while, trying to gauge what lay beyond. Then he opened his mind cautiously, and all his sinews stretched taut, like a man listening hard.

'That smell,' he said after a while. 'It's worse than a cesspit. What is it?'

He tried to compose himself again, but his concentration was disturbed by a big, fat bluebottle that buzzed down the passageway. Then he heard a sound that sent a shiver down his spine. It was long and high and indescribably sad. It seemed to come from a long way off.

They looked at one another, and Will said, 'What was *that?*'

Gwydion shook his head, listening, but the sound was not repeated.

Just then two men came through the yard, carrying something large, but running because of the rain. They did not notice the visitors and went into a doorway on the far side. What they carried seemed to be a gilded war saddle of red leather, but it was enormous. Its arches were high front and back and its girth straps so long that they trailed for three paces along the ground. As they passed, the carthorse tossed her head and stamped uneasily.

When Will turned back again he saw Gwydion had stepped to the end of the passage, and was silently motioning him to follow. One passage led to another, and then another, and instead of turning left he turned right and came out into a larger, darker courtyard, which had tall gates on one side. In the centre of the yard stood a large cage made of elaborate ironwork. The bars were all as thick as Will's wrists. This was definitely the source of the bad smell. Despite the rain the stink was more noisome than that of a boar's sty. It seemed that some gigantic animal had been caged here, but that was impossible because the only way in or out of the courtyard was through the narrow passage through which they had arrived.

'Pssst!' The wizard beckoned him. 'We must go before we are discovered!'

'But look at this,' he said, intrigued by the cage.

'Come! This is no time for distractions.'

With a muttered incantation and a final flick of his hand, Gwydion caused the rain to slacken and then to cease. They went back the way they had come, then made a show of preparing to leave in case anyone was watching them.

This time, Gwydion followed after Will, who opened his mind and tuned himself to the stone as much as he dared, letting his talent steer his feet ever closer to it. They tracked along the side of the Great Hall in a tightening arc, until Will's shoulder brushed against the building and they stopped.

The door they had first come to opened again, and the bald man came out. 'The rain's stopped. You must go now,' he said. Then, looking at Will, 'Is he drunk? In the middle of the day?'

'It may be that he is *unwell!*'

'Unwell? Then why did you not say so before bringing him through our gates?'

Gwydion rasped, crooking a finger at the man suddenly, 'Do you think the disease is contagious? Uncharitable knave!'

'Charity has no meaning when it is forced upon folk!'

'I shall tell the Elders at Cirne that your cheese stinks and your bread is hard!'

'Aye! You tell them that! The fewer of your sort we get here the better!'

The man watched after them until they were gone from sight. Once out of Clifton Grange they followed the path up the hill as if they were taking the Crowle road, but as soon as they were out of sight of the manor they doubled back and headed into the woods above the village of Aston Oddingley. On the way Gwydion questioned Will about the stone.

'Did you scry it?'

'Yes. But it's bad news – it's under the floor of the Great Hall.'

'Then it is to the Great Hall that we must go tonight.'

They shed their false appearances then ate a supper of field bounty while they waited for night to fall.

'A shepherd's sky,' Gwydion said, looking up at a faery land above. There were crimson mountains and lakes of fire and golden valleys all sculpted in cloud. That world reigned for a moment then faded, and soon all was grey. It was a perfect sky for Will to contemplate as he kept vigil over his thoughts, armouring himself for the coming fight.

They returned to the manor no more than an hour after sundown, this time without disguise.

Will said, 'It seems likely the manor was built over the stone without the owners ever knowing of it.'

'I do not believe the present Baron Clifton or his late father ever tried to use the stone for their own ends. Indeed, I should think they knew nothing of it. Even so, their bloodline has been soured – they have harboured a thing under their floorboards that would eventually drive each Clifton insane. Thus is harm propagated down the generations.'

For all Clifton Grange's seeming strength, the gates had been left unbarred. Even the doors were unlocked. There was no need to secure the house – none of the local folk would have willingly approached it after dark. Before night settled those who lived on the estate went home to their cottages, and the few servants who dwelt overnight at the manor took to their rooms in the outworks. Gwydion said he thought their doors would be shut tight. He doubted anyone would come out, no matter what noises they heard coming from the main house.

Once inside the Great Hall, Gwydion lit a dim blue magelight that glowed like King Elmond's Fire around the great candle holders that hung on chains from the hammer-beams above. The hall was a generous size and of the usual plan, with a huge empty fireplace facing high, narrow windows, and a gallery at one end. The walls were hung with tapestries and faded needlework that dated from a time when the baron's mother and her companions had spent their eyesight on such consolations.

Will felt the attacks of the battlestone falling against his mind. They seemed as distantly violent as the waves that broke against the Cliffs of Mor. He had prepared himself well. He helped

Gwydion push back the heavy furniture, then he scried the floor with particular care. He found a hatchet in the firewood basket and began to lever up the polished boards where the long table had been. The oaken boards groaned loudly against the iron nails that held them, but soon they had pulled up enough to show a patch of dry earth beneath.

Dusty webs and the husks of spiders clung to the wood, echoes of summers long past. This floor had not been disturbed in centuries, nor the ground beneath it.

They began to dig. Gwydion hacked at the hard-packed dust with his knife of star-iron, pausing from time to time to cast holding spells into the hole, or to apply binding magic to seal the bubbling seepages of harm that came up. Will took a small fire-grate shovel and dug, scraping out first dry dirt with his bare hands and then heaping up moister earth beside the hole. There were bits of sharp bone and charcoal in the soil and his fingers were numb by the time he began to notice a flat, hard surface appearing under them.

When he told Gwydion that he thought he had found the stone, the wizard muttered, *'Feh fris!'* in the true tongue, and produced a glow of magelight in his hands, before bending down to look closer. Will saw clearly the marks of the ogham as he began to scrape away again with his fingernails.

'This one seems to be very quiet,' Gwydion said, troubled.

'Yes,' Will said, 'I wonder about that. Maybe it's just deeply asleep, but maybe . . .'

'What?'

He swallowed drily. 'I don't know. Just be careful.'

Soon the edges of the uppermost face of the stone were uncovered. It was revealed as a block about the same size and shape as a child's coffin. Its sides were graven with marks, mostly lines, some square to the edge others slanting. As he saw them Will's heart began to beat faster. He wondered again why he had felt no further attacks upon his spirit from the stone, neither feelings of sickness nor shadows playing upon his mind. It was clear that this stone was powerful, yet it seemed willing to give up its secrets without a struggle.

'Have a care, Gwydion,' he whispered as he dug deeper. The wizard looked over the half-revealed marks with searching eyes. Ogham were carved along each of the four edges. Will called to mind the lessons he had received in 'tree writing' from Wortmaster Gort. It was called tree writing because each of the ogham letters was named after one of the thirty-three ancient kinds of tree. The very speaking of such words was a powerful magic in itself.

Will cleared more dirt from around the top of the stone, then worked his fingers under its head. He tried to lift it, but either it was too heavy or not enough soil had been broken away from its sides. He worked on steadily, knowing that the ogham were incised on each of the stone's edges and that to read them properly they must up end it. The inscriptions were set to trap the unwary, each open to two different interpretations; one read face by face, but the more important reading spiralled sunwise and upward round the stone.

After more scraping, Will tried to lift it again. He strained arms and legs to breaking before the dead weight would shift. It trembled horribly under his fingers, as if it resented being lifted from its slumbers. He released it, and as it fell back a sudden, intense fear overcame him and he jumped out of the hole. Gwydion was there immediately, standing over the stone, muttering and moving his arms, sending waves of hazy blue light into the pit to lull it.

'Are you hurt?'

'I lost my courage for a moment.'

He got down again and tried to lift the stone for a third time. He raised it half up and put his shoulder under it, but no sooner had he set it upright than a fearful howl froze his blood. It rose on the still air and split the silence of the night, a long, high scream, that echoed and died, a sound as cold as a dagger blade in moonlight, distant and plaintive as the call of the hag who portends war.

The wizard paid it no heed. He had already begun to dance,

to weave the necessary web about the stone, to mute and dull the rancorous emanations. Will watched the magic glowing and spinning in the air for a moment, then he turned and was horrified to see the door of the Great Hall swinging open. The nape of his neck prickled. His heart hammered. His eyes bored into the darkness. He could not believe what he was seeing, because there stood an old man in a nightshirt. In the pale magelight he seemed to Will to be no more than a ghostly apparition for he said nothing, just looked straight ahead.

Will turned to the wizard, but Gwydion was still dancing out the binding spell upon the stone, and could not pause. Not knowing what else to do, he leapt towards the door and tried to carry the old man out. But as soon as he was touched he sprang to life and fell down and began to shout out in bewilderment.

Will knew he had made a big mistake. He had foolishly tried to awaken a sleepwalker.

The man's yells were loud and pitiful. Will hoisted the struggling figure across his shoulder, wanting only to get him out of the Great Hall as quickly and quietly as he could. He put a hand over the old man's mouth, but his finger was quickly bitten.

'Agh! Serpent!'

Moans echoed through Clifton Grange until it sounded as if murder was being done.

Before Will could get his burden as far as the yard he heard feet running and doors banging and the noise of the whole household arming itself.

'Thieves! Outlaws!' the old man cried.

Will put down his wriggling burden in the middle of the yard and ran back the way he had come. He burst into the Great Hall.

'Gwydion!' he shouted. 'Gwydion, they're coming! We must get out of here!'

The wizard danced out the final flourish of the binding spell, then he pointed his staff. 'We cannot leave the stone here. And we must not move it until it is at least double-bound.'

'Move it? Are you mad? Before you can say "knife" the whole place will be swarming with servants!'

'The stone must leave with us, or not at all.'

Will stared back. 'Then we'll have to fight them for it!'

He leapt up onto the great table and tore down one of the tapestries, pulling out the ashwood pole from which it had hung. It was a good length and seemed strong enough for his purposes.

'Thieves!' he heard the old man cry. 'Thieves in the Great Hall!'

Armed servants were now gathering in the yard. Will could see a dozen or more of them clattering through the shadows, waving halberds and other pole-arms. He knew he must make time for Gwydion to apply the last of the binding spells. He looked for a way to bar the doors, but there was none. He thought of blocking them with furniture, but there was no time and nothing but a smooth, polished floor to brace against. Two or three men would easily be able to push their way in no matter what he piled up in front of the doors.

There was only one answer. He stepped out into the narrow passage down which the attack must come. His confidence rose as he made two practice lunges with his makeshift quarterstaff. The wood felt good in his hands. Fortune favoured him – here, just outside the doors, there was room to wield his weapon, whereas his opponents would have to approach through a narrower stone arch and fight where there was no room to swing.

He heard voices nearby. Three figures appeared in black outline. They were armed. Will gripped and re-balanced his staff and edged out to face the danger. The first man he surprised. He ran at him and turned him aside easily with an overarm blow to the jaw. The second man collided with and slipped under the first as he fell back, and the third tripped over and sprawled on top of them both.

'Back!' shouted a terrified voice. 'There's a whole pack of them! They're like mad dogs! Run!'

'Yaaaah!' Will roared, and sent them scuttling back in a panic.

As he stood foursquare in the passageway with his staff quartered across his chest, half a dozen faces peered into the darkness from the safety of the end of the passage.

'Better give it up,' a shaky voice said. 'We got you surrounded!'

'If you want us, come and get us!' Will boomed. 'Or maybe we'll come out and get you!'

He ran forward and whacked his pole at the nearest face. The wood thwacked against stone, and the other faces disappeared in a blink.

'Fetch lanterns!' another voice said. 'They can't get out 'cept through here. We'll trap them. Take word to Aston. Call out their lads!'

'Hold hard, my boys!' the first voice said. 'It'll be light soon! And the master's on his way home.'

Will knew his opponents were scared. By the feel of it at least one of them was very scared. But he could not say how long he would be able to hold a dozen or more men at bay. It would take only one lucky move on their part to bring him down. Soon the dawn would come, and his opponents' night fears would vanish. They would take heart once they discovered that he alone guarded the door.

He crept back towards the Great Hall and hid himself in the shadows, wondering what Gwydion proposed to do. Surely he isn't still imagining that the stone can be brought away, he thought. He was wrong about the manor being almost empty, and wrong about the servants being unwilling to come out. What a mess!

He waited in silence for the next attack, not daring to move. There could be no easy escape now. What if Lord Clifton's men bring archers? he thought suddenly. Or they might fetch dogs to flush me out! The best we can hope for is that Gwydion reads that inscription and gets us out of here before sunrise. Maybe he's in there covering the thing up again. I hope so!

As that thought flitted from his mind the hairs on the back of his neck gave a fresh warning. He knew he was no longer alone in the passageway. But before he could move there was a grunt and sparks leapt from the stone door pillar above his head. He pulled quickly back and felt the swish of a blade brush his cheek. Before he could lift his staff a kick to the side of his head sent him reeling from his corner. A great black shape loomed over him and he only just parried a tremendous slashing blow. The feint saved his life, but grunts came from the shadows and Will knew that the fearsome weapon was being swung again at his head. He twisted away. The steel of a broadsword rang off the stonework, then bit into his staff.

Will's head burst with pain as he felt the blade being wrestled from where it had lodged in the wood. The ash pole was old and dry and had little spring to it, not like the fresh-cut green oak he was used to. He hung on to the splintered wood, but there had been insane strength behind the blade. He felt himself kicked further into the narrow passage, so he had no chance to shield himself against the next blow. Down it came, biting deeply into his right arm above the elbow, shattering the bone and sending his forearm out at an impossible angle.

'Auuuugh!'

He felt the air leave his chest. His hand was useless now. He cried out as he felt the blood gush onto his chest and soak his shirt. His cry was not one of pain, but dismay – dismay that this was how his life would end, squalidly, painfully defeated, and in a dark place like this.

He knew that the next blow must dash his brains across the floor.

'Come out, my pretty cowards!' a thundering voice shouted. 'Cast a light in here!'

Will huddled on the floor, clutching his arm. He felt his eyes bulging from his head. Blood was spurting through his fingers. He saw now that his arm was almost severed. It dangled uselessly. His quarterstaff was hacked in two at his side and all the world was spinning and toppling into blackness. Oh, no! No! It can't be! his mind was saying, trying to deny what his eyes told him. A great wave of roaring noise was rising in his ears. He stared drunkenly into the lantern light, saw the lordly robes of red and gold and the badge of the wyvern. Blood patterned the blade that danced before his eyes, was smeared on wall and floor. There were footprints of blood – his blood – all over the passageway. A froth of it still gouted from his arm, despite his squeezing fingers.

'That's why I am your lord and you are my servants!' the great voice shouted, and Will felt the baron's foot crunch down further on his neck before releasing. 'Fetch him in here!'

Will gritted his teeth, gasping for breath as they crowded round with horror in their faces. As they lifted him up the helplessness of his situation assailed him. His arm lolled free on parted flesh, the opening bleeding in spurts now as he tried to nurse it hard to his side. They rushed him into the hall and dumped him down on the floor. He was sharply aware of the rattle of his own breathing and the lord's servants gathering in awe at the sight of a mound of earth and a strange, marked stone standing upright in a hole where the master's beautiful floor had been.

Some of the servants muttered oaths, others put their hands over their eyes in a gesture taught by the Sightless Ones.

At least Gwydion has got away, Will thought. He knew he was about to faint. He knew he was about to die, but he was unable to do anything to hasten or prevent either. He just waited for the pain to begin, but it would not begin and he started to tremble violently.

'Treasure hunting is it?' the baron said in a rage-filled yet distant voice. 'And in my house? That was a bad idea.'

Will's eyes rolled as he tried to follow the baron's walk around the stone. The blood that filled his hand was dark as wine and sticky as honey. He could feel the stone laughing at him, and he felt suddenly very cold.

'Well, you'll pay the full price for your thievery! We have a short way with the likes of you! Ready the victual cart!' He turned on Will again. 'What's this . . . a stone?'

Will tried to reply. He felt a big hand slap his face, squeeze his jaw so that his mouth was forced open.

'I asked you a question, thief!'

Despite everything Will felt a strange kind of peace settling over him. It was as if he had already begun to move beyond the warmth of the world. Yet something inside him fought against the snowflakes of peace that fell all around him. Master Gwydion! a part of his mind cried out suddenly in terror and desperation. Don't leave me! Don't leave me here to die!

His pale lips must have moved.

'What's that, thief?' the angry voice began again. 'What did you say?'

There was no answer to Will's silent plea, and as the world closed around him he was only just aware of the baron's rough voice issuing orders, of the stone being taken out and loaded onto a cart, and himself being lifted on top of it and bound to it with ropes that pinched off the flow of blood.

He sensed the starkness of the servants' terror, but they did as they were told. The stone seemed oddly warm under his back. He lay drawing his last shallow breaths as a halter was put around his neck and drawn tight. Blood caked his fingers as he flexed them. The cart shook and creaked as the baron got up to drive it forward.

'My lord, where are you going?' an anxious voice cried.

Through drooping eyelids Will saw the bald man who had first warned them away from the manor, who had given them stale bread and hard cheese.

'Where to, my lord?'

'To the lake, Gryth! To do as you should have done, craven, witless scum! I'm going to tip this thief and his booty both into deep water.'

'My lord, he's not dead!'

The baron's laugh brayed out. 'He'll not live long!'

'My lord, you must not kill him!'

The baron threw off his servant's hand and roared at him,

'Must not? *Must* not? What words are these from a man to his master?'

'But that would be *murder!*'

'And who is to witness this murder? The churl came here of his own free will. He has made a thief of himself. He will get only what is coming to him.'

With that he whipped the horse's quarters and made her pull. Will's body shook as four iron-shod wheels ground over the uneven stones of the yard. Still the bald man came after them.

'Have a care, my lord! Old Aeborn says the thief had an accomplice!'

'Let him interfere with me if he dares! Hyah!'

The cart clattered and shook as the baron goaded the horse to greater speed. Will stared groggily up at the broad back of the baron. His surcoat was redder than blood and the rings embroidered upon it in fine gold thread sparkled even in the pale dawn light. As Will lay bound and huddled on the stone, the warmth of it seemed to suffuse him still deeper, lulling him towards final sleep. The strength was fast leaving him now, and he began to see strange phantasms floating before his eyes as if he was close to death.

So this is what it's like, he thought, letting the dark close over his sight. How wrong Gwydion was all along about me being a reborn king. How strange that when I kissed Willow I did not know it would be for the last time. How can something as important as that happen without a person knowing? How I wish she were here with me now. At least there is Bethe to show that I didn't live my life in vain . . .

He forced open his eyes to take one last look at the beauty of the world, but all he saw was the baron's broad back. The phantasms swam all around and he doubted his sight, for what he was seeing now was a strange vision indeed. The mail collar around the baron's neck was unknitting itself one ring at a time, and the rings were falling away like apple blossom. And when the baron looked back, he was smiling and a beard was sprouting from his youthful face, which itself was slowly lengthening and turning older and kinder. And now the baron's hair was going from black to brown and from brown to grey, and his surcoat of velvet was fading and coarsening into a plain wayfarer's cloak of mouse-brown. And when Will looked down he saw that his half-severed arm was whole once more. There was no blood soaking his shirt and there never had been.

'Aagh!' Will said, looking at his arm and flexing his hand in astonishment. 'I'm alive! I'm – aaaagh!'

'Take that halter off your neck before you turn blue.'

'What have you done to me?' Will cried, tearing off the ropes and springing to his feet.

'The power of seeing,' Gwydion said pleasantly. 'It must be a disorientating discovery to find yourself in rude good health. I do not doubt that it is a most welcome one.'

'Aagh!'

'A simple spell of seeming. That is all.'

Will blinked and gasped, his heart bursting. He sat down astride the stone, careless of it now. All around him the world was bursting with birdsong and vivid colour. After a long time he asked, 'Gwydion, how could you have *done* that to me?'

The wizard looked over his shoulder, his face calm. 'You had to play your part. And that you did admirably.'

'But I . . . I thought I was dying . . .' There was a hint of reproach in Will's voice now. 'I . . . I thought . . .'

'And so did everyone else.'

'Gwydion, you betrayed my trust.'

'Oh? And would you rather I had left you behind?'

He turned away.

'I must say, your skill with a curtain pole is impressive, my young friend. But I fear your action was hasty for it only brought the whole household down upon us.'

'They were coming anyway. It was your fault if it was anyone's.'

'Absurd. In future you must use your wits a little longer before you resort to kicking and screaming. That is generally a good rule to bear in mind.'

Will stared around him. Still his lungs wanted to drink in the dew-moist air. His eyes wanted to feast themselves on the sight of great oak trees dark against the morning mists and the great violet dome of the sky as the last stars winked out.

'I thought I was dying.'

Gwydion chuckled. 'What were you thinking of, carrying off the old man like that?'

'I was trying to save your neck!'

'Were you, indeed?'

He climbed up beside the wizard, relief bubbling uppermost in the stew of emotions that churned inside him. 'I thought you told me you should never do magic so close to a battlestone.'

'*Unnecessarily*, is what I said. Seeming magic is not high magic, indeed it is little higher than conjuring or the art of subtle oratory. If you tell scared minds what must be believed, then fear will often work the trick. What you want to be believed will be believed without question. One man alone saw through the sham, but he dared say nothing, for all the rest were behaving as if things were otherwise. It is an important rede of magic that most men can easily be made to doubt their own judgment, and judgment is not far from sanity.'

Will looked behind him, into the bed of the cart where the battlestone brooded. It was still covered with dirt, but the dirt had dried in pale patches. 'It's warm,' he said. 'Warm and getting warmer. I don't know what holding spells you've put on it, but it seems to be fighting back wildly now.'

'Then it is to be hoped that we took it out of its grave in good time.'

'Where are we taking it? Ludford can't be far from here.'

'Ludford is ten leagues to the west.' Gwydion turned, sensing some new resolve in Will. 'Do you think I should make a gift of it to Richard of Ebor?'

'Perhaps not.'

'Hmmm. Nor do I.'

Will recalled the murderous and suicidal feelings that had overwhelmed his mind when he had been at Ludford before. 'Now I think back on it, another battlestone certainly seemed to me to be buried close by. Its power was very strong, though its music was confused.'

'We should not risk bringing this one towards it, in case both their powers are strengthened.'

Will rubbed at his arm, still unable fully to believe he had been saved. 'So where *shall* we take it?'

'In time, I hope, to the city of Caster on the Gut of Dee, and thence by ship to the Blessed Isle.'

He looked at Gwydion critically. 'But only when you've found a way to take it safely over the water, I trust?'

The wizard's chin jutted. 'That is a problem which presently remains to be solved, I will admit.'

'And what's to be done with it until then?'

Gwydion turned to look behind. 'I hope that we are many leagues away from here by the time Lord Clifton returns home, for when he does, he will learn an impossible tale from his servants. Then he will surely try to follow us, if only to find out what he has lost from under his hall and who might be wearing his semblance.'

'Gwydion,' Will sighed. 'You haven't answered my question. What's to be done with the stone in the meanwhile?'

The wizard nodded shortly. 'I know a place twenty and more leagues to the north of here where no mortal dares to go.'

CHAPTER ELEVEN

THE FLIES

The mists of dawn had slowly lifted and thinned, but whereas a blue sky had promised a sunny morning, high clouds had later rolled in from the west and the day had come on dull. Will yawned; he was very tired. He wanted to sleep but did not like the idea of making his bed beside the stone. The rough plank on which he sat afforded him little comfort. Besides, every time he so much as shut his eyes the horrors of the previous night made his heart beat so fast that he had to open them again.

After they crossed over the Saltwarp the road passed through dark elm forests that clothed a hilly land. Often they had to climb down from the cart and help their horse up the slope.

As Will pushed at the tail of the cart he asked about the ogham verse that had appeared on the stone.

'Did you read it?'

'I did.' Gwydion volunteered no more. He seemed watchful and expectant as he walked alongside the cart.

'Well, won't you tell me what it says?' When Gwydion made no answer he added, 'Don't you think I'd better know?'

'Why not try to read it for yourself?'

'How can I see the underside without turning it over?'

Gwydion sucked his teeth. 'What do you think it says?'

'Something about Lugh and a lofty palace. But on the other edge was nonsense: the false word of a king, or the word of a false king, or some such.'

'So much for your studies.'

'The true tongue isn't easy to learn when there's no one else around who speaks it. I did my best,' he said, knowing that was not wholly true. Then he added, 'Well, more or less.'

'Your best was all that was asked,' Gwydion said. 'More or less.'

The wizard cleared his throat and said in the true tongue:

> '*Lughna iathan etrog a marragh-tor,*
> *Amhainme feacail an eithichier do righ*
> *Ora fuadaighim na beidbe all uscor,*
> *En morh eiar e taier fa deartigh.*'

'*Lughna iathan etrog a marragh-tor,*' Will repeated, bending his mind to the problem. 'By Lord Lugh's waterfall—'

'Ford.'

'—sorry, ford. Beneath the tall palace, no, er . . . tower? By the false word of a king—'

'*Amhainme feacail an eithichier do righ:* by his word alone, a false king.'

'*Ora fuadaighim na beidbe all uscor:* shall ride his adversary under water. Oh, this makes no sense at all!'

'Shall drive his enemy the waters over!'

'*En morh eiar e taier fa deartigh:* and the home of masters they shall come into . . . the west?'

'Nearly. And the Lord of the West shall come home.'

'Um. What do you think it means?'

'Why don't you tell me?

> '*Beside Lugh's ford and the risen tower,*
> *By his word alone, a false king*
> *Shall drive his enemy the waters over,*
> *And the Lord of the West shall come home.*'

'Ah! Lugh's ford. That's surely Ludford!'

Gwydion sniffed. 'No great mind was needed to work that out, though this verse was made before ever King Ludd reigned. That is certainly true, and therefore remarkable in itself.'

Will stopped pushing at the cart and looked askance. 'And the "risen tower" must be Ludford Castle, which the verse foretells shall fall.'

'And?'

'And . . . could the false king be the usurper's grandson? King Hal?'

'We might suppose so.'

'But then, who is the Lord of the West? Some Prince of Cambray?'

'I would say it refers to the Lord Lieutenantship of the Blessed Isle. It is a false rank which the kings of this Realm have chosen to create.'

'Duke Richard, then,' Will said, knowing that the duke had once held the office of Lord Lieutenant. 'But that means the prediction is that a simple show of strength on King Hal's part will be sufficient to make Ludford Castle fall, and to drive Duke Richard across the sea into the west.'

'If your reading and mine are correct, that is precisely what it means.'

Will helped to heave the cart over a deep rut, wanting to know what clue the stone's verse had given on the whereabouts of the next stone. He asked, 'What about when you cross-read the ogham?'

'Then the verse ran thus – and this time I think it better if I do not trouble you with such tiresome matters as translation:

> 'Lord Lugh alone shall have the triumph,
> At the western river crossing, word of an enemy
> Comes falsely by the raised water,
> While, at home, the king watches over his tower.'

Will frowned. 'Meaning . . . what?'

'In this case, Willand, your guess might easily prove to be the equal of my own.'

'Then guesses will have to do. What are yours?'

'Only the beginning is clear to me: that Lugh, Lord of Light, shall be the only victor – that is an ancient form of words, an idiom which I had all but forgotten: it means that an outcome is not to be known beforehand, that the matter is safely beyond soothsayers and seers. I do not know the place that is meant by "the western river crossing". Perhaps it is a bridge across the River Ludd, or else the Theam. Or it may mean another river entirely. The rest of the verse is truly impenetrable.'

'Could the last line be about King Hal remaining in Trinovant? Being unwilling – or unable – to ride with his army and confront Duke Richard as his queen wishes?'

'Or perhaps it talks of Richard, sitting in Ludford Castle, deliberating upon what must be done.'

Will stopped pushing and, as Gwydion took the reins once more, he climbed back up onto the cart and drew a sleeve across his sweat-spangled forehead. He looked again at the stone. It was hard to believe that these works of ultimate harm had been created with a peaceful purpose in mind. Everything, as the Second Rede of Advantages said, had a greater price in the long run.

'I'm going ahead to see if I can't scry some more,' he said suddenly, jumping down. It was pleasant to walk among the wayside grasses. Here the cat's tails were still in flower and their long plumes waved at him, dusting his feet with pollen. He took his hazel wand out of his belt and made a show of divining, but as soon as he was far enough ahead of the cart he sat down and his fingers sought out the little red fish in his pouch.

He drew it out secretly and felt how it prickled his fingertips. Whereas his own green fish had always given him comfort, this one did not. It seemed as if some power was trying to enter him from the fish, or that the fish wanted to suck something from him like a lamprey sucked blood. It was an odd sensation. There was too much of a mystery here, too many questions unanswered, but when he thought about putting a few of them to Gwydion, his spirit shied away. He put the fish back in his pouch before the cart rumbled by and, feeling thwarted, turned his attention to the battlestone instead.

He got up and walked behind the cart for a while, and the stone stared back at him balefully. As for you, he told it silently, you've taken me away from my wife and child. And you'd do as much for everyone else in the Realm if we let you. That's why I'll see you emptied of all you contain – if I can.

As the cart passed under the shade of tall elms the ridges of ogham along its edges seemed to waver like the ripple that passes down the legs of a centipede. It seemed for a moment as if it was trying to crawl out of the cart.

You don't like that idea, do you? he asked the stone silently as he climbed up beside it. No, you don't.

'What are you doing so quietly back there?' Gwydion asked.

'I'm trying to see if it's got any other marks on it.'

'Well?' Gwydion said after a moment, this time looking over his shoulder. 'Does it?'

'It's hard to tell. But I think it's warmer than it was. We've had no sun all morning, yet it feels like the sun's been playing on it the whole day. And look at this—' He ran his hand over the stone, showing how it had bowed upward. 'It wasn't like this before.'

'Do you mean it has changed its shape?' Gwydion asked.

'To my eye it seems there's now a bulge in the middle that wasn't there before.'

'Are you sure?'

He looked again. 'Yes. When I was lying on it, it was flat. Don't you think I'd have noticed a curve like that?'

'That is hard to say.' Gwydion seemed amused. 'You were a little taken up with other matters at the time as I recall.'

'It's an obvious bulge, Gwydion. And it wasn't there before. Perhaps you should put more binding spells on it.'

'Perhaps.' The wizard's eyes did not move from the horizon ahead. 'But remember, not everything is what it seems. And it is the business of a battlestone to work upon the weaknesses of the mind.'

Though they saw many dwellings along the way, all had their doors closed and their windows barred. They met few folk and spoke to fewer yet. News of war was thin, either because those they met did not know, or did not want to say. By noon they had come among the western fringes of what Gwydion said were the Hills of Clent. He said they must cut west off the main highway and along a dusty lane to avoid Hag's Wood and Wychburgh Hill. Then, at Fiveways, they chose the most northerly fork and crossed the Stoore at the new bridge, making good speed now along the carrier's road until the light began to die.

Gwydion made much of the lightness of the traffic, and the fact that there had been no bridge-keeper to levy the toll. He got down and looked closely at the ground. 'A dozen horses were last to ride through here, all well-shod. I know the farrier and the smith who made the shoes. I know two of the horses.'

'That bridge worries me.'

Gwydion looked around, licking his lips thoughtfully. 'The local lord is absent. It seems the Commissioners have been scouring this neighbourhood too, for what lord would overlook a source of silver if he could spare a man to collect it?'

'The local lord, whoever he is, won't have missed much revenue today.'

'Yet this place is one that usually thrives. We have seen few young men along the way. Those going to market were women and children and old men. The flocks and herds have been led up to higher ground.'

'I thought there was little enough livestock to be seen. What's the reason?'

Gwydion cast him a knowing glance. 'If you thought an army of five thousand hungry men was going to pass close by your village, would you leave your flocks to graze in meadows beside the highway?'

'I see what you mean.'

They rolled on through the quiet landscape. The baron's carthorse was old and had given much, and Gwydion would not ask more of her than he should. When Will's impatience next got the better of him the wizard said simply, '"More haste, less speed." Think on it.' He said he could tell from the very silence how much rumour had been rife. He also said that with the harvest in and the tithes taken, lordly granaries would now be at their fullest. 'What better time is there to have a harvest of men?'

Will cast an eye at the stone and shuddered. It seemed that the further they took it from its proper place in the lorc the hotter and more bulbous it grew, but the change was happening so slowly that he could not be sure of it.

'What if we cross a lign with it?' Will asked suddenly.

'Did we cross ligns with the Dragon Stone?'

'I don't know. Probably. But this one's different.'

'How so?'

'It's active. It's doing things.'

They stopped eventually at Oakey, where Gwydion entered the famous grove and stood under the Thousand Year Tree in whose shade he said a famous king of old had once been crowned.

'That was in days now long gone,' he said, his eyes misting with memories. 'And Great Arthur hunted here each year. He gathered acorns for the royal planting ceremony. It is foretold that another tree, grown of an acorn shed by the Thousand Year Tree, shall in future time turn the fate of the Realm.'

'How can a tree do that?' Will asked, checking again for any further changes in the stone.

'By hiding in its branches one who shall be pursued. So the seers have said.'

'It's a mighty strange business, prophecy. And little enough was said of it in the book you gave me.'

'Little enough is known. Seers do not understand their talent.

They are rarely able to give more than misty clues as to what will be. And some things are hidden from them entirely. But time is a cartwheel, which, though it rolls onward, also rolls around. And there are wheels within wheels, for that is the essential self-similar nature of our world, so that events repeat themselves time and again, and through this we may learn much and even prophesy after a fashion through the use of experience alone. Likewise, we may learn much from the experiences of those that have gone before us. That is why the wise man pays close attention to the rede, "History repeateth itself", for that is a great truth, be the wheels of a man's life ever so great or ever so small . . .'

Gwydion's philosophies meandered on and Will yawned. In the failing light it seemed to his eye that the stone moved and then lay still again. He watched it for a while longer, but it did not move again and so he decided he might just have imagined it.

They spent the night in the grove, out in the open, yet Will felt wonderfully safe and secure. He recalled to Gwydion the night they had rested in Severed Neck Woods, and the marvellous dream he had had of the Green Man coming to him with his kingly retinue of elves and his earthy embrace.

'Perhaps modesty has changed your memory of that night into a dream,' Gwydion told him as they settled down by their fire. 'It was no dream. You were given the freedom of the wildwood, and that is a very great honour. That is why I steered us here. We will sleep soundly tonight, despite our burdensome cargo.'

As Will laid his head down he said, 'I think you should tell me where we're going.'

'To a place where we already know a battlestone may be stored in some degree of safety.'

'Where? A castle?'

'To the cave of Anstin the Hermit.'

He propped himself up on one elbow. 'But you said the Plaguestone killed him.'

'So it did.'

'Then how would this stone be safe there with no one to watch over it?'

'No one but the Sister who fetched Anstin's food knows he is dead. And she has pledged herself to silence.'

'But if Maskull should learn about it, will he not be drawn there to tamper with it?'

Gwydion's expression hardened. 'I hope he will not learn of it.'

'But if he does?'

'Maskull knows much, but he never knows as much as he believes, for he is arrogant. In the matter of the stones he has tried to follow me, then, whenever he thought it possible, to leap one step ahead. But this has done him little good. He reached the King's Stone before us, yet he did not try to raise the battle-stone or harness it to his will. He thought only to lay dangerous spells upon it to entrap me.'

'Then you think he knows less than we do about the lorc?'

'He does not behave as if he knows more. Perhaps fear is preventing him from using the harm he knows lies within the stones. Certainly he did not have the courage to lift the stone he had found at Tysoe.'

Will laced his fingers behind his head and lay back. 'You once told me that Maskull knows where I came from. Is that true?'

Gwydion took a long time to answer. 'He knows more than I.'

'But how can that be?'

'I cannot tell you that.'

'Cannot? Or will not? Gwydion, I deserve to know.'

'Recall what the rede says: "A little knowledge makes fools of most men, and is a danger to us all."'

'You think I'm unready? That I'll let whatever it is floor me? That it will lead me astray from my true path?'

The wizard shifted slowly. 'Inappropriate knowledge often does lead people astray.'

'But so does a lack of it! You've already told me that. I must know who I am and where I'm from.'

'You are the third coming of King Arthur.'

'But you know more about me, and you're not telling.'

'Not yet. And you must hope that my decision is well judged.'

'Gwydion, I'm not a child any more!'

'Trust me, Willand. Trust to my judgment, as I trust to yours.'

He clamped his teeth together, angry now. He had thought about telling Gwydion of the conversation he had had with Morann, but now he decided against broaching that difficult topic. The jewelmaster had said as much in one night as Gwydion and Gort had managed in six years. The next time he met Morann he would find out all he wanted to know.

'Good night, Gwydion.'

'Good night, Willand. Sleep well tonight and you shall rise tomorrow all the fresher.'

All the next day they moved the Aston Oddingley stone northward across a land of open heath that was dotted with gorsethorn bushes and distant meres shining silver under a milky pale sky. These lakes reminded Will of the false water he had often seen shimmering far ahead along hot summer roads, and served to remind him that not everything a man saw was what it seemed to be.

When he turned again to check the stone, he saw that it had certainly grown fatter around the middle. When he put his hand out to touch it he was forced to draw it away quickly. When he spat on the stone to test it, his spittle sizzled. That was enough.

'Gwydion! The stone! It's boiling hot! If we don't do something the cart's going to catch fire!'

The wizard turned. 'Take one of the empty casks and fetch water.'

'I have a better idea: I'll empty everything we have over it now. Go on just a little further. We'll soon have all the water we need.'

Will had seen that up ahead the branch of the River Mease which they had been following drew nearer to the road. While he emptied their drinking water over the stone he told Gwydion to drive into the ford and then stop. The stone seethed and steamed as he made a pad of his cloak, and put it against the end of the stone to protect his feet. He braced his back and pushed with his legs, until the stone began to slide towards the end of the cart.

Gwydion turned and saw what he was trying to do. 'Stop! It must not be allowed to touch bare ground!'

Will stopped. 'Why not?'

'What would stop it feeding on the earth streams hereabouts? You say it is already active. It must have been close to fulfilling its destiny when we lifted it. Much closer than I thought.'

Will abandoned his efforts and jumped down into the sluggish, shin-deep stream. He cupped his hands and began splashing water up and over the back of the cart. Vapours swirled up from the stone like escaping ghosts. He kept on splashing until the bed of the cart was drenched and no more steam would rise. Then he filled their casks and watered the horse, watching silently as Gwydion stood once again over the stone and began to tighten the magical bonds that enclosed it.

The wizard seized his arm. 'And now I must ask questions of it.' He climbed down and danced out interrogation spells in the river, splashing, muttering, crying out as his feet trod the slimy stones of the riverbed. The water rose dark up the hem of his robe as he whirled and kicked in a kind of rapture. At last he collapsed to his knees in the stream, arms raised above his head.

'Let me help you.' Will reached out.

'We must go on with all speed,' the wizard said intensely, taking his arm. 'We must not linger here. I can feel Maskull's presence as surely as a sweathound picks up a day-old scent.'

'Maskull?' Will looked around, feeling suddenly naked to the sky.

'He is not here now, but he has been here lately. And he knows we are here now. The waters have told me that much.' Gwydion's eyes seemed to track something in the middle distance, then they snapped back to Will's own. 'We must get on!'

The wizard gave the dripping stone a dagger glance. 'I was right. We did not lift this menace from the lorc soon enough. It is drawing close to the appointed time.'

Will rubbed at his mouth, knowing what Gwydion's words meant. 'I hoped things wouldn't come to this.'

'Unfortunately, they have. Courage, Willand! We can still reach safety, but we must attempt a draining the very moment we reach Anstin's cave. There we will have our best chance of success, for I know well the ground thereabouts.'

Gwydion unclasped his cloak. 'Our casks are full. Let us soak our mantles and wrap the stone in them.'

When it was done, Will led the horse out of the stream, then he climbed up alongside the wizard and hoped his fears were not showing.

'How far?'

'Seven leagues, no more.'

Seven leagues! It seemed a very long way, but Will knew he must try to raise good cheer in his heart. He began to sing, not a great song of heroic deeds as told by the courtly balladeers, but a little ditty repeated by children to learn their measures,

> *'Thirteen inches are a foot,*
> *From three feet a pace is cut.*
> *Two paces clear a handspan make,*
> *Long as a fathom, pole or rake.*
> *Eleven fathoms yield a chain,*
> *Ten chains doth a furlong gain.*
> *Of these furlongs, twenty-and-four,*
> *Comes a league, and not an inch more!'*

When the song was done he looked back along the road and told himself they had already come twice seven leagues so far. 'We can do it!' he said. 'We'll just take it like the horse does – four legs at a time!'

Gwydion smiled a chastened smile. 'I can think of no better

travelling companion than you, Willand. Though I presently wonder what might be the cause of your unreasonable optimism.'

'There's nothing wrong with looking on the bright side, Gwydion.'

'Indeed, there is not!'

Later that day the clouds parted here and there, showing patches of blue sky. Then the sun began to come in and out as if it could not make up its mind what to do. It patterned the farmland around with light and dark that moved across their path from left to right. Will found it unsettling travelling a road in the certainty that Maskull had come this way only a short while beforehand. And Gwydion had said the sorcerer knew where they were.

Will tried to clear his mind of that idea as if it was the stone's doing. To distract himself he watched a sparrowhawk hovering up ahead by a small hill. It plunged and vanished.

'The men of a hated master are easier to confound,' Gwydion announced as the cart rumbled on northward across the quiet land.

The words had come out of the blue and Will repeated them. '"The men of a hated master are easier to confound." Is that a rede of magic?'

The wizard shook his head. 'Merely the inscription on one of the gold coins of common sense.'

'And what's written on the tails side?'

'Probably that men fight best for love.'

'Is that true?'

'Certainly. Why else is so much effort put into making them love bright banners? For once that is done they can be made to fight under them. The rede you are probably thinking of says: "He who rules by fear rideth the tiger cat."'

Will thought about that for a while, then he said idly, 'Are they fierce creatures, then, these tigers?'

Gwydion raised his eyebrows. 'Have you never seen one?'

'You're becoming forgetful: we do not have them in the Vale.'

'A pity! It would keep your Valesmen on their toes if they were to have the odd tiger stalking Pannage Woods. Perhaps I shall bring one for you. There are tigers in the king's menagerie in Trinovant. They are somewhat like brindled cats, only a dozen times longer, and fierce and delightful all at once.'

Will grinned. 'Like stripy lions, you mean?'

'And what do you know of lions?'

'Again, you're forgetting – there are four of them caged at Ludford, by the gates of the castle. Gort told me they were brought out of the south, the gift of a sea merchant who hoped to win trade favours of Duke Richard at Callas port.'

'The Wortmaster spoke the truth. They are a royal symbol, a living advertisement of the duke's continuing hopes that one day he will sit the throne of the Realm, that his blood shall be restored to its rightful—'

Suddenly, the wizard broke off and looked fixedly ahead. Though there was no threat that Will could see, he called the horse to a halt. Then he leapt from the cart and put his arms up like the branches of a tree.

'What is it?' Will asked. He followed the wizard's eye. There was some cultivated land, a stand of trees to their right, the trace of a waterway, nothing very remarkable. 'Gwydion, tell me what ails you!'

But Gwydion made no reply, and when Will turned round he saw vapour rising from the cloaks that they had wrapped around the stone. It seemed like vapour, but then he sniffed the air and realized that all the water had boiled away, and what was rising was smoke.

'Oh, by the sun and moon!'

He leapt down and pulled the bung out of the nearest of the casks. Water gouted over the singed cloaks as he shook it over them. The stone underneath began sizzling and steaming again like a frying pan.

'Stop that confounded noise!' Gwydion shouted.

'The cloaks! Look, Gwydion! They're nearly afire!'

'Never mind them!'

He looked in amazement to Gwydion, but the wizard only knelt down and pressed the side of his head to the ground.

'What are you doing?' Will demanded.

'Tshhh! Mounted men! Many hundreds. Coming . . .' he said, then he stared up at the sky and his eyes rolled up inside his skull and he fell backwards like a man who had been shot through the heart by a crossbow bolt.

'Gwydion!' Will shouted. He looked around again, but he could see no sign of danger. 'Gwydion!'

The wizard had fainted.

Will knelt over him, called loudly, slapped his cheek. But there was no response. He thought to untangle Gwydion's legs and lay him on his side, just as Wortmaster Gort had once showed him was best to do, but the wizard came awake and threw him off, before leaping up into a strange crouch.

'Gwydion, what's the matter with you? Speak to me!'

There was no response. The wizard gazed back at him, slack faced and bewildered, hardly blinking.

Will tried to pull him upright, but he drew away and would not come out of his crouch. He splashed a little water from the cask over the wizard's face, and instantly Gwydion took off in a crazy, squatting run, with one arm trailing behind him.

'Gwydion!' Will's voice rose in panic now. 'What's happening to you?'

He tried to master his fear, but now Gwydion was trembling and twitching, his lips opening and closing, his teeth grinding together.

Not knowing what else to do, Will pounced and grabbed the wizard around the waist. He lifted him up and laid him across the seat of the cart. Then he climbed up behind him and began driving the horse forward. 'Gwydion, if mounted men are coming,' he said, 'then we've got to get away from here! It's the baron! Oh, come on, Gwydion! Get up there! Hyah! Puull!'

The cart jolted forward suddenly. He urged the horse to pull faster, coaxing her out of a walk. A plan had formed in his mind. If he could get the cart to the nearest stream, this time he would push the stone in and hang the consequences. It would be hidden and cooled at the same time. Then he would unhitch the cart and ride off on horseback, taking Gwydion to the woods that hemmed in the stubble fields to the east. There they would have some chance of escape.

'Wake up!' he shouted at the wizard. Gwydion's head lolled and his mouth fell open as he was shaken by the shoulder. 'What's happened to you? Is it a spell? Is it some trap that Maskull's caught you in?'

But when he looked back he saw a sight that worried him even more. A column of men were spilling out onto the road to the south, a line of dark figures emerging from the afternoon's haze. They were many, for they were raising a lot of dust. Will could not make out the banner that streamed above them, except that it was red.

It *is* the baron, he thought. And if they're galloping we'll soon be overtaken whatever I try to do. There's not going to be enough time!

'Gwydion, wake up!' he yelled, but the wizard slumbered on like a man seized by a falling fit. The cart bounced and jumped as the horse gamely gave her best and took them off the line of the road. He hung on to the wizard. 'Gwydion, by the moon and stars, if you don't wake up I'll . . . Oh, this is bad!'

The sun glittered now on the dark mass of horsemen, and Will saw blued-steel helms. They were not coming at a gallop, but still their approach was swift and they were closing. He guessed their number at five hundred.

Something was wrong. Too many were knights in full harness. Even if Baron Clifton had called out every last one of his vassals and all the knights of the Middle Shires he could not have mustered so many armoured men. And why would they have wasted time donning mail and plate just to chase down a pair of thieves?

'Hyah! Puull!'

What made Will urge the horse on again was a trilling trumpet note. He looked over his shoulder. A second column of horsemen was now closing on the first, also at a trot. Many banners of red and blue and green streamed out above them as they came on. Dozens of banners flying and hundreds of riders.

'What's happening?' he shouted angrily. Then the terrible truth began to dawn on him.

Gwydion twitched, then convulsed and began to cough. Will hung on to him as the cart bumped again over uneven ground. Will steadied the wizard as he tried to sit up.

The wizard gave Will a dark glance and wiped a little blood and spittle from his mouth. 'Stop the cart!'

'I can't – we're being chased!'

'Of course we are! Pull up!'

The wizard tried to snatch the reins, but Will resisted.

'You don't understand!'

The wizard thrust him back and wrested the reins from him. 'Fool! Why did you leave the road? Can you not tell an *army* when you see one?'

Will looked back wildly. 'Hey . . . ?'

'It is the stone that's drawing men to battle! It is pointless to try to outrun them – wherever we go they must follow!'

Gwydion slowed the horse to a walk. Ahead was the brook Will had been heading for, but now it served only to bar their way. All around it was soft, tussocky ground, the sort that carthorses did not like. Columns were gathering at their back amid a great cloud of dust. More horsemen appeared by the moment, drawn unknowingly towards the cart that was in their midst.

'Their commanders understand nothing of us or of our cargo,' Gwydion said. 'They do not see that all their actions are being controlled by the stone!'

'Gwydion, what happened to you? I was scared. I thought you were going to die. I thought Maskull had landed some kind of spell on you.'

Gwydion scowled. 'It was a trance. My awareness left my body momentarily to change places with a skylark's.'

'A skylark? You mean a *bird*?'

'Of course a bird! What better place to go than up into the middle airs if a man wishes to find out what is happening below? From that vantage, I saw much. These squadrons of horse are but the outriders of a far greater army that is on the move all around us. And for every rider there are a dozen footsoldiers. Look! Thousands are coming across the meadows.'

'Are they from Ludford?' Will asked, seeing more men emerge from the cover of the woods. He tried to identify their war banners and liveries. There was one of gold-over-red that carried the device of a severed head. Another showed a green lion with a forked tail rising up against a yellow background. 'I'm sure these aren't the badges of Duke Richard's allies!'

'Alas! The host is commanded by Lord Ordlea, and under him is another of the king's Commissioners of Array – Lord Dudlea. Twice as many men are in this army than all who clashed at Verlamion put together. It is my guess that Maskull has persuaded the queen to send them along this road to intercept the Earl Sarum. He is trying to bring his own army south from his castle of Wedneslea, hoping to join with Richard at Ludford.'

'Earl Sarum?' Will asked, knowing he was one of Duke Richard's two greatest allies. 'How many men does he lead? Did you see them?'

'The tail of his army was but half a league to the north-east. Its head is coming now through Loggerhead Woods. He has spotted his enemy, I would say, but he has fewer than three thousand men at his command. It is hard to say what he will do, for he too has been drawn unwittingly towards the battlestone.'

'But they'll be massacred,' Will said starkly. 'They're outnumbered three to one.'

He shouted the tired horse on towards the small brook, but the wheels of the cart had already begun to sink in the damp ground and Will looked around him despairingly as they lurched to a halt.

'It's no good. We can't go any further.'

And there they waited while Lord Ordlea's great, raggle-taggle army engulfed them. Squadrons of armoured horsemen went rushing by to left and right, marshalling themselves to guard the flanks. Three lumbering masses of footsoldiers were now packing in tightly with one another ready for the attack. Drums were beating and men yelling as they clashed their weapons. 'The king! The king!' they shouted, for most were simple farmers who had been told they were doing no less than King Hal's bidding against a wicked rebel lord.

For a while the cart was surrounded by a sea of running men who wore no helmets or breastplates but only yellow hoods. They were carrying bills and axes and fearsome hooks on long poles. Their faces were filled with a fierce eagerness to kill. Half-armoured men-at-arms with drawn swords led the charge and urged men on with shouts. Then footmen began massing along the line of the brook, holding the margins of the boggy ground until archers could come forward. It seemed to Will that many of these lads were fresh from the field. They were frightened and could not help their fear. Some were white-faced, shocked even by the sight of so many men together in one place. Some knew they were being herded like sheep towards a slaughter. But there were others still, weakminded and savage of heart, who had listened to the stone uncritically and knew very well where revenge was to be found. They wanted only the chance to draw blood, to bear down upon their enemy and wreak havoc.

A mounted knight's esquire with a mace in hand came up and snarled, driving his men on. But then he wheeled about and called out to Gwydion, 'You there, drover! In the name of the king, what are you doing here?'

Gwydion played the helpless man overtaken by calamity. 'Carrying, sir.'

'Carrying what?'

'Naught but a stone, sir. It is our . . . business.'

The squire looked them over, but there was nothing in the cart his soldiers could use. He saw them only as an obstruction to be got around. 'You are between armies,' he said, as if talking to a fool. 'Get-out-of-the-way!'

'That we would do, sir – if we was not stuck fast!'

As the horseman galloped away, Will jumped down to help haul the cart out of the mud, but it would not move. Heat was pouring from the stone now, rippling the air above it like flame. Will could feel it like an oven against his cheek. There was swirling smoke and the smell of charred wood. He put his back against the nearest wheel and heaved, but it was no use. His feet slid in the sodden ground. Despair overcame him as he saw the Earl of Sarum's army spreading out along the rise to the wooded north-east. There were few men on horseback among them and some were dismounting ready to fight. Most were men-at-arms but there were many archers wearing red and black, and they came to the fore, all driving in sharp wooden stakes to stand behind in case enemy horsemen should charge down on them. They had come along the road and emerged in widely spread companies from Loggerhead Woods, trying perhaps to give the idea there was a far greater force in reserve. They hung back like seasoned men who had been in such a fight before. Gwydion was watching them, muttering subtle words and gesturing broadly towards the earl's army like a man willing them to disperse.

Will felt the cart lurch, then flames began to leap up from the back of it.

'Gwydion! The cloaks! They're burning!'

He jumped up into the back of the cart once more and began beating the flaming cloth against the stone. But then the stone itself began to thresh from side to side, and when Will pulled away the second cloak he saw to his horror that the stone was a stone no longer. Now it seemed to resemble nothing so much as a giant, grey maggot. It wriggled from side to side as if trying to escape from the cart.

He gasped in disgust, his flesh crawling as he saw the thing writhe in its smoking bed.

'It's starting!' he shouted. 'Gwydion, there's no more time!'

Flames leapt up from under the stone. Will sprang away and began to unharness the frightened horse. In a moment the whole cart was engulfed in flame, and there was now no way to prevent the maggot falling to the ground.

'Get back!' Gwydion said, gripping his arm. 'Once this overripe thing touches the earth it will begin spewing forth all the harm it contains!'

He danced about the flaming cart, staff in hand, calling down spells of ever greater power to combat the monstrous grub. A hundred paces away the mass of Lord Ordlea's army watched a cart burn. They saw a madman dancing about the flames and many laughed to see it. Few, if any, of these common soldiers had ever been to war before, doubtless some thought that a cart was burned before every battle, and many were still in good heart, not having seen blood spilled yet.

But Will knew better. He had seen the way war arrows skewered men, how edged weapons sliced through their flesh. And he had seen the effect a battlestone had on the minds of men who heard its whisperings. His own heart squeezed in his chest as the triumphant stone vented its glee. His head filled with the sounds of laughter and another, more terrifying sound. And his spirit quailed. He had heard that dread noise before, and his own voice ebbed away.

What a fool you were to imagine you had broken the Doomstone . . .

Then came the familiar sound of tearing air. He cowered in fear, for he knew it as the harbinger of bloody death. It filled the sky as a thousand arrows sped over his head, carrying murder to those beyond. A few score fell short, appearing suddenly in the ground around him, the nearest of them three paces away. It stood up in an instant like a strange white flower brought magically into being. When he looked up, he saw Lord Sarum's men stretching in an unbroken line across the wood, and many archers loosing volley after volley. He could make out their faces. He could hear the footsoldiers behind them coming forward.

For all that Lord Sarum had been touched by the battlestone's influence, he was a canny soldier. He had the advantage of higher ground, and he remained wary of the trap that awaited his outnumbered army two meadows away. Fearing he might be outflanked by a swift cavalry charge, he had planted his left wing against the boggy ground that ran down to the stream. Any horse ridden across it would sink up to its hocks in the mud. Any attack would stall. The earl had covered his right flank with a barricade made of a double line of victual wagons, and that was manned by billmen whose long weapons could unhorse any rider who came near.

Will knew the character of Lord Sarum from the weeks and months he had spent at Foderingham and Ludford. The earl was almost sixty now, one of the richest men in the Realm and as wily as any fox. He understood the art of war very well, yet here he was fighting for his life. He had been manoeuvred here by the queen's insistence, set upon by a newly raised rabble and brought to an ill-considered fight by the judgment-destroying powers of an ancient stone.

All this came in a flash to Will's mind as the air above tore with deadly sound. The arrows came so thick that Will heard their shafts clattering one against another in mid-flight. He crouched down, unable to do otherwise, for once experienced, the terror of being under an archers' volley never left a man.

But there was no protection to be had from an upflung arm. Screams began as the first deadly rain struck home against the advancing body of footsoldiers. Men fell down and screwed them-selves up on the ground in agony, but still the mass walked forward regardless. Then, a count of six later, the second volley struck and there were more screams. Another count of six and the same again. And on it went, with each volley taking a fresh crop of men until at last, the advance faltered and they were ordered back, leaving the field to the hundreds of dead and dying who had been struck from their ranks.

Will turned away, more compelled now by Gwydion's struggle. The burning cart sent its flames high above the wizard as his voice thundered out spells which he still hoped might restrict the stone's menace, but Will knew that without any chance to lay hands upon it all Gwydion's efforts were doomed. Amid the wreckage of the burning cart, the maggot seemed to rear up as if looking for the one whose dance tormented it so.

Amid the shouting and bleeding and dying Gwydion stepped out his magic powerfully and with courage, but perhaps he now drew too close to the stone. For a moment a blue glow haloed it, locking it tight, but then a mouth opened in the maggoty flesh that began to shriek out words that murdered the true tongue. Words of power, they were. Dire words that called down a renewal of pain and death upon the field.

The wizard reeled back, shielding himself from the twisted magic as it gushed forth. Now the mouth opened out like a broken jaw and spewed forth its black cloud. At first Gwydion's magic caught the cloud, confined it and controlled it, as if in an invisible net, so that it rose up into the air: a great swirling, whirling mass, angry and seeking escape surged out.

As if obeying some general signal, men and horses surged forward. Will stared at them disbelievingly. Had Lord Ordlea ordered a charge up the hill? If he had, he had surely written their death warrant. Hooves thundered the ground as the attack gathered, and a thousand horse were sent hurtling up the slope against the enemy. The first wave drove straight against the centre of Lord Sarum's line, and Will watched, thinking that the attack must now succeed. But then a thousand yew bows twanged and a hundred horses fell down or reared or turned aside, and the power of the charge was broken. Those who followed on behind were thrown into confusion, and there was chaos until they were able to fall back.

Then Lord Ordlea rode forth from his disordered cavalry with

drawn sword, rallying them to a second charge. His banner of
yellow and red flapped free and streamed out as he and his
personal knights gathered and threw themselves hard against the
enemy. But once more the charge failed, broken by the deadly
sting of the Sarum archers. Down went more horses and men.
When Lord Ordlea himself fell to an arrow, a foot attack was
ordered, this time by Lord Dudlea. Obedient soldiers advanced
across the meadows. They ran, yelling up the slope, but when
the first of their number sank under a storm of arrows the rest
threw down their helm-axes and made off like rabbits scampering
on the Downs.

Will knew that Gwydion could do nothing to stop the
monstrous slaughter. He had thought the wizard might put up a
show of fire into the sky, but all his skills had been consumed in
trying to contain the battlestone's malice. Will, though he had
studied much, had not the art himself to send thunderbolts
through the air to amaze the armies into quitting the field, and
he dared not interfere with Gwydion's attack upon the stone. He
crouched and flinched. On an impulse he drew out the red fish
from his pouch, muttering words of the true tongue over it, but
it was no good for giving courage as his green fish had been.
Instead, he felt only guilt – this stone had beaten them by stealth.
It had sneaked in through their defences, thrown them.

He shouted, railed angrily against the madness and the senseless bloodshed. Outrage seized him and he ran about, a lunatic
crying out against the storm. Many an arrow that had fallen short
he found stuck in the ground nearby. He began pulling them up
and snapping them across his knee, casting them down as if this
vain show would stop the killing. But then a stray horseman, a
man filled with fury or fear, or just wanting to kill, rode him
down and he was thrown to the earth.

When he raised himself up, it was only to his knees. He looked
on the battle with hopeless eyes now, seeing there was nothing
more to be done about it. Wars were never stopped by fools
shouting into the void, no matter what they said. A lack of

foresight and vigilance had been to blame – his own as much as Gwydion's. They had tarried and dithered and missed their chance.

But now the problem towered above him and the terror of it gripped his heart. He stood up, empty-handed, staring awestruck at the sky. A raucous humming filled all the air around him, but this time it was not the sound of arrows. The rising mass of malice that was being forced upward like smoke by the wizard's magical grip was revealed now as countless millions of carrion flies.

They were streaming from the stone in teeming numbers, as if the battlestone was the spout of some huge underground cave. The flies rushed out in a torrent, but still they were swept up and confined by Gwydion's magic. Those few that escaped the vortex swirled out over the field unable to do much harm, but as the stone continued to empty itself into the sky Gwydion's power to oppose it began to fail. Will watched how the wizard was overcome as the unstable column of darkness grew ever more gigantic. It began to twist then fall apart. Then the flies burst out and spilled across the sun and sky until the light of day was turned grey by their teeming numbers.

But below the vast tower of blackness the battle went on regardless. Another volley of arrows arched high and sped down through the darkness, doing murder among Lord Ordlea's men. Then two bodies of opposing footmen clashed, and the fighting became bloody and hand-to-hand. A thousand armed men crashed into one another, opposing colours crushed together as if by gigantic forces. The shafts of pole-arms and billhooks spilled this way and that, inclined at all angles as men were hacked and stabbed and forced to the ground to be trampled and die underfoot. At the fringes of the melee the fighting was most furious, for here men had the room to wield their weapons. Daggers and axes did the bloodiest murder. Horses reared as armoured captains slashed at their antagonists from the saddle. Footmen tried to unseat riders with their pole-arms, tangling their pikeheads among mail and plate, and when they succeeded, a dozen men fell on the hapless victims. They raked them with great hammer blows, or cut away their helmet straps then ripped out the strings of their necks so they were drowned in gushes of blood. Will saw arms and legs cut off, heads cloven in two; even though one blow came through the rim of a steel bonnet it was given with such force as to open the skull beneath. He saw men frozen by terror, men with no stomach for killing, men grey-faced and wide-eyed who had lost control of their actions and wanted to run. And there were other, rarer men, men who enjoyed the killing. But whatever kind of man came into the fight, and whatever his thoughts and feelings, still there remained a white-hot place at the centre that consumed all who approached it.

The struggle washed around Will, became a disorderly morass of shouting and screaming, with flurries of extreme anger showing in bursts of intense violence. It was horrible to see, and worse to smell, for when men's bodies are ripped open what spills across the grass is pungent and vile. He staggered through it untouched, and it seemed as if the killing would go on forever, but at last the sun was eclipsed as if by a giant hand, and to Will's eyes it seemed that night had come suddenly upon the valley. All the sky turned black and the noonday sun was blotted out, and he heard nothing now beyond the screams of dying men and the sourceless hiss and buzz that enfolded him. There was a great concussion upon his body and he dived down to find escape in the blood-sodden earth, but the flies found their way into his eyes and up his nose and into his mouth, choking him, making him spit and retch in increasing fear. All around, soldiers were waving their arms in frenzy, caught in a storm of stinging black snow. Footsoldiers threw their arms to the ground, horses ran madly, riders were blinded and thrown. The timeless torment went on, in agony, in insanity, beyond all endurance, while men danced openly with Death.

But Will had not died. He managed to scoop the flies from his mouth long enough to draw breath. He wiped them from his eyes sufficient to see the pyre that had been their cart. Flame sheathed the stone now, flaring and crackling as thousands of black motes blundered through its flame. It was a stone once more, shrunken and dying, its rage spent.

At last the darkness began to clear as the blow flies settled widely over the field. The swarm dropped on the fallen who sprawled and grovelled all around. It lay in drifts, covering everything in a thick, black blanket. Wounded horses whinnied in terror underneath those drifts, their legs kicking out. Wounded men were smothered in it, drowned, reaching up for air they could not find. When Will forced himself to rise he saw just how intimately he had been caught up among the slaughter. All around him men were crying out. The battle was over. The main butchery had lasted less than an hour, but the harm that had issued from the stone had slaked itself only by emptying life from the bodies of seven times three hundred men.

CHAPTER TWELVE

CAPTIVES

Across that hideous place, which forever after was known as Blow Heath, the flies settled then melted away until all visible sign of them was gone. Soon, as the wizard had said, they would vanish in like manner from human memory.

The conflict had been the work of half an afternoon, but it had been enough to change everything, and Will and Gwydion found themselves passing among an unexpectedly victorious army that had now begun a most brutal celebration.

'So it is, when the bloodlust comes upon men,' Gwydion said, his eyes searching the heaps of bodies that lay all around. The wizard looked very old and worn thin by his failure. 'I have seen this so many times before. Savage fools! Sarum's men knew they were the day's underdogs. They believed they were going to die. Yet look what thanks they now give for their lives! How easily men glory in the deaths of others who are so like themselves! Is there never to be a saving of humankind?'

Will sat in the trampled grass, dazed, sickened, filled with horror. The murderous rout had flowed past, leaving them unscathed. Whether that was by chance or by Gwydion's art or through some other reason, he did not know. He looked around at a scene that had been unimaginable just a few hours before.

Through the morning this place had been just another peaceful green meadow, one scattered with daisies and buttercups and dandelions. Now so many hundreds of men were heaped here like sides of meat – the disgusting dead. Many more were bleeding and destined soon to die, and horror hung over the place along with the shocking reek.

The embers of the cart smoked nearby, and in the midst of it all stood the burned-out battlestone. It had shrugged off all the bonds that Gwydion's magic had placed upon it. It had fulfilled its purpose. Now, it seemed to be laughing at them.

Will rose to his feet. Anger boiled up inside him and he sprang at the smoking stone. He gnashed his teeth and beat wildly at it with his fists until his knuckles bled and until the ashes flew around him and his rush of rage was sated. And then he began to weep. He put his arms around the warm shell of the stone and hugged it, and slowly sobbed the hurt out of himself.

And the stone understood. It forgave him, for each had, in their separate ways been emptied, and Will's heart beat in rhythm with the thimbleful of kindness that remained inside the stone now that the fountains of harm were spent.

At length Gwydion came to him and took him gently away. A spent battlestone was a thing of comfort, a stump that would confer mild boons upon the world. It was hard for Will to release it, and harder still to walk away, but he did so. There was now much needful work to be done and a deal of suffering to walk among.

In the next hour he witnessed the deaths of many men. He went from corpse heap to corpse heap, looking for those who might yet be saved, and no one tried to stop him, no matter how weakminded or savage was their own foul business among the dying. Soon a sweet stink hung over the field, and he was reminded of the smell of the bodies that had been laid out in rows after Verlamion, faces grey yet reposing in apparent sleep, many of them bright with splashes of blood, many others whose flesh had been torn in horrible ways. Yet some still fair of feature and seem-ingly untouched.

Will saw again the miasma that hovered over the heaps like a ghostly mist, as if the dead were preyed upon by spectres and the other boneless presences that were said to dwell in the lower airs. But as he watched, he saw that it was not so, that there was something sacred present, something lingering and reluctant to leave.

'Come, Willand!' the wizard's voice called to him. 'We must work with good despatch and do what we can.'

Will bent to his task. As a healer he knew how much greater was the kindness required to repair a brief moment's harm. Harm, it seemed, flowed too readily through the world, as freely as blown breath or the water in a mountain stream. Whereas kindness – kindness was an altogether slower quantity, thick and sluggish as honey.

Gwydion turned back the bands of men who went among the terrified wounded like wild beasts intent on doing cold murder and butchery. Will soon saw where comfort and healing might best be offered, but most of the wounds he found were grievous. 'I know what you're suffering. I know what it's like,' he told a youth whose arm had been struck off at the elbow. But the lad's lips were blue and his eyes shone bright with shock and held a contrary certainty as he counted Will's two good arms. Even so, he welcomed the incantations that lessened his pain and would in time help to heal the ragged flesh.

'How old are you?' Will asked before he moved on.

'Nineteen years, Master,' the lad said, still gripping Will's hand. 'I have been a shepherd since I was seven. But today I was a soldier. And from this day forward it seems I am to be a beggar.'

A brute of a man who waited nearby said, 'At least a crow pudding has not been made of you!' But then he bethought what he had said, seeing the word 'crow' was used by many to speak ill of wizards. He quickly muttered, 'Begging your pardon, Master. I didn't mean that to sound as it did.'

But Will did not care about insults. He saw the wounded lad offer a brave smile as the blood stopped and his flesh made a miraculous start on the long road to healing.

It was a long time before the leaders of the victorious army were able to draw their wilder men back to good order, such was the booty to be had from the routed foe. Horses and helms, swords and purses, lordly shoes and coats of heavy cloth – all were here aplenty, and more besides. There was still much to be got from men by murder. Such luxuries as a golden buckle or a knight's saddle were counted worth a year or two of work in a field, so looting was rife and the healing went on alongside a far grimmer business. Where Gwydion could not stop them, men went from friend to foe alike, saying loudly that injured dogs would never have been left in such misery. Many a throat was cut with a false excuse of mercy. Opportunists crept among the fallen, looking for whatever it pleased them to have.

Will heard it called out by Lord Sarum's heralds that a mere two hundred was the count of his dead, but that ten times that number at least had been slain among the opposing ranks. At that announcement a cheer was raised by the victors.

'What is to become of the bodies of the dead?' Will asked the wizard in a voice raw with outrage.

Gwydion said, 'They will be left here, fly-blown and rotting, until the local folk are driven here to bury them.'

'Driven?'

'By the Sightless Ones. They will see to it that these dead are heaped together in common graves. They will take this golden chance to rant about death and so terrify and catch hold of the minds of those village folk they fetch here to do the digging. And the people will dig and endure speeches, for those who would put out the people's eyes love to reproach them for their blindness!'

Will looked one more time across the heath with its thousands of dead. When the victorious army began to assemble again,

Gwydion stood up and thrust out his hands like a scarecrow. He called a cleansing spell over the battlefield, then sang out:

> *'Crow, caddow, pie,*
> *Rook, raven, fly!'*

A hundred birds flew up from the field at his words. But it could have been the beating of drums and the blast of trumpets and the thunder of hooves that sent them into the air, for the next moment Lord Sarum came bursting through the ranks on his great charger, standing stiff in his stirrups, his whole body shining in steel. His standard bearer and his chief captains galloped at his back. He raised his sword as he rode and whirled it again and again above his head. A wild shout went up as he paraded in triumph, back and forth before his army. His visor arched above his shining sallet-helm. Thousands of eyes were fixed upon the man. This, Will knew, was one of those moments a warrior lived for. What passed between lord and man was the pure, hard light that shone at the heart of a soldier's glory.

But Will turned away. His spirit rebelled against the cheering mass of men. He bent his mind instead to his healing. His arms were bloodied to the elbow, but at last he was pulled away by insistent men-at-arms who cried, 'Tell my lord's herald who you are!'

'A healer, that is all. Leave me be.'

'He is a wizard!'

Lord Sarum's herald looked on. 'Then are you not the same wizard who laid a blessing upon our victory? The one who brought us the wondrous stone?'

And when Will looked where they directed him he saw men surrounding the spent battlestone, touching it and delighting in it.

'I'm no wizard!' he told them angrily. 'And I'd not call this a victory!'

'Are you then our *enemy*?' they asked him, taken aback at his sternness.

'Who's your enemy? Look around you! A dozen times as many men have died here as were killed at Verlamion! What kind of victory do you call that?'

But they cried, 'Fetch the wizard! Bring him to the magic stone!' And they pulled Will away from his tender work.

Lord Sarum came now, to see for himself the miracle at which his men were marvelling, but Will stabbed a rude finger at him and accused him hotly. 'See, my lord? Look what happens when our work fails! For the want of a two-horse cart and a half dozen men to help us bear the stone smartly away, this terrible thing has been brought upon you!'

The lord's braver retainers threatened to throw him down for his insolence, wizard or no, but he shrugged them off and stood mutely by the stone, watching to see how easily men's hands reached out to touch it. It was shrivelled and crazed and it had gone dark now. Its surface was pitted and puckered, or perhaps it was just that its power to cast illusions as to its true shape and size had died.

Lord Sarum walked three times about the spent stump. 'So this is one of the magical stones against which the Crowmaster used to warn! Where is he?'

Gwydion stepped forward then, haggard and stumbling in his singed rags and looking to all who saw him like a mad and filthy beggarman, but his voice was thunderous. 'I warned Richard of Ebor! I asked him for help in finding these stones – *and I was denied!*'

Lord Sarum countered dismissively, 'Then ask again, Crowmaster, and this time permission may be granted to you, for it seems this stone at least has brought us victory!'

Hundreds goggled at the idea.

'Imbeciles! Does not one of you understand what has happened here this day?'

But they laughed at him, making light of his insolence. After all, he was a wizard, one driven half mad by a life dabbling in corrosive magic. The earl laughed. And his soldiers laughed, and

there was cheering all around, men glad in their deadly achieve-
ment, praising one another as if it had been their prowess that
had decided the fight. Their war chants rose now until they blotted
out the cries of the dying. Will pressed his bloodied hands over
his ears, but the tumult only grew. He was jostled away, and the
stone taken up and borne aloft by many hands and carried off.

'Where are they taking us?' he asked Gwydion as they were
borne away also.

'To Ludford!' the soldiers said, laughing. 'We must go from
here! Before the evil queen sends another army to punish us!'

CHAPTER FOURTEEN

THE KINDLY STUMP

They were brought along to the carts that were to carry the wounded at the tail of the baggage train.

'Get in,' the soldiers told him.

'Why?'

'You are to come with us.'

'By what right?' Will said, pulling away.

'Right? It is my Lord of Sarum's order.'

'We are not Earl Sarum's men. We choose to stay here!'

They were quickly surrounded by men who drew blades, and though Will raised his stick ready to resist, Gwydion waved him down with a tired gesture. 'We will go wherever the greatest need presently lies, and that is with those who are hurt.'

'But what about the next stone?' Will hissed. 'We must hunt it down.'

'Be easy now. First we must ponder on the true meaning of this stone's verse.'

Will did as he was told, for he saw no gain in resisting. He watched sullenly as the army formed up along the road. The line of men stretched ahead into the far distance, three thousand of them, marching forward, slowly at first and with many delays, but then faster and with many of them singing of a triumph which two hundred of their number had purchased through sacrifice.

The earl's carts were laden with all that an army must carry, and now much booty besides. Nor did they leave the spent stone behind. As they creaked along there was an escort of men packed close about the cart in which it rode. The soldiers walked bareheaded. Some wore their helms slung on their backs. Some had bound up small wounds. Their faces and jackets were stained from the fighting, but the eyes of those who reached through the bars of the cart to touch the stump were full of wonder. They were already calling it the 'Blow Stone'.

Will tried to stop them, but Gwydion caught his hand.

'Let them do it,' he said hollowly. 'For there is no harm left in it, and if it pleases them why should you prevent it?'

'There was a time,' Will said, 'when you would have called this a superstitious abuse of magic and you would have tried to stop it yourself.'

'Just let them be, I told you!'

'I will! And I'll let you be too!'

His anger having fizzed up, he turned away and fell silent. Shorn of their hair, the soldiers looked like so many dirty-faced children. Some were already drunk, others carried jugs to sup from. But Will knew he could find no peace in dulling his thoughts, and so he worked on, healing where he could, and so did the wizard, though he seemed to Will like a man disgraced in his own esteem, and working only to make amends for his own shortcomings.

As night stole over the land, Lord Sarum's scouts steered the army to wood-sheltered high ground which they had chosen above the valley of the River Mease. The night was cool and dry and the weald around very dark and gloomy, without even a single star showing in the sky. Fires were lit and tents put up, and there was food aplenty – tons of fine victuals had been found among the enemy's baggage.

'Don't blame yourself,' Will said, sitting down.

But it was as if the wizard saw deeper troubles among the dancing shadows of the fires. Will sought to comfort him again, but Gwydion would not let himself be comforted. Not even the kindly emanations of the spent stone could give him back his usual countenance, and it seemed to Will that this time he had stretched himself beyond the limit of his powers.

'I am at a loss,' Gwydion admitted at last in a distant voice. 'The binding spells were the same ones I called down upon the Dragon Stone. And on the Plaguestone. Yet this time they did not hold.'

'It's no fault of yours that the stone grew hot. Nor that we were forced to drive into muddy ground.'

Gwydion's hard, grey eyes seemed like stones in the firelight. 'Why do you talk of blame and fault, Willand? I want only to decide what must be done.'

Will withdrew then, and left the wizard to his cold thoughts. He wrapped himself in a blanket and quickly drifted into sleep. But no sooner had he closed his eyes than he began to dream. And what he saw was a dream within a dream, for it began with the feeling that he was waking up. In the inner dream he knew that something had been hidden from him, but he did not know what it was. There had been a haunting beauty all around him and a feeling of joy of such richness that he had wanted to shout out. But then he had remembered his waking life, and that had seemed in comparison very mean and disappointing. In the inner dream the air had been warm and soft and summery, there had been sun on his skin, the birds had been singing in the trees and the colour of the grass had been greener than any green he had ever known in waking. In the inner dream he felt glad and at peace with himself and he knew it was the feeling of home, of the secret, happy world of the Vale. Yet he knew he must wake from it. But how could he waken, for was he not now already awake?

When he really did open his eyes it was to draughts and shadows. His feet were stone cold and the blanket rough and damp under his chin. He got up to walk among the dying fires and came at last to the edge of the camp. Here dark woods loomed thick with undergrowth. Uppermost in his mind now was the decision he had made to send Willow home. He wondered how she had fared and what Morann must have had to say to persuade her to stay in the Vale. Despite all that had happened, that at least had been for the best – Willow had not had to brave the dangers of battle, nor witness its horrors. And there was a more selfish reason to be glad that she was back in the Vale – she had not seen their dreadful failure with the battlestone.

His heart gave a squeeze – how he missed her.

He peered into the black stillness and recognized that it echoed the void inside him. When he saw how his thoughts were tending, he stood up to them. *Wallowing.* That was what Gwydion called it when a person surrendered to his own weaknesses and then helped them drag him lower into despondency.

Will turned his thoughts deliberately towards the sorcerer. He had half expected Maskull to appear as the battle raged, but had he even been aware of the battle? More likely he had been watching it from some remove. This time there had been no fountains of fire, no plume of violet flame. But had there been more subtle magic at work? A sorcery that made things turn out the way Maskull wanted? One, maybe, that worked without Gwydion's knowledge? The stone had certainly achieved what seemed to be far too easy a victory against them.

He shook off the last thoughts as unanswerable and dangerous. Unanswerable, because only Maskull knew the truth of it, and dangerous because it helped his despondency to deepen.

'I know you're out there, Maskull,' he whispered fiercely. 'Show yourself!'

But no one came, and not so much as a badger or a fox stirred in the inky night.

He tried to look deeper into the blackness, still weary in body and spirit, but wherever his mind led him he ran up against a single name – Arthur.

If Gwydion's right about me, he thought, then I'm the third and final incarnation of Arthur, and that's that. But what does it mean? How can I be linked with a hero who lived and died a thousand years ago? Are we the same person? And how can we be that?

But there was something else that he did not want to acknowledge, for it was certainly true that he knew more about Arthur than ever he had learned.

'Well, whoever I am,' he told the night, 'I still feel as if I'm me. How could I be Arthur, when Arthur was a king of the Realm?'

He tried to find his way back to his sleeping place, but it was not as easy as he had hoped. Many fires still burned, there was the hum of conversation in the camp. Round and about there was singing and some raucous laughter, but most of the drunkards had obliterated their memories of the worst day of their lives by pitching themselves headlong into sleep.

He wandered towards the centre of the camp and found the painted tents of Lord Sarum and his captains. Their standards hung limply in the windless air. Cressets burned. Sober night guards in kettle hats leaned on their poleaxes, enduring their wearisome duty. Will did not want to draw a challenge so he kept away from the earl's enclosure. Even so, he saw nearby the cart that carried the spent stone, and beside it a wagon on which was mounted a cage. The covers were half drawn back, and sitting inside the cage, looking as forlorn as any man could, was the figure of Lord Dudlea.

He was clad only in a long shirt and seemed to have suffered some hurt to his shoulder and arm. Will wondered what would become of him, but even as he watched the figure stirred, reached through the cage and placed the tips of his outstretched fingers on the nearby stump. Will did not yet know what powers the stone might now possess, nor what boon it might confer, but the gesture touched him, and as he crept away he added his own wishes to those of the captured lord that mercy might yet be alive at Ludford.

★   ★   ★

A long morning's march through hilly lands brought the earl's army first to the crossing of the Great River of the West, then shortly after, turning south-west at the village of Mart Woollack, they went by a good, hard road along Luddsdale, and eventually came upon the way to Ludford.

Will watched over himself and worried much upon his mood that morning. A day's healing and a night plagued with horrors had left him drained. He walked or rode along in the carts that carried the wounded as the condition of the men allowed. The churlish soldiers were grateful for his attentions, but the captains whose business it was to escort Lord Dudlea would not let him approach the nobleman.

'But he's wounded,' Will said. 'I should tend him.'

The guards shook their heads. 'His wound is slight. We were told that no one is to speak with him for he is to be questioned at Ludford.'

'About what?'

'He has made a bargain for his life.'

'In what way has he bargained?'

The biggest of the guards brushed him aside. 'Begone! It is not the part of captives to question their keepers.'

'I am no one's captive!' Will said hotly.

'At least let us inspect our stone,' Gwydion said, hushing him.

'No man may see it,' the guards replied uncomfortably. 'The order was given last night by my Lord Sarum himself.'

And that was an end to it.

As soon as they were out of earshot Will asked, 'What shall we do?'

'Nothing.'

'Nothing? Let's walk away. They can't stop us.' He was still bristling.

'Be easy. I would rather we went to Ludford.'

By mid-afternoon Will's powers of healing were running low again and his spirit had become faintingly weak.

Gwydion, grave of face, still laid tireless hands on the wounded.

Will quoted the rede at him. '"By his magic, so shall ye know him." Aren't you drawing Maskull to us by doing so much healing?'

'What would you have me do? Fail these men again?'

'Again . . .' That word said much. 'You told me off for doing the same at Eiton. For healing.'

'Healing was not your crime, but the fame that you spread about by doing it. A little healing will not in itself draw Maskull to me. Healing is not great magic and so much of it is done every day by thousands of Sisters up and down the Realm that the chatter of it drowns in the ether.'

Will asked permission of the guards, on his honour, to go and walk alone, and when word was granted to him he drew apart from the column a little way. The soldiers still watched him but gave him respect and a kind of liberty, for they knew that wizards were by repute strange creatures who needed their own company at times.

And it was true that a deep part of Will craved refreshment. As he walked he listened to what the trees told him. The leaves of the oaks were in the last of their three seasons now, being darkest green and heavily galled. Soon they would brown and fall. The life the trees had put forth was already drawing back into their trunks as they prepared for winter. The dry, gentle rustling of their leaves told much about the powers that were moving below in the dark streams of the earth.

The nearer they came to Ludford the closer the moon crept towards the sun, and the stronger the earth powers waxed in the lorc. He could sense a lign running deep within the hills to his left. It crossed the Great River of the West, Severine's Flood, at almost the same place as the army crossed. Deep in a wooded gorge where a fine stone bridge stood, he had seen an unmistakable glimmering in the waters. Now that same invisible green lane seemed to shadow them ever closer as they walked on towards Ludford.

The sensation was unlike anything he had felt before. It rose and fell as he drifted along so that, had the feeling been music, it would have grown louder and softer every few paces. He could not be sure, but it seemed as if there might be at least one other lign running through the land nearby, one somewhere out beyond Appledale, beyond the cliffs of Woollack Ridge. It seemed that the two ligns were coming closer together. If so, at some point, they must cross. And in that place another battlestone would be found.

It was an uneasy thought. He remembered Ludford as a strongly walled town with a castle on the west side. The fortress stood above the place where the waters of two rivers joined. He shaded his eyes against the setting sun. I was overcome with confusion when last I came to Ludford, he thought. What will happen to me this time? Am I to be driven completely mad? Is that to be the nature of my sacrifice?

The town walls rose up, and they came to the Feather Gate. To Will's surprise, they found the tall, iron-bound doors flung wide and all the maze of streets and alleys lit up.

This was a town that had been forewarned of great news. The earl's heralds had ridden ahead. All Ludford's cressets were burning bright and all its people had been turned out to welcome the victorious army of their lord's great ally. Everything was in uproar as Will and Gwydion entered the goose market. The six town waits strolled ahead playing their instruments. Woven in with the cheering Will heard the festive song of tabor and mandolin. The bullring was filled with more folk, the torchlight red on their faces. The Duke of Ebor's trumpets sounded and Earl Sarum's drums beat their warlike reply. Will watched as the troops, marching five abreast, proudly carried their poleaxes in parade. Children took up the beat, skipping alongside. Bells pealed and girls cast baskets of pale rose petals by the handful over the soldiers from balconies and windows.

Will looked away from the wild cheering as they passed under the jutting upper floors of neat lime-washed merchants' houses. Here were many prosperous dwellings that sported carved timbers and faced the streets leading into the market square. Will said, 'Anyone would think we'd just saved them from a great disaster.'

'My guess is that Richard has told them a far-fetched tale. What use is truth to a lord when a war is in the offing?'

Now they rounded a corner and Will's eyes were drawn to the spire of the Sightless Ones with its great iron vane and mysterious letters – A, A, E, F – and the device of the white heart, ghostly in the night. He caught again the curiously scented foulness which he had smelled at Verlamion. And he heard the voices of forlorn men hidden behind their walls of stone and tall windows of black glass. They were adding their discord to the din. As Will passed through the cloth market he noted the morbid stone monument that stood outside the chapter house. As always, it was decked with red-shaded candles, and Will's flesh crept to see the hooded Fellow who watched blindly from his niche, standing motionless in the shadows beyond.

In the excitement of their entry into Ludford, Will had forgotten about the chapter house, and the freedom Duke Richard gave to the Sightless Ones to come and go, not only in the town, but also inside his castle. Will wondered if the Fellows had yet heard the rumours about the 'wondrous stone', and the wizards young and old who had helped bring the earl victory.

Ahead, two familiar white castle towers soared, their stone rippling in the glare of the torches. Will felt his heart beating faster. His skin tingled, and an unusual sensation gripped him. He pushed it away, denying it as no more than his own tiredness and the enthusiasm of their reception. Outside the castle, the procession split into two parts. The bulk of the army peeled away, marching out of the town again by the Durnhelm Gate. They were going down towards the river where a part-prepared camp waited. But the earl and his party continued on up, into the open mouth of the castle.

Will and Gwydion went with them, past the four lions that he remembered. When last he had seen them they had lain slothfully in their cages; now they were roused, pacing back and forth and making growling sounds deep enough to send a tremor through a man's ribs. The animals had been made anxious, and not just because of the activity. He felt the need to open his mind and try to make some sense of the tangle of earth streams that ran under the cobbles of the market square, but he did not dare to do it.

He said suddenly, 'What are we going to do about the Blow Stone? Have you been able to catch sight of it?'

The wizard smiled. 'I have. And a most remarkable change has come over it.'

'What change?'

'It has continued to shrink. It is now no more than half its original size. And it has taken upon its surface a pattern. It appears, so to say, *carved*.'

'You mean with the verse?' Will said, alarmed. 'In plain words?'

'Nothing so straightforward as that. In the words of the archer who told me, "It is impressed by the very mark of the Lord of Ebor's signet."'

Will's eyes opened wide, and he marvelled. 'Do you mean the device on Duke Richard's ring? The one he wears all the time on the little finger of his left hand?'

'You may have seen its impress on the letters he sends. It shows a four-leaf clover, and below three pike flowers on long stems.'

Will felt an eerie chill pass through him. 'What do you think that means?'

'I only repeat what I have been told. As to its meaning, that I cannot yet speak about. Ah, but look who is here to greet us!'

Will followed Gwydion's staff and saw a shambling figure with a mass of unruly hair and a beard all striped like a badger.

'Wortmaster Gort!'

Gwydion seized his friend by his shoulders and hugged him. Words of the true tongue passed between them and Gort offered a respectful gesture, not of the kind offered by a servant to a lord, but rather like one that might pass between brothers.

'Master Gwydion! Tsk! tsk!' Gort said, beaming and laughing.

'Well met! And look who walks by your side! Willand! Hey-ho, my dear friend! Welcome! Welcome to poor old Ludford again!'

What little could be seen of Gort's face among his heap of unkempt hair was red cheeks and smiles. He was the Duke of Ebor's herbalist and healer and gardener and much more besides. He had not changed a whit since Will had last clapped eyes on him. He still wore his robe of oaken green and the same shapeless grey hat was perched on the top of his head. Will moved forward to embrace him. 'It's good to see you, Wortmaster!'

'Not scared of castle gateways any more, I see!' he said suddenly, tugging on Will's arm.

Will only realized now that he was standing under Ludford Castle's great suspended portcullis. He looked up and a stab of fear passed through his heart. The last time he had been at Ludford he had been unable to shake off the vision of himself being impaled by the great black spikes that hung so precariously. There was a yell and the hairs on his neck stood up stiff as bristles.

'Hoy! Look out there!'

As he stepped aside a large ox-cart rumbled through the gate. But the beasts that hauled it were struggling, hooves slipping and sliding on the muddied granite of the threshold. The panicked driver shouted for Will to get out of the way, then something snapped on the cart and it lurched sideways.

Will flattened himself against the stone of the guardhouse wall just as the cart tipped. One of the great iron-shod wheels leaned towards him and threatened to give. He pressed his nose flat to the wall and sank down as the rim gouged a crescent-shaped groove in the guardhouse arch beside his head.

'Get out of the road!' the red-faced driver shouted. 'You want to get yourself killed?'

Bare inches further and the wheel would have caught his head and burst it against the stone like a ripe berry.

'Are you hurt?' Gwydion asked, lifting him up.

'It missed me.' Will blinked at the cart, unsure if it was the one that carried the spent Blow Stone. He wondered suddenly if the accident, or perhaps his escape from injury, had been the stone's doing.

'My flapping mouth! Speaking too soon!' Gort fussed and brushed Will down with his hand, tearing a cloak that was already burned into holes. 'Oh, dear!'

'Never mind!' Gwydion thrust out a warning finger. 'Keep your eyes and ears open, Willand. And all your wits about you! Remember where you are come to.'

He nodded tightly, cold inside. The vision of the portcullis had been more than just an idle fancy. It was a long-standing fear connected with the prophecy that said 'one would be made two'. Will had often thought that it must mean that one day he would be cut in two. And even Gwydion had said that it was likely to be a premonition that foretold his death. He looked back at the deadly portal and reproved himself for having put it out of his mind. At the same time he acknowledged that his joy at seeing Gort again might just have come at a most crucial moment.

Once they had moved away from the gatehouse, the cold feelings went away. He hugged the Wortmaster once more. 'Oh, Gort, it's very good to see you again!'

'And you, my lad! But look at you, you're a lad no longer!'

'Married now, and with a fine daughter.'

'You don't say!'

'I do say. And proudly too. Bethe, we named her.'

'Good choice! Oh, for a certainty!'

'She's halfway through her second year and already looking as beautiful as her mother.'

'Ah, young Willow! Now there's a willing spirit and as handsome a girl as ever I saw. Where is she?' He craned his neck, looking back past the lines of the earl's baggage carts.

'She isn't with us,' Will said, his spirits guttering. 'Gort, didn't you hear about the battle?'

'Ah. That. A little bird told me. And after that Earl Sarum's men came here about noon today, all with the same news. Come along and you can tell me what I've missed. Are you hungry?'

'Are we hungry?' Will repeated, looking at Gwydion.

The wizard inclined his head. 'As weevils.'

'But who is this?' Gort asked, pointing at the cage that carried Lord Dudlea as it swayed and creaked in through the gate.

'That is John Sefton, called Lord Dudlea,' Gwydion said. 'He was caught upon the Heath commanding the enemy after Lord Ordlea was slain.'

'Oh, I would not wish to be in his shoes!' Gort said.

'He has none,' said Will bleakly. 'All but his shirt has been stolen. What do you think they'll do with him?

'It's no supper and a hard bed tonight, I'll be bound,' Gort said. But Will knew the Wortmaster's levity covered a serious possibility.

'Will they execute him?'

Gwydion steered Will away. 'Duke Richard would not slay a fellow noble in cold blood, for that would set a dangerous precedent.'

'But will they not torture him to learn what he knows?'

'Unnecessary. The nobles of this Realm are not such fools that they would not willingly shout out a hundred secrets at the sight of a hot iron. The problem is not too few words, but too many. Already, in his solitary misery, Lord Dudlea has been squirming like a maggot. He will speak eloquently enough in order to gain his release.'

'What has he said so far?' Will asked.

'He has spoken with Earl Sarum about a certain secret weapon that the queen now possesses.'

Will's eyes widened. 'Secret weapon?'

'So he calls it.'

'He's just trying to save his neck!'

'Maybe,' Gwydion said. 'Though there is a safe haven which I shall show Friend Dudlea in time should negotiations fail.'

'What safe haven?'

'I have learned there is a sorrow underlying Lord Sarum's triumph. A soldier told me that while the battle was being fought upon Blow Heath a second army raised by the queen lay not three leagues distant. It seems that two of Sarum's sons, Thomas and John, were captured while pursuing a band of the enemy in the rout. They have been borne off to await the queen's pleasure at the city of Caster in the north. Dudlea does not yet know this, nor will he learn it from me until he has coughed up enough morsels to satisfy his captors. Yet he will eventually have Sarum's voice to plead for his release even if things should go badly for him with Friend Richard.'

Will smiled, seeing how skilfully the wizard planned to manage things, but then Gort drew them both aside and steered them through the commotion of the outer ward, before showing them across the inner moat. They went by the inner gatehouse and threaded their way among the cluster of buildings that crowded the inner ward. Lodgings had long been prepared for them. Servants met them and took their burned and ragged cloaks away to have their scorches and holes patched.

When they were settled in Gort's parlour bread and stew were brought, and afterwards a pot of Gort's medlar cheese appeared and a platter of sweetcakes to spread it on.

'Hunger is surely the best relish!' Will told him, munching with a full mouth.

'"An empty belly maketh even hard beans taste sweet!" as the rede tells it,' Gort agreed.

The Wortmaster's rooms were intricately decorated, the walls pained with vines and meadow plants of many kinds. It was work with great depths to be discovered in it, Will decided, work painstakingly done by a man who knew about his materials and the effects that a lifetime of honest practice could achieve. But there was magic there also. In daytime, walls and ceiling showed blue sky and clouds, while at night there were stars in a black sky. And the whimsical figures that peeped from the twists and turns of the vines gambolled and grinned. In the firelight they danced and made rude faces at one another, and one put his tongue out at Will and winked at him.

Gort sang a tuneless verse as his nose savoured the odd, musty aroma of the medlar cheese:

> *'Just as the pedlar,*
> *Who taketh the stripe,*
> *The medlar turns rotten,*
> *Before he turns ripe!'*

'And do you have an equally bad verse about the quince?' Gwydion asked. He turned to Will: 'Gort makes the best jelly of quince that I have ever tasted, but his poetry has always been woeful.'

'Well, I like it!' Will said, springing to the Wortmaster's defence.

Gort swept off his hat and bowed low at the compliment. 'Ha ha! Well said, my friend!'

Gwydion grunted. 'Alas! Our young friend has little discrimination when it comes to the poesy!'

'I know what I like, Gwydion! And that's good enough.'

Gort waved his hands. 'Well, I have plenty of silly songs, but no quince jelly. Sorry to disappoint the Phantarch, but all my sealed jars remain at Foderingham.'

They made do with a bowl of hazelnuts and a jug of cider, sitting comfortably at Gort's untidy elmwood table. Then they moved closer round the fireplace. The mood changed as Gwydion let Will tell their host what had taken place upon Blow Heath.

'Oh, that's not good,' Gort said, frowning back at them when Will had done. 'No, no, not good at all. Oh, my. What does it all mean?'

'It means there's danger coming this way.'

'Oh . . . danger! That's not nice.'

'And more fighting if we don't do something.'

'Armies trampling down the land . . . oh, my!'

Gwydion raised an eyebrow significantly. 'You see, Wortmaster,

Willand here says there is a battlestone buried here at Ludford.'

'A battlestone? Here? Oh. Are you sure?'

Will took a deep breath. 'I've always known it. Don't you remember the last time I was here? It nearly drove my wits clear out of my skull. Back then, I didn't know what I was up against. The feelings were so strong I began to think that Duke Richard had fetched the Dragon Stone here out of some kind of lordly mischief. I wanted to kill him, and then to die myself. I was in a mess, until Gwydion came and flushed the foolishness out of me.'

Gwydion and Gort exchanged weighty glances.

'So now you'll scry this battlestone out pretty quick, hey?' Gort asked.

Will scratched his unshaved chin. 'I . . . hope to.'

'You *hope* to?' Gwydion said with some surprise.

'I mean, I hope I can pick up the true patterns again. If I can, then I might be able to find the stone.'

Gwydion seized on his faintness like a talon. 'Doubt is not your friend, Willand. Do you not understand that you are the best scrier ever to have walked the earth? No other man can do it. I cannot. Gort cannot. You have found three battlestones since we left the Plough, and that was not so many days ago.'

Will bit back the remark that came too readily to his lips – that he may have found three battlestones, but they had not yet dealt with any of them. Still, he felt warm and full and grateful to be in buoyant company again, and so he said, 'If I sound doubtful it's only because scrying depends on so many things – you know it yourself, Gwydion: the season, the shape of the moon, the lie of the land – and this is an odd place. All the stone buildings that stand around here complicate matters. They seem to affect not only the earth streams themselves, but also my ability to feel them out. If those old Slaver roads act like looking-glasses when it comes to the flows in the lorc, then Ludford's no different. There's something buried here. Something big.'

Will recited the Blow Stone's mysterious verse.

'Beside Lugh's ford and the risen tower,
By his word alone, a false king
Shall drive his enemy the waters over,
And the Lord of the West shall come home.'

Gwydion gave the cross-reading:

'Lord Lugh alone shall have the triumph,
At the western river crossing, word of an enemy
Comes falsely by the raised water,
While, at home, the king watches over his tower.'

'What do you think of that, Wortmaster?' Will asked.

Gort shook his head, and at length he sighed like a man tired of thinking, and said, 'Well . . . there's an awkward piece of riddle-me-re to end a supper party, and no mistake!'

CHAPTER FIFTEEN

A THIEF AT LUDFORD

The following morning Will rose early and went out with Gwydion to search for the Ludford battlestone. He had slept badly again, plagued by visions of doom and fed upon by the horrors that haunt a man's thoughts between the second and fifth chimes after midnight. But whether his night sweats were prompted by the battle or by the nearby battlestone he could not say.

A great mass of men was encamped outside the walls. The duke's army was already mustered at Ludford, and their number had swelled to eight or nine thousand overnight. Since dawn, men had been ranging across the land, hunting out and bringing in food, or spending their labours on the felling of trees and digging of ditches and earthworks to defend the poorly protected eastern approaches. All the town gates except one had been barred and propped with heavy timbers. Inside the walls there was a mob of townsfolk and soldiers milling at the far end of the market square. Will saw several black-hooded figures among them – red hands from the town's chapter house. They were standing around the cage in which Lord Dudlea had been brought to Ludford. At first Will imagined the nobleman had been executed and his corpse exposed for the jeering pleasure of the crowd, but the mood was not one of prurience or ridicule, but rather one of wonder.

Gwydion raised his staff and pushed his way to the fore, and Will went after him, noting that the Sightless Ones who had been goading the crowd were hastily withdrawing. When Will reached the cage he saw that it held not Lord Dudlea but the Blow Stone, and several folk were down on their knees before it.

'*What are you doing?*' Gwydion demanded of those trying to reach through the bars.

' 'Tis a magic touchstone!' they cried. 'It gives *powers* to all those who lay hands upon it!'

'Stand back!'

A bright-eyed young soldier raised fervent hands. 'It bestows qualities! It makes men proof against wounds. It will give us victory in war!'

'Have you touched it?' Gwydion demanded.

'Aye, Master!'

The wizard struck the man hard across the face and sent him reeling.

'Agggh! What's that for?' the man said, holding the side of his head.

'Such invulnerability as this you may have any day, my friend!' Gwydion's voice was enormous and wrathful. 'Who ordered the stone put here?'

They cowered. ''Twas the duke himself!'

'Soldiers of Earl Sarum! Go back to your camp! And you, good townspeople – repair to your homes as fast as you may! Go now! This stone must not be violated thus!'

The crowd groaned, angry and disappointed.

Gwydion's authority hardened. 'Go, I tell you! For you do not know the dangers you court here!'

'The stone heals the sick! We have heard it plain!' a brave voice called back.

'It makes the faithless husband confess his deeds!' a woman at the back shouted.

'And it will crush our enemies!'

'It will do none of those things,' Gwydion told them. 'Do as I bid now, or I will compel you!'

A one-eyed old man glared up at him and spat. 'It is said to protect against *wizards*!'

Gwydion raised his staff, unwilling now to be gainsaid. 'I have warned you! Leave this place! Get about your business, all of you! There is nothing to aid you here!'

Some recognized the power vested in the oaken staff that was raised on high above them. They made signs of respect and began to turn just as sheep obey the shepherd. But others stood stubbornly for a moment, and only when the greater number had melted away did they lose their courage.

At last Gwydion called Will along and they too left.

'What about the stone?' he asked. 'You can't just leave it there. They'll be back like mice as soon as blink.'

'What can I do? It is there at the duke's order.' He looked over his shoulder to where a group of beggars had already begun to steal back towards the cage. 'We must part. While you scry, I will go to Richard and try to persuade him to take the stone away.'

While Gwydion went in search of the duke, Will did as he was told. But he wondered at Gwydion's actions, thinking darkly that things had turned out badly again. If Gwydion had done as I warned and nipped this in the bud when we were back on the road, he thought, then the false fame of the stump would not have been blown up so large.

He took himself out beyond the barricaded gates of Ludford town, and walked the whole sward back and forth. It was his aim to try to feel some hint of the place where the next stone might lie. But there was now such a maze of earthworks in the land outside the town walls that he found it impossible to form any picture in his mind or even to know with any certainty where the lign must run.

After a while Gort joined him. By now it had become clear

that Will would be able to do no useful scrying today, so they went together to the Wortmaster's leech garden, where many different medicine plants grew.

'Herb and stone and wholesome word! These things are richest in healing powers,' Gort said. 'But the greatest is the herb! And as among men, so among herbs: some are common, others most rare, and some even precious. Let me show you my little treasures, eh?'

He pointed out a plain plant with dark, prickly leaves, pulled it up and knocked the soil from its gnarled root. 'In warmer climes this bears a yellow bloom,' he said. 'But here it grows unregarded, though it is powerful against enchantments. In the Marches they call it "haemony".' He rubbed the leaf of another wort that had first sprouted up where innocent blood had been shed. Yet another, he said, had been brought from over the sea by birds. And yet another had a silver flower that only appeared once every thousand years.

'Many a healing herb grows out of the grave of a good man,' he said ruefully. 'There are rosemaries and lavenders and whortleberries in this garden which I have gathered from the barrows of a hundred of the great kings.'

'And why is that pear tree's trunk painted with whitewash?' Will asked. 'And why is it growing behind an iron fence, where no one can gather its fruit?'

'Oh, beware that tree!' Gort said in a loud voice. 'For the plucking of that fruit will turn a man into a dove!' Then he whispered, 'Taproots and tubers! We don't want creepy-crafties climbing up our best pear trees, do we, eh?'

As two of Gort's undergardeners smiled up at their master, Will realized that his own fingers had gone unbidden to his pouch and had taken out the red fish. He muttered, 'It's a shame there's no herb here to heighten my senses when it comes to finding stones.'

'Alas! That is indeed a shame. But there has never been a herb with that power. Your talent is one of a kind, and hardly to be tampered with.' Gort peered at him closely. 'But . . . are you feeling quite well in yourself?'

'Quite well.'

'Are you sure?'

'Why do you ask?' He did not know why, but be resented the question.

'Oh, well, if I can't help . . .'

'I'm healthy enough. A little light-headed maybe, now you come to mention it, but there's nothing you can do to help that. And I think in any case I'd like to be on my own for a while.'

Will wished Gort good day, then went out into the inner-most ward and from there up onto the walls. He took the air deeply, looking down across the land from a corner of the great square tower of the keep. The various pitched roofs of the castle showed maze-like patterns in green and purple slate. Ravens circled the tower top, cawing warily at the duke's blue and white standard as it snaked out in the breeze. The banner showed the falcon and fetterlock, the golden bird straining for freedom. Beside the duke's standard was a flag bearing the white lion of Morte, and now flying alongside that was the Earl Sarum's banner of red and black upon which stood a fearsome golden griffin.

To the south-west was the dark Forest of Morte, brooding upon its hillside. It was ablaze now with autumn colours. Away to the east was Cullee Hill and on its summit the rocky crag they called the Giant's Chair.

Up here under a milky sky the morning breeze was cold. Will was without his cloak, and he felt all the colder leaning against stone and listening to the hungry ravens' croaking cry. He saw the guards, blear-eyed, silent, dishevelled, their blood still fired by last night's red wine and mutton marrow. But Will was feeling the world around him with a strange crispness. He took a deep draught of cold air, and then a familiar voice behind him said, 'Now then, Master Willand, how goes it?'

His hand clasped guiltily around the red fish, hiding it from view. When he turned, he saw a face that was known to him. 'Why . . . Jackhald . . .'

'Hey-ho, Willand. It's been a long time, has it not?'

Will forced a smile and they clasped hands. Jackhald had been one of the duke's castle guards at Foderingham. Since the battle of Verlamion, he had been raised to the rank of sergeant of the guard. He had noticed Will's interest in Cullee Hill, and said, 'On a clear day half of the Middle Shires can be watched from that place.'

Will looked in vain for a wisp of smoke rising from the beacon. 'And does the duke keep watchers up there?'

Jackhald grinned. 'Aye. Ludford's in Marcher land, which means it's close to the borders of Cambray. Cambray, with its hard mountains and blind valleys – it was ever a dangerous place to enter uninvited. Its rule is still disputed by the hardy princes of the west. They are often in a state of war.'

'That's no doubt the official reason why the duke has men sitting up on top of the Giant's Chair,' Will said quietly. 'But I expect the real reason is to keep a watch out for the approach of Queen Mag's allies, is it not?'

Jackhald folded his arms. 'They say there's a second great army out there as big as the one Lord Sarum beat off. They say it's coming here. Is that not true?'

'I've heard nothing.' It came into Will's mind to mention Earl Sarum's captured sons. Instead he asked, 'What's happened to Lord Dudlea? I saw his cage in the market place but there was a block of stone in it instead. Has he escaped?'

'No, his lordship is safe under lock and key.' Jackhald glanced sidelong at him. 'The two younger sons of Earl Sarum have been taken.'

He feigned surprise. 'Earl Sarum's sons? You don't say.'

'No doubt Lord Warrewyk will be angered to hear of his brothers' fate. When he arrives . . .'

Will looked up suddenly. 'Lord Warrewyk is coming here? From Callas?'

'He's already set sail across the Narrow Seas. He'll be here soon enough. And in great strength as likely as not.' Jackhald gave an encouraged laugh. 'With his lordship's army here, Ludford will be able to withstand any power the queen may send against us.'

Will said nothing, feeling no urge to share what he knew with the duke's man. He pointed down towards the inner ward, where a tall young man with trimmed blond hair stood, clothed in lordly style. He was surrounded by half a dozen men.

'Isn't that Edward down there?' He put fingers to his lips and made as if to whistle, but Jackhald pulled his hand away to stop him.

'Now, don't you be showing no rude manners here, Will. And don't you be calling a plain name on an earl in general hearing.'

Sudden anger snapped his patience and he shook Jackhald's arm away. 'And don't you lay hands upon me without leave!'

Jackhald looked back, surprised at Will's haughtiness. 'I only meant to say that the Earl of the Marches has his dignity to think of. If you would speak with him you must go formally to make a petition in writing and beg an audience of him.'

'Beg an audience? With Edward? We grew up together!'

'I know that. But don't forget who is the master here now.'

Will said no more. Ludford Castle was indeed Edward's by title, since he was his father's heir and therefore Earl of the Marches. Will recalled the Edward of old, the many lessons they had endured together and the day they had fought one another to a standstill in their tutor's room at Foderingham. That had made them firm friends, yet later, here at Ludford, Will had conceived a jealousy for the duke's heir that had been hard to set aside. He had clearly seen that Edward was angling to take Willow away from him. And the last time they had met had been at Verlamion, where Will had played the peacemaker while Edward had been anxious to blood himself as a warrior. It was then that their paths had parted, as he had always known they must. Parted forever.

Down below, Edward paused at the entrance step of the Round House, the place where the duke conducted all public business. Edward seemed to be giving orders. Among those who joined him were two knights. One was unknown to Will, but the other's colours showed him to be Sir John Morte of Kyre Ward, the man who had first taught both Will and Edward the practicalities of war. Will almost did not recognize him, for he had lost much of his fine head of dark hair. Also crowding upon Edward was his seneschal, a scrivener, a notary-at-law in dark green robe, two merchants waiting to hand him petitions and a black-robed Elder of the Sightless Ones.

'He's now quite a busy man, I see.' Will's eyes followed like a crossbow as the duke's heir disappeared inside the Round House. He felt a strange, vinegary pang biting at him. 'Tell me, does he still like to play the paragon of chivalry to please his father?'

Jackhald looked quickly askance at that. 'Sir Edward does not play at anything. He is all that his father wished him to be. More, if I'm asked about it.'

'And Edmund?' Will asked, meaning Edward's younger brother.

Jackhald shifted uneasily. 'Sir Edmund is still but sixteen years old.'

Will thought he heard a hint of shame in the soldier's voice. He pursued it. 'Come on, Jackhald. Tell me: is Edmund as kind and thoughtful a lad as ever he was?'

Jackhald stiffened, his voice hard now, affronted. 'What do you mean by that?'

And it even alarmed Will to hear the sneer in his own voice. He knew he sounded meddlesome and insulting, but he could do nothing about it, for when he tried to repair the damage his words began to sound wheedling. 'You know how much I always liked Edmund, how much I liked them all. They were like brothers and sisters to me, for I had none of my own. I just want to know what's happened to them, that's all.'

Jackhald looked at Will's sweating face and guarded his views with a plain reply. 'Sir Edmund still studies under Tutor Aspall.

The Lady Margaret and the Lady Elizabeth are all grown up now and promised in marriage.'

Will wiped at the moisture on his face. The red fish was burning in his left hand, but somehow he could not open his grip or put it away. 'Is the Duchess Cicely here?' he asked, meaning Duke Richard's wife, a woman he had once liked very much. 'She was always so *attached* to the duke as I recall. She always wanted to be near him no matter how important the business that took him away.'

'Her grace is here. And her two younger sons. She did not want the boys falling hostage to her husband's enemies.'

'She should fear for her children the more if there's to be a siege,' he said. 'But let's hope it doesn't come to that, eh?'

'Aye. Let us hope.' Jackhald's eyes narrowed. He searched Will's face carefully. 'It looks to me like you're sickening for something, Master Willand.'

He was not and he knew it. But whatever was moving within him sent his mouth running away with itself. 'It's nothing. Tell me about the others. The two younger boys.'

'Sir George is ten now, and Sir Richard is eight.'

'You might tell me more about them than their ages. You don't like any of the duke's children much, do you?'

Jackhald balked at that. 'They are my lord's kin! I would not speak ill of them to anyone!'

Will burst out into edgy laughter. 'Oh, be straight with me, Jacky. I'll not speak your opinions aloud. They are despicable young brats, are they not? You've always thought it, but never had the guts to say. Isn't that so?'

Jackhald's jaw clenched. He turned on his heel and left. Will watched him, the sweat streaming from him now, the red fish burning his palm like something held in a blacksmith's tongs. He couldn't open his fingers. He went down from the keep as soon as he could, staggering, yet still as furtive as a rat, and trying not to draw attention. As he reached Gort's rooms he burst in and could no longer contain his agony. He let out a gasping yell, bit hard against his lip and peeled his fingers back with his free hand. Once he had picked the talisman out of his flesh he jammed his hand in a basin of water in which herbs were soaking.

Relief washed over him, but it was a long count before he dared to look at his palm. When he did there was no sign in it that anything was amiss. He flexed his fingers, rubbed at the ball of his thumb. There was no pain at all, no mark or angry colour.

He went over to the corner where he had flung the red fish, and gingerly picked it up by the tail. Its green eye stared up at him innocently enough.

'What are you?' he asked it.

He felt unwilling to put it back in his pouch, and instead he shut it in a box and hid it under his bed. Then, still feeling more than a little jittery, he went out and sought refuge in Gort's now empty leech garden. Here was a comfortable bench, set down in a good place to think, and he began wondering at the way he had lost control of himself and what had urged him to so ill-judged a conversation. It was all too reminiscent of the last time he had been at Ludford. Something here was leaning on him, trying to drive him out of his mind.

Knowing he must meditate on the problem, he began to consider the weaknesses and the failings, examining himself closely on each point, and paying particular attention to the failing called vainglory, or pride.

According to the magical redes, the three great weaknesses were jealousy, hatred and fear. These gave rise to the seven failings, urges which, when carelessly indulged, led to injury and affront to others. The three lesser failings were pure – greed, cruelty and cowardice. Each of these arose from one weakness alone, greed from jealousy, cruelty from hatred, and cowardice from fear. Then came three greater failings, each of which were made from two weaknesses in combination, like the colours of a painter's board. Tyranny was blended from jealousy and fear; wrath was a mixture of hatred and fear; and sloth arose from jealousy and hatred. But the king of all failings was vainglory, compounded as it was of all three weaknesses in equal measure.

At last, he decided he must go to find Jackhald and apologize without delay. He took another circuit of the walls to look for him, and as he came to the parapet near the gatehouse he spied a black-robed figure breaking from the cover of a stone wall no more than fifty paces ahead of him. One glimpse made the hairs tingle on the back of Will's neck. The face was masked, yet there was something familiar about the way it moved.

'Hoy!' Will called, but the figure was already running. It entered the upper storey of the gatehouse and passed out of sight. Will ran after it, but found only a slammed door. He burst into the gatehouse, dodged past the great rope-wound drum and wind-lasses that raised the portcullis, then he hauled open the far door. By the time he had emerged onto the parapet on the far side, the figure had made its escape.

'What are you up to? You have no business here!'

He spun. It was one of the gatekeepers, a bumbling fellow in a dirty cap and apron, coming out of a side door.

'I saw someone. Chased him here. Did you see where he went?'

'Who?'

'A man. Dressed all in black.'

'I saw no one come this way, in black or otherwise. Here, you can't just come up—'

'There's mischief afoot! Raise the alarm. Put out a call for Master Gwydion. And another for the Wortmaster.'

'Eh?'

'Well, *go on, man!*'

The gatekeeper started into action and disappeared back the way he had come. Will searched warily now, listening and watching for a sign. At last, when he looked down over the wall he saw a rope dangling free by one of the round towers. Whoever had come by here had vanished into the bushes below.

By the time Will returned the other gatekeepers had appeared. Then Gort and Jackhald came and listened to his account.

When he had finished Jackhald said stiffly, 'Perhaps you imagined it.'

'Jackhald, you were right to think that I've not been myself today, and for that I ask your forgiveness, but did I imagine this?' He stepped to the tower and hauled up the rope.

'Probably just some serving maid's sweetheart making himself scarce,' Jackhald said, unimpressed.

'I don't think so.'

'Black-hooded? Black-robed? One of the red . . . ahem!' Gort came close and put his mouth close to Will's ear. 'One of the eyeless brethren, wouldn't you say?'

'I don't think that either.'

Gwydion appeared at the doorway to the stair. 'Then tell us. What *do* you think?'

'I think it was the same man who attacked me at the Plough.'

Gwydion closed his eyes for a moment, then he opened them and said, 'Are you sure?'

'No, Gwydion. How could I be? But I'd say there were at least six chances in seven that it was the same man – if I am to trust my feelings as you constantly remind me—'

Jackhald gave him the same searching look he had given him earlier. 'His feelings don't mean much. Our young friend's not been feeling too well today. Quite out of sorts, Master Gwydion, if I'm any judge.'

'Willand's feelings may mean more than you think, Jackhald,' Gwydion said. 'There is more to this than meets the eye.'

Will looked to where he had first caught sight of the figure. Nearby was the great wooden housing that held the iron time engine which kept the hours. It made Jackhald jump by loudly clanging out the first of nine strokes.

'Come with me now, Willand,' Gwydion muttered in a way that brooked no objection. 'We must attend the duke in council. There are important matters to settle for which I have sought an audience.'

Will felt disappointment at that, wanting instead to pursue the matter of the rope. 'Must I come too?'

'I think you would profit by it.'

They went back through the gatehouse and down off the walls and once they were alone Gwydion took him sharply towards Gort's parlour, ostensibly so he could don his newly patched cloak. But what greeted them in their quarters was not what Will had expected.

'Oh, Gwydion! Look at the mess!'

Gwydion stood at the door and surveyed the wreckage of the room. The table and all the chairs had been turned upside-down. A goose-feather pillow had been slit open, the mattress upon which he had been sleeping was slashed and his second-best shirt torn. Even his scrying wand had been snapped. The room seemed to have been ransacked by someone in a hurry, someone who did not care what he damaged.

'Why pull a good shirt in two?' Will said, unhappily holding up the ragged remains.

'That will mend. But who has done this? And why? Those are the important questions.'

Will pointed in the direction of the gatehouse. 'Our visitor, of course. Don't you think it was him?'

Gwydion's glance was impassive. 'Is anything missing?'

Will hunted through his belongings. After a while he said guardedly, 'Nothing of any real consequence.'

'Nothing? Your face tells me otherwise.'

He shrugged. 'Well, I can't find my silver coin.'

'Silver comes and silver goes. That is no matter.'

'I care nothing for its amount, Gwydion. But this coin was in the nature of a keepsake. I used to keep it for luck. It was given to me by the man I'm accustomed to call my father.'

'Then it is indeed valuable. But thieves are weaklings, and seldom respecters of real worth. That, truth to tell, is the chiefest harm they do in the world, for some things that are stolen can never be replaced.' He pushed the foot of his staff through a jug handle and lifted it up, as if expecting to see something underneath.

'What are you doing?'

'Sometimes, when we seek for what has gone missing, we find instead what has been left behind.' He bent and picked up a small white thing from the floor by the fireplace. It was flat, but too big to be a coin, and too white.

'Let me see that,' Will said, coming over. Then he gasped, for it was a bone badge made in the shape of a white heart. 'That's the token of the Fellowship!'

'I take it this keepsake is not yours.'

'Of course not.'

'Then it would seem that we have our answer. But now we must bend our minds to a new challenge. We're late for Friend Richard, and he is not a man to wait.'

Will sighed. He put on his mended cloak and looked at it, pursing his lips. 'Hardly fit to wear before a duke.'

'Why do you say that?' Gwydion adjusted the folds of his cloak as it hung. It was clean and neatly mended. 'I do not think any garment the worse for patches. Each patch is a piece of kind-ness, something done with care and oftentimes love. My own garb is ancient – it is nothing but patches – like the old broom that has had six heads and seven handles.'

'I can't see any patches in your cloak.'

The wizard laid a long finger beside his nose. 'That, Willand, is just a matter of seeming.'

Will sniffed. 'Ah, then you *do* think appearances are impor-tant.'

'Only when it comes to persuading fools to think better of what it is that I have to tell them. Come along, it is past time I brought Friend Richard to book.'

They hastened to the meeting, and when they entered the Round House Will was dismayed to find the duke's chamber already packed. All the senior officers of the castle were here, every knight and nobleman, the duke's chamberlain, his seneschal, as well as Earl Sarum and his most trusted lieutenants. Edward was here, but the Elder of the Sightless Ones whom Will had seen earlier was not. The duke himself sat on a great carved seat that was raised up three steps. There were lions' heads with flowing manes carved on the armrests. Around the circular chamber, twelve carved faces – women's heads set with crowns – stared down. They were the Twelve Austere Queens whom Will knew from history. Their images appeared in all courts of government in the Realm and were meant to guide the consciences of those who sat in judgment upon others. Then Will's eye fastened on something resting by the duke's seat, an ivory rod. With a start, he realized that it was an item he had seen once before, a piece of unicorn horn that Edward had shown him. Duke Richard, he now saw, used it as a pointer when he sat in council.

The duke looked every inch the rightful king. He said, 'Master Gwydion, welcome to you.'

The wizard opened his arms in a gesture of friendship. Will did not know if he should bow. He saw Edward look his way, but there was no acknowledgment in the glance.

'I thank you, Richard of Ebor,' Gwydion replied with formal dignity.

'You have asked to speak with me about my stone. You will pardon me if I insist that such a talk be conducted before my friends and all my people.'

Gwydion's hand slid down his staff, and he leaned its head against his shoulder. 'I did not request any secrecy, for I come to speak about the true cause of the disaster at Blow Heath.'

There was a tense shuffling at that, and the duke smiled. Earl Sarum, at his elbow, did not. 'True causes, Master Gwydion? Disaster? A strange choice of words. You speak as if the bravery of my staunch ally, Lord Sarum, was not responsible. Do you not agree then that it was he who brought us our great triumph against overwhelming odds?'

The chamber fell utterly silent now.

Gwydion stirred. 'The colour of the warrior blood that flows in your heart has never been in doubt, Friend Richard, nor the bravery of your kinsmen or servants. They were surely the masters in the late battle. But I ask you: what profit is gained by the death of so many innocents?'

'Innocents, he says!' Lord Sarum scoffed. 'Who, in this life, is that?'

The wizard's eyes glittered with a cool fire. 'My friend, near three thousand simple men of this land lie dead upon a noisome field not a dozen leagues from here. It was no quarrel of theirs that laid them low, but an intractable dispute raging between their lords.'

'Then it *was* their quarrel,' the duke put in.

'Aye,' Earl Sarum added, 'and by far the greater number of the dead were our enemy! Ten to one at the least, or I am a blind man!'

Gwydion waited for the mutters of assent to echo away. 'How many times have I repeated this rede to you, Richard? "It is always possible to avoid war, and war is always best avoided."'

'A fine sentiment, Master Gwydion, but the injustice that has been heaped upon me is plain for all to see!' Duke Richard stabbed an angry finger. 'Queen Mag has ever sought to play me like a fish upon a line. She has baited me these past four years. Behind every gesture of friendship there has been some malicious scheme, behind every smile some poisonous whisper. She has enchanted the Great Council with false promises and lies, so that now half the lords of this land are up in arms against me. I am denied my appointed office by these enemies. I am driven across the Realm by men who seek to imprison me, to dispossess me, to impeach me on false charges, and all so that they may have what is mine!' He banged the arm of his chair. 'The she-wolf wants me dead! Do not forget to mention this, Master Gwydion, when you speak of true causes!'

Those who listened clapped their hands and stamped their feet, and gave voice to their approval.

Gwydion bore it all and waited for silence. Then he said, 'All that is undeniable, my friend, and I have no argument to set against you. But the true cause of war lies deeper than individual greed or jealousy. It is harder to understand than power or wealth. It is less clear to the eye than the disputes between rightful king and pretender or usurper.'

Richard's eyes narrowed. 'Then say your piece and be done with it.'

Gwydion gave a gesture Will had seen so often before. It seemed to say that here was a lone wise voice struggling to be heard in a madhouse. 'I have warned before about certain malicious stones. I have told how they must be found if the Realm is ever to be at peace with itself. The stump that was brought here is one such that has been discharged in battle, but, Friend Richard, you must not think of it as *your* stone.'

The silence bore down on them all.

'Master Gwydion, the stone is graven with the mark of my signet. It has come to me as a gift from my kinsman, who won it in battle. Therefore, it seems to me whatever magic it contains can fairly be called mine.'

'How many times must I tell you, Richard? Magic is selfless. It cannot be possessed, and it must not be abused. Though the stone was indeed taken by Friend Sarum, it was not his to give.'

'Then, to whom does it belong?' The duke's stare was unblinking. 'Is it *yours*, Master Gwydion?'

'Mine?'

'The Old Crow stole it!' a voice called from the back.

When Will looked, he saw that it was Lord Dudlea who had spoken. He was no longer imprisoned in his cell, but stood haggard, in a stained shirt, loaded with chains and under close guard by two of Lord Sarum's henchmen. Will realized that he had been brought here for a purpose.

'Bring the prisoner forward!' the duke said. 'Let him speak.'

'He stole it from the house of John, Baron Clifton.'

'Is this true?' the duke asked.

Gwydion tried to wave the point away. 'The battlestone has lain buried at Aston Oddingley for thousands of years. Baron

Clifton knew nothing of it, though it was what drove him and all his forebears insane. My main point is this—'

But Will saw one of the duke's yellow-clad advisors whisper. The duke's fist clenched on his unicorn-horn rod, and he cut in on the wizard. 'But if you admit you dug the stone up on Clifton land, then the case is clear, Master Gwydion. As landowner, Baron Clifton was the owner.' He smiled for the benefit of those who hung on his words. 'Mad Clifton is my sworn and notorious enemy – his men joined battle against my allies – therefore whatever else may be said, I cannot be accused of partiality. However, this means the stone is now become a rightful spoil of war. It was in turn gifted to me through lawful means, therefore I deem it to be mine and see no reason why I should not use it as I see fit.'

There were cries of assent. Gwydion nodded ruefully, conceding the decision, but then he said, 'Friend Richard, deeming does not make matters so. Whatever you may say, the stump is not yours to be milked like a cow, or used to give false hopes of invulnerability to your people. If you persist in such a course, then trouble will surely befall you.'

That sounded like a curse, and breaths were sucked in at its pronouncement. The hum of voices echoed in the chamber, and the duke seemed swayed for a moment as he deliberated further upon the matter.

Gwydion said softly, 'Bring it in, Richard. It should be set up in my lodging—'

Sarum exploded. 'He wants to have it for himself!'

Gwydion's voice rose louder. 'Give it to me for one turn of the moon, while I squeeze from it the secret it holds. I can make it give a clue as to where the next stone lies. Surely you would like to know where the next battle will be fought?'

But the Blow Stone has already yielded up its verse clue, Will thought, jolted by the wizard's words. What's Gwydion's game?

The duke bit on a knuckle and made his decision. 'Have the stone brought to this chamber where the eyes of the Twelve

Austere Queens may rest upon it. In this place, Master Gwydion, and not in any dark den, you may enquire of the stone as you will. That is all.'

Lord Sarum flashed the duke a hard glance, but he did not speak out against the decision. Gwydion excused himself, and strode from the chamber. Will turned and followed close behind. The wizard, as usual, had quietly got exactly what he wanted.

CHAPTER SIXTEEN

MOTHER BRIG

At Gwydion's command Will spent the next few days looking for the Ludford Stone. Some days he went with Gort, but mostly he walked alone in the hope that his senses would clear. But there was something going on that played against his talent and frustrated his best efforts.

When he went to the Round House he saw that the emblem of the duke's personal signet was still clearly graven in the stone's surface – a four-leafed sign surmounting three long-stemmed pike flowers. When he asked, he was told that no art of the wizard's, or of the Wortmaster's, had been able to shift it.

'But don't we already know the Blow Stone's verse?' he asked.

'Do we?' Gwydion replied archly. 'I have drawn no verse from it. What we read was given to us by the stone itself, offered when it was in its harmful prime. Do you think we should trust such a gift?'

Will pursed his lips, then said slowly, 'Then you think it was given out to mislead us?'

Gwydion's look was shrewd and careful. 'That is a possibility. On the other hand, the stone may have told true. Do not forget the rede: "Harm often comes of an unwisely told truth." We uprooted the stone and took it far from its proper place. There is still time for a predictive verse, no matter in what spirit it was originally offered, to be made real by events.'

Will thought about that until his head ached. 'Just tell me why you didn't tell Duke Richard about the verse.'

'I may tell him. In time. If and when the need arises. But for the moment I can think of no better way to keep what remains of the Blow Stone from being offered up as a source of false hope to the people than to work on it here.'

'What about when we rode here?' he said. 'You didn't prevent the soldiers from touching the stump then. I wanted to turn them away, but you said there'd be no harm in it.'

'Well, then – you were right and I was wrong.' Gwydion's eyes were calm and his look unresisting. This was purest guile, and Will knew it.

'Oh, don't treat me like a child!'

'Then don't behave like one. And think before you speak. There is a great difference between comforting men who have lately fought in a battle and deliberately preying upon townspeople's credulity. The whole Realm is tumbling headlong into an abyss. Rather than question me you would do better to go out and scry for the next stone.'

Humbled, and with nothing more to say, Will went outside and did as he knew he should, leaving the wizard to his arcane labours.

As the days passed, Will settled into the rhythms of castle life. At the fifth chime of the morning, the guard was changed and smoke began to issue from the bakehouse chimney. At the seventh chime, the morning meal was served. At the eleventh hour, merchants were admitted to the outer ward. At the noonday bell, a troupe of Fellows were let in to the inner ward to kneel at their little shrine, to wash and wail for an hour at the spigot by the Round House. Folk came and folk went, and there seemed a neverending stream of lordly business. Will saw Edward many times, but always from afar. It seemed that many of the duke's routine tasks had now fallen to his elder son. Edward shouldered them with a serious demeanour and was always surrounded by at least a dozen men to whom he must listen or issue orders. Will wanted to approach him but, as Jackhald had said, they had grown apart.

Another man to be seen increasingly in the castle grounds was Lord Dudlea. At first, Will was surprised to see him at liberty. Two guards watched over him as he worked down by the sheep pens. He was dirty and dishevelled, but the chains had been taken from his wrists and neck, if only to allow him to shovel ordure. When he met Will's eye there was a look of such malice in his own that Will recoiled.

The intensity of that look caused Will to wonder if he had not misinterpreted it. Perhaps what he had really seen was a mixture of misery and disgust. Will wondered too about Lord Sarum's sons, and whether a deal of exchange had yet been offered. But the next day, momentous news came that drove all other thoughts out of Will's mind – a royal army had been spied heading up from the south.

Gort said that meant a siege must now follow, and Will agreed.

'It was bound to happen sooner or later,' he told Gwydion. 'The next stone is surely here at Ludford. And that means the next battle will be here too – unless I can find it.'

'An inescapable conclusion,' Gwydion said.

'Oh, yes! You must do your best, Willand,' Gort agreed. 'Everything now depends on you.'

And so for three more days Will wandered unhappily from the Durnhelm brewhouses to the Linney, out of the Broad Gate and all along the banks of the Theam, and from Galfride's Tower to the Portal, but to no avail. Thousands of men laboured in sun and rain, digging entrenchments, scouring the land for food, emptying village granaries, herding great numbers of oxen, sheep and geese into the town and filling the outer ward with materials. Stockmen wove willow hurdles and put up a maze of animal pens in the market square. Nearby houses were turned into grain stores or filled with fodder. The air around the castle became filled with the stink of dung, and the sound of much lowing and bleating and honking. Inside the keep, Will found a sinister traffic as men brought out of store quantities of rusty-headed arrows and sorcerer's powder ready to greet the enemy.

As the moon's last quarter neared, Will was ever more troubled by fears. They clouded his mind hourly, but he combated them by fixing his thoughts immovably on Willow and Bethe. Even so, there were real worries – had Morann delivered them home without mishap? Was the Vale really safe from the devastation that had been visited upon Little Slaughter? And even if everyone at home was out of harm's way, how long would it be before he saw them again?

'Is Morann coming?' he asked the wizard. 'Does he even know where we are?'

'He will have read the marks I left for him, marks that only a loremaster can read. Never fear, he will come if we should stand in need of him.'

But Will did fear – time was running out. He looked up now at the unkind sky. Over the last few days of grey, damp weather, soldiers had been sharpening stakes and heaping higher the muddy outer defences, lines they would have to man when the queen's army finally came for its revenge.

He stretched, tired after three nights of broken sleep. The brightness of the moon had joined with the whirling in his brain to keep him from rest. And last night he had heard a strange, chilling wail coming from the direction of Cullee Hill. It had been a sound so unearthly that he had got up from his bed and gone over to the window. He had waited a long time, standing naked in that cold draught, thinking that if another battle began it would be his fault, but the Morrigain cry, if that was what it was, had not come again.

Now, angrily resolved to find the Ludford Stone, he climbed another earth bank and vaulted over a half-made log barricade before plunging down into a filthy ditch and scrambling up the far side. Here he tried again. But still the hazel wand felt as good as dead in his hands. He snapped it in two and threw the pieces down. Then instantly regretted his childishness, because now he would have to find a hazel tree and the only ones near grew down by the river.

As the rain came again he sat near the end of the earthworks, under a soldier's canvas shelter, squatting on an upturned pail, watching big clear drops of water falling down from the sagging canvas above. Time and again he went over the Blow Stone's verse, and tried to find some way to learn for sure if it was true or false.

> *Beside Lugh's ford and the risen tower,*
> *By his word alone, a false king*
> *Shall drive his enemy the waters over,*
> *And the Lord of the West shall come home.*

Surely the meaning was clear enough, but perhaps he only thought that because the stone already had him hard in its grip. He looked around, feeling too thick-headed and stupid to puzzle any longer over the subtleties that must lie in words. A hundred fears had rushed into that space in his mind that he must keep open and empty.

Cold, wet fingers went to his pouch to fetch out the piece of cheese he had put there, and maybe one or two of the hazelnuts, but something was wrong.

The red fish . . .

It was missing.

I can't just have dropped it, he thought, looking around, alarmed by the loss. I can't have. Can I?

He stood up, checked his pouch again. Nothing. He retraced his steps across the Linney as best he could – nothing. All the way back to the town he searched the ground. Still nothing.

'What have you done with it?' he demanded of himself, unable to remember when he had last seen it. 'You've managed to lose it, you fool!'

When the anger drained away he felt empty and exhausted,

because there was no chance of finding it now. No chance of comparing it with the green fish that Willow had been asked to bring . . .

Suddenly he felt very alone. A wretched, self-pitying fear overcame him. The rain had stopped so he trudged back to the town walls and went in through the Feather Gate. A beautiful white cat was washing its paws in a sheltered corner. The cat looked at him and seemed to smile.

'Pangur Ban?' Will said in wonderment, his heart lifting. 'Pangur Ban, can it be you?'

In answer, the white cat stretched daintily and turned back on himself so that his tail curled and brushed against a rough wooden post. Pangur Ban had come to him three times before. Once in Wychwoode, once in the Blessed Isle, and the last time was just after Maskull had defeated Gwydion at the Giant's Ring. He was so blemishless and so beautiful that Will knew he could be no earthly creature.

'Pangur Ban! Where are you leading me?'

The cat paused and seemed to understand him. Will followed, up through the goose market. Pangur Ban padded lightly ahead, rubbed his face against the corner of a merchant's house, and stared momentarily at Will with big, golden eyes. When Will looked again to see where he might have gone there was only an old beggarwoman dressed in rags.

He put his hand to his pouch and pulled out the piece of cheese that was still there, but as he offered it he felt his wrist seized as if by a claw.

'I thank you for your kindness . . . Willand.'

He was startled to hear his name. Two milk-pale eyes looked up at him. The last time he had seen the crone she had been Queen of the Ewle, her long grey hair twined with holly and ivy.

'Mother Brig!'

'Ah, your memory is keen!'

'It's good to see you again.'

'Has Master Gwydion neglected to teach you the proper

greetings. Say: "By the boar, the tree, the wheel and the raven!"'
She broke the cheese in two and sniffed at it, then put the smaller
piece in her mouth and sucked it with evident enjoyment.

Will did not know who – or what – Mother Brig was. Now
that he thought about it, she seemed to be a witch, one of the
Sisters, perhaps even their queen, though she chose to appear as
no more than an old, blind beggarwoman. Embarrassed, he said,
'How is it that a famous Wise Woman sits begging for her bread
in this damp and draughty place?'

'Do you not yet know your redes of magic? Begging is a way
of doing kindness in the world.'

'Doing kindness? What can you mean by that?'

'Aye, kindness! Begging is giving bliss,' she laughed. 'Don't
you know even that much?'

'Begging is giving bliss? How can that be?'

'Have you never fed ducks before? Have you never felt the
enormous pleasure there is to be had from their gratitude?'

'Ah, so you're a seller of gratitude, are you? I never thought
of begging like that before.' He laughed, but then grew serious.
'Surely you're of more consequence than this. I remember that
once you entertained Duke Richard to your Ewletide feast. And
when he came you laid a rule on his head and sat in judgment
upon him. You even told him his future. How is it then, that you
enjoy no better ease than a cold corner to sit on and dry crusts
to eat?'

'There is no ease better than this and no place more important in all the Realm!' She scowled and shifted away from him.
'Do you think the gift that beggars give is to make others feel
superior? That is dirty charity. And what is this "consequence"
you speak of? You should go away and think deeper thoughts
about the world. Think hard about wealth and power and influence and wisdom, then come back to me and tell me what they
truly are.' She laughed suddenly. 'Perhaps one day you will even
know what foolishness is.

'Birch and green holly, boy!
Birch and green holly!
If you get beaten, boy,
'Twill be your own folly!'

While she laughed and sang and cackled to herself, he shook his head. 'Truly, Mother Brig, you must be the wisest of the wise, for I never have any idea what you're talking about.'

'Then you are still a young fool! Can you not feel all the eyes in the Realm turning this way? We are in the thick of it here, Willand! This is now the hub about which the whole world turns.'

She cackled again, then slapped lightly at his braids with her stick and repeated the eerie omen that she had spoken to him once at a Ewletide feast:

'Will the dark,
Will the light,
Will his brother left or right?
Will take cover,
Will take fright,
Will his brother stand and fight?'

He listened, then spoke the verse back to her. 'Mother Brig, what does it mean?'

She laughed again. 'What does anything *mean*? Oh, how the Ages decline when we must make do with such heroes as you!'

He remembered the red fish and the problem of the Blow Stone, and a foreboding came over him. He said, 'Mother Brig, there are things I must attend to. I have to go.'

'Of course, for I am but an ugly old crone with a laugh like a cinder, while you are a handsome young man.'

And when he looked again, she seemed no longer to be an ancient beggarwoman, but a young woman as fair of face as Willow. He recoiled, blinking.

'What's the matter, Willand? *Something in your eye, perhaps?*'

When he looked again she was as she had been before.

'I . . .' Urgency pushed him on. 'I . . . I'll tell Master Gwydion I saw you.'

'Tell him my favourite food is salmon!'

'Salmon, did you say?'

'Leastways, *this* beggar is a chooser!' She wagged her stick at him, then, as one remembering an afterthought, she said, 'Now think on all that I've said! Beware your brother! Hah ha ha ha ha!'

He left her then, and went back towards the castle, looking ever for a white cat that had once more gone its own way.

CHAPTER SEVENTEEN

THE HOSTS GATHER

Anxious days passed. Every sunrise, Gwydion went alone to the Round House, but his report to the duke every sunset told that no matter how he worked the Blow Stone's stump he could not make it shift its shape or reveal the resting place of the battlestone they must now so urgently find.

Every day Gort brought powders and flasks of dew. Gwydion danced around the dead stump with absorbed concentration. 'There *must* be a secret within,' he told the impatient duke. 'It remains only for me to find it. But these things take time.'

As for Will, he told Gwydion about meeting Mother Brig, but said nothing about the red fish or its loss. That was partly due to shame over his foolishness, and partly that he had begun to tell himself the fish was of no consequence. It had passed easily into his possession, and passed out of it again just as easily.

Instead he fretted over Willow's likely return and watched all that passed in and around the castle. He saw Lord Dudlea near the water cisterns. He was looked after by no guard, and Will saw that he no longer wore chains, even on his ankles. He was carrying a yoke from which hung two full pails of water, and he looked askance at Will, but made no comment, except to seek his gaze and to make a *baa* sound, like a ewe calling to a lamb.

Will hurried to the Round House, thinking it no more than some kind of curious insult. He thought again about what he had heard concerning the captive, and noted the improvement in his treatment.

'Of course,' Gwydion said. 'It is Lord Sarum's doing. Friend Dudlea has offered to trade knowledge about the queen's secret weapons.'

'What has he said about them?'

'Very little, as yet. Nor will he without first receiving certain guarantees.'

'Why don't you *make* him talk?' Will said.

But the wizard turned his attention back to the Blow Stone, saying, 'Foolish words. They make you sound weak, like a torturer.'

And Will left the Round House, feeling an intolerable pressure building in his head.

Not long after the noonday bell, a fast messenger galloped into the outer ward and threw himself down from a lathered horse, unstrapping his satchel as he ran. The duke came out from his solar. His knights and Edward, his heir, were with him. Will approached, but Edward looked at him as a man who sees only a stranger, and the bodyguard came forward with their bills and helm-axes. Not wishing to confront them at such a moment, Will drew back from their challenge.

His decision was wise, for within moments a commotion took hold of the whole castle, and a whisper began spreading abroad: *'The earl's son has come at last!'*

The looked-for army of Lord Warrewyk, Earl Sarum's first-born son, was reportedly no more than two leagues distant. The welcome prepared in the town for the son was even greater than that which had greeted the victory of the father. Jackhald said that a large host of men had come across the Narrow Seas and had landed in Kennet, where more had joined the march. The army had swung widely to the west, avoiding the great city of Trinovant. Three engines of death came in pride of place with

Lord Warrewyk, three ox-trains of twenty yoked pairs, each hauling a great fire-belcher.

Will and Jackhald watched as the army approached and the town was called out to receive it. Throughout the afternoon, Ludford more than doubled its strength so that a formidable company was now gathered without the walls, and the joy of the townsfolk at that was real enough.

'Now we shall see whose arms are the greater,' Jackhald said with satisfaction.

'There's nothing to be cheering about,' Will told him gloomily.

Jackhald grinned back, robust. 'Down in the dumps again, are we? You're beginning to sound like a proper crow. You should ask Master Gwydion to see if a spell hasn't been placed on your head by some witch or another.'

Will let the comment pass, though he reflected on the rhythms of his increasing discomfort. It was no wonder, for here he was sitting atop a flowing lign, yet trapped among stone walls that shattered it like a fountain. His mind quickly became bemused whenever he tried to make sense of the confusing patterns. Dread feelings rose and fell twice a day, and came later every day like the tides of the sea. During a nondescript phase of the moon the rise was bearable, but at every sharp quarter the pain and confusion threatened to swamp his sanity. And as the lorc continued to fill with power the pressure on Will's thoughts increased.

He watched Lord Warrewyk's army entering the town by the Broad Gate. Now, just as before, a great mass of men marched down towards the soldiers' camp, while others came up into the castle precincts. The nobles rode under three banners. The first had three white bucks upon bars of black and gold. The second flew two silver lions upon red. Between them, there was a red banner with a muzzled bear in silver. The bear, Will knew, was the badge of Lord Warrewyk himself, but he was unsettled to see the two silver lions, for they were the arms of John, Lord Strange.

Almost seven years had passed since the summer when Will had learned to read and write in Lord Strange's tower in

Wychwoode. It had been some five years since Lord Strange had appeared among the king's forces at Verlamion. Now, true only to his own inconstancy, he had switched sides. No matter how much water might have flowed under Evenlode Bridge, it seemed, nothing had been able to wash Lord Strange clean. Will shuddered at the thrill of horror he always felt at the sight of the half-man. From the neck down Lord Strange was like any other lord, but his head was that of a wild boar. And it had grown even bristlier and more boarish – his tusks were yellower, his snout more pointed, and a stiff ridge of grey bristles now ran right over the top of his head.

'Filthy crow!' he grunted as he turned into the outer ward and saw Gwydion standing near the duke.

As the Hogshead strode towards him and launched out his sword, Gwydion did not turn, but suddenly raised his gnarled staff. 'John le Strange, I warn you – approach me no closer.'

'Gnngh!' Lord Strange snorted in his wrath. His sword was lifted, made ready to chop down, but when the time came it did not move. The razor-sharp point only circled irresolutely in the air while Gwydion's back remained turned.

'Show your face to me, wizard, for I would speak hard words to you!'

The hundreds who were gathered saw Gwydion turn about. His eyes were dark and his voice soft. 'Speak then. What have you to say to me?'

'You have cursed me! And now you will cure me, or else, as I swear by all the rotting stumps of Wychwoode, you will die at my hand!'

'Hear me, John le Strange, and hear me well. I do not deal in curses. Nor do I bear you ill will. I have told you as plainly as I dare that you have only yourself to blame for your misfortunes.'

'You told me my blood would fail!' The pig-voice rasped out. 'You said girls would be born to my line! Girls! So my title would pass to the son of another! Since you spoke those words, I have sired naught but daughters! What is this if it be not a curse?'

'Be content, John le Strange. For daughters are a joy denied to many. And surely they are the equal of sons.'

'Four daughters!' he sneered. 'You have cursed me!'

'My words warned what would befall through your own failings. You allowed the sacred grove of Wychwoode to be destroyed, though you were its appointed warden. Did you think such a deed would go unpunished? What goeth, goeth about again! Greed and ambition are what destroy you.'

'Then pity me my misfortune!'

'Is it any wonder that misfortune attends one as obdurate as you?'

What Will knew but Lord Strange did not, for it could not be told to the Hogshead directly without killing him, was the true nature of his curse. The spell had been laid by Maskull, concocted from the dregs of Lord Strange's own inconstancy and made as a flag to show the sorcerer how the winds of change were blowing in the Realm. The spell forced Lord Strange's face to show the greed and corruption that lay in the hearts of his fellow lords, but so fashioned was the spell that he could have restored himself at any time, simply by rooting out his *own* failings. Yet he had remained deaf to all the wizard's hints.

The Hogshead brandished his sword again, but impotently, for it was as if his elbow and shoulder were both locked tight.

'Gnngh! Sorcery! See how he practises sorcery against me!'

Gwydion hooked a little finger. 'I warn you, defiler of groves – if you shake that stick at me one more time I shall scatter no more acorns for you to eat.'

Those who watched now goggled and gasped, for the sword suddenly seemed to become an oaken branch, one laden with acorns that began to drop all around as Lord Strange shook it.

Nervous amusement began to ripple among those who saw. Then laughter broke out. Will felt Lord Strange's spirit falter under the burden of humiliation. The Hogshead cried out as his anger was trodden down by Gwydion's ridicule, then his courage failed him altogether.

As Gwydion walked away, the Hogshead's sword – a sword once more – fell in the mud, and he shouted after the wizard, 'Master Gwydion, I am heirless!'

At Will's side Jackhald guffawed. 'Well, that's a pretty sight, ain't it? They say it's called vanity when a person looks in a glass and sees what's not there. But hairless? Him? Ha! Ha! Ha!'

Will could not help but feel for Lord Strange. His appearance and manners were far worse now than they had been six years ago. That fact, more than anything, warned how close the Realm must have come to degradation.

As Will watched the Hogshead go, ill-boding thoughts simmered in his mind, but then he felt an unexpectedly gentle touch on his shoulder. He stiffened, turned and found himself staring at a face that was far easier on the eye than Lord Strange's.

It was Willow's.

PART THREE

MADNESS AT LUDFORD

CHAPTER EIGHTEEN

HONEY MEAD

Supper was over and night had fallen. The wizard, the two lore-masters Gort and Morann, and the little family that had been reunited all settled down in Gort's wonderful rooms. Willow had brought the green fish talisman. Straight away she handed it to Will, who hung it next to his heart where it seemed to belong. It felt very good to have it back, and he pressed it between palm and breast and closed his eyes briefly like a man savouring the moment.

'Are you all right?' Willow asked

He smiled at her. 'Oh, yes. Better than I've been for some time.'

She squeezed his hand and smiled back. 'Me too.'

As darkness deepened across the ceiling and walls, they gathered close together round the fire while Gwydion sketched for the newcomers a picture of what had taken place in their absence. When talk of the dreadful battle on Blow Heath was done, the Wortmaster opened a bottle of his sweetest honey mead.

Willow smiled and touched her husband's face. He looked back at his wife now as she nursed their child, and found himself filled with the same contrary emotions he had felt back at the Plough – great joy that his family were with him, but an equal fear for their safety, for now here they all were bottled up together in Ludford and their enemies bearing down on them.

Morann recognized Will's misgivings and laid a hand on his arm. 'I'm sorry for the delay. These are dangerous times and I had an errand of my own that would not wait. But it's good we left when we did, because we were not long out of the Vale when we happened upon the queen's host.'

'You saw them?' Will said, struck with horror.

'We saw them all right,' Willow said. 'But they never saw us. That was through some craft of Morann's, I suppose, for they came right by us. Then, as soon as we could, we rode west, and ran straight across Lord Warrewyk's army.'

Morann nodded. 'Willow went up as bold as you please to the earl. She pushed aside his bodyguards and warned him to his face that he was heading for a wrathful meeting with a far larger army.'

'And what did he say to that?'

'He thanked me, of course,' Willow laughed. 'Wouldn't you have done?'

'The king himself rides with the royal host?' Gwydion asked.

'He's at the head of it,' Morann said. 'With the queen and Henry de Bowforde at his elbows.'

Gwydion stroked his beard. 'You say a *larger* army? How many soldiers were with the king?'

'A very great many,' Willow said. 'More than enough to make Lord Warrewyk and his twelve thousand turn aside, and he struck me as a man who'd give battle at the drop of a hat if he thought there was the smallest chance of winning.'

Gwydion nodded. 'That is not far from the truth. Lord Warrewyk is warlike, but I fear he is persuaded here by a greater strategy of which he remains wilfully ignorant. He has more than doubled the strength of Ludford. Now perhaps the Ebor falcon is too big to be locked up, even by the fetterlock which the queen has brought with her.'

'I wouldn't wager a wooden spoon on that,' Willow said. 'You should have seen the king's army! We thought there must be forty thousand men if there was one.'

'Forty thousand?' Will said sitting up. 'Surely that can't be right.'

'At least,' Morann said. 'And it'll be fifty thousand by the time it arrives, for it's swelling all the while as it goes.'

Will whistled as he looked to the wizard. 'Fifty thousand? Is that possible?'

'My guess is that it will be sixty,' Gwydion said flatly.

'Am I dreaming?' Will looked from face to face. 'How many men are there in the Realm?'

'Sixty thousand would account for one in every seven men of fighting age,' Gwydion said.

Willow grimaced. 'Men certainly flock to the king's banner, though most have been driven to it like sheep.'

Gwydion drained his mead. 'The common men of the Realm do not regard their king badly. To most, he is the embodiment of Sovereignty. Do not forget that he has now reigned over everyone, man and boy, for more than thirty-seven years. Hal's father was king before him. And his father's father before that.'

'No one speaks of it openly, of course,' Gort said, 'but among the Duke of Ebor's people all three generations of King Hal's blood are thought of as tainted – a usurper's line, you see. Our duke doesn't dare to make an open claim, oh, no! But by the strict law of blood he is the rightful king and that knowledge eats at his heart as a codling grub eats at the core of an apple.'

Will felt the comfort of the talisman next to his heart. He drew it out. 'Tell me, Morann, what do you make of this?'

Morann took the little green fish and examined it closely, setting it on the flat of his long dagger, then turning it over between his fingers and rubbing it against one of his front teeth to test it. At last, he cleared his throat and said, 'Seven times seven score crystal forms are found within the earth, but I never have seen the like of this before. It is no earthly stone.'

Will looked to Gwydion. 'Then where did it come from?'

Morann said, 'As to the maker – the craftsmanship seems to me magical. And if there might be a meaning to whatever's graven upon it – I cannot read it.'

Morann gave the talisman back and Will felt Gwydion's eyes bore into him as he prepared to make an admission. He told them all about the red fish and how he had managed to lose it.

'It must have fallen out of my pouch.'

'Why did you hide it from me?' Gwydion asked.

Will felt foolish. 'I don't know. Several times I was going to tell you about it, but I couldn't. And then after I'd lost it, well . . .'

'You did not lose it,' Gwydion said.

Will looked at him. 'What do you mean?'

'It was stolen.'

The others stared, but Will knew straight away what Gwydion meant. His eyes flashed away from the wizard's own. 'The Sightless Ones!'

'Oh, not them, I think.'

'But what about the white heart token that you found?'

'Perhaps it was left only to mislead us.'

'Do you think so?'

'It is a probability.'

Will turned his own talisman over in his fingers. The honey mead was settling his belly. Firelight danced on the blue and gold painted walls. A beaming moon inched across the dome of the ceiling and hid among the plaster vines twined about the chimney.

At length, Will broke the silence. 'I have a bad feeling about Lord Strange.'

The wizard's eyes glinted with firelight. 'Lord Strange is the author of his own downfall. I have already offered him three good chances to redeem himself. He has refused them all.'

'I know he hates you, Gwydion, but can you do nothing more to help him break his curse?'

'Oh, Lord Strange!' Gort said. 'Poor creature. But pity the poor piggy that has my Lord Strange's head too, hey? Will's right, though, Master Gwydion – the Hogshead does believe you've put that curse on him.'

Willow said, 'What I don't see is why you had to reveal his future to him? Wasn't that cruel?'

Gwydion inclined his head. 'Cruel? Howso?'

'It seems cruel to foretell a person's doom.'

'It is only so if that person decides he cannot avoid his fore-told doom.'

'But Lord Strange is pig-headed,' Gort laughed, 'isn't he?'

Gwydion said, 'Lord Strange is stubborn, but he is not stupid. He is a wilful schemer. When I made my warnings to him he was not past redemption, though I fear he may now have reached a depth from which it is impossible to return.'

'But I still don't think you should have foretold his lot,' Willow said. 'It's like knowing the day you're going to die.'

The room was quiet save for the soft crackling of the fire. Flamelight played in Gwydion's eyes as he allowed Gort to refill his goblet. 'How else could I have given him a chance to seize his own true destiny? The spell that infests him is such that he must help himself, or die an ugly death. I cannot do more than I have done already.'

Willow said, 'Well, I feel sorry for the Hogshead. It must be terrible to carry such a burden.'

A look of sympathy settled on Willow's face. It was such a mix of strength and kindness that Will felt his fingers tightening again on her hand.

He looked to the wizard. 'You once foretold my own doom in this very place. You said that I was to die under a portcullis. Yet I have not.'

'I did not say you would die under a portcullis.'

'You said "one would become two".'

'That was, and is, a prophecy of the Black Book.'

'Just as it is that "two will become one".'

Gwydion's eyes moved to Morann's face. 'You should not have told him.'

Morann's gaze was unblinking, guileless. 'It was there to be told.'

'So was the portent that Edgar de Bowforde "should beware castles", so also that Lord Warrewyk shall "die by the star" – I have told one, yet I have not told the other! I always choose my words with care. I never gave Will to believe that he could not escape his doom.' Gwydion's eyes sank into the shadows of his face. 'This shows well the difference between him and Lord Strange. When I took him to dwell for a season with Lord Strange it was partly in the hope that he might learn to read and discover the redes of magic from the Sister of Wenn, but I also had hopes that his presence might teach Lord Strange enough to redeem him.'

Will said, 'You mean, you put me there as encouragement? To show him what it would be like if he could have a son of his own?'

'That was . . . one aspect of it, I suppose.'

'Oh, Master Gwydion!' Willow snorted. 'How you do dare to meddle so in folk's lives.'

The wizard's chin jutted. 'Willand is a true Child of Destiny. He must not forget that!'

'However could I do *that*?' he said wryly, then asked, 'So, do I have the power to overturn portents too? Need I fear the portcullis' teeth no more?'

'I did not say that.' Gwydion spread his hands.

'I'm going to my bed now if you don't mind, Gwydion,' Will told him as he got unsteadily to his feet. 'Your talk makes my head spin.'

'Me too,' Willow said, following him. 'That mead's gone straight to my head.'

Gwydion called after them, 'All I was trying to say, Willand, was that one difference between you and Lord Strange may be that you truly believe you can shape your own future, whereas he does not. But there is still time enough for a portcullis to fall on you!'

CHAPTER NINETEEN

A TOAST BY THE DUKE

It was early in the morning grey two days later when Will looked to the beacon upon Cullee Hill and saw it trailing dark smoke – the king's army had been sighted. But it was not until the day after, when the duke's scouts had made their report, that the lords of Ludford sent men out to rouse up their forces.

As the moon swung higher Will's feelings of disquiet had begun to rise again. He began to feel feverish. His eye ranged along the lines of fresh earthworks and trenches – great heaps of brown soil had been piled up and many young trees cut down and hauled away to make breastworks and timber walls to secure the approaches to the town. The Earl Warrewyk's great guns had already been drawn up to face the place from which the attack would most likely come.

The wizard too looked out over the cold, misty morning. Smudges of smoke rose in the distance, marking the place where the king's host now rested. A thousand camp fires had flared through the night, tainting the air. Down below, the earthworks were manned and everything stood in readiness.

'Hearken to Friend Richard's voice,' Gwydion said, looking down from the town walls near Broad Gate. 'Do you hear how he goes at it too loudly? Such strength of conviction often bespeaks an inner doubt.'

Willow cuddled her daughter close to her. 'You read folk deeply, Master Gwydion. Do you think Duke Richard believes Ludford will fall?'

'Not yet. The castle is strong. And Richard has stout confidence – in himself and in his kinsmen. Nor is it without cause. It has been a good harvest and his granaries are full. He believes he can hold out here as winter begins to bite. It is then, or so he thinks, that the king's host will begin to falter and dwindle.'

'Do you think it will be otherwise?' Will asked.

Gwydion's expression gave nothing away. 'What I have been telling Richard may soon give him some pause for thought.'

'What have you told him? Has the Blow Stone spoken to you?'

The wizard continued to measure the town with his eye. 'My interrogation has revealed nothing more. The badge it carries is the duke's signet. That seems, in itself, to be the message.'

Will wiped his face. 'Do you think so? Perhaps the stone warns of the duke's death.'

The wizard turned back. 'Willand – you are sweating.'

He nodded, feeling suddenly much worse. 'The moon is moving towards syzygy. It happens tonight. This is where the lign of the birch crosses the lign of the rowan. These feelings come upon me like waves. Each is worse than the last. I don't know how long I can resist.'

'Let me help you,' Willow said, trying to take his arm.

'Come,' Gwydion said. 'Let us breakfast together.'

But Will did not feel hungry. He let them go, saying he could not bear to come down off the walls. All seemed hopeless. Now that the king's host had arrived he could no longer safely scry the ligns more than a hundred paces or so from the castle or the town walls. Yesterday, hidden archers had taken a dozen unwary defenders, and the report of their ambushes had thrown a pall of fear over the defenders. The queen was setting a ring of iron about Ludford. Will knew it was her intention to stamp out her enemies once and for all.

That afternoon, the hunt for the battlestone continued. Despite Will's increasing agitation, he tried again, walking up and down the trenches and breastworks with his split hazel wand. But after an hour or two Willow's concern for him had grown.

'I just can't scry here!' he shouted. 'It's these great towers and curtains of stone. What comes from the lorc gets broken up by them and lost and changed like light in a forest.'

'Come inside, Will. It's affecting you badly.'

'Oh, it's so powerful! I can feel it pressing on my mind all the time. I'm having to fight to keep a grip!'

As she hugged him he stiffened and turned away.

'Willow, I'm sorry! My thoughts are going round and round so fast it feels as if my head's going to come off!'

She chewed her bottom lip and pressed her head to his chest. 'Poor Will. Come on, let's see if the Wortmaster can't do something for you.'

He shook his head. 'Gort's already done what he can, but his powders and poultices are too mild. He can't make the medicines stronger without dulling my senses. I'll be able to survive this because it's only the moon's last quarter, but a week from now it will be at the full. That'll drive me to the very brink.'

'At least you have your talisman now.'

He breathed a little easier. 'Yes. That's a great comfort to me. Thank you for bringing it.'

She put her hand in his and they walked further along the walls. They looked out across the broad sweep of farmland that surrounded the town. He said, 'I told Gwydion that two ligns cross here, but it feels more like three.'

'Three?' Willow said, realizing the importance of his words. 'Three ligns crossed at Verlamion.'

'Yes.'

'But . . . they marked the Doomstone. You don't think Ludford Castle might have a Doomstone of its own, do you?'

He tensed, shivering, sweat streaming from him now. 'All I know for sure is that I'm glad you're here.'

'Come on, you'll get a chill and catch your death.'

They started down, but two disappointments awaited them. When they came to the outer ward a crowd was gathering. Willow got the rumour from the gateman. 'Water's been poisoned a-purpose,' he said. 'Some bad-hearted swine's thrown a dead sheep down the well!'

They hurried to the inner ward. Below the walls men were rigging up barrels and awnings to catch whatever rain might fall. They found Jackhald arguing loudly with the cooks, then they saw Morann leading a horse. He was wearing long riding boots and travelling apparel.

'You're going away?' Willow asked, crestfallen.

'There's an errand I must accomplish. It cannot wait, and I must make my escape before the postern is closed. I'll be able to get through the Forest of Morte if I leave now.'

'Did you hear? They're saying the well has been poisoned,' Will said.

'So Gort told me.' He leaned forward and softened his voice. 'Don't tell anyone, but he's had a sheep's carcass hauled out of there.'

'It's already common knowledge.'

'Aye, well this place is a-flush with gossips.'

'Morann, where are you going?'

'I'd better not say.'

Morann kissed Willow's hand, clasped Will like a true friend and wished them well. Then he mounted up, clattered across the drawbridge and was gone. When they reached Gort's quarters they found Wortmaster and wizard closeted together. The two were grinding something aromatic in a mortar that sparked and spat back at them.

'I think we might have solved the problem,' Gort said, sniffing his fingertips. 'Yes, yes. Solved the problem. Hmmm. You know, it's rumoured there's a traitor among the duke's household. Now then! What about that, hey?'

'Who says that?' Willow asked, unimpressed.

'The duke himself does,' Gwydion said. 'But I doubt it. He is trying to concentrate minds for the coming battle.'

A bell pealed out, and there was shouting outside. That was the signal, Gort said, for everyone from the household to muster in the inner ward, and soon there were hundreds of folk crowded around the well. It was deep, one of the deepest castle wells in the whole Realm. Its mouth was a round, stone-lined hole, eight or nine feet across, with a stone lip shin-high running around it. An iron rail stopped folk from falling in, and a winding handle and drum were set above. From that there dangled a bucket.

Everyone watched as Gwydion leapt up onto the stonework and made a great show of dancing out magic around the well. Gort muttered as he blew powder from his hand. It glittered and crackled and filled the air with a minty smell. When they had finished, everyone packed in closer around the well-head, until Duke Richard's personal bodyguard appeared and began to clear a path for him, urging lesser folk back with the handles of their helm-axes. Duke Richard came in procession, bringing the duchess, Edward and his other children. His chief allies came too – Lord Sarum, Lord Warrewyk and Lord Strange. The duke spoke privately with Gort, then stepped up onto the lip of the well.

'I have heard it said by malicious folk that the water in this well is impure. That it gives a gripe to the guts of those who taste of it. That it will kill children. That it is not fit for a dog to drink!'

'We could smell the stink of it this morning, your grace!' one of the younger cooks ventured.

The duke ignored the remark. 'I promise you: the water is now wholesome.'

The duke's seneschal held up the well-pail for all to see, then threw it down the hole. The long rope snaked after it into the blackness, the winding handle twirled and squeaked then there came a splash from far below and one of the duke's guards began hauling the rope hand-over-hand. It took a long time for the pail to reappear, but when it did it was full of water. The duke took it and showed it to the crowd, who gawped at it. 'You see – it is now quite clear!'

But when the duke raised it up a warning of great power overwhelmed Will and he started forward.

'No, your grace! You must not!'

The duke's bodyguard tried to intercept him, but he leapt forward and made a grab for the rope, trying to tug the pail away.

'Your grace – no!'

The rope was snatched from Will's fingers. One of the brawny bodyguards caught him and thrust him back into a corner, forcing him to his knees. Instantly four helm-axes were pointed at him.

'Leave him!' the duke commanded. All eyes were on him as he dunked a drinking cup into the pail and raised it to his lips. 'To our victory!'

But as he put his head back and downed a deep draught from the cup, those who watched cried out.

The duke drew the back of his hand across his lips defiantly, but he saw that even the two earls were staring at him aghast, and when he looked at his bloodied hand he recoiled.

The duke spat a mouthful of bright red gore onto the ground and cursed. Gwydion stepped forward, his voice calming the horrific moment. 'Easy! Do not be afraid. It is only an illusion. He has taken no harm!'

The duke's shock turned swiftly to rage. He grasped Gort's robe briefly as he passed him, then thrust him away. 'Old fool! You promised me the water was clean!'

'Your grace, I . . .'

But the humiliated duke was already striding away with his hands over his mouth, his entourage following him.

CHAPTER TWENTY

THE MADNESS GROWS

T hat night, as the moon headed towards the full, Will found himself slipping helplessly into nightmare. He had dreaded the coming of the dark. His half-waking thoughts teemed with visions of wells that turned into human mouths, of shrieking in the night, of fissures that yielded up fierce flying creatures, of figures swathed in dark rags slipping in over walls and running noiselessly along the ramparts of the castle . . .

When morning came he awoke to find a beautiful white cat curled up on his bed, but as soon as he reached out to it, it vanished.

Gwydion, who had sat in vigil with him most of the night, came in and laid a sign on his forehead and offered him kind words and a powder. 'Gort says to drink this in water. Do you want me to bring Willow in? She's worried about you.'

'I'm all right.' He croaked drily. His eyes swam. 'What about the duke?'

'He blames Gort for the embarrassment, though it was not his fault. Friend Richard must bear the responsibility himself. I told him he should have set a guard on the well, and a closer watch over Lord Dudlea.'

'Dudlea? You mean—'

'He made his escape yesterday.'

'Then he's the one who dropped the sheep down the well . . .'

Will got up. Paradoxically, he felt better than he had for days. But he knew it was only a brief respite. Already his senses were starting to feel out of kilter. Willow brought him a filling breakfast, which he wolfed. Soon after, he complained of feeling sick. Despite her protests he went out as soon as he could to cut himself a fresh hazel wand, then he spent the rest of the day doggedly scrying the approaches beyond the outer ward. Once more, his efforts proved fruitless, but just before sunset, as he lingered by the lion cages near the main gate, he felt twitches in his thighs and he began to feel there was something flowing in his arms.

At his back the moon was appearing above the eastern horizon. He felt a weird sensation prickling all down his neck and across his shoulders. It made him shudder violently. An old beggar at the gate grinned up at him and, as he passed, called out to him, 'Somebody's walking on your grave, stranger!'

He turned to look at the old man, but the madness seized him, and a great roaring and grinding filled his head. There was the clanging of steel on stone. The next thing he knew he was thrown down on his left side by an irresistible force. When he put out his hand to lift himself up he was amazed to find that a lattice of thick timbers had appeared beside him. The portcullis had come down. Its great weight had driven its iron teeth hard into the mud-filled gutter designed to receive them. Two gatemen on the far side dashed from their door to discover what had happened. One of them asked if he was hurt. The other's face was upturned, examining the recess from which a dead weight of timber and steel had unexpectedly dropped.

'It's nothing,' he said, testing his left ankle. It was a light sprain, no more. He looked up in wonder at the portcullis. If he had not paused a step when the beggar had spoken to him he would have been impaled. But when he looked to find the old beggar, the man was nowhere to be seen.

★   ★   ★

It was dark by the time he hobbled up with Gwydion to the winch house above the gate. Together they looked at the winding drum. Gwydion showed him where the rope had been cut.

'Did you foresee this last night in your dreams?' Gwydion asked, picking up a hatchet from where it had been allowed to fall below the winding drum.

Will took the axe and ran a finger along the rope. 'I don't know.'

The charms about the wizard's neck clattered. 'Recall what I once told you about the nature of premonitions.'

'You said they're warnings sent back from the future.'

'Then you know what you must do.'

Will closed his eyes, and for a moment he was one with his memories, back in the past with his former self, feeling what he had felt then. An eerie flow connected across a gulf of time, and he made an effort to cross that gulf with his thoughts. When he had projected the warning, he drew a deep breath.

'Who was the old man who spoke to me?'

'Who do you think he was?'

'When he first spoke to me, I thought perhaps that it was you again. In disguise. Testing me.'

'It was not I. What did he say?'

'He called me "stranger", and said someone had walked on my grave.'

'Ah! That is the usual form of words used hereabouts when a person sees someone shiver. Did you shiver?'

'I suppose I must have. The moon was rising. It's almost at the full.'

'As the flows rise and fall in the land so do dark currents move in our bodies and minds. Believe me, I am not wholly blind to your sufferings, Will.'

'Someone chopped the rope,' he said, meeting Gwydion's eye. 'Who did this? And why? Is it because of who you say I am, Gwydion?'

'Certainly.'

'What do they want with me?'

Gwydion said, 'Maskull wants to kill you because you are the one who will prevent the fulfilment of his desires.'

That was too much, and his mind turned away from it. He sat down beside the great windlass that raised the portcullis. The pain in his ankle throbbed as he bent to pick up the severed rope. 'Perhaps someone else did this. Or perhaps what Maskull really wants is to get at you through me.'

'Perhaps . . .'

He let the severed rope fall. 'And there are hundreds of red hands at the cloister. Their Elders are admitted into the castle. Maybe it was one of them.'

'Maybe.'

Will put his finger into the groove where the axe blow had fallen, then positioned himself by the drum and moved as if swinging an axe himself. 'Well, that's something we can say at least,' he said, looking up at the wizard.

'What?'

'Whoever swung that axe was left-handed.'

As Will prepared alone for his ordeal, the moon opened a great, bloated, unblinking eye over the world. At the tenth chime of the castle clock it was riding at its highest, flooding wan beams across the stars of the south, and Will's terrors began to grow unbearable. He sat upright, drenched in sweat, his breathing fast and shallow. And when he sprang from the bed he almost fainted from the pain that knifed through his ankle.

On Gwydion's advice much of the room had been cleared and Willow had taken herself and Bethe into the adjoining chamber. But now, unable to ignore his cries, she broke in on his solitary agony and helped him into a chair. Gort's magical walls were alive with flames – the world was burning, as giants and dragons disputed for possession of the land. She fought him as he raved, comforted him and calmed him, nursed his head to her breast.

He was as tense as harp wire, feeling the violence of the currents that moved within him. It seemed that running madly through the moon-drenched fields was the only thing that would take away his fever. It seemed like death to resist.

Pangur Ban was in the room, watching him unreadably. Willow brought an ember from the fire and blew on it. Soon a gentle candlelight had filled the room. But now her voice mocked him. He tore at himself, rambling about his wizard's mark.

'Behold!'

'Calm yourself. You don't have any wizard's mark.'

'*Then what am I?* Where do I come from? Help me!'

'I'll fetch Gort.'

'No! Gort was never one of the nine! He had a mark once, but it faded! He no longer has the power!'

She gripped him. 'Let me bring Gwydion, then.'

'I've tried to ask him! He won't tell me!' He felt his eyes rolling in his head as he looked over his own body. He tried to twist himself about, to see what could not be seen. 'I cannot find a mark anywhere! But what if it lies in the middle of my back? Or under my hair? Willow, what if it's under my hair. Look there! Under my foot? A dark patch! A dark patch on my sole!'

'The duchess has a looking glass. Tomorrow, we'll ask her—'

He raved with sudden panic, seized his foot in both hands. 'No! The mark will not show in a glass!' His staring eyes met hers as she bent to mop the sweat from his face.

'Try not to trouble yourself . . .'

Her voice was as soft as butter. It humoured him. When she reached out to touch his braids, he recoiled. His eyes were wild and fevered as he forced himself back into the corner of the room.

'I must find it! *I have to know!*'

'Hushhh . . .'

Again she calmed him with gentle coaxing. And when he subsided, she took out a knife and tore strips from a sheet. She bound him hand and foot to the chair, fearing that when the next outburst came she would not be able to hold him.

His eyes opened wide and he laughed madly. 'I have tried to be a *good* man!'

'Will . . . it'll soon be midnight. Then the feelings will go away. I promise.'

But she could not promise. She did not understand. His muscles were taut, his limbs rigid. He would not – could not – control them. When she held him he suffocated.

She closed his fingers round his talisman and let him be, but she would not leave him, and so they waited together in the unwavering candlelight for his affliction to break.

When the next wave came he began to writhe and scream, and though she fought him with all her strength she could not keep him down. His hands spasmed. Blood welled in his eyes. Still she clung to him, and thrust him down. She put a stick between his teeth, fearing that if she did not he would bite off his own tongue.

'Nnnngh! Nnnnnngh! Nnnnnnnngh!'

But just as his shouts reached a pitch of agony that she feared he could no longer bear, the castle clock tolled midnight. The sound was like a charm. The fight began to go out of him, and within moments his struggles had died away. A bead of sweat trickled down her temple, dripped from her chin onto his face, and her own terror began to fade. Pangur Ban jumped up onto the bed and looked with serene golden eyes at the naked, sweat-drenched man. He put one white paw on Will's chest, and at the sight of that, Willow began to cry.

Will's breathing eased. His thoughts slid back into focus as the moon started its long fall away into the south-west.

'I've found it!' he said with rapturous, limitless gratitude, still tied, still grasping the leaping green salmon in his wet hand. 'Oh, Willow! I've found it.'

'There, there. Of course you have,' she told him, knowing the fever had made him believe he had found the stone. 'Sleep now, if you can.'

He drowsed for a little while and twitched once or twice, like a man who jumps in his sleep. In his dreams he saw a large black slug oozing from the Blow Stone. It wriggled up the snout of Lord Strange . . .

Will coughed as he came awake. He wiped his mouth on the back of his hand and blinked. There were red marks on his wrists. Cool light was streaming through the window and Willow had just finished feeding their daughter.

'And how are you this fine morning?' she asked, reaching out to touch his face. 'You've been asleep for a long while. That's good.'

'How long?'

'Since just after midnight. The castle clock has chimed six bells. How are you feeling?'

'As twitchy as a squirrel. And my head's still filled with bits of dream, but I'm sane again.' He kissed her hand, then her forehead, then her mouth.

'Good. I'm pleased about that. Gort looked in on you. He's made up another powder for you to drink.'

Bethe looked at him, grinned and reached out a small hand. The innocence of the gesture went straight to his heart.

'Da da da da.'

A tear filled his eye. 'By the moon and stars . . . I love you, child.'

There was a moment filled with warmth and light, then Willow, practical as ever, took Bethe for a wash. As he lay back he found he could put facts together seamlessly without everything flying apart inside his head. He began to think about his attacker at the Plough. Why did he have no memory of the man's face? The answer had to be magic. A spell of concealment. Then there was the gargoyle creature he had saved, the ked. Having tasted his blood it had been able to lead the would-be killer to him. Gwydion had said that the creatures were often kept by the Sightless Ones . . . and the Sightless Ones often mixed up left and right!

He sat up, excited by his partially connected insights. Here was another clue – when he thought about the fight at the

Plough, two things stood out. The first was that he and his attacker had been evenly matched; the second was that he had equalled the strength of his attacker's right arm with his own left, yet at the same time his own right arm had been unable to overpower the other's left. That could mean only one thing – his attacker was left-handed.

He told Willow that he had finally worked it out.

She gave him a hot infusion to drink. 'Are you sure?'

'Don't you see? It fits with the left-handed axe stroke, the one that sent the portcullis plunging down. Before you arrived here I saw someone escaping over the walls. I chased him through the upper floor of the gatehouse. His face was masked, but I recognized him.'

'Rest,' she said. 'Last night has taken a lot out of you.'

He blew across the surface of the hot brew and sipped. It tasted of lavender honey and summer strawberries. 'Gwydion told me not to doubt my inner feelings so much. They're telling me it was the same man who fought me at the Plough. Whoever loosed that portcullis was the same one who stole the red fish. I think he's been sent by the Sightless Ones. Where's Gwydion?'

The leech garden was bleak and windy. Blackbirds hopped in the bare autumn beds, turning over dry leaves. He heard their fluting cry of warning as Gwydion and Pangur Ban came by.

'You must find the Ludford Stone, Willand. And you must find it soon.'

He stroked the cat's head then nodded at the wizard. 'I'm doing my best. If you want to help, you might try buying us a little more time.'

'You are forgetting that the battlestones were made by fae magic. The tune of worldly events moves to their beat, not the other way round. There is no more time available to Ludford than that which the lorc will allow.'

Will pushed the complication away from his thoughts, eager instead to tell Gwydion his latest idea. 'Look, I think it's the

Sightless Ones who've sent the assassin,' he said. 'And here's why I think it.'

He explained, and as he explained the certainty he had felt slowly drained away from him and his clever ideas seemed thin and threadbare in the cold, hard light of morning.

Gwydion gauged him, then turned away. At last he said, 'I think it may be the right time for me to tell you what I was really looking for when we visited the village of Little Slaughter.'

'What?'

'A sign. A sign of someone called the Dark Child.'

Will blinked. 'Who?'

'In prophecy he was called the Dark Child, but his name is Chlu.'

'Clue?'

Gwydion's finger moved extravagantly in the air, making Will think for a moment that he might be about to step out a spell. 'In the plain speech of today the name can be spoken that way, and perhaps spelled C-h-l-u, but the true name is ancient, it comes from one of the old tongues of Cambray. It means "he who controls or steers". The Dark Child was hidden in Little Slaughter. He was the reason the village was destroyed.'

'But you told me Maskull destroyed it because he thought I might be living there.'

Gwydion's back straightened. 'I dare not tell you all that I know or suspect, and you know very well the reasons for that, but I now believe Little Slaughter was destroyed because the Dark Child was there. At first I thought the village was wiped out in order to kill him, but now I do not think that could have been the reason.'

'Then, why?' Will said, his eyes narrowing.

Gwydion trod with great care. 'For exactly the *opposite* reason – to preserve the Dark Child's life in secret. Chlu was taken away, and the village destroyed to disguise his removal.'

An unwanted vision flashed inside Will's head: a purple sky, livid lightning flashes, a pretty village smitten into ruin at a single stroke. 'But to kill all those people just to cover one man's where-abouts?'

'Maskull is more than capable of it.' Gwydion's eyes hardened. 'He holds but one idea in his head. An idea so gigantic and so blinding that it blots out all other ideas. Remember the rede which says: "Unkind means are not improved by kind ends."'

Will let out a long breath. 'This Chlu – whoever he is – must be very important to Maskull.'

'He is.' For a moment Gwydion seemed disinclined to make further comment, but then he said, 'I believe Chlu is the one whose face you cannot remember.'

Will stared back. 'You mean he's the one who's been trying to kill me?'

'I believe he is the instrument that Maskull is now using to find you.'

'Then he wasn't sent by the Sightless Ones?'

'Not if I am correct about his true place in the scheme of things.'

CHAPTER TWENTY-ONE

A GLIMPSE OF THE ENEMY

Will followed the wizard out of the garden, then out of the castle and town, and soon they came to where Duke Richard's personal banner flew. There, splendid in shining armour, the duke stood with his allies. Will quickly saw that the duke was prepared to trust the strength of Ludford's walls despite being outnumbered three to one.

Gwydion raised his staff portentously and recited the Blow Stone's curious verse.

> *'Beside Lugh's ford and the risen tower,*
> *By his word alone, a false king*
> *Shall drive his enemy the waters over,*
> *And the Lord of the West shall come home!'*

'What treason is this?' Earl Warrewyk asked. He was resplendent in shining armour and crimson surcoat upon which was embroidered in fine-wrought silver a muzzled bear and a butchered tree.

The duke's hand stayed him with his rod of unicorn ivory. 'That was no treason, but a portent of the enemy's doom, eh, Master Gwydion?'

'Alas!' Gwydion called. 'Is the day not come just as I told you it would? Hal's host advancing upon you? Sixty thousand men within sight of these walls?'

Lord Sarum laughed. 'So many? To show us the futility of resistance?'

Gwydion cut him a dark glance. 'And you, my lord, mean to see your sons again, whatever the cost to Ludford and your allies' cause!'

Lord Sarum bristled and took a step forward. 'Explain yourself!'

'Your men were guarding the walls over which Lord Dudlea escaped, were they not?'

Lord Sarum's hand went to his sword hilt. 'Speak plainly, Old Crow!'

'Let us be civil,' the duke muttered. 'Let us agree that it is the way of wizards to talk in riddles.'

'And it is my way to make them speak their minds,' Lord Sarum growled.

Gwydion struck back. 'If Lord Dudlea had not found his way unaided over the ramparts, then we might have persuaded him to speak plainly – of the secret weapons the queen is reputed to be keeping.'

Lord Sarum's teeth gritted and he began to inch out his sword, but Gwydion stayed his arm with a compelling gesture that was made in a moment. 'Do not presume upon my patience, *my little lord*!'

'You dare to call me—'

'Enough!' The duke stepped between them. 'My Lord of Sarum, be easy with my wizard, I beg you. You know well the power he disposes. And you, Master Gwydion, it would please me if you would speak politely to my friends. I have never seen you behave like this. Are you not forever telling us that you are a guardian of the land and a peacemaker?'

'Friend Richard, I do not make peace in this Realm. Peace is your king's concern. I simply offer my counsel which warns of the disaster that will swallow you up if you do not agree to parley with Friend Hal.'

As the wizard let his words hang, the duke's fears stood revealed. His face flushed and his jaw clenched as it so often did when his thoughts turned to King Hal or his queen. Still he waved a dismissive hand towards the enemy's tents. 'It takes no wizard to see that those who serve the she-wolf have chosen to put their trust in a vain show of arms. Tell me, Crowmaster, what proof do you have of the queen's triumph if I decide not to talk with her husband?'

'Dudlea was poised to tell about her secret weapons—'

'Dudlea?' Lord Warrewyk exploded. 'He's nothing! There are no secret weapons! He was only trying to buy himself time with lies!'

Gwydion faced him down. 'And what if I have lately gained definite knowledge concerning the nature of these weapons?'

'Can they smash down walls such as these?' Lord Warrewyk scoffed.

Gwydion's hands produced a hard-to-see gesture in the air, ending with a snap of his fingers. 'One of them can sail over a wall as if it was not there at all.'

'He speaks once again of magic,' Lord Sarum said. 'Nothing he says may be proved.'

But the wizard shook his head. 'The queen's secret weapon does not rely on magic of any kind. Come, Willand. Let us withdraw a little way and allow our gracious host to talk with his friends.'

Will watched as the duke and his kinsmen looked to one another and deliberated. The duke put a mailed hand to his chin. Indecision weighed upon him heavily. Will knew that, as ever, Gwydion was knocking heads together with infinite care.

When at last the wizard judged the matter sufficiently debated he rejoined the duke. 'Will you not speak with the king, Richard? For the sake of the Realm, of all you love, and of all who love you?'

'How can I treat with Hal when that she-wolf uses him as her stool-servant? I do not see why I should oblige her. She wants only to have the fight over and done with. She knows that every day our forces glare at one another, hers must needs grow the weaker. Her army will bleed away. Ours, on the other hand, has nowhere to desert to. Therefore, let them come to us, cap-in-hand, to parley terms if they desire to undo what they have begun.'

Sarum and Warrewyk brayed with laughter at that. Their warrior hearts were lifted to see their leader continue blithe and unconcerned in the face of a fearsome and numerous enemy, and stand so solid against the subtle manoeuvrings of a wizard.

'Then that is settled,' Gwydion said, gathering in the vital point. 'I have your word that you do agree to meet in a parley.'

The duke gripped his ivory rod and spread his arm wide. 'Crowmaster, let me show you why I have such faith in our position. Do you see how well prepared we are? I have kept our town walls in good repair. We are well gated and strongly defended. Our flanks are covered by water. At our back stands my mighty castle. See there! Double trenches dug on our right. Lord Strange's good men have made a moat to protect our centre. And look where those parapets of timber are set above it – an archers' bank now stands there so that the enemy cannot charge suddenly upon us. A stream of death will pour down upon any fool, mounted or afoot, who dares to approach any of our breastworks. And greatest of all, see here – these are the pride of my lordly kinsman: my Lord Warrewyk's three bombards!'

'Ah, the bombards . . .' Gwydion allowed the hint of a scowl to show. Earlier he had pointed out the guns to Gort, saying, 'Those filthy rods of iron have the reek of eastern sorcery about them!'

'Meet my three spokesmen: "Trinovant", "Toune" and "Tom o' Linton"! They have mouths of fire.' The Earl Warrewyk offered his flat smile, then turned and called out, 'Master Gunner! Are we ready to speak to the foe?'

'Aye, we are, my lord!' The gunner, stocky and round as a powder barrel, swept off his leather hat and bowed his head.

'And what is the surprise you have for the queen's horsemen?'

The gunner grinned. 'These three are full-charged with nails and horseshoes and other pieces of sharp iron that will harvest the enemy by the bushel if they come near!'

Gwydion made a gesture the uninitiated would have seen as no more than a shrug of his robes, but he drew close to the duke and took him aside, his voice persuasive and low. 'Richard, I accept your pledge. What hostages do you care to exchange that are sufficient to guarantee your parley with the king? Give me their names.'

But now pride welled up in the duke's breast and he fought the subtle words. 'The time is . . . past when talking . . . can heal the wounds . . . the insults I have suffered . . .'

'But if mere words alone could make this great host retire from your walls, then would it not be worth an insult or two? Remember what I have told you,

> *'Beside Lugh's ford and the risen tower,*
> *By his word alone, a false king*
> *Shall drive his enemy the waters over,*
> *And the Lord of the West shall come home.'*

The duke's private struggle went on for a long moment. His glance fell upon his lordly captains, then he turned back to Gwydion and opened his hands in a broad gesture. 'It matters not to me. Let them come a-begging. Let them go away with their tails between their legs. We shall tell the she-wolf that if her people try to approach us in arms they will be taken off at the ankles by the reaper's blade!'

'Then give me a horse. I shall do as you have bid. I shall go now to see the king and speak with him in such terms that a parley cannot be avoided.'

The duke summoned an attendant who wore an expectant face as he rose from his bow. 'Give him whatever he wants!'

'Yes, your grace.'

Will watched as a good destrier was brought. Gwydion mounted up and galloped down the lane of grass that stood between the hosts. Clods flew up from the killing ground. It seemed to Will that the duke's words were correct – no easy approach to Ludford was possible, and any attack that came this way would fast become entrapped and put to a murderous rout.

And in the trap lies our best hope, he thought. For Ludford must seem to any experienced eye a very tough nut to crack. The queen has schooled her henchmen to hate Gwydion and to pour scorn on all he proposes, but still there should be enough cool heads among her retinue who understand the massacre that awaits them . . .

Will caught his thoughts and grounded them savagely. He was thinking like a lord, not like a wizard's helper. For all the strategies and preparations, the underlying trouble remained. He bent his mind to consider the battlestone, fizzing and fuming undisturbed in its pit. Wherever it was, it had brought this calamity. And it would drive coming events forward, no matter what the lords had planned and despite whatever game Gwydion chose to play.

The wizard returned within the hour and gave his report that the king had agreed. Duke Richard was not pleased, but he nodded all the same.

'That weaseling wizard!' Lord Sarum jeered. 'It's because they've found us so strong that they dare do no other now than flap their chins at us.'

The king's heralds came up with the six hostages that had been agreed from each side. They were exchanged, these sons of noblemen, and paraded in plain view under a guard of drawn blades. If treachery was attempted in the parley tent they would be slaughtered at a word. They sat in camp chairs, drinking and chatting among themselves as if in the secure knowledge that all would go well, but their faces were pale in the morning light and their thin laughter betrayed them.

The waiting among the soldiery was also tense. Will saw the

fear, the impatience, the grim whetting of daggers and the tightening of buckles by those convinced that the fighting must soon
come.

Will found himself approached by six troopers.

'Off with his coat!' one said, and took him by the shoulder.

'Who are you?' he said, instantly on guard.

'Who are we, he says! We do his grace's bidding, and we need
to have them rags off you.'

'Rags?' He threw the men off roughly, spat on his knuckles
and prepared himself for a fight.

'Now, then!' one of them said, grinning. 'No need for struggles! You're to be shaved, and your hair cut.'

'When Ludford Castle falls in a heap I will!' he warned them.
'Or it's a fight you've got!'

'It is to be done. We have our orders!' they cried.

'Well, I'm nobody's man. And I'll make you eat your orders
before I give up my braids!'

'Be easy there!' Gwydion called to him. 'Let them dress you
as they will. They know their business.'

'Dress me?' he said indignantly. 'Why should I?'

'Because I have a task for you, and you must look the part.'

'But my *braids*, Gwydion! By the moon and stars!'

'The braids will be no great loss. You have lost them before
and doubtless you will again.'

'Last time you called me a young savage for doing it!'

'That was not for what you did, but for the reasons you did
it.'

'And I suppose your subterfuges are a better reason!'

'Willand, be easy with the barber now. You can have your braids
or you can be a peacemaker. Make your choice.'

'Then hand me your secret knife, Gwydion,' he said, half out
of a wish to make the wizard pay a price also. 'If it's to be done,
it's better that it be done by me.'

The wizard drew forth the sheath that contained the precious
star-iron blade, and passed it across without a word.

Will let the duke's men seat him on a stool. The barber shrugged an apology as he watched Will lop off both braids in one sawing cut, then he set to bobbing Will's hair in lordly style. He shaved his cheeks and the back of his neck close, up as far as the tops of his ears. Then he was shown rich clothes and shoes of soft leather and dressed up as a minor knight's esquire, a proper junior member of the Ebor household.

'This is *ridiculous*!' he told the wizard. 'I feel like a . . . I feel like an idiot! You changed your own appearance back at the Plough, why couldn't you apply a magical disguise to me?'

'We must not condone the unnecessary use of magic.'

'*Unnecessary?*'

'You're to be attached to the duke's retinue. Now put this on and stop complaining.'

Will ignored the proffered scabbard of dark leather. There was a steel blade within. He said, 'After all you've warned against the carrying of steel? What's this in aid of, anyway?' For the sake of the disguise he allowed the sword to be girt on at his waist. 'Gwydion, will you answer me?'

'You're to come to the parley, of course. Everyone gives up their weapons before a royal audience. A great show is made of it, so you must have a blade to give up.' The wizard put a sly finger alongside his nose. 'Remember: eyes of a hawk, ears of a hare.'

Then he was gone.

The parley itself was in a great painted tent that had been hastily put up a bowshot and a half from the town walls and halfway between the facing armies. It was in a place that Gwydion had chosen, near a big oak tree that had not yet shed its leaves. It felt like a place of good aspect.

When the herald's signal told that all was ready, the duke's party rode out at an unhurried pace. There was a haggling with the heralds over the weapons. At first, the duke's party refused to recognize the custom and Gwydion had to intervene. Eventually a royal permission was issued concerning weapons, and each man was allowed to go armed with the symbol of his rank, but was to surrender his helmet and throat-guard.

Will managed to speak an indignant word to the wizard. 'What are you thinking of? Trying to broker a peace while the Ludford Stone is still in the ground? It's impossible.'

'I have learned an important lesson,' Gwydion said archly.

'What lesson?'

The wizard stooped near. 'That these battlestones contain a malicious intelligence that may be played at their own game!'

'What do you mean?'

'You will see.'

'I just hope you know what you're doing.'

'Trust me.'

'I always do – fool that I am.'

The parley tent was ruled by the formality of royal protocol, and it was decked like a throne room prepared for audience. Because the nobles of the duke's party had insisted on carrying broadsword and dagger, they were not allowed to approach the king's person beyond a double rope of red and gold which was strung six paces in front of a pair of high-backed chairs.

Will's eyes swept across the important men in the ranks opposite. Dozens of knights and squires and pages crowded to the rear, many with the badge of a white swan on their chest, or in enamelled pewter on a ribbon. Will wondered what it signified, for it was no badge that he recognized.

Royal attendants stood in a line, holding cushions on which sword and helm and gilded crown were set. Many of the noblemen present, Will knew, had fought at Verlamion, and thoughts of revenge clouded their faces. He watched the king as he took his place in one of the ornate thrones. He was sickly, pale-faced and with downcast eyes.

Beside him his queen, his consort and keeper, sat upon a throne of equal measure. Her blemishless, chalk-white face shone in the muted light of the tent. She was striking – dark eyes, raven hair, ruby lips, and clad all in crimson velvet. Her gloved hands glittered with gold rings, each set with a black diamond. And never far from her, Henry, Duke of Mells, stood proudly in his dark-burnished armour. On the far side also stood the king's generals, foremost among them the commander of his great host, Duke Humphrey of Rockingham, grim-faced, for his son had been slain at Verlamion by a Warrewyk arrow.

All wore the white swan device, and as Will came forward and his eyes reached further he found the reason; for there, in a child's seat or little boat, shaped into the likeness of a white swan, sat a sturdy lad of six years – the heir.

That's his badge, Will thought, imagining how this new fashion, this new way of showing loyalty, must have swept through the court. But he did not have long to think about it, for as his eyes left the heir his heart skipped a beat – the bearded brute nearby with fierce eyes and five yellow rings on his scarlet surcoat was the mad baron, the one whose murderous semblance had cut Will's arm off. He looked away before those crazy eyes latched onto his own, tried to steal a reassuring glance at Gwydion, but then thought better of it. His hand clutched at his arm, and he realized that it was no easy thing to set aside the power of illusion.

Wherever Will looked now it seemed that a new surprise lay in ambush for him. Over there, bold as brass, stood Lord Dudlea. He smirked at his erstwhile captors, enjoying the moment and eager to show off.

Will looked away again, hoping he would not be spotted. This time he fixed his eyes on the walls of the tent itself. Seen from inside, the painted canvas showed the heraldry and mottoes that adorned it as if in a looking glass. He tried to idle his mind, reading the crisply lettered words as they rippled gently in the breeze, blanking out what his heightened senses insisted on bringing to him. Even so, he could hear the barking of dogs in the distance. The smell of bruised grass was keen on the air. The play of sunlight passing through the branches of the big oak tree gave the tent a curious, dreamlike quality that paralleled the murderous undercurrents of the moment. The palms of Will's hands sweated. He caught hold of his thoughts as they began to slide – his mind's eye had glimpsed a mass of archers surrounding the tent, making ready to shoot a volley of arrows through the wavering canvas into unseen targets. It was clear nonsense, he knew, for how could archers mark their targets blindly? But all the same the fear was exact and inexplicable and hard to dispel. It seemed to have the force of premonition about it, or perhaps it was just the stone reaching out to him again in its eerie way.

By now the tent was half-filled with Duke Richard's henchmen. It was time for him to make his entry. At the king's command, the audience would begin. Duke Richard carried with him his customary rod of unicorn ivory. His men came forward gravely and, to Will's surprise, they approached the king immediately and knelt, as one, before him.

It was a gesture calculated to unsettle the queen and her advisors. Among the duke's retinue were Earl Sarum, Earl Warrewyk and the softly grunting Lord Strange. Seeing them, Will suddenly remembered Edward. He was not here. A chill ran down his back. Perhaps Edward had ridden out earlier, to be exchanged as one of the hostages. It was not impossible, given the importance of the parley.

Only now did Will see Elders of the Sightless Ones come in to accompany both parties. The robes of the two groups of Fellows were of different colours and cuts, and Will wondered if that was significant. Perhaps they were rival sects. Perhaps different chapter houses vied with one another in matters of influence. It was a question Will had never considered. The Fellows themselves gave little away, for their doings were arcane and their public face always as cold as alabaster.

Will's eyes darted back to the queen, and he felt again the pungency and ill-temper that emanated from her. It was worrying to realize that one misplaced word spoken now, one dagger produced in wrath, and a running fight would break out that would see them all dead. Will's toes, clad in their leather shoes, felt the muffled currents running in torrents through the earth nearby. His eyes settled once more on the king, and he recognized a man labouring under a spell.

Gwydion stood solemnly to one side, watching the opening formalities closely. The hoods of many of the Sightless Ones were turned to him, as if the Elders were gauging the wizard with some unnatural sense.

'Your king receives his loyal subjects in audience . . .' Though King Hal was near two-score years in age, his voice was eerie – part child's, part that of an old man. He spoke in short, stilted phrases and seemed not to know the meaning of what he said.

Duke Richard's eyes were steely as he returned the empty formulas that protocol demanded. He added, 'His grace's loyal duke, Richard of Ebor, humbly bids him welcome to this, his strong castle of Ludford. Yet he must enquire the reason so many have come hither, and ask why so great a host stands ready in arms . . .'

Will almost cried out then, for his wandering eye had recognized another face among the king's retinue. There, standing not far from Lord Dudlea, was one dressed in the style of a lord of the Blessed Isle. He wore trews and the *leine*, a belted shirt of linen, and a cloaked *feile*, or mantle, of black and moss-green chequered wool. He carried the two-handed sword slung at his back, and on his hand was a silver ring studded with a gem of glistering green.

Morann!

The loremaster kept a straight face but winked at Will, who could not help but show his surprise.

By the moon and stars! he thought. Gwydion must have planted him in the king's court as a spy. So that was the *errand* that couldn't wait.

The diplomatic exchanges went on.

'. . . and therefore, Sire, this duke must ask for what reason his kinsman was prevented from going upon his lawful way and was outrageously attacked upon Blow Heath by men whose loyalties have never . . .'

Will grew impatient with it. Everyone knew that the king was an empty shell who did little more than repeat lines whispered to him by his queen. But as Will changed his mind's focus a thrill of danger stabbed him without warning. His eyes moved to the dappled light that at first seemed no more than sunshine filtering through dying leaves. But now he saw something else. A strange rippling had started a little way behind the queen's throne. The light there scintillated and glistened like the fur of Pangur Ban when he walked in moonlight, like the hood of the old man at the Plough Inn who had once turned into Gwydion . . .

The more Will concentrated on the sparkling light the less he saw. He cautiously opened his mind to it, and then a dark shape began to spin together. It was horrible. A pang of terror ran to earth down his spine, raised all the hairs on his neck. A cautious glance at Gwydion showed that the wizard's attention was on the parley. No one but the queen suspected the figure that whispered behind the thrones. He knew with a hammering heart that it could only be Maskull.

Once before, Will's inborn talent had enabled him to penetrate Maskull's wiles. Years ago, at the royal hunting lodge of Clarendon, while Jarred, the king's conjuror, had juggled coloured fire in the air, Will's innocent eye had looked straight through Maskull's shrouding sorcery. His newborn sensitivity had emerged clean and keen, and had perceived Maskull shimmering like the spectre of Death.

That time, Will had not understood, but now he did, and the knowledge that Gwydion's great enemy was here unbeknown to him jolted him like a blow to the face. He stiffened, prompted by insistent warnings in his mind. He longed to kick off his borrowed shoes and run. Sweat ran down his freshly shaved neck and prickled under his collar. He felt smotheringly hot under the lordly velvets. He dared not look back towards the sorcerer. He could not stop the visions flooding back of the dreadful time when Maskull had raised him up in magical fire to roast him and make him scream high above the Giant's Ring. He swallowed, resisting an overpowering desire to wipe away a drop of sweat that had started down from his hairline. Then his left hand strayed to his sword, and he grasped the counterweight at the end of the hilt.

It was the worst thing he could have done. Instantly two dozen eyes snapped towards him.

He took his hand away again, very slowly. That wasn't very clever, he told himself. What if Maskull had seen? What if he'd recognized you?

He noted the questioning look from Morann as all his senses began to rage and his face paled. He could say nothing, could offer no warning to Gwydion as his courage shrivelled. What was preventing Maskull from acting? Surely, he could strike here and now with impunity. All it would take would be a surprise bolt of purple fire – Gwydion, Duke Richard and all his henchmen would be burned. Even the troublesome duke's heir would die. And all at the cost of a few young hostages who had no more value to a sorcerer than wood lice. What was he waiting for?

But for all Maskull's advantage, he did nothing. The meaningless lordly talk went on, back and forth, counted against a thousand of Will's heartbeats. He ignored the high-flown words, and instead he let Morann's steady gaze bolster him until he could get a grip on his panic.

Maskull, veiled in invisibility, remained occupied behind the queen's throne. His suggestions were spoken to the severe beauty who in turn muttered replies for the king to speak aloud. Slowly, Will began to gather together the shreds of his calm. He forced himself to look at the king whenever he spoke, and to keep his glances natural. He closed his mind to the tantalizing ripples that tore the air near the thrones, and bit by bit the sorcerer's ghastly shroud repaired itself under his gaze.

'. . . therefore, Duke Richard of Ebor, hear our solemn promise. We invite you to come again into our royal presence at the hour of terce upon the morrow, and here receive at our hand all the guarantees that you ask of us.'

No! Will wanted to shout out. Don't agree to that. Don't pledge your word to come here a second time.

But he could not speak. He watched, dumbly unable to intervene, as the duke made his promise. Richard of Ebor gave his word that he would show himself before the king again tomorrow. And then the parley was done.

You must say something, Will told himself. But his throat was as dry as dust. You must warn Gwydion. And he must warn the duke. The king is not speaking in good faith. Maskull is here, and we're all caught up in a deadly trap!

That the duke's party rode back to the castle in good order and in safety was Gwydion's doing. The wizard kept Will's mouth closed until they had crossed the moat and the inner ward and had hurried to Gort's rooms.

Neither Gort nor Willow were there as the spells began to fall away from Will's jaw. But they did not fall fast enough and he slammed the door behind him in frustration. 'Mmmmmmmmmmh!'

Gwydion seized him angrily. 'What are you trying to do, you young fool? Did you mean to bring down the whole negotiation? Did you not see how delicately things were balanced?'

'Gwydion!' Will whispered fiercely as soon as the spell released his throat. 'You don't understand! *He* was here! In person! In the tent!'

The wizard started as the truth slammed home. He let go of Will's shoulders. 'Maskull? *Maskull* was in the parley tent?'

'That's what I was trying to tell you when you muted me!'

Gwydion stared, shocked. He seemed unable to believe it, and shook his head. 'This cannot be. It was some kind of falsehood. You were suffering from an emanation of the Ludford Stone. It was a *vision!*'

'It was no vision, Gwydion, I swear it! You must believe that! Maskull is here!'

The wizard sat down, his face grimmer than Will had ever seen it. 'This changes much that I had planned. Truly he must have bathed in the Spring of Celamon . . .'

'He must have had a reason not to blast us all where we stood – though I really can't see it!'

Gwydion's brow knotted. 'He is at pains to remain hidden because he believes I am, as yet, unaware of his return. He does not know I was called by you to witness the destruction of Little Slaughter. He does not know that I found the door through which he emerged from the Realm Below.'

'You did *that*?' Will asked, astonished.

'We both did, for you were there, Willand. You watched me examine the broken door.'

'I don't remember any broken door . . .'

'Come, now! The gold vault under the ruined chapter house. The one we visited near Nadderstone.'

'That?' Will recalled the twisted iron that had barred the way into the dark chasm beyond, and the dank airs that had risen up from the hole. The smell had been redolent of a whole dark world down below.

Gwydion put his face in his hands momentarily. 'Those bars were torn apart by Maskull's magic. The Fellows must have been surprised, though far from pleased I imagine, to find one such as he appearing in the bowels of their house.'

'Maybe that's the real reason Isnar decided to pull the chapter house down.'

'We shall never know.'

Will's mind was spinning. 'You say Maskull didn't begin a fight in the tent because he didn't want to show himself to you. But what would that matter if a surprise attack had killed everyone who stood in his way?'

Gwydion's eyes were half-lidded. 'A surprise attack such as you describe could not have succeeded.'

'Why not?'

'Because it would not have killed me. I possess many charms against Maskull's array of magical weapons.'

'They didn't save you when you duelled with him at the Giant's Ring.'

'A well-prepared attack was made against me at the Giant's Ring, but even that would not have killed me, only denied me form and therefore delayed me. Also—' The wizard motioned Will to sit down. 'Also, Maskull knows that a violent stroke such as you suggest would not have the desired effect in the long run.'

Will rested his weight on the table's edge. 'You'd better explain.'

'Maskull believes he has found a way to live forever. He was once like me, one of the Ogdoad. You know that, well enough, but you still do not fully understand what it means. We are not immortal, Will. We live only so long as there is enough magic remaining in the world to sustain us. That is why our numbers have declined as the Ages have declined.'

'You make it sound as if there's a great hole in the world through which all the magic is escaping.'

'You are not so far from the truth in your guess. However, the task of the Ogdoad has always been to act as pathfinders for men. It is our job to bring about the best of all possible futures as magic inevitably leaves the world unprotected. In these latter days Maskull turned against the Old Ways. By the time Semias made his choice, it had become clear to Maskull that he would have to take the long road to the Far North himself and leave me to become the last phantarch. He cast about for another way until he had found the means to switch the fate of the world onto a new path. This, he hopes, will bring it to the destination he desires. He intends to guide the world along that path, though it will bring the Old Ways to final ruin. He cares not that there will in consequence be war lasting five hundred years. He cares not that every man who lives in the world will be forced to suffer for his sake. Such is the blinding power of his one great idea that he cares only to reach the end that he has set his heart upon.'

Gwydion stood up and tugged his robe higher across his shoulders, signalling that there was no more time to talk. 'It is almost the hour of noon. You must open your mind as you have never opened it before, Willand. You must find the Ludford battlestone, and I must deal with it before it can unleash the attack that Maskull so desires.'

'I'm doing my best,' Will said, more frustrated than ever. 'But what's to be done about Maskull?'

Gwydion looked sideways, his glance deadly dark. 'Do not spend any part of your mind on him. Do not be tempted to game with him either. Leave him for me to deal with. In the same way that he has sought to keep me in the dark about his return, so we must keep secret our own knowledge about him. Fear not! He does not know who you are. You are under my protection and he cannot recognize you.'

'And what about the faceless one who tried to kill me? The one you said was called Chlu, the Dark Child. You said he was Maskull's agent.'

'Chlu is Maskull's *instrument*, not his agent. The difference is important. Maskull has, by some as-yet-unknown means, discovered Chlu and set him at large in the knowledge that he will try to find you. Chlu, he believes, has reasons of his own to want to do that. He is under no compulsion.'

Will shuddered and stood up. 'I don't know why this Chlu should want to murder me. I've done him no harm. I don't even know who he is.'

'And yet, though you have looked upon his face, you still cannot remember it.'

Will shook his head. It was true. Try as he might, he could not call the Dark Child's face to mind.

'You say you have done Chlu no harm, but perhaps the harm he fears from you will be done in the future.'

Will snorted. 'Well that's a fine thing, if a man may be attacked because of what he *might* do one day!'

But Gwydion chose to steer the discussion another way.

'Whatever the case, there is a strong compulsion at work. But I think that Chlu is not a willing sorcerer's slave. Indeed, he is quite unsuited to the task that has been set for him. If I know Maskull, he will have bound Chlu upon a magical chain before letting him out into the world. One day soon, I think, he will try to reel him in and begin to wring the truth from him about you. Fortunately, that day has not yet come – or you would not be standing here.'

Will numbly followed the wizard into the innermost ward. But as Gwydion marched away to the Round House, Will lingered, and as soon as he was alone he put his hands to his temples, opening his mind recklessly wide and with no regard for the moon's phase.

It felt like stepping off the battlements of the keep with only a hope that thin air would support him. A terrible fear flashed through him and began to wrestle with his spirit for possession of his mind. It was a wave of such sudden despair that it took him by surprise. It punished him for his stupidity, and revealed nothing in return. Once again, there was no direction in what he saw, only a perplexing maze, a thousand impressions, glancing, shattering, splintering, lost like drops in a fountain . . .

'It's the stone! It's the stone! It's the stone!' He shouted at the sky, feeling exultation and fear in equal measure. 'It's here!'

He closed his mind sharply. Reality coalesced like figures emerging from a fog. Understanding resolved itself into five senses again. He spat thickly, his eyes filled. He felt close to vomiting as he listened to his own yells still echoing off the high walls. Cooks and bakers and serving folk gathered in a knot by the kitchen door, looking at him anxiously, driven to silence by his raving.

'What are you looking at?' he demanded.

'Sir?' said one of the brewhouse boys, seeing the lordly style in which Will's hair was now cut and the clothes that had been borrowed for him from Edward. 'Sir . . . please . . .'

When Will looked closely at them he realized their faces were white and ghastly. Then one of them, a young woman, had the courage to say, 'Sir, we would have our Wortmaster come to us. Do you know where he is?'

'Gort? He's gone to – auuugh!' And the filthy smell hit him, and he drew away for fear he would retch. 'By the moon and stars . . . *what's that?*'

He saw their fear. They were going against the direct order of their lord in making the complaint, but they had to tell someone of the horror they had found.

'Sir, it's the well. It's happened again, and we can't bear it no more. Look!'

The head cook lifted a pail and poured blood out of it. It splashed crimson across the cobbles.

'Bring ropes and lifting tackle!' he told them. 'Take me to the well! And fetch the wizard too!'

CHAPTER TWENTY-TWO

RAW MEAT

'There's sometimes poisoned air down deep wells,' Gort said. 'Why, at Castle Beaston up by the city of Caster, there's the deepest well in all the Realm—'

'Thank you, Wortmaster,' Will said, 'but I'd rather not hear about Castle Beaston just now, if you don't mind.' He watched the smith hammering on the rail that ran round the well. A section of it had already been pulled away and part of the winding mechanism taken down.

As Will prepared to climb into the stinking hole, he tested the loop of rope on which he would have to make the journey. It was thick, the same rope that had been unwound from the portcullis drum under Gwydion's supervision a few days before. Strong spells had been laid on each of the strands in turn, and a loop big enough to hang a man had been expertly whipped into its end. A second rope, almost identical to the first, had also been prepared. Now a dozen of Jackhald's steadiest men were gathered in the innermost ward. They had been told to act closely on the wizard's instructions.

Gwydion questioned Gort about the depth of water that usually stood in the well.

'Weeds and worts! Why, it goes up and down with the seasons.

Knee-deep in a dry summer, then up to a fathom. Or more at times. With the weather we've had? Oh, no further than Will's handsome new haircut, I'd say. Enough to drown him in at any rate, hey?'

'Thank you for that kind thought, Wortmaster,' Will said.

Jackhald urged the wizard, 'Let me send one of my lads down. It's our job when all's said and done. Last time—'

'This time's different,' Will said shortly.

When Jackhald shook his head and asked why, Gwydion muttered over his shoulder, 'Because this time we are not looking for a dead sheep. It would not matter who you sent down, they would not come up again.'

That was enough for Jackhald. He cast a glance at Will and fell silent. Will was already taking off his belt and pouch. He handed them to Gort, then stripped off his borrowed finery and pulled his shirt over his head.

Gwydion attached a second rope to the first and made it fast, then Will climbed over the stone lip of the well, fitted his left foot into the loop, and the lowering began.

He took with him no lantern, but descended the twenty or more fathoms in a blaze of blue magelight sent down from above. He was naked except for the greenstone talisman that hung at his neck. He put a linen pad to his nose and mouth that had been treated with some aromatic drops of Gort's devising, meant to combat the stench. It worked after a fashion, but it could not fully disguise the foulness of the air that wafted up from the butcher's sewer below.

For the first fathom or so, the inner part of the well-head was round and smooth. It was made of dressed stones neatly fitted by masons. Then, for another couple of fathoms, the walls were of rough stones laid upon one another without mortar like a country wall. Below that, the well was hewn from the red sandstone ridge on which the castle stood.

Will felt the air on his bare skin growing cooler. To take his mind off the steadily worsening stench, he fixed his thoughts on a strong memory of bumble bees flying between the long stalks of purple lavender that grew in his garden at home. It was a pleasantly distracting thought, but part of his mind remained watchful and aware that he must not let himself drift into a daydream. His eyes saw chisel marks slipping by, marks that were two or three hundred years old, marks from the well's first making, and among them magical sigils that had been carved here by some practitioner of old. One of the marks, he saw, was to ensure the purity of the water. Another was set to discourage water drakes from infesting the well. The first of them crumbled at his touch.

At least drakes are one danger I won't be facing, he thought wryly as he bounced a little lower, twisting slowly on the rope. A sudden, vivid image came to him – he imagined a gigantic spider letting itself down on a thread above him. Cautiously he forced his mind tight closed, countering the stone in case it was already probing his fears. He found his hand straying to check the talisman on its thong. As ever, it made him feel better to touch it with his fingers, but it seemed to be alive with warnings now.

As he saw the surface of the water below rising up to meet him, he took the pad from his mouth and shouted for the rope team to hold. His order was relayed too quickly and he stopped too soon. Echoes returned, and he hung for a silent moment in that unbearable reek, suspended a little way above the surface. He shaded his eyes briefly from the blinding brightness of blue light shining from above and reflected from below. There, almost beside him and lying at an angle against the side of the well, was the battlestone.

Its top stuck out of the bloody water. Magelight cast sharp shadows and its colour turned the oozing blood that seeped from the stone's surface black. Will carefully untied the second rope and tugged on it until it began to pay out. Bracing his right foot against the wall, he bent forward ready to pass the rope behind the stone.

'That's enough! Stop!'

There was a delay. Echoes filled the shaft. But then the rope jerked to a halt. The cloying stink seemed to intensify suddenly, driving him to want to get out of the narrow space. A sudden lightheadedness assailed him as he fought the impulse, and he thought he was going to faint. He straightened, felt his knees buckling. Now he was sure he was going to faint. He just had time to realize the danger he was in when his foot slid out of the loop. He plunged down into the cold slime below.

Every part of his skin crawled with horror as his head went under. He thrashed, then felt slippery stones under his feet, and when he pushed against them his head broke the surface again, and he gasped for breath.

The shaft was full of noise, anxious shouts folded back on themselves until they were meaningless.

Fetid air rushed into his lungs, but the cold splash had brought him out of the faint into which he had been falling. He wiped his face.

'Nearly . . . but not quite!' he told the stone fiercely, then slammed his mind closed again.

He scooped more of the stinking blood from his eyes and looked up. The blue light glared back unwaveringly as the rope loop snaked and dangled like a noose a few feet above his head. He jumped for it, but it was beyond his grasp.

Gwydion shouted a question, but again its meaning was lost in echoes. He called back and heard his words lose themselves too. He was chin deep, his arms raised, fingers dripping blood. Then, slowly, something broke the surface next to him. It thrashed, twisted.

He cried out in fear. But the fear immediately dissolved when he realized what had come to the surface. It was not the snout of some fierce water drake, but the end of the second rope that had dropped into the water in the stone's shadow.

As relief broke inside him, he drew on his courage and began to convince himself that he could counter the stone's best efforts. He tied the second rope round it, tried his full strength against the bowstring knot that Gwydion had told him to put in it, then he shouted up the shaft again for them to ease the loop on which he would ride to the surface a little lower.

Once again his message was garbled by echoes.

Just a few feet more . . .

Still the loop hung too high for him to reach. There was nothing for it but to climb up the stone itself, but it was slick with blood. His fingers and toes found a purchase on the spiral figures that were carved on its sides, but as soon as he laid hands on them his mind filled with the coldness of dead flesh. He almost lost his grip, but his hand groped for the loop, touched. Once he had grabbed it he was able to steady himself. As the rope stretched under his weight, he wiped his hands on the dry, fibrous twists and set his mind as firmly as he could on imagining the journey back.

'Pull!' he shouted.

As the echoes began to die away, the loop jerked under his foot and he began to rise up the shaft half a fathom at a time. It was a long, long ride. When he came near to the surface the magelight sputtered then burned out. He saw Gwydion looking down anxiously. The wizard dragged him bodily out over the lip of the well, where he slid onto the floor of the kitchens, looking like some strange newborn thing.

'Are you hurt?' Gort cried.

The draught of good air made Will retch. He tried to rise to his feet, but skidded in the blood he had puddled on the stone flags. Now that it was over the horror of it hit him.

'What happened?' Gwydion demanded.

Gort splashed a bucket of water at him.

Will spat. He was shaking. 'Never mind me. Pull the stone out, Gwydion. Do it quickly! But don't break the rope or drop it. Whatever happens, I can't go down there again!'

The men began to haul on the second rope. This time, the effort they made was much greater. When the stone appeared in the mouth of the well Gwydion would not let anyone approach it. The rope was tied off securely, and Jackhald's men were warned away. Then a stout wooden beam was lifted up and together Gwydion, Will and the Wortmaster levered the stone up and out of the well-head. It crashed heavily to the floor, scraping the flags as they hauled it like a sled into the brewhouse. Gwydion insisted they lift it upright as quickly as they could.

The wizard stood back, his gestures looping loose rings of magical influence over the stone. Will pressed another of Gort's kerchiefs perfumed with honeysuckle and woodruff to his nose as he ran his eyes over the moist stone. The vile stink in the brewhouse doubled and redoubled, though it seemed to Will to be as sweet as mountain air compared to the reek down below.

'We're lucky it wasn't cracked in two by the fall!' Will gasped.

Gwydion said, 'The question is: how did it get into the well? Was it always here? And if so, what effect must its malevolence have had on the castle and those who have dwelt here?'

'It was thrown down,' Will told him. 'And recently.'

Gwydion looked more closely at the stone. It was the colour of raw meat. Blood wept from it continuously and soon began to pool on the floor. There was damage to its corners where it had rattled down the well and struck the bottom. The wounds oozed pus like half-healed flesh.

'Where are my clothes?' Will asked. When he went to the door he saw serving folk loitering in the innermost ward. He stared back, drenched in blood and slime, and looking like a man who had been flayed alive. Cries went up at the sight of him.

He allowed Jackhald to lead him to a corner of the ward where he washed in water pouring from the cisterns. Will's clothes were brought, but as he put them on and began to towel his hair he felt fresh pangs begin to assail him.

The dislocated stone was awakening by degrees, slyly, just as the Blow Stone had awakened, and with the same inevitability. Maybe the lorc was learning to counter the attacks they were making on it. Maybe the stone had read their method and knew their minds, maybe it had read their minds and now knew their method. But how could that be so? For they had none.

He laughed humourlessly, then stopped, abrupt.

The moon was swinging higher and the Ludford madness was returning. He knew he could fight it for a while, but he would need help tonight. Now that the stone had been raised there would have to be a confrontation.

The nauseous wave passed. Lucid clarity settled on him. Sharp thoughts pricked his mind. He called Jackhald to him. 'I want to speak with the man who went down the well before me, the one who pulled the dead sheep out.'

Jackhald's eyes narrowed. 'Why?'

'Gwydion needs to prove how the stone came into the well, and how long it's been there.'

A man was brought. He was dirty and his huge jaw was unshaven. He eyed Will suspiciously. 'Pooh! Master, it stank worse than a dunny down there.'

'This one's a waster and a whiner, and none too bright at that.'

'Jackhald, please . . .' Will turned to the man. 'What's your name?'

'Edwold, Master. But let another man go down there this time, for I won't!'

'Edwold, I don't want to send you down the well. Just tell me what you saw down there.'

Edwold stared blankly. 'Nothing.'

'Nothing at all?' Will rubbed his chin. 'Was there no water?'

'Ar. Water. 'Tis a well.'

'Was there . . . was there by any chance a large stone? Like this?' He drew a shape in the air.

Edwold grinned toothily. 'Ar! But 'twas bigger by twice than what you're showing there.'

'That's right.'

Jackhald growled. 'You said nothing before about no stone.'

'I said naught about it, for 'twas but a stone!' Edwold looked from face to face, fearing he was about to be blamed for something he thought was no fault of his. He turned to Will. 'Master, I thought it no great matter for a stone to be down a well. I was sent down to hook out a sheep, was I not?'

Jackhald growled. 'What you mean is, you said naught about any stone because you was afeared of being sent down again to fish it out!'

'Calmly, Jackhald.' Will spoke again to Edwold. 'Just tell me all about the stone and how it got there.'

'There's been a lot of peculiar goings on since the new people come here,' Edwold said darkly. 'The accursed lord come here with a dozen men in his company to the outer gate a few nights back. He starts banging to be let in. We opens up to him and we sees who it is right well.'

'Accursed lord? You mean Lord Strange?'

'Ar! Says he's come to speak with his grace, so we lets him in. And why not? For we all knows the Hogshead for who he is, and 'twern't none other, eh?'

Will smiled encouragingly at him. 'Go on.'

'Well, then, see, there's these dozen liverymen of his comes in carrying something big.' He spread his arms vaguely. 'Three men goes before it. And three men goes behind it. And three goes upon either side, like it's a coffin maybe with a dead man inside. But 'taint no dead man. I sees what it is – no more than a big, carven stone, and all muddy like.'

'The truth of it now!' Jackhald said angrily.

Will went on. 'You mean, it looked freshly taken out of the ground?'

'Ar. That's it.'

'And then?'

'Well . . . that's all. Except Dorric. He's the second gateman. He tells me next day that the Hogshead's men happened upon that stone in the earth while they was digging trenches out yonder.' He pointed towards the river.

'Did you know that he'd put it down the well?'

'Not I! I swear it!'

'Truly, now!' Jackhald demanded, and threatened a blow at Edwold.

'Only yesterday did I know that! Maybe I did know before, but I weren't like to speak of it to nobody. I heard it were a magic stone, see? Like the one that done the healing after the battle. Dorric, he says the Hogshead's men hid the stone down the well on the say-so that it would henceforth give good ale in place of water.'

Jackhald nodded with grim satisfaction. 'Now we're coming to it!'

Will let out a gasp of exasperation. 'Is that what Lord Strange's men gave the servants to believe?'

'Ar.'

'And that's why nobody spoke much of it.'

'It seemed like his grace the duke knew, and that Lord Strange's promises would come very well to pass.'

'And no one dared say anything after the duke drank blood.'

'Ale. That was the promise. Though, by the stink of it, it's not much like any ale that I ever tasted.'

Will dismissed Edwold and when Jackhald had taken the gateman away, he steeled himself to return to the foul brewhouse. Gwydion was treading lightly, dancing binding spells about the stone. Will, knowing he must not interrupt the sequence, waited silently for the wizard's acknowledgment.

'Well?'

'It seems Lord Strange's mattock-men found it while digging entrenchments along the banks of the Theam. He took secret possession of it, had it brought here days ago. It was put there before Lord Dudlea put the sheep down.'

Gwydion's lips pursed. 'Oh, but this is bad news indeed. For Lord Strange is a weakling spirit, a man of too-pliant loyalties. If he has engaged with the stone then—'

Will waited for the wizard to finish, but he did not. 'What is it?'

Gwydion put up his hand as if waving away an unworthy

thought. 'Only that a mind such as his would be driven to *treachery.'*

Will's thoughts crystallized as he recalled the vile dream that he had had in which a large black slug had come out of the Blow Stone and crawled up Lord Strange's nostril. In the clean light of day he had shaken the horror of that dream off and forgotten it, but now he realized he should not have done so without first questioning its meaning. Perhaps that had been the Blow Stone's gift to him – its way of telling him what would happen with its successor.

He said, 'When Willow was a young girl she lived close by Lord Strange's tower in Wychwoode. She told me how little respect his foresters had for him, how he always blames others for his own shortcomings. I myself have seen how all along he's failed to heed your warnings. I fear for us all if the battlestone has whispered in his ear.'

'It is an odd flag that turns about on its flagpole and thereby causes the very wind to change direction!'

Gwydion stroked his beard. He seemed about to say something else when the castle chimes clanged out, sounding the first hour of the afternoon. Instead of replying, he waved Will away, turned and went to stand by the window, and when Will ignored the dismissal, he said, 'Willand, I would be grateful if you would leave me alone for a while.'

Something in Gwydion's tone alarmed Will, but he began to do as he was asked. He saw that as soon as the brewhouse door was closed, the wizard would begin the hazardous business of draining the stone. It gnawed on Will that he no longer trusted the power of Gwydion's binding spells. That bloody day on Blow Heath, his failure had been made plain. He had not even been able to contain the harm of a battlestone that was active and ready, and to draw one out was a vastly more dangerous undertaking.

'I ought to help,' he said.

Gwydion shook his head. 'It will be best if you sent Gort here and then left matters to us.'

'Gwydion, I—'

'Go to your wife and child, Willand! Be with them in this dark hour. There is nothing more for you to do here!'

The snub burned. Having found the stone and brought it up, it seemed his usefulness was at an end, but he bowed his head obediently and withdrew. As he emerged again into the inner-most ward he quailed at the gamble Gwydion was taking. The destruction that would be wrought inside the castle and the town if he failed would be tremendous. It seemed suddenly to be a desperate gesture, the act of a wizard whose powers were failing, whose time was nearing its end.

Will found Gort, who asked for Jackhald to stand a guard on the brewhouse door.

'Where are Willow and Bethe?' he asked.

Gort looked over his shoulder. 'They're indoors. Shall I fetch them out?'

'No, leave them be.' Will fingered the talisman at his neck. The green stone was smooth under his fingers. He looked long and hard at the mark – three triangles set one within another. Gort gathered up a bundle of charms and headed for the brewhouse.

'If only Morann had left them at home,' Will muttered. Lightheadedness ghosted through him again. It was dreadful to know that so fearsome an array of enemies were so close at hand and all means of escape now blocked. 'As it turned out, Gwydion was right – they would have been much safer in the Vale.'

CHAPTER TWENTY-THREE

THE BLOOD STONE

D espite the agreement to parley the next day, the king's army was being readied to launch an attack. All afternoon, drums had been beaten and banners ridden up and down the lines, provoking the enemy with brave defiance. Will walked the circuit of the town walls with Willow and his daughter. He carried Bethe and found her weight in his arms a great comfort.

In the distance, across the fields, men in red livery guarded the banks of the River Theam and the postern gate that was the back door of the castle. He watched a detachment of them carrying a log up the slope towards the castle. Some wore the badge of the white bear, but others wore on their chests the silver lions of John, Lord Strange.

'Strange by name, and strange by nature,' Willow said. 'That's the best they used to say of old Hogshead. My father told me it was a stolen book of magic that first got him into trouble. He meddled where he shouldn't have.'

'That doesn't surprise me.'

Will recalled the shelf of books that had belonged to Lord Strange. There had been among them a bestiary – a book of animals – in which an unknown hand had written spells. Now Will realized where those jottings had come from. Lord Strange must have copied them from a 'key', a true book of magic. He had probably not known at the time that every key that was ever made was protected by ferocious spells set to trap those who had no business looking at them. 'I wonder where he got the key, and what kind of a spell it was that afflicted him?'

Willow laughed humourlessly. 'I'd say it was likely the girl he jilted. She suffered most from his ambitions. She must have taken her revenge on him, though it cost her her mortal form in the end.'

'Gwydion always told me it was Maskull's doing – that the Hogshead was made as a yardstick against which Maskull might measure the state of corruption of the Realm. Perhaps Gwydion has got it all wrong.'

Will's gaze wandered along the earthworks where great numbers of Duke Richard's archers and men-at-arms were disposed. They were enjoying the autumn sunshine as if it was their last chance.

'What'll happen if he tries to drain the stone and fails?' Willow asked.

'Then the harm that lies within it will escape. Unless it's prevented, such harm can come together in a demonic form that spends itself viciously in the world. Such was the emanation that chased Gwydion and me halfway across the Realm the night before the battle at Verlamion. Had we not lured it after us, who knows what destruction it would have wrought?'

The castle clock chimed the sixth hour. A grey dusk had begun to gather. As Will spoke, movements caught his eye and he thought there was something not quite right about Lord Strange's men. It was as if a whispered word was passing among them from man to man. Those who heard it picked up their weapons and put on their kettle hats and went about fully equipped, despite the warmth of the day. If they had been warned of an attack, why was the news not being carried to the duke's men?

Willow daintily wiped her daughter's mouth. 'And if Master Gwydion *doesn't* try to drain the stone?'

Will's eyes remained fixed on the men dressed in Lord Strange's livery colours. There were three thousand or more of them, and they all seemed to be stirring at once. 'If the battlestone works out its destiny on the field, then the queen's host will attack and many thousands will die here.'

He hung his head and breathed deep, knowing that he must not tempt fate while he was within reach of the Blood Stone's influence. He could feel uncomfortable thoughts creeping around him like wolves around a dying man. Already his mind was turning to face the ordeal ahead. When he looked to Willow he saw her expression was desolate. She asked, 'When will we know if Master Gwydion has succeeded?'

'Only when some woeful horror bursts from the inner ward with Gort held in its jaws.'

'Oh, don't say that!'

She was right to warn him. He stroked her hair. 'Gwydion won't begin until nightfall. I'm sure he'll come striding from the brewhouse in triumph come first light and tell the world there's nothing more to fear from the infamous Blood Stone.' But that sounded too much like empty bluster – another way of tempting fate. He added lamely, 'I suppose we'd better keep our fingers crossed, eh?'

She bit her lip. 'Can I do anything?'

'Tonight will be hard. Take Bethe to secure quarters and stay with her. Lady Cicely will not begrudge you that.'

She saw how deeply it pained him to feel he might be a danger to his own daughter. 'Poor Will,' she said. 'I'll see you through it.'

He took her hand. 'I'll be all right. I'd better go now.'

Bethe began to mewl.

'Hush, now,' Willow said, taking her from her father. She began a song to lull her daughter back to sleep.

> *'Butterfly, butterfly,*
> *Where do you go?*
> *When the sun shines bright,*
> *And the rose buds grow . . .*

'Butterfly, butterfly,
Where do you sleep?
When the sun does down,
In the shadows deep . . .'

As her soft words drifted on the air, they held him and he did
not want to leave. He began to engage his thoughts and feelings,
tried to disentangle his real fears from the effects of the stone.
No matter what happened, tonight was going to be miserable –
he must prepare for it as rigorously as possible. He did not want
to worry Willow any more than he already had, but it seemed to
him that Gwydion had taken an unnecessarily long time to prepare
the Blood Stone for draining. All along, he had been behaving
oddly towards the stone.

As they headed for the steps he watched the men in red who
were ranged below the walls. A powerful conviction suddenly hit
him and he ran back to his wife. He said, 'I'm sure Lord Strange's
men are getting ready to make a run for it.'

'What?'

'I think they're going to go across to the queen's side. Look at
them!'

Willow followed his gaze. She watched the men closely for a
few moments, then looked to him. 'You're right. They're all waiting
for a signal from him. What shall we do?'

'If Lord Strange goes over it'll mean disaster for the duke. I
must warn Gwydion right away!' He dashed off.

'What about us?'

'Take Bethe. Find Lady Cicely, and stay as close to her as you
can.'

He drew a deep breath and opened the brewhouse door, but still
the stench hit him like a wall. The battlestone was in the middle
of the room exactly as he had seen it last. Blood still seeped from
it as if from grazed flesh. Gwydion was standing a little apart
from it, by one of the great mash vats. He was unmoving, deep

in thought. Will waited with a sinking heart, anxious not to disturb him, but Gwydion said, 'I have been waiting for you.'

'Waiting? What do you mean?'

The wizard turned and faced him, a curious half-smile on his lips. 'You have come to tell me that the stone must have whispered into Lord Strange's ear after all. That he is about to turn his coat and lead all his men over to the enemy. You are going to say that his treachery will leave a great gap in the middle of the duke's defences. A hole that cannot possibly be closed up.'

Will stared. 'Why . . . yes.'

Gwydion laughed. 'Oh, Willand . . . forgive me. It was the only way.'

There was a noise outside. The sound of many feet running through the inner ward. Trumpets sounded. There was shouting and the clopping of hooves on stone. It sounded like many men were entering the castle.

'What's that?' Will asked anxiously.

'Fear not, Willand, they are the duke's own loyal men.' Gwydion said it with a serenity that Will thought did not sit well with the moment.

'But—'

The wizard looked out at the courtyard. 'Lord Strange's treachery has put them in a fine panic. Gort has already advised Richard to fly and await a better day. That is, I think, what he will do.'

Will stared at the stone as it quivered and seeped pathetically. 'Gwydion, you've not even begun trying to drain the stone. You've been with it for hours, and apart from a few binding spells you've cast nothing.' He seized the wizard's shoulders, concerned for him. 'What's the matter with you? Have you lost your mind?'

Gwydion did not turn away from the window. 'They are running around like ants. Do not worry. Leave me. Go and do what must be done for your family.'

Will hesitated. The wizard's unnatural calm unsettled him

mightily, but he glanced at the repellent stone and stood his ground. 'No, Gwydion, I won't leave. Not until I get a proper answer. The moon's going to rise in less than an hour. If you won't try to drain the stone, then I'll have to.'

Gwydion shrugged and said, 'You are a kind man, Willand. But in matters of high deception, kindness is often blindness. I did not drain the stone *because my plan depended upon it*.'

'*What plan?*' The hairs stood up on the back of Will's neck.

'Harm used against harm, do you see? I have made the offer of an easy way out. I have been permitting the stone to use Lord Strange as it would.'

Will's shoulders fell. 'You've done *what?*'

'I could not stop it, so instead of trying to drain it I decided to allow it to spend its power – long enough, at any rate, for Lord Strange to fall deeply under its influence.'

Will threw his hands wide in appeal. 'But why? Surely that plays exactly to the stone's purpose! You've helped it to do what it wants!'

'I have. But this time what it wants works to our favour. Lord Strange's betrayal has made it wholly impossible for Richard to remain here in defence of Ludford. Listen to the verse the Blow Stone gave us:

> '*By Lugh's ford and the risen tower,*
> *By his word alone, a false king*
> *Shall drive his enemy the waters over,*
> *And the Lord of the West shall come home.*

'And so it has come to pass! Hearken to those flying feet! This castle will fall, not after a battle, but after a parley! The word alone of a false king – King Hal – shall drive the Lord of the West across the seas and into the Blessed Isle!'

'You mean you've delayed the draining just to ensure the prophecy comes true?' Will shouted. 'Surely that's against every rede of magic. If that's what you've done, then we're doomed!'

'We?' Gwydion said. 'How many times must I tell you – our aim is not the victory of either side in this shabby little war.'

'I know that! It's peace we're fighting for!'

'Oh, it is more than peace. It is the winning of the best of all possible futures for the world. Tell me now, which of my actions is against the redes? For it seems to me that you are trying too hard to blame me.'

It was not possible to argue with a wizard. 'This doesn't feel like the way to win the best of all possible futures, Gwydion! To me it feels like the frittering away of an opportunity. It feels like sacrifice and the wrecking of all our plans. Gwydion, what's happening to you?'

He put out a hand, but the wizard stepped beyond his reach. 'Your instincts do you credit, Willand, but beware! This stone is alive. It still interferes with your mind and spirit. There is much you may yet learn from those who move more slowly, for it is often said amongst men of wisdom that more haste seldom means greater speed. Consider, if you will, the meaning of the second reading of the verse:

> *'Lord Lugh alone shall have the triumph,*
> *At the western river crossing, word of an enemy*
> *Comes falsely by the raised water,*
> *While, at home, the king watches over his tower.*

'All this has come true on its own and without any help from me. The unknowable future against which we have struggled was this: at the western crossing, the crossing of Ludford's river, word of an enemy comes – that is Lord Strange's betrayal. Falsely by the raised water – meaning this castle well. At home, the king in his tower watches over all: not King Hal but *Richard*! Richard, do you see? Richard, sitting here in Ludford Castle, deliberating upon what must be done. In the end, it becomes clear: there will be victory for neither Richard nor Hal. And so I have proved it is possible to outplay these stones on their own ground. Go,

Willand, for I still have work to do. Whether you like it or not, you must leave me with this wanton stone. Get out now, or you will not be able to save your sanity!'

The wizard began to drain the stone in the last remaining hour before the moon rose. It died shrieking in welters of blood, while Will sank deeper into the mind-fever he had kept at bay for so long.

This madness was nightmarish. This time Willow could not help him, and he sank alone into a breathless despair. He howled and writhed, haunting the innermost ward. No one dared approach him, for it was said among Ludford folk that the sight of a lunatic on the day of the full moon had the power to rob all who listened to him of their reason.

In truth, the men of the duke's household had sufficient cares of their own. Through some fleeting gap in his nightmares, Will glimpsed the Lady Cicely and her entourage hurrying behind a row of bodyguards. They seemed to be running for their lives. And there, Edmund, the duke's second son, all in blackened armour, limping and striving with a withered arm. He spat in Will's face, shook him briefly by the shoulder, and spoke words to him that had no meaning, then he dissolved . . . like smoke.

No one had come to save him. There were numbers of heavy chests all around, iron-banded coffers, chests studded with round rivets. Stout poles were thrust through their rings. They were carried along by eight men each, like great, black spiders. Edmund in black steel frothed and jerked and shouted as he limped through the inner ward. The duke's officers shouted warnings, but again the words washed over Will as they would an unreasoning beast.

As the treasury of Ludford was loaded into carts, Will's thoughts disintegrated. Shafts of moonlight shattered the shapes of the castle walls. Men ran through the darkness, carrying off all that could be moved of Duke Richard's belongings. Will remembered a voice from the past. He sweated and cowered in his corner, hugging the cold stone wall, beaten down by the emanations that assailed him. And through all the violence and agony the one thing he could not forget was the beauty and goodness in Willow's face.

When at last the inner ward was emptied, there was quiet for a while, but then the peace was suddenly destroyed. At first there was only a looming shape, then something huge flashed overhead. A monster with crimson wings glided over the castle. It filled the sky. But it wasn't real. How could it be? It gave out blood-chilling screams that seemed to speak Will's name.

'It's the madness!' he shouted. 'It's naught but a terror raked up from the dregs of my mind!'

He shook his fists at the sky, but the monster came again and this time circled lower.

'It cannot be! There are no more dragons! Not here! Not in the Realm!'

He watched in fear and loathing as the beast flew down. The dragon stretched out a great talon and plucked a bolting carthorse from between the shafts of a wagon. Will felt the draught of its wings on his face as it launched itself back into the sky and dashed the cart to pieces against the wall. Then it raised itself up and flew off, while the horse kicked and whinnied pathetically in its grip. And there on its back was the figure of a man wearing mail of red dragon scales and long cock-spurs. He rode above the wings, sitting in a golden saddle placed at the base of the long neck, where the threshing head and fearsome teeth could not reach him.

Raving in his madness, Will's eyes popped. He hid his face, then he forced himself to stare at the empty courtyard, trying to believe that what he had seen was no more than a figment conjured by the Blood Stone. It seemed real, but then so had Edmund.

Then a carthorse's head slammed down in the yard close by him and splattered him with gore. He threw up his hands in horror, telling himself now that there must be catapults outside the walls. Then he heard the bones shatter and the innards rupture as the rest of the horse burst in a heap nearby. Entrails stretched across the cobbles towards him. A single eye stared at him from the head. Foaming lips peeled back from yellow teeth. Then blood began to trickle from the nose and run between the stones towards his feet.

He watched the gore flowing towards him for a moment, and when he looked to see where it had come from there were Willow and Bethe, lying dead on the ground.

He ran screaming into the night, but then something hit his head with tremendous force, and he fell down, winded, broken, unable to bear the pain any longer. The world became a red haze, then a black void, and then the void closed over him and swallowed him whole.

CHAPTER TWENTY-FOUR

FLESH ANEW

'I should have tied you down.'

Gort's voice was something to hold on to as Will's mind struggled back from the darkness.

'Here, drink this!'

He dashed the bitter cup from Gort's hand and tore open his shirt. Then, with the power of three men, he rose, struck Gort to the ground and began to stagger away.

'Stop him!' Gort shouted. 'Somebody stop him!'

But there was no one who could. He remembered that the castle had once been full of terrified men, but now they had gone. He pushed through into the inner ward. Near the Round House some men were trying to pull something out of a cart. The ground was littered with valuables abandoned in haste – bolts of cloth, broken chests, sacks of grain, barrels. The very walls seemed to blaze, though there was no longer any fire lodged in the torch holders.

He keeled over, hit the ground hard. There was the sound of running feet.

'Lost! Lost! All is lost!' someone cried. 'Run! Get out while you may! The enemy is coming!'

'Cowards!' Will screamed at the empty gate. 'The beast has killed my wife and child!'

He rose up, filled with fury, determined to fight the dragon to the death. But where was it? High overhead the moon crept on towards the moment of fullness. He pushed the wreckage of the cart aside and went back into the innermost ward, drawn now by the fearsome noises that emanated from the brewhouse. Groans and thunderous rumblings echoed off the walls as the stone still contested the fight.

'*Agh lasadha an tsolais . . .*' Gwydion's voice rose thin above the clamour as he cast and danced his last shreds of defiance at the merciless stone. Blood-red light bubbled at the window. A shade loomed huge over the cowering wizard. Even in the midst of raging madness Will's senses told him that the stone was ready and poised to force its will upon its tormentor.

Around Will's neck the leaping salmon talisman shone so bright a green that his eyes could barely stand to see it. He flung the door open and cast Gwydion away from him. A great gust of vileness rushed at his face, blasted him like the flame erupting from the maw of one of Lord Warrewyk's engines of death. But he drove carelessly onward against it, onward until his outstretched hands were planted against the palpitating surface of the stone.

'My wife! My child!' he cried, seeing only their corpses. 'Bring them back to me!'

He tore the talisman from his neck and, at the very moment of syzygy, plunged it into the stone's side, driving his fingers deep and forcing his grip to close. Then he gave a shout of savage joy, as he ripped out the stone's beating heart.

The Blood Stone shook wildly. It roared and screamed. But, in Will's hands, the heart of the stone was dead and cold and the stone was a battlestone no more. Yet the killing had taken some terrible toll on the killer. How much time passed before his eyes saw the world again, he did not know. There were only voices, swimming in a sea of sound.

'Quickly!' Gwydion said, pulling him across the blood-flooded floor. 'Soldiers are coming!'

Hands struggled to support him. He tottered, fought for command of his legs. Despite the passing of the climactic moment, he remained in the grip of some stubborn affliction.

'Stand back!'

Gort dashed a bucket of rainwater over him. Together, Wortmaster and wizard lifted him to his feet as the cool light of the full moon glistened on the stones of the inner ward.

'It hasn't gone away!' he raved, reeling like a drunkard. 'The influence is still there! I can still feel it!'

'It cannot be,' Gwydion told Gort. 'Calm him! He's moon-struck!'

'No!' he cried. 'The stone lives, I tell you! I can hear it. I can feel it! The soldiers are fighting on!'

Gwydion took hold of his head. 'The soldiers are fled. Listen to me, Willand! The battlestone is done for! You tore out its heart. The battle ended before ever it began. The castle is fallen.'

'What is it you hear?' Willow's voice asked, looking into his eyes. 'Is it truly the stone? Oh, Will, let me help you!'

His eyes rolled as Willow held him now. But Willow was dead!. Killed by a dragon!

'Willow?' His eyes started out from his head.

She hugged him. 'It's all right, Will. I'm with you now!'

'Oh, Willow! You're alive. *You're alive!*'

'Can't you do something for him, Wortmaster?'

'Not here.'

Gort and Gwydion each took an arm, Willow lifted his feet and they rushed him back inside Gort's rooms and laid him on the bed. Willow sang,

> *'How can another ever know,*
> *What weight of woe,*
> *Breaks the heart of a friend so?'*

Gort put a piece of heath-pea root in Will's mouth. 'Bite on it! Tsk! Tsk! Harder! Chew it up. Oh, that's better.' Once the bite was made he pushed Will's lips back and poured a burning liquor over his teeth. Will choked at the foulness of the taste, but then they pushed him flat and the rigidity began to leave his muscles. He began to float inside his own body.

'That's gooood,' Gort soothed. 'Very good. You've done well tonight. All you could have done and more, eh? Now you just lie there and leave everything to us. Everything to us . . .'

Gwydion muttered incantations over him, but through it he could hear a fearful booming. It sounded through the castle like the footfalls of a giant, and he feared that somehow the harm in the Blood Stone had finally been made manifest. But then the glory of the full moon dropped steeply away, like a cliff under a soaring seabird. Numbed by the medicine, Will's mind rose up and up, beyond his body. His spirit flew out beyond the walls of the inner ward, beyond the castle and the town. Darkened lands rolled away beneath his senses. Hill and river, forest and dale, stood out, colourless, washed by the brightest moonlight he had ever known. His mind's eye saw the ligns as clear as could be: two broad green lanes, one paler than the other, two streams of earth power confined by ancient magic to run straight and true across the land. And where they crossed was the riverside earthworks that had been dug by Lord Strange's men.

His floating mind perceived waves of light running along both ligns. It was so easy now to see them. Effortless, where once it had been impossible. He saw that one of the ligns cut straight through the middle of the castle. There it shattered like sunlight on water. It filled both inner and outer wards with a million scintillas of moving light. But the waves that travelled along the ligns were greying, dimmer now. The power seemed to be pulling back, running away to southward, withdrawing – or being withdrawn – towards a presence that lurked on the southern horizon.

The understanding stole over him that a disastrous bloodbath had been avoided. Lord Strange's going over to the enemy had fatally weakened Duke Richard's position. At first, the duke and his allies had stubbornly refused to fly. But then the duke's warrior

335

resolve had broken. His troops had been ordered from the barri-
cades and entrenchments. With his plans in tatters, the duke's
main force had hastily made off, while a small party of horsemen
and wagons went by unfrequented ways into the wilds of the
west, into Cambray, where the queen's forces could not easily
follow.

Boom! Boom!

Will's mind swooped and dived like a house martin over a
night land that shone as bright as day. He saw how Ludford had
been given up, castle and all. The great host had already closed
on the town and the undefended gates were thrown wide to admit
the queen's army. The delighted rabble had doubtless been promised they could take what they wanted in place of unpaid wages.
Men were looting all that could be found instead of pursuing
their enemy in rout.

Boom! Boom!

And here was the source of that thunderous booming. An
engine of war, hauled in to knock upon the locked gates of the
castle. A great oak trunk mounted on chains in a timber frame,
lifted by two crews of men hauling on ropes, then let fall until
its mighty crash rang to the echo.

> '*Hemlock, belladonna, mandrake deep,*
> *Bring him home his thoughts to keep . . .*'

Gort's chanting brought Will's roaming mind back into the
room. The crucial moment of the full moon had long passed and
its ebbing power allowed Will to return steadily to himself. The
artful stars of Gort's ceiling replaced those of the real sky as Will
opened his eyes.

Boom! Boom!

'We can't linger here,' he heard Gwydion say.

He tried to sit up, but Willow steadied him. She seemed on
the point of tears and only one thing could have filled her face
with such anguish.

'Where's Bethe?' he said, coming to.

'Will . . .' Her tears flowed. 'She's gone.'

'Gone?' He struggled up.

'With the duchess! Will, I couldn't do anything.'

'Why didn't you keep her with you?' he demanded.

'Steady!' Gort said, laying a hand on his chest. 'That's not the way. It's nobody's fault. Willow made sure that Bethe was safe with the duchess before she came down to tend you, and in the meanwhile—'

'Willow . . .' He felt her agony overwhelm him.

'When I found you, you were out of your mind. And when I went back the duchess was gone. It all happened so fast. Oh, Will!'

He pulled her to him as she sobbed. 'Willow, Willow. I'm sorry. It's not your fault.'

'She'll be well tended,' Gort said. 'The Lady Cicely's been a mother seven times over.'

'How could she have taken her? And what if the queen's soldiers catch them?'

Gwydion stepped into the circle of candlelight. 'No one from the queen's army will dare follow Richard into the west. Or if they do they will not get far along the mountain roads, for there is great magic still in the land of Cambray. They do not suffer the uninvited in those hills.'

Boom! Boom!

'That's a battering ram,' Will said.

'I hope Lord Warrewyk took his guns along with him,' Gort muttered. 'And his casks of sorcerer's powder, too. If those engines of destruction are ready to be turned upon us, then this fair castle will be slighted to ruins in half a day!'

Will told Gwydion, 'I saw a great army in retreat to the south. But there was a line of carts going swiftly westward, towards the mountains of Cambray.'

Gort nodded. 'The princes will allow Richard through to the coast, for he pays to keep ships in more than one port. These days he knows not to keep all his eggs in one basket. I think he will head for Caerwathen.'

Will stroked Willow's hair. 'Did you hear that? Our child is to pass over the seas. She will be safe in the Blessed Isle.' He looked up. 'And Edward? What of him?'

'Most of Richard's army are with the hosts of Lords Warrewyk and Sarum. They have been sent south, and Edward will be with them.'

'Where are they going?'

Gwydion pursed his lips. 'My guess would be Belstrand on the south coast, for there waits the fleet that brought Lord Warrewyk over the Narrow Seas. He and his father and Edward will take ship once more for the fortress port of Callas. They will easily outmarch an army that is intent on looting Ludford. Do you see now how Richard's power has been dispersed, but not broken? This is the best of all outcomes. We have carried out a most satisfactory day's work! Most satisfactory!'

'I wish it felt like it.' Will's eyes narrowed at the wizard's enthusiasm. 'What about the stump of the Blood Stone?'

'I did the only thing possible if Richard was not to have it.'

'You dropped it back down the well?'

'I did. I do not know what boon the drained Blood Stone will confer, but confer a boon it now must. Perhaps the good ale that Edwold hoped for will one day make Ludford famous for its brews.'

'And what about the other spent stone?'

'Richard's men have taken the stump of the Blow Stone away with them.' Gwydion made a dismissive gesture. 'That is a small matter, for I would argue that it is right in principle for all battle-stones, spent or not, to be returned whence they came. My concern there is only to prevent Richard misusing what he has taken.'

Boom! Boom!

Bestial cries and the great heaving and slamming of the iron-shod trunk against the gates almost drowned Gwydion's words.

Willow pulled away. 'I can smell burning!'

'We must see how the land lies,' the wizard told them.

They followed as he went up to the walls near the inner gate-house and looked out over the ruined outer ward. It was eerily deserted and ghastly to see. A lone unsaddled horse galloped in circles, its ears pricked, nostrils flaring. Many of the goods of the castle had been strewn about, carts were overturned and the dead bodies of men and animals littered the ground.

Beyond the shadows the sky was red and the din dreadful. Will looked skyward, remembering the nightmare dragon that had tormented his stone-fevered mind. It had seemed so real. He shivered, shielding his eyes against the glare of flames. Beyond the castle walls the town was being torn apart by the queen's forces. Many houses were already sheathed in flame and there was screaming. It was as if Maskull had cast a spell over the queen's soldiers. Many townsfolk too slow to run would die tonight, and Will heard their despairing cries. Their lord had deserted them, and many would rush into the clutches of the Sightless Ones, for the chapter house was the only building that would remain inviolate.

The great castle was especially unsafe. Without defenders to guard the walls and gates and towers, they could not stand for even an hour. And Will knew there were those among the queen's forces intent on searching out booty more valuable than that which the town afforded.

Boom! Boom!

Will turned at the sound of the battering ram. The gatemen would have secured the entrance before disappearing over the walls. That would have given more time for the duke's party to make their escape. There was the clang of iron, the shattering of roof slates. Will saw the flukes of a siege hook scraping up the wall on its rope. At last the hook found a purchase on the stone and the rope pulled taut. Then other iron hooks flew over the walls and hung momentarily like spiders before they too dug in tight.

'Grapnels!' Gort cried. 'They're climbing the walls!'

'We must go now,' Gwydion said, as if in answer to the latest splintering sound of the ram. He began to shepherd them back towards the spiral stair that led down into the inner ward.

'Are we going to get out alive?' Willow asked, her upturned face smudged. 'And where will we go if we do?'

Will could give her no answer. He let Gwydion lead them past the Round House, and then back towards the kitchens. There they picked up three loaves and filled a large earthenware jug with water. 'I must go to Trinovant,' the wizard said.

'What about us?'

The wizard handed Will the water jug and pushed him on into the innermost ward. 'I must find a way to solve the verse that points the way to the next stone.'

'The verse . . .'

Will gasped. He had forgotten about the Blood Stone's vital message to them.

Gwydion spoke it in the true tongue:

> *'Faic dama nallaid far askaine de,*
> *Righ rofhir e ansambith athan?*
> *Coise fodecht e na iarrair rathod,*
> *Do-fhaicsennech muig firran a bran.'*

'What does it mean?' Willow asked, awed by the sound of the words.

'Its meaning is a matter that requires much thought.' Gwydion cast an eye at the ramparts where dark figures were already beginning to appear. 'And rather more time than we have at present.'

Gort said, 'Master Gwydion! I think these inner gates might hold the queen's soldiers back for a little while, but we should make haste. Follow me! There is a secret way down to the river.'

'Stop!' Gwydion said, gesturing them to go a different way. 'Wortmaster, you and I will take our leave together. We shall do so by a route which none can follow. But Will and Willow – you must stay within these walls.'

Will halted and stared at the wizard. 'Did I hear you right?'

Willow grasped the wizard's robe. 'Where can we hide? They'll search everywhere!'

'Oh, it is best not to be hidden,' Gwydion said, handing her the loaves. 'What is hidden may always be found. Take the bread, you'll soon be glad of it.'

Gort looked anxiously towards the inner gate which he knew must soon come under attack. 'Master Gwydion, those who are presently knocking upon the outer door will easily scale these walls too. They may kill anyone they find here. Do you want Will to defend himself by magic?'

'There will be no need for that. Indeed, he must not resort to magic at any cost!'

'I'll stay,' Will said, seizing the wizard's sleeve, 'but only if you take Willow with you!'

'No, Will!' Willow shouted. 'I won't go without you!'

Gwydion laid a reassuring hand on her arm. 'The plan I have is quite simple. And safer than any other.'

He led them down to the dungeon under the keep. Gwydion struck up a pale light and they saw storerooms that had been part emptied by the duke's household servants. Here was the cell in which Lord Dudlea had spent his nights. It was vacant now. Inside, the cold stone floor was scattered with filthy straw. There were rusty chains hanging from the walls and a thick iron door with a small, barred window. Will recalled how here, years ago, he had heard a baby crying where no baby had been. Now, with Bethe taken away from them and the pain of that parting keen in their hearts, he marvelled that their predicament could have so affected him before Bethe had even been thought of.

'Must we go in there?' Willow said, her lips a ghastly blue in the magelight.

'You must,' Gwydion told her, ushering them both inside. 'For they will not murder their own.'

341

'You're making a joke,' Will said. He set the jug down and stared at the wizard in the noisome darkness. 'But I don't see the humour in it.'

'It is no joke.'

'How can we pose as captives? What about the parley? Half of the king's host know me by sight. Lord Strange certainly does. A haircut and a fresh suit of clothes will be no protection here.'

Gwydion braced his feet widely, put his hands to his temples, muttered. He began to dance and twirl in the straw. Words rumbled deep in his throat, words that were not in the true tongue, nor any tongue that Will had heard Gwydion use before. He recoiled from the wizard's magical caress, felt something dry being dashed across his face, something like a powder, a pepper that stung his eyes. Then a blinding brilliance almost knocked them both down and left them in utter blackness apart from the colours in their heads.

'Lord Strange may know the sight of you, Willand, but he does not know the Maceugh!'

'The . . . *what*?'

Will's own voice sounded odd in his throat as the wizard struck up the magelight anew.

'When the magic settles fully upon you, you will begin to know who you have become.'

Willow dropped her loaves, and when Will turned to her he was amazed to see another. 'What's happened to us?' he said, shaken to his marrow. 'What have you done?'

Willow put a floury hand to his cheek. 'Oh, Will, look at your face!'

'Do not be alarmed,' Gwydion said. 'You are now not merely dressed as a lord and lady of the Blessed Isle, you are clothed in flesh anew. It is not an illusion. I have employed an ancient magic that might have been made for the purpose. It is a transformation that will deceive even Maskull's eye. It's one of my best skills.'

'What purpose?' Will roared, looking at his own strange hands and again at the stranger who was his wife. 'Whose purpose?'

The booming of the ram and the cracking of huge timbers forestalled the wizard's answer. Gwydion took him by the shoulders. 'Do not blame me, Willand. I have done this to save your lives. I must have eyes and ears at this crucial moment. You will be an ambassador. Seek out Morann, he will know what to do.'

'No! Gwydion! Not that wretched trick again! You can't leave us like this!'

But Gwydion had already withdrawn from the cell and was sliding the great iron bolt across that locked them in. His face appeared at the small, barred window.

'I am sorry not to be able to stay with you longer, but Gort needs my help now and this is no time to tarry. I warn you against exercising magic while you are in the guise of the Maceugh. Any cast, no matter how trivial, will put your life in jeopardy and swiftly bring enemies down upon you.'

The wizard's face vanished.

'We cannot pass for folk from the Blessed Isle!' Will shouted. He reached a vain arm through the bars. But his words already betrayed themselves, for they were spoken in the accents of another shore.

'Do not seek for me, Willand. I promise that I will come to you before the spring turns to summer. Until we meet again, tread softly!'

The wisp of wavering magelight faded to become steady, fire-reddened darkness. He pulled his arm back inside the cell and sat down.

'*Deoheir gathe, ar Saille,*' he said at last, marvelling as he did so that he knew the speech of the Isle. It sounded to him straight away very comfortable and somewhat like the true tongue only a great deal more straightforward.

'*Deohshen muire gath, ar Gillan,*' Willow said, returning the greeting. Then she asked, '*Ceornaise teuh teone?*'

'You might well ask how I am! In truth, I am so angry I could spit blood!' He put a hand to his chin and was dismayed to find a neatly-trimmed beard had sprouted there. 'He talks about

343

bringing about the best of all possible futures, yet he's taken away my child, he's made a stranger out of my own wife and a different man out of my own self too. And if that's not enough he's left us locked in a dark dungeon with the enemy about to begin rapping on the door! Oh, Gwydion, you call yourself our friend. How could you have done this to us?'

PART FOUR

THE TURNING
OF THE TIDE

□ □ □

CHAPTER TWENTY-FIVE

TURLOCH'S RING

Of all the lords who surrounded the king, Henry de Bowforde, Duke of Mells, was the most powerful and the most dangerous. The old Duke of Mells, Duke Edgar, had died in the fighting at Verlamion, after which his son, Henry, had inherited both the dukedom and the queen's special favour. And now he had granted Will an audience.

'We must be very careful with Duke Henry,' Will warned his wife in a murmur as they waited in their cell to be interviewed for their lives. 'He's no fool. He recognized me once before, just as the battle was starting at Verlamion. He was nearly the death of me then, though I might say that his catching sight of me at that moment separated him from his father and probably saved his life. However, I doubt he'd see it that way if it came to it.'

Willow took his hand. 'Have faith. If Gwydion's magical disguises are strong enough to serve against Maskull, they'll deceive Henry de Bowforde.'

He laced his fingers with hers. 'If only magic worked as reliably as you suppose. I'm tired of sitting in this filthy cell. I'll murder Gwydion when I see him next.'

'Oh, don't say such things, Will. It's uncomfortable, but it could have been worse, and Morann told me that Gwydion has a knack for finding the best path forward.'

'He told that to me too.'

He sighed, wishing there was a little more of their water left. They had been in the dungeon three days now, confined all the while as a riot of looting raged through the castle. Since their discovery by drunken soldiers from whose sight Will had hidden his wife, they had lived on a diet of stale bread and cistern water. The next day he had shouted angrily through the cell door to the soldiers who ventured near. After being discovered they had waited again while more important matters were attended to.

Will looked at Willow in the dim daylight that crept into the cell. She, at least, seemed unrecognizable. The change was astonishing: she was taller, had fuller lips and more prominent cheekbones and she now had a curling mass of auburn hair.

When she saw him studying her she looked back penetratingly with green eyes and shook her head at last, saying, 'I don't know if I'll ever get used to you looking the way you do.'

'What's wrong with me?' he asked.

'That long, russet hair and that beard! A straight nose and piercing olive eyes. You look like a fox!'

'A *fox*, is it?'

'You're far too handsome to be my Willand.'

'Well, thank you for that kind thought!' He grinned. 'You're not so bad to look at yourself, I might say. I could almost forgive Gwydion his high-handedness if I was not so angry.'

His shirt was a *leine* dyed a pale saffron yellow, and his garb was of the same brown and black woollen broadweave as Willow's dress, being pinned in place by a silver *delch*, a brooch which had a lustrous brown stone set in it. He knew – though he could not say how he knew – that it was a form of dress made after the fashion of the Clan Maceugh. The brooch signified his leadership of that clan. He was the man known simply as 'the Maceugh'.

Approaching footsteps sounded. This time they were purposeful and disciplined. Then came the sound of the stiff, rusty bolt being slipped. Will stood as the soldiers entered the cell, and suddenly he and Willow were being brought out into strong morning light by men wearing blue and white livery.

They marched out of the keep and took their charges down through the inner ward. The light hurt Will's eyes, but he strove to take in everything he saw. A thin wisp of smoke was issuing from the bakehouse chimney. The castle was now in good order, showing that men of rank had taken control once more. Will knew what to expect. For a day now the engine that called forth the castle chimes had been ringing the bells regularly once again. The bells sounded now, and Will counted the hours – twelve noon. The device borne on the chests of the escort was the silver portcullis – badge of the dukedom of Mells.

As they waited under guard, Will watched lines of soldiers being ordered hither and thither. Gort's fears about Lord Warrewyk's guns being used to slight the castle had so far proved unfounded, making Will suspect that Ludford Castle had already been marked down for new ownership. If so, there was still much clearing up to be done, and a great deal else to be set in train.

Will pondered the coming interview and wondered what his best approach might be. Willow took his hand during much of the long wait, but as the castle chimes marked the second hour of the afternoon, two dozen men in black sallets and blue and white iron-studded jackets appeared and stood to arms near the Round House. A procession of nobles emerged from it and was escorted through the inner ward towards the doors of the Great Hall. Among them was Duke Henry. It was not long before Will's guard ordered him to follow.

The sergeant said that Willow must remain outside, so Will took his leave and walked on alone, with conscious dignity despite his dishevelled and unwashed state. The Great Hall had been partly stripped, but it smelled as it always did, an odd mix of stale food smells, woodsmoke and beeswax. Autumn light slanted through the tall windows, sending diamond-shaped splashes of colour across the scrubbed floorboards. The side tables had been pushed back against walls that no longer displayed their great tapestries. Much had been taken away and much assembled here from other parts of the castle ready to be taken away.

A dozen or so men sat at the high table – scribes and others sitting among parchments and papers. Henry de Bowforde had seated himself in Duke Richard's favourite chair. His eyes were flickering to left and right over his documents like a viper's tongue. He was a long-nosed, unsmiling man with an unhealthy pallor, twenty-one years old and dressed in a suit of blue with ermine trim and a blue hat which hid most of his straight, dark hair. The back of his pale neck was shaved high from ear to ear in lordly fashion, and now the burnished armour he had worn in the parley tent was gone he seemed less of a soldier and more like a sheriff's clerk, except that two gold and enamel chains of office clanked against the fluted velvet breast of his doublet. It was his habit to play with his dagger, which he turned over now in gloved fingers.

A recorder in legal green spoke quietly at the duke's side, but the cutting tones of his voice carried to Will's ears. 'The captive claims to have been travelling in embassy from the Blessed Isle, your grace, and to have been illegally detained by the Duke of Ebor and imprisoned by him. He was discovered by your men along with a woman whom he claims is his wife. They were both locked in the oubliette.'

'Locked in, you say?'

'That is so, your grace.'

Henry's eye fell on Will and searched his unfamiliar clothing critically. 'Who are you, my good man?'

'Whoever I may be, I am not your good man,' Will said, astonished at his own effrontery and his own heavily accented words. He brushed a piece of straw from his cloak and added, 'As for how my friends know me, I am called by them the Maceugh, Lord of Eochaidhan.'

'The "Muck You of Yokee-an"?' Henry repeated. His voice was soft and dangerous. A smirk fleeted across his mouth, then vanished. 'Quite a mouthful.'

Will made no reply, but stood unmoved as the intimidating silence stretched out.

'And . . . who *are* you?'

Will's blood ran chill. His back straightened and his eyes kept their challenge. 'Do you say that I am not the Maceugh?'

The duke rearranged his papers and muttered, 'The man appears unable to understand what I'm saying to him.'

'I own that I speak your language less than perfectly,' Will said quickly, 'but I dare say I speak it better than you speak mine.'

Henry's eyes dwelt upon him for a long time, then cut away. 'Well . . . whoever you are, I've had you brought before me to enquire as to the reason the Duke of Ebor did not kill you, or at least take you with him when he left.'

'You must ask Richard of Ebor that.'

'Yes, well, I am asking you.' Henry leaned forward, resting his chin on the heel of his hand. 'So hazard a guess.'

'Duke Richard did not strike me as a cold-blooded murderer,' Will said evenly. 'And perhaps he did not relish landing me back whence I came for fear that I might blame him for his actions.'

'Blame him?'

'Aye. For his incivility to me and mine. And for his interference in my mission, which was to bring news to your sovereign lord.'

Duke Henry shifted and he consulted his papers once more. 'Oh, yes, I'm forgetting. You claim to be an ambassador of some kind. Well . . . what is it you want to say to our gracious king?'

'I am ambassador to your king – and to no other.' Will spoke the words pointedly and the duke stirred with irritation.

'We do things a little differently here. Those who would speak with his grace must speak through me. And I warn you that if you speak to me insolently again you will be taken to the top of the keep and shown the quickest way down. Now is that clear enough for you?'

Will held the duke's gaze proudly. The man dressed in legal

green whispered, and again Will's keen ears caught what was said. 'He claims to have vital news for your grace.'

The duke gave a nod of understanding, then said, 'What *vital* news do you have for me?'

'That would be best told in private.'

In truth, Will had no idea what news he was supposed to have. He had made the claim when he had been at his most desperate to get out of the dungeon.

'We are among friends. You may speak freely.'

Will's mind raced as he looked from face to face. He saw no one he would have regarded as a friend. Nor did free speaking seem like a particularly good idea. Yet he knew he must say something, and something convincing.

'I wanted to inform you of the port that Duke Richard was making for, that you might have intercepted him.'

That jolted the duke and his eyes narrowed. 'You know the port? Then tell me the name of it.'

'It is called by the princes of Cambray Caerwathen.'

The duke sat up stiffly as he recognized the name. Beside him, the recorder nodded slightly. 'Sadly, Ebor has already sailed from there. It's a great pity you did not speak up sooner.'

'You cannot with justice blame the Maceugh if his news has gone stale. Your men were too busy ransacking the wine cellars to listen to a foreign voice pleading to be released from a dark cell.'

There was absolute stillness in the hall and the guards that flanked the doors seemed to be straining to make stones of themselves. The duke had cultivated a reputation for ruthlessness. He sat back, his dark eyes appraising the difficult upstart who stood alone before him. Whispers passed between the duke and his men. Papers were shuffled, pointed to, amendments made by the scribes. Will heard himself debated, the Blessed Isle referred to, and many a glance came his way. Throughout the ordeal he stood patiently.

At last the duke said, 'I have a surprise for you.'

'A surprise, your grace?'

'Yes. It's in the nature of a little test.' The duke laid down his dagger and spun it about like a pointer. It came to rest point outwards. 'A test that will determine what we are to do with you. I need to know what truth there may be in your story. You see . . . I cannot quite put my finger on where I've seen you before. But I'm sure I know you from another place, and that worries me.'

Will's blood ran cold, but he did not let a flicker of doubt escape him. 'You do not know me, your grace. You have never met the Maceugh before.'

'You sound rather too definite about that.'

'I am wholly certain of it. I would have remembered you.'

The duke glanced at him sharply, winnowing the remark for the trace of an insult. He seemed about to speak again when a man in the robe of the Isles appeared at the far end of the hall. He walked briskly down the hall, his *cadath* cloak billowing black and green in his wake. 'You asked for me, your grace?'

'Yes.' Henry picked up his dagger again and pointed the tip at Will. 'This . . . captive . . . says he's a lord of the Blessed Isle. Speak to him in his own tongue. Explain that we're undecided what to do with him. Invite him to give proof of his claim, for without proof we cannot admit him and must put him back where we found him at the very least.'

Morann, for it was he, bowed shortly and turned to Will.

'Now look at the fix you're in,' he said in the tongue of the Isle. 'Did I not tell you you're no better than you should be?'

Will allowed himself the hint of a smile, for in the tongue of the Isle the expression made perfect sense. 'That you did, Morann. And I'm very pleased to see you're in the same boat with me.'

'Well, try not to look as pleased as all that, my friend.'

'How did you know me?'

'I thought I heard an owl in the early hours three mornings ago. Gwydion paid me a visit. He said he was away to Trinovant, and that I was to look after you as best I could. Though what

I've done to deserve such a cruel fate I don't dare to think. Play along with me now.'

'That I will.'

Morann strutted back and forth all the while talking in the tongue of the Isle. He kept up the pretence of a full and searching interrogation, knowing that all eyes were on him. But Morann's questions were flippant and Will began to enjoy himself.

'I'm away myself soon to the Blessed Isle,' Morann said. 'So you'll have to fend for yourselves here. I'll give you silver enough for your needs, and the court are obliged to offer you a place to stay if they do not send you packing.'

'That's if Black Harry here doesn't have me flying from the battlements instead.'

'He won't do that. He'll think you the dearest friend he ever had by the time I've finished with you.'

'There's no need to go quite as far as that. But listen, if you're going across the water will you fetch us news from Richard's camp of what has become of our daughter? Willow has been beside herself with worry.'

'I will, my good friend. You may depend upon me!'

Will smiled. It was wonderful to speak so fluently in a language which he had never learned, and to understand every word that was spoken in return. But the enjoyment stopped short when Morann suddenly turned in front of him and punched him hard in the face.

The blow was powerful enough not only to wipe away his smile, but to lay him on his back also. He found it hard not to react. 'Moon and stars! What was that for?' he said angrily, getting up. He began dabbing blood off his mouth.

Seeing that Will was preparing to give as good as he got, Morann thrust out his arm and spoke quickly. 'Have you forgotten what I told you about the ring of Turloch of Connat? It's a tale I related to the young duke here a couple of nights ago. Now do what you must with it!'

Will shook the stars from his vision and tried to bring to mind the story that Morann had once told. It was that Turloch would strike anyone suspected of being a traitor, and if the accused could not bring himself to kiss the ring then he was guilty.

As the duke watched, Will knelt, seized Morann's hand and pressed his lips to the big *smaragd* stone. Morann laid a hand on the top of his head, keeping his lips there. He muttered, 'Well, we do have to make it look good now, don't we?'

As soon as Will was let go he murmured, 'It's nice to know who your friends are.'

Morann turned to the duke and said, 'You may trust the Maceugh as deeply as you trust me, your grace. He is a friend. Of that, I am full sure.'

CHAPTER TWENTY-SIX

CASTLE CORBEN

And so, as winter came and the season of Ewle approached, the men who had joined the army of Queen Mag to see their sovereign's will done at Ludford began to melt away. Vaunting oaths were offered against the Duke of Ebor's name, his war banners were torn down and the royal standard raised in their stead. The troublemaker himself had been driven over the seas, so in many men's eyes there was no further cause to stay. Through what remained of the autumn the royal host that had amazed the Middle Shires with its great size and strength steadily dwindled. While lord, knight and churl alike returned to distant estates well pleased with the lesson they had taught to a rebel and a traitor, others were better satisfied with the booty they had taken.

So far as Will was concerned, the killing of the Blood Stone had certainly set back the rising of the lorc and bought the Realm a little more time, but it was impossible to know when the next stone would awaken, and to be forced to wait idly and without news in such circumstances was a kind of torture.

Throughout the winter the shrunken royal army left Ludford and shuttled from castle to keep and from keep to castle all around the Middle Shires. Will could not understand why the court did not return to Trinovant, but no such move was ever considered. First the queen ordered them to the royal stronghold of Afonwykke, and when food and provisions ran short there, they moved on to Kernelwort. Finally, as spring drew on, they came to the dread Castle of Corben, where the queen announced there must be a reckoning.

It was in this place that three waters joined; the Findon Brook met the Rivers Sow and Afon. Above the torrent stood King's Hill and upon that grew the infamous Corben Tree, an ancient great-leaved lind that shed curses as other trees shed autumn leaves. The sward about it was perpetually churned. It seemed trampled and pig-broken, though no pig had dared come near this place for over a thousand years. This was ground consecrated to the ritual dances of warlocks and pig blood aplenty had been spilled here in long ages past. It was, Will thought, a place of very bad aspect. Even so, it was at Castle Corben that Morann, Loremaster and Lord of Connat, finally returned to them on a wet and dismal spring day in the month of March.

It was on the afternoon of the spring equinox when Willow, on her way to fetch a loaf of bread for supper, saw a strange rider coming up through the grey drizzle. Rain dripped from the brim of his hat, and he looked more than a little starved in the face, but there was no mistaking who it was.

'You'll be happy to learn of your little girl, I'm thinking,' Morann said straight away, making Willow drop her loaf in the mud.

As soon as he had entered the castle precinct by the postern gate, she led him aside and took him up to their quarters. It was a single room up a stone stair at the meanest end of the castle, in fact as far from the royal apartments as it was possible to be. She pulled him quickly inside so that no one saw.

'Let's get you out of the cold and rain!' she said.

Will had been sitting alone in the gloom, worrying and watching the rain beat down outside. He had been willing the green king's-spears to burst yellow at the tip in the gardens, but without magic to draw on they had remained stubbornly closed. He had been thinking about his daughter and how he had now lost six precious months of her infanthood. He had been thinking about Gwydion too.

As the door slammed he leapt up, taking Morann's hat and shaking out his sodden cloak for him.

'Oh, Will!' Willow burst out tearfully. 'Morann says Bethe's in good health and fine spirits!'

'My darling girl! That's what we've longed to hear! Morann, a thousand welcomes to you.'

They clasped one another close.

'I've been three days and nights sat in the saddle or huddled under a hedge. To clap eyes on you both again is very good!'

'He says Bethe's the heart's delight of Lady Cicely. She's treating her as one of her own!'

'Did I not tell you she would charm the duchess with her smile?'

Morann grinned. 'Her little cheeks are as rosy as Woollack apples. She already speaks two dozen words of the true tongue, though none of her nurses knows it for what it is. She is quite the little fairy princess.'

Willow burst into tears. 'Oh, Morann! I wish I could see her now!'

'You will soon, I'm sure of that.'

Will hugged her close and wiped away her tears, then he clasped Morann again by the forearms and passed a grateful greeting in the tongue of the Isle, as seemed only natural, before asking what news there was.

Morann loosed a soaking wet sack from his belt and dropped it on the floor. He took crystals from his pouch and set them by door and window and on the hearth. 'To foil eavesdroppers,' he said. 'All Duke Richard's family, except Edward, are safe in exile in the Isle.'

'And what of Edward?'

'The duke's allies, Sarum and Warrewyk you'll remember, marched down to Belstrand and sailed for Callas. Edward went with them, as did the bulk of the Ebor army. The duke's other castles, Castle Foderingham and the Castle of Sundials in the North, are ordered to hold aloof from all requests by the king to open their gates. They are prepared for a long wait under arms, as are his allies' other strongholds. Unless a siege train is brought to crack them open, each will stand for months or years if necessary. I do not think the queen will order them slighted – she'll not want to destroy what she covets for her friends.'

'What news of the stones?'

Morann wiped his face; it was lined and careworn. 'As for the Blow Stone, it's back in the Blessed Isle where it belongs. At Gwydion's request it has been set up in the oak groves of Derrih where it confers as fine a neighbourliness upon the people as ever you did see. I don't know what happened to the Blood Stone.'

'That's not what I meant,' Will cut in. 'Has Gwydion any notion of where to find the *next* battlestone? Has he found out anything? You *have* heard from him . . . haven't you?'

Morann staggered, and Will saw that his face was pinched and wan. 'All in good time. Can't you see a man's trying to catch his breath here?'

Will relented immediately. 'Forgive my bad manners, old friend! What a poor host you must think me. Sit yourself down by the fire and get warm and dry, and then we'll talk.'

While Willow combed Morann's wild hair, Will fetched out a jug of cider and three tankards and a large shred pie. Morann sniffed at it and closed his eyes like a man in love. 'Hmmm. I'd say I'm quite ready for this.'

'What on earth is in that old sack of yours?' Willow asked, picking at what had been dropped by the door.

'That, lovely lady, you shall presently know. But first I must have meat and drink and plenty of it, for nothing much more than a powder of Albanay heath-pea root has passed my lips in three days.'

Morann ate his fill like a champion. When he had downed a goodly portion of the pie and swallowed his first tankard of cider, he belched and sat back. Only when Will saw that a little more colour had come into his face did he ask what news there had been of Gwydion.

'I've not met with him all winter.'

Willow said anxiously, 'Do you think a silence like that could be anything other than a cause for concern?'

Morann, creaking like a saddle-sore man, pulled off his boots with a groan. 'Who can say? He has many concerns. This is usual with wizards.'

'But surely,' Willow insisted, 'he would have sent a message to us by now – if he could.'

'Well, if you think that,' Will said, 'then you don't know Gwydion. Giving and withholding is how a wizard manages the world.'

A basket of green firewood – wrist-thick branches sawn into foot-long lengths – stood drying by the grate. Willow pulled the basket aside to let more heat out into the cramped room, then she sat down beside Morann. 'Didn't he say anything to you about when he'd return? Or what more we should do in the meanwhile? Our silver is almost spent.'

Morann shook his head. 'Gwydion's last words to me were: "Whatever happens, you'll hear from me by the feast of Imble at the latest."'

'But Imble was seven weeks ago!' Will said.

Morann sat back and loosed the enchanted knife from his belt. 'The Ogdoad were ever guaranteed to stand by their word. Even Maskull was wont to do so in times past.'

Mention of Imble made Will shudder. It was an ancient fire-day, and an important festival, marking as it did a time of thanks offered to the land. In the Vale it was marked by the Festival of Lambing, but amongst lordly society it was the day the Sightless Ones chose to celebrate their Fast of the Purification of Mothers.

At Imbletide it had been especially hard for Willow to bear the separation from Bethe. For the sake of appearances, she had had to attend the Fellowship's joyless ritual meant for women who had borne children. She had hated it, and had almost broken down in tears when questioned by the Elder about what children she might have. Will sighed. 'Sitting here is achieving nothing, but what else can we do? I suppose we must all wait for Gwydion's word, whether it's coming or not.'

'This war is none of his doing,' Morann said, setting his wet boots by the fire. 'And he cannot be blamed for the frustrations of it. Were he Jarred the Juggler he would be putting a score of balls into the air all at once, and we had best be hopeful that he chooses for our sakes to continue doing it.'

Will knew he had been set straight. 'Forgive me,' he said. 'I know Gwydion will be doing his best, wherever he is.'

'There's nothing to forgive,' Morann said with better cheer. 'Impatience was ever the young man's vice, if my own life's lessons have taught me anything. But tell me, what has passed with you?'

Will explained everything that had happened with the king's court, paying special attention to their constant moves and the way the army had melted away to less than a sixtieth of its number. 'Speaking of life's lessons,' he said, 'one truth fast became clear to me – a great army carries with it a fearsome burden of cost. Nor can it stay in one place for long. When an army moves, it lays the land bare for seven leagues around. By Ewletide the king's army had diminished to a thousand.'

Willow poured more cider. 'I don't understand why the court doesn't return to Trinovant where it properly belongs.'

'Because,' Morann said, 'most of the people there admire Richard of Ebor. When news of what happened at Ludford arrived, the burgesses and aldermen of Trinovant closed their gates against the court's return.'

Willow showed her surprise. 'They closed their gates against their own king?'

'"Until redress and remedy is found for the injustice heaped upon Duke Richard of Ebor's head." That was the wording of the proclamation they nailed to the Luddsgate.'

Will glanced at Morann. 'Or until the king raises another great army to force a way into that city, too, I suppose.'

'Gwydion once told me that the churlish folk of the Realm dearly love their king, despite his shortcomings,' Willow said. 'Are they so different, those who dwell in Trinovant?'

'Oh, they love Hal too. But they want him free of his queen and all her luxurious friends. Her retinue has run up great debts with many of the Trinovant merchants, debts they boast of paying when Duke Richard's estates fall to them.'

'They're that open about it?' Willow said.

Morann nodded. 'When news came of the shattering of Ludford the merchants of Trinovant were not best pleased. There is a kinship among merchants. At Ewletide, Trinovant rose up and the mob would have burned down the royal palace had it not been for the Sightless Ones who issued forth from the Great Spire and drove them back with curses. Even so, there was much destruction and lawlessness.'

Will sighed. He had always believed there was no dispute that could not be settled by two people of good faith and ample forgiveness sitting down together over a pint or two of best beer. Such was always the way in the Vale, where nothing was thought important enough to rise above a wholesome compromise.

Morann drew out his long, thin knife, and began thumbing the edge. 'Tell me, was the move to Kernelwort made at the prompting of the Fellowship, or did it come from Maskull?'

Will made a wry face. 'Maskull, I'd say. Though he's been going away for weeks at a time on business that I can only guess at. And then, as sudden as you like, he returns. At such times the court's always thrown into a flurry and a panic. Half the time he goes cloaked so that no one save the queen can see him, and half the time he walks in plain sight.'

Willow said, 'He's due to return here soon, if his other absences may be taken as our guide. Every time he does appear he uproots the court and sends us all on to a worse place.'

Morann studied the flaring emerald in his ring, watching the way it reflected in the surface of his blade. 'That may be the best news yet.'

'You wouldn't say so if it was you who was being dragged around all the Middle Shires,' Willow said.

Morann took the point. 'It seems to me Maskull is trying to gain magical advantage by choosing his ground. It looks like he's playing a grand game of checks with Gwydion – he's moving his king and queen for safety. I hope that's so.' He gestured roundly, but half of it, Will thought, was to cover his misgivings. 'And so you came at last to Castle Corben. Do you know aught of the Corben Tree or its dark history?'

Will shrugged. 'I don't, but it feels like a place of bad aspect to me.'

'You shall not hear much more about it from my lips, for it was a place of dubious and debatable magic in the reigns of Cynsas and Orelin, a thousand years ago, though later it was famed for its fleet-footed horses. Some say these steeds were bred with the blood of pards in their veins. Not in the way a pard is bred half-and-half with a lion to make a leopard, but with just a drop of pard blood to give the horse a fiery nature. Such things are possible only on tainted ground.'

Willow shivered. 'More than once I've heard a cry in the night. I took it to be a griffin, though maybe it was a pard.'

Will turned quickly to her. 'You said nothing to me before.'

'I thought it was just a fancy. I wasn't sure what I'd heard, and now I'm even less certain. But I guess it must have been real enough, for it put the shivers right through me.'

'It came from afar,' Will said softly, remembering. 'Borne on the chill of the north wind, a high, keening sound that passes through the heart like the slenderest of knives.'

'That's it exactly,' Willow said, glancing at him. 'How do you know?'

'I've heard it before.'

'It could not have been a griffin,' Morann said flatly. He shifted so that the light dulled in his ring. 'Griffs of all kinds have deep, growling voices. And pards have no voice at all, except it may be a sort of hiss much like a swan has when there are cygnets to guard. Anyway, pards have long since vanished from these parts.'

But Will continued to think about the eerie sounds that had come to him. The call he had heard near Aston Oddingley, and again while he had looked out from the battlements of Ludford. But his mind refused to connect them with the horror of another night when a huge red-winged creature had appeared in his night-mares.

'Perhaps it was the Morrigain,' he said distantly. 'The hag who portends war. Gwydion warned me that she walks abroad boldly at times. She favours the night.'

Will got up and went to the window. Outside the damp day had plunged into an early gloom. It was already as dark as twilight and the rain clouds were like a grey lid pressing down the sky. There was a long silence, while fire shadows danced on the walls, then Morann said, 'Tell me, has Will had words with the king yet?'

Willow shook her head so that her long wavy hair shone with red highlights put there by the fire. 'The Maceugh has not been given leave to approach the royal person to present his emissary's credentials.'

'I'm pleased about that,' Will said. 'Because, in truth, I dare not approach King Hal too closely.'

'Dare not?' Morann said, his finger tapping on his tankard. 'Why do you say that? He is as mild a fellow as ever there was. One to be pitied rather than feared.'

'I know he means me no harm, but there's something about his glance I've come to think might penetrate the disguise that Gwydion gave us. For all its subtle art, it seems to me that this shape was woven chiefly to deceive Maskull, and there are times when some men – Duke Henry for one – are able to look through it.'

Morann put down the tankard. 'Then you're wise to be wary. For no spell of magic is foolproof, and Henry de Bowforde looks like a fool to me.'

'It's a dangerous mistake to believe that where Duke Henry's concerned,' Will said. 'But there's one thing I don't understand . . .'

'Only one?' Morann grinned.

'"By his magic, so shall ye know him." It's one of the deepest redes of magic. It says that spells betray their makers. So how is it I'm not lit up for Maskull by Gwydion's handiwork?'

Morann's smile broadened. 'I could hazard a good guess at that, but I will not. If Gwydion has promised that Maskull will not be alerted to your disguise, then you may rest assured he has arranged it so.'

Will gave a nod and glanced at Willow. 'That makes me feel a little better. But only a little.'

Morann drew out an elmwood whistle and put it to his lips. For a while he blew a haunting melody that spoke of green meadows and grey hills and shafts of sunlight that lit a blessed land. As he did so a profound peace settled over the room, and Will felt a lump form in his throat. He locked fingers with Willow as he listened, and the lump dissolved away and once more he felt the ancient power begin to flood him. While many men took more than they gave, there were some who gave more than they took. Morann was one such.

They murmured their thanks when the last strains of the Connat air drifted away from them. The music was yet another gift from the man who had been looking after Will, one way or another, all his life.

'I'm going to have to leave the court,' he told Morann. 'We can't wait for Gwydion any longer. Maskull has been interesting himself in the battlestones.'

'What?'

When Will told him about the stone they had found at Tysoe and the sighting posts that pointed to it, Morann stopped him. He got up and went over to the wet sack that he had left by the door. He produced from it what looked like an old Ewle wreath. It was made from hundreds of dead leaves.

'What is it?' Willow asked.

'A letter from Gwydion. It was left for my attention at Worfwyken Bog near the Crossing of Northbridge on the

Severine.' Morann threw it down onto the floor. 'It's in the ogham of the Ogdoad – each leaf is from a different tree, each represents a different letter. This is the last word I've had from him.'

'What does he say?' Will asked.

'He confirms your fears. Let me see . . . "Maskull has now taken possession of the battlestone that was buried below Dainspeirhafoc" – that would be Sparrowhawk Hill in the present speech of the Realm.' Morann sighed and shook his head. 'Why didn't you take charge of the stone there and then?'

'Gwydion said we ought not to. We'd already found a stone near Arebury, but the ground about it was a stinking mire, and our task was made all the harder by the nearness of a stream. As for this one, Gwydion said we mustn't bother with it, for we had bigger fish to fry.'

'So for want of a knot a whole ship may have been lost.'

'It was plain to Gwydion the Tysoe stone was not the one we sought.'

'But you left it unguarded, knowing that Maskull had been there. That was a very great risk. What can Master Gwydion have been thinking?'

Will shook his head like a man overwhelmed. 'I don't know what else we could have done. It's not easy for anyone to use the harm that lies within a battlestone for his own ends. Maybe Gwydion thought that leaving it as a temptation for Maskull might be a way to hinder him. At the time Gwydion was more concerned to find the stone that marked the next battle. And rightly so, for there we succeeded – we found the Blow Stone. And you know what happened to that. But what if Maskull has taken the stone that the Blood Stone points to? The one that's due to come alive next?'

Morann stared back at him. 'Was it a battlestone? Or a stone of the lesser kind – the kind that only guides and connects the others?'

'I don't know.'

'Then our only clue is the Blood Stone's verse,' Morann said.

He picked up the leaves and began to riffle his fingers through them. Will saw among them birch and oak, hawthorn and rowan, ash and holly. Morann spoke the verse in the true tongue and the sound of it was awesome.

> '*Faic dama nallaid far askaine de,*
> *Righ rofhir e ansambith athan?*
> *Coise fodecht e na iarrair rathod,*
> *Do-fhaicsennech muig firran a bran.*

'*Faic dama nallaid far askaine de* – what does that mean, Will?'

'Er . . . See the . . . see the wild little deer on his rope?' Will offered desolately.

That broke the gloom. Morann laughed so hard he almost fell off his chair. 'The wild little deer, you say? Ha ha ha! On his rope! Ha ha ha-ha!'

'Where's the joke?' Will asked, bemused, but then grinning back. He looked to Willow, but she was laughing along with Morann whose howls were now resounding.

'Oh, that tickled me. It truly did!' Morann choked.

Will's cheeks coloured. It was a habit that his new face had, and it was mightily annoying. 'I'm not the scholar that I might be, I'm afraid. Gwydion only conferred the tongue of need upon me with this fine disguise. He abided by the redes and refused to throw in the true tongue for good measure.'

'Oh, you can say that again! Ha ha!' Morann's face was red now.

Willow said, wiping her eyes, 'Well, tell us, Morann. How should it be?'

'Come on, Will! Even in the tongue of the Isle you should know what is meant by the expression "wild little deer!" Think!'

Will scratched his head. 'I . . .'

Willow said, 'Spiders! It must be spiders!'

'So it is. Willow, you're a marvel. And so we have . . . now let me see . . .

'Watch the spider upon his thread,
Who shall be the next true king?
He walks abroad to seek the road,
And sees not the raven upon the wing.'

'It doesn't mean anything to me,' Will said. 'How about you?'

'I can't say it does,' Morann said, sucking his teeth. 'At least nothing that jumps right out and hits you between the eyes.'

While the fire spat, and sap sizzled and seethed at the log's end, they looked at one another blankly.

'Let's hear the other reading,' Will suggested. 'That's the one that should tell us where the next stone lies.'

Morann looked through the leaves again, then spoke the lines.

'Dama nallaid rofhinn e coise do-faicsenh,
Farhe righe fodechtan a muig a de an.
An firr ansambith iarraier skainne,
Faic ath na rathod dalha na brann.

'A spider indeed walks unseen,
While the king is yet abroad.
But he who seeks the flaxen thread,
Shall ravens find beside the road.'

Willow poked the fire and watched the red sparks fly upward. 'A spider who walks unseen – I think we all know who that must be!'

Will nodded. '"While the king is yet abroad." The Blow Stone spoke of King Hal as a "false king", and Gwydion thought the part about "the king watching over his tower" was Duke Richard defending Ludford Castle.'

'The stones do not seem to speak well of the usurper's line,' Morann said. 'Perhaps it is soon to die out.'

'Then let's say that the "king" here means Duke Richard, since there's no mention of falseness this time.'

Willow met her husband's eye. 'And the duke is out of the Realm, as we know. But I wonder who's seeking the flaxen thread. What *is* the flaxen thread? And what are the ravens beside the road?'

Once more they sat back in silence, but then Will said, 'The lines don't seem to fit with the Tysoe stone or the stone at Arebury. That's something, at least.'

'The word "skainne",' Morann said. 'In the true tongue that means something very particular – a fibre of harl.'

'Harl?' Will asked. 'What's that?'

'The fibres of a flax plant. When flax is harvested the stalks are soaked in water and rotted until only the harl remains. It's the harl that's spun into flaxen thread.'

Willow said, 'That doesn't get us very far.'

'Perhaps this might.' Will gave the loremaster the green stone fish from around his neck. 'Gwydion told me it was with me when he first found me. I used it to crack the Doomstone, and then to kill the Blood Stone. You can see why I'm keen to try it on the next stone.'

Morann took the fish and examined it briefly before handing it back. 'It's a strange token, your little salmon. And I'll admit there's not much else I can say about it, though I've been a jewel-master for a fair old time.'

'If only Maskull would cause the court to progress southward,' Willow said. 'Then maybe we'd get into country that Will recognized better.'

'Perhaps we're doing what we should by watching and waiting here, but it doesn't feel right.' Will frowned, and turned to Morann. 'Would you encourage me to go against my promise to Gwydion?'

Morann looked back gravely. 'Your promises are your own concern, Willand. I cannot give you better counsel than your own on what you must do for the best.'

'You sound like Master Gwydion when you speak like that.'

'Meaning . . . what?'

Will took Morann's challenge. 'Oh, come on. You know he tells

me far less than he knows. He keeps things from me very deliberately.'

'He keeps something from everyone.'

'But why me?'

'Don't you know?'

'No. He makes me wonder sometimes whose side he's really
on!'

Morann shook his head. 'Don't say that, Will. You should never
doubt him. He's a wizard, and he cannot tell you all that he knows
– no, not even about yourself. The reason is that he is a mover
and a shaper of events. He knows cause and effect very well, and
he knows that whatsoever he tells men causes them to move this
way or that. But he does not reveal to you all that he knows, for
he dare not interfere with your fate.'

'But he does that equally by *not* telling me what he should!'

'Let him be the judge of that. And if you're in any doubt, recall
our friend, Lord Strange – the solution to his problem has always
been within his own grasp, yet he may not be told where to find
it by another.'

Will stared back. 'Are you trying to say there's a spell like that
upon my head?'

Morann drew a deep breath. 'After a fashion, Will, maybe there
is.'

'Explain!'

'Easy, Willand. All I meant is that Master Gwydion might see
his way clear to tampering with *your* future and *your* fate, but
would you expect him to play so freely with the future and fate
of Great Arthur and therefore the Realm?'

Will sat back, collapsed into himself. Despite his frustration,
he could see that Morann had made a crucial point. He said, 'At
this moment I surely don't feel like I'm Great Arthur.'

'At this moment,' Morann said, not cracking a smile, 'you surely
don't look like him either. And maybe you are him and maybe
you're not, but all I know is that you'd better be him, for time is
moving on apace, the lorc is turbulent and too many battlestones

remain in the ground. As for me, I have an ungrateful task too. Tired as I am I must leave again, and soon. Where I'm going I don't expect to run across Master Gwydion, but if I do you'll surely be the first to know.'

CHAPTER TWENTY-SEVEN

THE DRAGON'S JAWS

The weather turned warm and springlike for the next week. The splash of otters was heard in the Afon's waters, while the flash of kingfisher blue was seen among the reed mace. Buds burst and flowers began to brighten the grounds of Castle Corben. Even the dour walls of the keep were lightened by the warmth of sunshine.

As Willow had supposed, Maskull's next reappearance heralded a burst of activity around the king, but it was not another move that was in the offing – there was to be a gathering.

Will was glad. For all its austerity, Corben Castle was not troubled by the same joining of ligns that had made Ludford a place of madness and misery for him. Even so, whenever he cautiously opened his mind to his surroundings he could taste the odour of tainted magic hanging like a mist about King's Hill and along the banks of the Afon. Over the roofs and towers of the castle a ghastly power writhed with a glow like King Elmond's Fire, and Will wondered what events could have left so long-lasting a mark on the place.

Before Morann had left he had reluctantly given something of the history of Corben, telling what had taken place a thousand years before. He had spoken of royal brothers, Cynsas and Orelin, ninety-eighth and ninety-ninth kings of the line of Brea, who had first raised the sceptre here. Cynsas had reigned for fifty years, and Orelin for thirty-two, and when the latter died, in his ninety-second year, he was succeeded by the grandson of his younger brother, Robilax. This was the hundredth king and his name was Uther, later called Pendragon. It was a time of upheaval, for the famed wizard, Merlyn, had lived in those days and had come to Corben to consult with the birds of the air and to work his high magic – magic that would bring about the second coming of Great Arthur to the land. But later, in the time of the greatness of Arthur, madness had afflicted Merlyn, an insanity brought on by the death of a friend, which drove him first to the Forest of Arden and then eastward to the linden woods and the solemn rookeries of Corben. There, in the mystic glades, Merlyn had wandered many a year, living on roots and berries, riding a stag for his steed, and suffering only the company of wolves and other wild beasts. And in those days, Merlyn sought out the warlock's doom-ground and talked with the stars and danced magic that was akin to sorcery, though it was not quite sorcery, for Merlyn had been mad and his intentions uncertain.

'You see, Master Gwydion once knew what it was like to be a man in torment,' Morann had said. 'He has known love and death, for in those days he took himself a wife and then he lost her. In his madness he killed a man, the one whom his abandoned wife would have married. And what was the reason for it? It was because he thought himself the betrayer of the Ogdoad. Some beliefs a man cannot live with. They rot the mind. The blame was what sent him mad.'

On tempest nights, Will could hear the echoes of those dangerous times still hanging in the air. And he could feel now that a delicately poised web of magic enfolded the royal court, centred on the king. Regardless of where Hal went, Maskull's spells and Gwydion's counterspells remained locked in place about him, always vying, blocking, exerting precise magical force to and fro, the one always counterplaying the other. Although the sum of those spells was nil, Will appreciated that was not the same as there being no magical forces in place at all. And it seemed that King Hal's spirit was wholly weary of the tensions. He appeared strained and drained and afflicted by a terrible pressure, so that what fragile sanity he possessed seemed overready to crack. And yet something prevented it. Will wondered at the unguessed personal strength that lay within the king's heart. He was no weakling, but an embattled spirit, one enduring a monstrous burden. Perhaps that was what the churlish folk saw in him and loved.

Yet Will was able to see, as few others could, why Maskull had brought the court to Castle Corben and held it here as if in preparation for some crucial event. It was not only a place of bad aspect, but the very place where Gwydion had faced his sternest personal test. And the crucial event seemed to be connected with an announcement. There was to be a banquet, or so it was rumoured, a banquet to celebrate the king and queen's fifteenth wedding anniversary.

But was that just a pretext? Beyond it, as yet, lay only more debate and uncertain rumour. Will had come up here to the Long Gallery to decide what must be done. Beyond the gallery was an uninterrupted view across the greensward that lay between the castle walls. A hundred paces away stood the lind tree that Morann had spoken of – the infamous Corben Tree. He had slept on Morann's words for a week, but no clear way had yet emerged. Should he go, or should he stay? What to do for the best?

Will's thoughts were reaching for an answer when he passed close by a stocky man with an unsmiling demeanour and an archer's arms. The man lingered at a corner, and when Will came close he whispered, 'Hsst, my lord! A moment, if you will!'

Catching what he thought was his real name, Will turned sharply, his hand giving warning on the handle of his dagger. 'What did you say?'

'Easy, my lord . . .' The man's eyes strayed briefly to the dagger, then he took a step back. He was no lord or squire, but if he was a servant he wore no livery colours or badge to show who he served. 'I have a message for the Maceugh of Eochaidhan.'

'A message from whom?'

'I'm to ask the Maceugh if he'll come along with me.' The man seemed overeager, agitated. He looked around as if he did not quite like the business he was about.

'Why should the Maceugh come with you?'

'To attend a private meeting.'

'Private, you say? Or secret?'

'That's all I am to say. Will the Maceugh come?'

Will calculated swiftly, thinking that if it was Duke Henry who had sent the man there might be deadly peril at the end and no simple way of avoiding it. But if it was not Duke Henry, there might be something interesting to be learned. He nodded and followed the man across the castle court, up a flight of stone steps and along a short, open gallery. He sweated as he approached the door at the far end. When the servant opened it Will was surprised to find Lord Dudlea waiting for him.

'Greetings to you, Maceugh,' Dudlea said. He dismissed his servant, then invited Will to sit down, an offer Will declined. He also refused the cup of wine that was poured for him.

'Have no fear,' Dudlea told him, 'we're quite alone here.'

'That's what worries me. Plots are hatched in private meetings. If you have something to say to me, you should say it in public.'

Lord Dudlea's eyes were unmoving. 'The duke has asked me to speak with you – in private.'

'The duke—' He stopped himself, suddenly feeling danger close in on him. For some reason, when Dudlea had said 'the duke' his thoughts had flown straight to Richard of Ebor – and to Bethe.

Dudlea looked hard at him for a moment, then he said, 'The duke needs to know where the Clan Maceugh stands in our present struggle.'

Will returned the stare, but he was thinking furiously. He knew he must tread with care. After what seemed like an age, he said, 'My clan stands where I stand.'

'And where is that?'

Will stiffened. 'That remains to be seen. I was sent into this Realm as emissary of the High King. So far, I have not been allowed to present my credentials to your sovereign, and this is an affront.'

'Come now, Maceugh. You know the reason for that, or we are both fools.'

'If you mean that your king has the mind of a child and is ruled by others, then I must agree with you. But he is still your king, and I can speak with no other.'

Lord Dudlea gave his guest a withering look. 'Don't make this more difficult than it need be, Maceugh.'

'Take my words as you will.' He decided to gamble. 'I have two eyes in my head, my lord. I can see that you are loyal to your king, but that you have little time for the queen and her manoeuvres. Now what of the duke? Has he a message for me, or not?'

Dudlea's face became stony once more. 'Maceugh, you're a candid man. Therefore I will not beat about the bush with you. Duke Henry does not want Richard of Ebor to cross from the Blessed Isle. To that end we have been looking to acquire an ally who is prepared to prevent his leaving.'

'And you want the Clan Maceugh to be that ally?'

'Not . . . quite.'

'Then what?'

'We need someone to get close to Richard of Ebor.'

'Close?'

Lord Dudlea drew a breath. 'Close enough to slip a knife between his ribs.'

Will let the astounding moment run through him. 'By that, I guess you would have me kill Richard of Ebor.'

'Yes.'

'And why should I agree to that, when it would mean certain death for me?'

Dudlea put his fingertips together. 'In truth, it will be the death of you if you refuse.'

Will bristled. 'You threaten me, my lord!'

Dudlea gave a world-weary laugh. 'What you do not know is that I was a prisoner at Ludford in the weeks before the castle fell. There was no emissary of the Blessed Isle imprisoned in the dungeon there, for I was housed there myself. Therefore, what you told Duke Henry about yourself cannot possibly be true. I don't know who you are, or what your game is, but you are certainly a liar and a fraud, and I know from long experience that men who are that can generally be persuaded to do the bidding of others.'

'You're talking of blackmail.'

'Yes. And your choice may be simply put – do this hazardous thing for Duke Henry and succeed, and you will be rewarded richly. Try his cause, and fail, and your wife will at least outlive you. But refuse him, and you both will die painful deaths.'

Will's blood flowed cold in his veins. He reminded himself that Dudlea was only doing the dirty work of another. He made sure his face gave no clue and said, 'I have heard your offer.'

'And?'

'And I will think on it.'

'Do.' Lord Dudlea sat back, a tight smile on his lips now. 'But do not think overlong, Maceugh, for affairs are now beginning to move again. Duke Henry cannot afford to wait long for an answer.'

Will turned, bringing the interview to an end. At the door, he nodded the slightest of bows and withdrew. He knew that finally he had been put in the dragon's mouth, and already he could feel the dreadful jaws closing on him.

The Great Hall of Castle Corben was ablaze with candlelight. Servants loaded the long feasting tables with a spread of meat and drink fit to honour those who had gathered. There were many nobles present – two dukes, six earls, a dozen barons, a hundred knights, all with their ladies. Many had come in haste to the royal summons, to show fealty to their king and his beautiful queen, for this was a banquet none dared miss.

Willow had listened closely to the gossip that circulated among the queen's ladies-in-waiting. She had learned that a mysterious 'advisor' had told the queen that she must take every opportunity to show her closeness to her husband, and that the fifteenth anniversary of the royal marriage would provide the perfect setting for an important announcement.

But before the announcement must come the feast. Jarred, the queen's conjuror, danced a parody of magic in the hall. The conjuror always painted his face for his performances, making it unnaturally pale, reddening his lips and rimming his eyes in black. It was also his habit to stick a little silver moon on one cheek and a little golden sun on the other. He blew coloured fires and made doves fly up from his hands above the laughing revellers. As the hall waited for the king to arrive festive music played. There was juggling and tumbling by a troupe of acrobats and dwarfs, and lastly a poor bear trained to dance, or at least to move its limbs to the orders of a fearful wretch with a whip.

Will suspected that it had been brought in as a joke, scorn aimed at Earl Warrewyk's heraldic badge, which was a muzzled bear. He was sorely tempted to bend his skills in favour of the animal's plight, to utter a spell that would break the muzzle from the bear's collar and send the beast bounding free towards the high table, but he remembered Gwydion's warning that he must not do magic unless he was also willing to risk his disguise. The time for that was not yet come. To Will's eyes, the Great Hall was a landscape of shifting quicksands that might easily swallow him. Not to have turned up tonight would have roused everyone's suspicions, but sitting here among so many enemies had already made him uncomfortable, and the arrival of Maskull had made him sweat.

Now trumpets blared and the conjuror, Jarred, danced a semblance of magic before them all as they prepared to feast and to drink. Will paid the entertainments scant heed – poor Jarred, who wanted only to be admired, though everyone had seen his tired tricks a dozen times. He little suspected there was one moving invisibly among his audience tonight who could have burned him to a black skeleton with no more than a fierce glance.

Maskull was known to be at court, though he had chosen to remain unseen by everyone save the queen. But Will had the knack of seeing him too. The sorcerer threaded his way through the feast like a black viper as the queen made her entry on the king's arm. All saw how she turned her head this way and that as she walked, and many surely counted her movements as haughty watchfulness, though she was in truth listening to what Maskull told her. The king himself, mute, wan of face and seemingly bewildered beside her, tried to shut out the voices in his head. He carried a daffodil in his thin fingers, and the badge of the white swan had been pinned on his breast. He seemed remote and unworldly, living deep within himself now, in an inner dungeon that was the only refuge of his spirit.

At high table, King Hal took his place beside the queen. And, on the other side of her, Duke Henry sulked, severe in his lordly fur-trimmed velvets. Rich, heavily pleated robes hid an undershirt of mail that he always wore against the unlooked-for dagger. The queen's allies had been foregathering so there were many seated at high table whom Will did not recognize, but there were also many whom he did. Beyond the king sat Lord Strange, tossing his long head and grunting temperamentally. His grey lady ate little – she sat insipid and unsmiling at his side. And there, Baron Clifton, whose wild stare showed the damage that had been inflicted upon his mind by the Blow Stone. The last guest Will's gaze fell upon was Lord Dudlea, watchful and calculating, and accompanied now by his wife, a woman who was reputed to be his shrewdest advisor.

As the Maceugh sat down beside his own wife he may have seemed serenely untroubled, but the matter that Lord Dudlea had put to him was still turning inside his head. The plan to hamper Richard of Ebor's return was all-consuming. Dudlea had already said he would not wait long for the Maceugh's answer, but there were things that must be thought through before Will could make any move. What, for instance, if the deadly plan had not come from Duke Henry? There was only Dudlea's word that it was so. True, the plan carried the odour of Henry of Mells about it – it was simple and violent and against all the rules of chivalry, but that was hardly proof that it was Henry's idea.

Had it perhaps come from Maskull? Much else that stank of treachery did. This plan was simple, and meant to be final, but it seemed unlikely to be the sorcerer's doing, for, surely, if Duke Richard died in exile, the Ebor claim to the throne would vanish and the war would cease. According to Gwydion, that was the last thing Maskull wanted, because the war was the chief means by which he was steering the fate of the world along its collision course.

Then, might the plan have come from the queen? Or even from Dudlea himself? The first seemed more likely, but it was hard to tell. Either one might think that killing Duke Richard offered the best hope of putting an end to the war, but that was to ignore the part played by the battlestones. While those troublesome nuggets of malice remained there could be no peace. And so perhaps all attempts to kill Duke Richard were already doomed to fail.

Will glanced at his wife. She ate sparingly, taking only a token of the food that was set before her. Her gladness over receiving news of Bethe had already turned into a pressing desire to see her daughter again. He could feel the torment she was suffering, and his admiration for her doubled again – she would not agree to leave the court without him, not even now that her own life had come under threat.

The sacrifices we make for you, Gwydion, Will thought bleakly. If Morann had brought better news – or worse even – then we'd know where we stood.

Morann had, in the end, done little to help him make up his

mind. All day Will had been tempted to gallop out from Castle Corben on an errand of his own. Nothing magical, just a day's ride to try to find the nearest lign, to make a start getting onto the track of the next stone. Sometimes, when the moon's phase was fat and gibbous, when it rode the ecliptic like a great misshapen pearl set in a silver ring, he could sense the lorc calling to him. When the flows were strong he could feel something a few leagues to the east. It seemed like the Tanne lign – the lign of the oak – the same one on which they had found the Plaguestone. And on nights of exceptional clarity there were hints and echoes of other stones further away to north and south. But the one that lay almost due east was the strongest.

A tongue of flame flashed out as Jarred ate fire and then spewed it forth again like a dragon. He stepped and strutted for the feasting lords. Silken scarves appeared from ears and mouths, playing cards and coins flew and vanished, wine was poured from empty vessels. How Jarred delighted in the applause and bewilderment of those who watched. Will saw the oddness of the man, the need that had driven him to become master of a hundred petty illusions and sleights of hand that Gwydion said held true magic to ridicule. And while Jarred diverted the crowd, Maskull preyed upon it. The harm-doer walked the hall unseen, sliding lightly from place to place, listening to private talk, to those who had taken too much wine, hearing what passed in confidence between the dangerous Lord Dudlea and his bright-eyed lady, now whispering secrets to the queen, whose nostrils flared and whose black eyes flashed at what was reported.

Willow put her mouth close to Will's ear. 'There's a new rumour among the ladies.'

Will noted the sorcerer lingering near Lord Strange, and nodded almost imperceptibly. 'Go on.'

'They're saying that this time Maskull has returned to court and brought a creature with him.'

He turned. 'A *creature*?'

'They are all terrified of it.'

'Of it . . . or the idea of it?'

'I think it's real enough.' Willow's smile broadened, making it seem to anyone who watched that what she was saying was amusing and trivial. But even her gaiety attracted dark glances. Unlike most of the ladies present, her hair was uncovered and fell in glossy auburn locks, following the style of the Blessed Isle. Will saw envy in the eyes of many, and most especially in those attired according to the code of modesty recommended by the Sightless Ones. The knife-eyed women with whom the queen chose to surround herself were plain and mousy, and all of them delighted far too much in destructive gossip.

'So far as I can tell, no one has yet seen the creature,' Willow said, dabbing at the corner of her mouth. 'But there's supposed to be a reason for that.'

Will frowned. 'There would have to be.'

'They're saying Maskull has brought something so hideous that the very sight of it turns people to stone. Is that possible?'

Will took a sip of wine. 'It's not impossible. Our absent friend has in the past spoken to me of a creature hatched from a cock's egg by a toad that has the power to kill by its glance alone.'

'Do you think Maskull's brought a cockatrice here?'

'I doubt that. He is a subtler mover than that.'

Will's glance now took in the web of shifting alliances that tied the court together. He was aware of the eyes that regarded him with interest. Which of them knows about the plot to kill Duke Richard? he wondered. Which of them knows that I've been approached?

His skin prickled as the sorcerer came closer. Maskull was hard to see, a creature of all appearances and none. His lithe movements caused Will to shudder as others were made to shudder by the movements of a spider.

Though he was not present in plain sight, Will could see that his suit was of midnight black set with silver signs. He wore spurs like a knight, yet he moved as soundlessly as a sneak-thief. Will's mind dug deeper into the sorcerer's face, sensing another duplicity there. It recoiled from the ghastly death's-head that shimmered beneath the fair and youthful appearance which Maskull kept on show for the queen's eyes.

Will deliberately looked elsewhere – to where the queen and Duke Henry spoke to one another like lovers. Beside them, pale, sad Hal stared mournfully into the middle distance. Will saw the full shame of the king – the footman who stood by and dabbed at the corners of his mouth with a cloth, while under the table the queen touched the thigh of the young duke so that he leaned in on her ardently. Yet while the mother of Henry's half-brother encouraged Henry's desires, her glance also flirted with his two foremost rivals. And all this was played out while poor, half-mad Hal gazed on.

As the sorcerer came within a dozen paces Will made a special effort to look through him. It was hard to do. Maskull's eyes were black vents that led into another world. Not dead, nor yet like the glassy jewels of the violently insane, but eyes with a strange, compelling quality whose glance was unavoidable. Maskull moved away, and Will relaxed, only then realizing the assault he had been under. He squeezed Willow's hand, glad that she could see nothing of Maskull, but then he looked casually back and found with a shock that he was staring directly at the sorcerer.

He looked away again quickly, but he had been charmed and maybe caught too. Maskull was now on the other side of the hall, but he danced quickly around the room, moving like a black flame. Will's eyes steadfastly did not follow. He turned again to Willow who was the safest of havens, but she was not looking his way. He dared not touch her for fear his gesture would be misunderstood as his calling attention to some inexplicable oddity he had seen shimmering in the air. He dared not mark his talent that way and said something jestful to a knight who sat nearby. The man laughed and Will laughed back, hoping that his braying would break the spell, or mask his fear. But, no. Maskull turned as if into the attack. He roared soundlessly into Will's face, forcing a flinch.

But Will rose to his feet and with a smile walked directly at Maskull who danced nimbly away, avoiding contact by the smallest of fractions. Will did not turn aside. Instead he stepped to the window and closed it, saying calmly, 'Is it just me? Or is there a cold draught in here?'

When Maskull broke off his inspection and whirled away, Will felt a weakness in his knees and was glad to sit down again. Then Jarred swept away the danger by leaping up onto a table top and shrieking, then diving off into . . . *what*?

Into nothingness it seemed.

He vanished. In a black flash. Gone. Through a hoop into nowhere. Not even a wisp of smoke remained.

Those who saw it happen grabbed their neighbours and pointed to where the conjuror had disappeared. Astonishment was on many faces. 'Did you see that? *Did you see what Jarred just did?*' And, as if the queen's conjuror was still there to receive it, they yelled their applause and stamped their fists into the table tops and waited for him to reappear to take his bow, which he did a moment later high on the gallery that overlooked the far end of the hall.

Minstrels took their places. There was much movement in the hall. Only half those present were seated now.

'Let the music begin!' Jarred called down to them all, spreading his arms wide.

'That was real magic,' Will murmured as the music struck up.

'I thought so,' Willow answered, pulling him behind a pillar. 'I wonder where Jarred learned a trick like that.'

'I can guess. But if he learned it from Maskull, he'll live to regret it.'

The moment Will looked away, his eyes ran into Maskull again. He turned suddenly, making it seem as if he had forgotten something. Then he swooped on one of the fruit dishes and took an apple. He lounged beside another pillar and began to pare the skin from it with his knife as Maskull's attention focused on him. After a long moment the sorcerer's eyes slid away. Will's heart beat faster, then faster again as he realized the queen herself had moved to the other side of the pillar. He had never before been so close to her. He could smell her perfume – lilies. He heard Maskull speaking insistently. Like his eyes, his voice was at once intense and seductive. He spoke at length and Will heard it all.

'. . . once I was known as a maker of weapons, but now I have fashioned a thing of rare beauty. It is a device of greater power than any that has yet been made. It shall be my gift to you.'

The queen looked to her advisor with a steely eye. Her fist tightened and she said softly, 'Final victory!'

Will inched a little further round the pillar. Queen Mag's face was rapturous, her eyes upcast towards Maskull's own, her lips barely moving as she spoke. 'I will not – cannot – rest until Ebor and all his spawn are dead.'

'You shall be asked to make no peace until that is done.'

The queen smiled. 'I have already promised Henry of Mells the quill I shall use to sign the peace. I have told him it is to be dipped in Ebor's blood!'

Maskull's voice changed. Malice rippled through it, so that it almost matched the queen's own. 'You see? Events are unfolding as I have always told you they would. Even the most painstaking of balances may be thrown down. And remember this great truth: "In all things it is more difficult to build up than to tear down." That is why we shall win. The very nature of the world works in our favour!'

Then Duke Henry came to speak with the queen, his eyes suspicious to find her alone yet in such an exultant mood. He wore a querulous expression. 'When will you tell them?'

'Soon.'

'When?' he repeated sulkily, unaware that Maskull was observing him from a distance of less than one pace. 'I must know.'

'Henry, your impatience is showing.'

'It's past Hal's bed time. He's blubbering. He must have been at the wine again—' Then, with sudden venom, 'You! What are you doing there?'

Will stiffened.

'I asked you a question, Islander!'

'We are all here at the queen's command.' Will felt Maskull's adamant gaze fall upon him.

'You're eavesdropping . . .' The duke's eyes narrowed to two slivers of jet. 'I'm sure I *know* you.'

What saved Will was the banging of a heavy candle holder on a table top to quell the noise. Henry turned on his heel, leaving an intangible threat hanging in the air. He and the queen moved quickly through the crowd towards King Hal who was still enthroned in pride of place. The gathering parted before them. It backed away as the queen turned about and came to a halt beside her husband. Sensing more vital prey, Maskull joined them.

The queen's eyes glittered brightly, and then she smiled. 'My lords – the king and I welcome you to this happy celebration of the fifteenth year of our marriage. However, a matter has arisen that requires our immediate attention . . .'

Will took his wife's hand and drew her close in beside him. The queen was an expert at twisting words. She wormed her way into naive hearts, showing by turns helplessness and gratitude. She flattered and she promised, told everyone what they most wanted to hear before exacting her price. As she spoke Will thought again of the rede that warned against believing what showed on the surface and advised instead taking a close look at what lay below.

'. . . and therefore, my lords,' the queen concluded, 'his grace the king announces a Great Council against treason to be held here at Castle Corben in seven days' time. At that Council you will be able to show your loyalty to your sovereign.'

As the plucking of lutes and the beating of tabrets and timbrels started up again, a hundred excited conversations began. Willow said, 'What did she mean by a Great Council against treason?'

'It's Maskull's doing.' Will glanced at the sorcerer, who lingered near Lord Dudlea. 'He's going to try to gather all the nobles of the Realm here against Duke Richard.'

Willow's eyes widened. 'But why?'

'They're going to attaint him in his absence.'

'Attaint? What's that?'

'His fellow lords will try him and find him guilty.' Will wondered how this latest turn of events affected what had been asked of him.

'And when that's done, what will happen to him?'

'Then everything he and his allies own can be legally confiscated by the Crown.'

'Everything?'

'The queen will demand that Foderingham and the Castle of Sundials in the North, and all the other estates be given up.'

'And the duke?'

'After he is dispossessed, he will be declared an outlaw and an official bounty placed upon his head.'

CHAPTER TWENTY-EIGHT

JASPER

.

W ill had a knife in his hand when he first saw the monster enter the castle gardens. He was whittling the semblance of a pine cone into the bulbous end of a stout staff as he sat in the bright midsummer sunshine. The weather was warm and fine, and the sky a wispy blue. What clouds there were flew high and thin overhead and the sweet smells of summer were on the air. Chairs and benches had been placed on the sward of grass that lay between the castle and the Corben Tree. Many were occupied now, mostly by the clerks and servants of the nobles who had arrived for the Great Council.

Since the night of the royal banquet rumour had grown that Maskull had a strange creature locked in his tower – not a cockatrice after all, but a man-creature, a monster of the sorcerer's own making. The gossips swore that the man-creature was so ugly that his face had to be wrapped whenever he walked abroad, that the merest sight of him would turn a man to stone.

Will felt a shadow pass across him. It was Jarred the conjuror, who dawdled for a moment, then sat down on a bench not ten paces away. He had been drinking.

Just then, the hairs began to rise on Will's neck, and he knew

Maskull was coming his way. It took all Will's strength not to leap to his feet, but when he saw what was approaching, he could not help but let a gasp of surprise escape him.

Maskull was cloaked in invisibility, but a doleful figure was hobbling in his wake in plain sight. Its walk was awkward, like one struggling impotently against some hard-gripping compulsion. The figure was shrouded from head to toe in black gossamer, but tightly, so that its form could be seen though no part of it showed. There was a strong whiff of magic about its movements – it was being directed to go where it had no wish to go.

Will looked away. A surge of fear flashed through him. No one ran away or called out. No one dared to speak. Only when the sorcerer had gone did Will's flesh stop creeping. Only then did the scent of roses come back to his nostrils. Folk turned to one another, muttering fearfully, asking what it was that had passed among them.

Will's eyes settled on Jarred. When not preening before an audience, the conjuror was usually as fidgety as a ferret. But he was not fidgeting now. He had seen Maskull go by.

Will was sure of it. He recalled the trick Jarred had pulled at the banquet. The need for admiration was what had made him a royal conjuror, but the queen, captivated now by the powerful magic of a real sorcerer, had tired of poor Jarred's caperings. Perhaps his desire to rekindle her interest had driven him to meddle with powers that were beyond him.

When Will turned he saw something that interrupted his speculations. Lord Dudlea's servant was approaching.

'I have a message for the Maceugh from my master,' the man said flatly.

Will shaded his eyes. 'And what message is that?'

The man's face was empty. 'My lord asks that you come to meet with him.'

'On what business?'

The other did not move. 'I do not know what business. Only that the Maceugh must come.'

'Must?' Will stared back, but did not stand up. 'What language is this in which to frame a request? Tell your master that the Maceugh will meet with him at noon tomorrow.'

The other edged closer. 'My lord means to meet with you now.'

Will got swiftly to his feet. 'The Maceugh is not at your master's beck and call. If he says he will come at noon tomorrow, then that is when he will come!'

Heads turned at the sharpness in Will's voice. Seeing the whittling blade, the lord's man took a pace back. 'Your pardon, Maceugh.' He put his hand to his chest and bowed his head, but the bow was shallow, and his apology unmeant. 'I will take your reply, but I warn you that this will not satisfy my master.'

'Noon tomorrow,' Will growled. 'And tell your master that his servants have poor manners.'

The other nodded shortly, then left. But Jarred's curiosity had been stirred. The conjuror gestured at him. Will shrugged as if to dismiss the disturbance, but Jarred said, 'Beware Lord Dudlea. He's dangerous.'

Will shifted to avoid the splash that leapt from Jarred's flask.

'Want some?' Jarred said, thrusting out the flask.

'What is it?'

Jarred laughed. 'Does it matter?'

Will put the flask to his nose, then to his lips. It turned out to be cowslip cordial, powerful and over-sweet. He looked closely at Jarred's face. Without his face-paints and conjuror's tokens, he appeared ordinary and prematurely aged. His skin was papery and creased by lines. Tiny veins could be seen coursing beneath the surface. His hair had withered to grey wisps and his teeth had yellowed. He looked to Will like a man who had given so much of himself over to appearances that his heart had died inside him.

'Are you . . . *unwell?*' Will asked.

'There are to be no more performances,' the conjuror told him. 'Her grace has tired of Old Jarred. When he protested she banned him from court. She sent her sergeants to turn him out an hour ago. Two filthy brutes. They said his quarters were needed by an earl, that he must make do with the hayloft above the stable if he would stay.'

'That's not so bad.'

'Not so bad? It's a lodging fit only for peasants!' The conjuror stared desolately at the castle walls. 'Why has she sent me away?'

But Jarred knew why, and Will knew why too.

The conjuror tried to rise from the bench, but failed. 'I'll take my revenge upon her,' he murmured darkly. 'On all of them!'

'Don't tell everyone your plan,' Will said, alarmed at his open treason.

But Jarred would not be hushed. He became maudlin. 'When first she came to court she always called for me. My three blind mice illusion was always her favourite. She used to love my magic. But ever since *he* arrived, she's treated me like an old shoe.'

Will shook his head in sympathy. 'Who do you think *he* is?'

'You don't know?' Jarred's eyelids drooped. He seemed to find something briefly amusing, then, 'I hate him.'

'Why? Because he does real magic?'

'*Real* magic?' Now Jarred's anger spilled out. 'What about *my* magic? That's the kind that takes a lifetime of practice. My skill is the sort that's hard won. Intricate. Difficult to do! It's not old-time sorcery, not some mystic power that flows out of the veins of the earth!'

Will's hands tingled. He wondered again at how little Jarred must know of real magic. How had such a man ever succeeded in uncloaking Maskull? But as Gwydion had once said, Maskull was arrogant, and arrogance often led to carelessness.

'Where does he come from, this sorcerer?' Will asked.

'He's another of those meddling wizards, those so-called lore-masters. I've seen their comings and goings. They're very good at giving advice, issuing orders to one and all, using the king's court as if it were their plaything! Who do they think they are?'

'You mean like that fellow . . . Gwydion? He comes at times to the Blessed Isle. He presents himself at the court of the High King in just the fashion you describe.'

'Yes, he's one of them. "Master" Gwydion, as he likes to be called. With his rings of blue fire and his disappearances. I was doing rings of blue fire years ago! I did rings of blue fire for the royal marriage! It amazed everyone. They talked of nothing else for days, weeks. But who remembers that now, eh?'

'They don't appreciate true talent,' Will said, watching Jarred knock back more of the heady cordial. 'But you were saying about Maskull . . .'

'I'll tell you something about him, Maceugh.' Jarred leaned on Will now as if he was an old friend. 'Nobody knows it, but he's here now.'

'No!' Will tried to appear surprised. 'Here?'

'Oh, yes. He thinks no one can see him. But I can. I know more than he supposes. He always keeps a private place for himself in whatever stronghold he brings us to. He has one here, a chamber in the south-east tower. He thinks no one knows when he goes there. But I do!'

'Doesn't he keep it secret?'

'He tries, but I use these!' Jarred pointed to his eyes. 'Any magician will tell you – folk who know how to use their eyes are very few. People always think they see, but they don't.'

'So Maskull has a chamber in the tower?'

'And the tower has a window. And every two or three nights he receives a visitor through it.'

Will pictured the tower. Its only window was an arrow-slit set high above the ground.

'What kind of a visitor?'

Jarred wagged a finger at Will's apparent doubts. 'It *flies* to him whenever it would speak with him. It grabs onto the sheer stone like a great big bat. Then it scuttles across the wall and squeezes in through the slit.'

Instantly, Will thought of the ked. That would be small and

agile enough to get in through Maskull's window. He asked, 'This flying thing – do you mean something like a goggly?'

Jarred's eyebrows lifted and his eyes closed. 'That is the vulgar name for such creatures, I believe.'

'But you said it *speaks* with him?'

'Of course it speaks with him. It's his spy. It does his bidding.'

'But . . . aren't such creatures always in thrall to the red hands?'

'Many are. But this one is wild.'

'Wild?'

'They come from the Realm Below.'

'How do you know it's wild?'

'A-ha!' Jarred tapped the side of his nose. 'Because this is the one that led Maskull out of the labyrinth of halls that lies beneath the earth.'

When Will heard that a pang of excitement passed through him. Until that moment he had not connected the ked with Maskull, but now it made perfect sense. The trouble was, the conjuror was now in a very loose-tongued mood. He could upset everything.

Jarred's red eyes swam as he took another swig of cordial. 'You didn't know? He's been down there for years. It's common knowledge at court. He was forced to dwell there in exile after a fight with one of his fellow meddlers. That goggly, as you call it, is the creature that guided him out, and he enslaved it for its trouble. Now he uses it as his night-eyes.'

'How do you know all this?'

Jarred yawned widely and sighed a deep, drink-sour sigh. 'I have . . . asked . . . the spirits.'

'You certainly have.' Will propped him up again. 'Come on, Master Magician, this day has worn too thin for you to enjoy any further. Let's get you to your new quarters. And I, for one, will hope you sleep like a man unburdened.'

Will took Jarred to his loft. By now it was early evening and the sun was golden in the west. With luck Jarred would not come to his senses until morning. But what then? Will climbed down the rough ladder, his new-carved staff in hand, thinking what to do about the black-swathed figure that Maskull had led through the garden. Then he recalled Gwydion's words: '. . . *If I know Maskull, he will have bound Chlu upon a magical chain before letting him out into the world. One day soon, I think, he will try to reel him in and begin to wring the truth from him . . .*'

He knew for certain that the figure must be Chlu.

Events were moving fast now. It was time to find Willow, so he headed back towards the castle. Dozens of noblemen had been arriving all day with their entourages, and the sward was filled with painted tents. Smoke rose from camp fires. Tethered horses were being attended to by grooms. Will recognized many of the colours that emblazoned the camp. Most belonged to lords who had marched their contingents to Ludford at the king's command, but there were many others now, attracted by the imminent break-up, not only of Ebor's possessions, but also those of his two rich allies. Maskull had succeeded in harnessing their greed, and it looked as if he must soon have his way.

Will's heart sank as he returned through the camp. Servants ate and drank, caroused, threw scraps to their hounds, rode horses up and down, practised with sword and buckler. A year ago, many of their masters had sworn that Richard of Ebor was justly trying to save the Realm from a wicked queen and her loathsome friends. Now they called Ebor a traitor.

As he tried to pass a large group of men drinking ale, he collided with one who backed hard into him and put an elbow in his ribs.

'What's this?' the man roared.

Will stepped away from a man of about thirty years of age, a westerner from his mode of dress, perhaps from Cambray. He had flaming red-gold hair and a face that was heavily freckled. Though Will recognized a princely bearing, the man held a drinking bowl in his right hand, and his left was poised on the hilt of a broadsword.

Will lowered his staff and put a hand on his breast, bowing slightly. 'Your pardon, sir.'

'My pardon?' the other repeated loudly. '*My* pardon, did you hear that?'

Will nodded slightly and began to move on.

'Islander! You spilled my ale! What do you mean to do about it!'

A hand was on his arm, spinning him, sending his staff flying from his grasp.

'If I've disturbed you, friend, then I apologize.'

The other cast his drinking bowl down. 'He spills my ale then calls me his friend!'

As Will recovered his staff he saw the drinkers nearby nudge one another. Their eyes brightened with anticipation as the Cambrayman stood in his path and kicked the staff out of reach.

'Let me pass,' Will said.

'Not until you've made amends. And if you refuse—' The stranger grasped the hilt of his sword and ran it half out of its scabbard. 'I'll make you pay in blood.'

The Cambrayman was showing off. His clothes were fine and raffish and his movements practised and showy.

Will's blank expression should have warned him. He said, 'Blood for ale? Only a fool would fight to the death over a mouthful of either.'

'Oh, *to the death*, is it?' the other demanded mockingly. 'Did you hear that? I speak only of blood, and he speaks of death!'

The eager crowd was listening gleefully now. Many were grinning. The rest watched as if they knew they were about to be treated to a spectacle. But, strangely, when Will opened his mind to the swaggering Cambrayman he felt nothing of the bully in him.

'If it's a fight you're wanting, then I'll not disappoint you. But even a meat-headed fool knows that a fight that's not to the death, isn't worth starting.'

The crowd hooted and jeered at that, but the Cambrayman

seemed intrigued by Will's words. 'An interesting point of view, Islander, but now you're adding insult to injury, and for calling me a fool you'll pay extra. You'll fight with me, or I'll ride you round this field like an Elder's mule.'

Will's shrug threw the suggestion off as unworthy. He gestured to where his staff lay. 'Now that you've deprived me of my plain stick of green wood, I'm unarmed, unless you call a whittling knife a weapon. So are you a coward as well as a fool?'

He turned away. At his back there came the unmistakable sound of a broadsword singing free. It set Will's teeth on edge, and as he spun, a scabbarded sword was flung at him from one of the eager watchers. He caught it, knowing he should not have used the word 'coward' with a man like this.

'Draw!' the red-haired man shouted, slapping him now with the flat of his sword. 'Draw, and we'll settle the matter like men.'

'Like men?' Anger surged in Will, but he controlled himself in dignity as he knew a real man should. 'Like children, you mean. You're drunk, my friend. And the matter's already settled.'

Another slap. 'I'm not your friend. And I'm not drunk. Draw, Islander, or I'll ride you like a mule, I swear I will!'

Will gritted his teeth. 'Now you're taking this joke just a little too far.'

The other prodded him, flicked the sharp sword-tip under a fold of Will's *leine* so that the fine linen tore. 'Draw!'

Will knew that if he drew the blade there would have to be bloodshed, but he could see no other way. He took stock again – his opponent was used to handling a sword, that much was clear. He was quick. He used his feet neatly, and Will saw from his eyes that he was not as rash as he tried to appear. Nor was he as drunk. This was no accidental meeting.

He was forced to parry the slaps, and as he did so the other turned his sword, so that now he had to protect himself from a range of practice cuts. They were delivered with frightening precision, and in a manner calculated to make an opponent look foolish.

'That's the way,' the other said, goading him. 'But you're

supposed to take the steel out of the scabbard first. Unless you'd have me carve it out for you.'

Those who looked on brayed loudly, but the brays turned to cheers as Will pulled his blade free. As soon as it was out the other aimed a full-strength blow at Will's head. He chopped upward only just in time to intercept it. Sparks flew, the blades rang and they pulled away.

'You're tall, Islander, and you're strong, but you're out of practice,' the other said, still playing to his audience.

Will slashed at him, but the last time he had used a sword had been at Castle Foderingham, years ago. His opponent warded the blow easily.

'Oh, come now! You can do better than that!'

Will ducked the other's reply stroke and rolled out of the attack. How could he avoid causing the kind of harm that could not be mended, when his hand was being forced?

The other circled, hawk-eyed. 'What's the matter? Isn't your heart in it? It soon will be!' He lunged and slipped under Will's guard, feinted left and slammed a hand under his chin to push him down. It was effortless, a consummate piece of skill, and Will landed heavily on his side. His sight blurred. Blood welled in his mouth. He knew he had bitten into his own tongue.

He spat red. The watchers yelled and roared. He was aware of more men running up to see what was happening until an arena formed around them. He got up, weighed the sword in his hand, disliking the shiny steel. But he could not afford reluctance for he dared not use magic.

'Had enough?' the Cambrayman enquired indulgently.

Will lunged in answer, sending his adversary skipping back out of range, even when Will slashed at him a second time.

But now Will's talent spoke to him. He could see that he had not been given just any sword. It was untouched by spells, yet a short, violent history flowed in it. It had been made by a smith who knew his trade well. The grip of dark red leather was sweat-blackened. The blade was springy and well-balanced, sharp enough, yet nicked where it had once been used to edge-parry a blow of tremendous anger. There was a weakness there. Will noted it all in a flash – this blade had seen much use by a skilled man, now dead. It had killed twice. Three lives had been entrusted to it. Yet in his own hand it felt awkward, and the waiting fault in the steel troubled him.

Another attack swept them together before they clashed then whirled away again to the safety of two swordslengths.

'I should at least know the name of the man I'm fighting,' Will said, circling to his right.

The other stepped back warily, then gave a parody of a courtly bow. 'My name is Jasper, son of Owain. Jasper, like the gem. What's yours?'

They met again on Jasper's initiative, heaved one another away. Shoes of soft leather skidded easily on grass, but what galled Will was that he could have brought the fight to an end by turning his opponent's steel into a set of horse-shoes in mid-swing. If not for his disguise.

The swords rang, swiped empty air. Blade tips bit into grass, were daggered and thrust. Will's sword tore open a nearby tent. The watchers laughed – all except the owner. Will stumbled over a three-legged stool. Their bodies dodged, swayed and swung away from blows, heads ducked. Kicks were aimed, an ankle was grasped and turned, a punch was landed. Blade bit blade. When next they clashed their foreheads knocked hard. Will forced words through gritted teeth as he shoved the other back. 'You already know my name,' he said.

Jasper heaved, but seeing that Will was the stronger, he had to cut away. He leapt lightly back, easily recovering his poise. Two swift counter-blows came crashing at Will. He knew that with neither mail nor plate to protect them the fight could not go on like this for long.

Jasper, son of Owain . . . The name meant nothing. Who was he? A prince of Cambray it seemed. A man as good with a sword as this must have won himself a wide reputation.

Three more quick swings to head, arm, leg. Then Jasper ran at him to charge him down. Will side-stepped and tripped him. He rolled, but carried the motion through and ended up on his feet again. Now Will knew for certain that this encounter was more than a kick at boredom or a show of deadly skill.

Then, why start it? he thought. Does he really want to kill me? Or is he trying to force me into magic?

But . . . a stumble!

Seize it!

Will brought to mind the fault in the steel. He smashed the flat of the sword against an iron cooking-pot, then held what was left of it aloft, broken off a foot from the tip. With a gesture of finality he threw it down onto the ground. But Jasper came at him with venom and he was forced to sweep up the steel stump again.

The crowd jeered at that.

'I can't fight with a broken sword,' he gasped.

'Then you should have been more careful!'

He felt the blast of anger from Jasper. It was fuelled partly by anger at his own slip, partly by annoyance at having been out-manoeuvred. He could not stand being made to look like a fool.

Will twisted away from a savage kick at his groin, rolled back, but then his hand found his staff. It came alive as he hefted and turned it. When Jasper ran at him he speared the end of it into his breastbone and stopped him cold.

The blow knocked the breath out of the Cambrayman, threw him down momentarily, but he leapt up, hacking, slashing, moving to left and right.

Nothing he did could shorten the distance between them. The staff stung his arm, elbow, breast, neck . . . There was no escape, except to step away.

Jasper's next blow would have cut Will in two, except that he reversed the staff and brought the other end of it up under the sword arm and jabbed it hard into an unprotected armpit.

Jasper's sword fell. It spun away and dug point-first into the damp earth. There it bent and swayed like a wheatstalk, as Jasper, legs split and off-balance, made a painful lunge for it. He missed. The pole menaced his face, and he sat down heavily on his rump, his hand pressed to his side.

'Now,' Will said quietly, hefting the staff like a man preparing to chop down a tree.

Those who watched bayed for blood, enjoying the vanquished man's fear.

'Do it! I have lived long enough!' Jasper said. His face was white, his voice almost indignant but he showed a brazen face. 'Kill me! I shall not ask for quarter.'

Will gave him a quizzical look. 'Kill you? Over spilled ale? What do you take me for?'

There were disappointed shouts from some of those who watched, and when they saw that no blood was going to be shed, they began to wander away.

Jasper stared up at him, his pride bleeding freely. 'Kill me. It's your right.'

'But not my pleasure.' Will watched him squirm.

At last, Jasper's anger evaporated and he threw out a hand. 'If you have no stomach to finish the job, then help me up.'

Will let him grab the other end of his staff and hauled him to his feet. 'Whose game are you playing?'

Jasper scratched his chin, shook out his bright hair, then laughed. 'You deserve to know – Henry of Mells.'

'You're an honest killer, at least.'

Jasper recovered his sword and wiped the soil from the end of it. 'Oh, if I'd wanted to kill you, you'd be dead. Henry wouldn't ask *me* to kill you – a couple of crossbow bolts are surer and cheaper and far more his style.'

Will spoke in a low murmur. 'Then why the fight?'

'Because he doesn't trust Islanders. He's not convinced you're truly an emissary of the Blessed Isle, despite what Lord Morann told him. As for me, I was once foolish enough to say in his hearing that a man's sword arm speaks more eloquently of origins than his mouth. He told me to make enquiries of you if I would win his favour. I need his favour, and so I did.'

'And what has my sword arm said about me?'

Jasper laughed again. 'Oh, I'd wager a silver crown to a chicken bone that you're not of the Blessed Isle. Though I'd say you've undoubtedly been there once or twice.' He punched Will's shoulder.

'Oh, is that a fact, now?'

'But don't worry, I'll say just the opposite to Henry.'

'Why did you agree to do his dirty work?'

Jasper gave him an appraising look. 'I told you, I want his favour. My father and I are not popular, and gatherings like these bring us close to our enemies. We need powerful protection.'

'Then why did you come?'

'It's the king's command, and if we're anything, we're loyal to Hal.'

It was a strange sentiment coming from a Cambrayman, but Will decided he liked Jasper. They shared a jug of ale. Will asked, 'You're quite a fighter. Where did your own sword arm learn its eloquence?'

'Let's say, I had a difficult boyhood.'

'You spoke of enemies. Do you have many?'

Jasper laughed. 'Enough. You see, when my father was in his young days he wooed and won the love of a lady. It was a love affair widely frowned upon.'

'She must have been some lady.'

'She was the late king's widow.'

Will let his amazement show. 'You mean . . . King Hal's mother?'

Jasper nodded. 'The same. Queen Kat. She's also my mother. My father's what you call a man of passion, see. One look at my mother and there was no stopping him.'

Will learned how Owain had saved Kat from a cloistered life under the lock and key of the Fellowship. There had been a secret marriage, both looking for a quiet life out in the west. And in return Jasper's father had got three sons. But it had not gone down well in many quarters. Owain's enemies had finally thrown him in prison in Trinovant and sent Kat to live in the Fellowship's cloister at Bermond. She had died there within the year, and her tombstone, Jasper said bitterly, made no mention of her marriage to his father.

'A law was even passed in Council against a king's widow marrying, so that such a thing could never happen again. You see, they thought my father was trying to gain power by making himself the king's step-father. But they don't know him. He did what he did out of love.'

Will was staggered. Jasper really was the king's unacknowledged half-brother. Yet two men more different in temperament and looks it was hard to imagine.

'Jealous lords have long memories and little forgiveness in their hearts,' Will said. 'It sound like you're lucky to be alive.'

'You're right about that.' Jasper looked at the tents that were spread all around. 'We try to live quietly in Cambray, but whenever the king declares a Great Council the law says we must attend. We are forced to travel from our own lands and come among a nest of vipers. My elder brother, Edwin, was killed the last time a Great Council was called. I'd rather not go the same way.'

Will picked up the two halves of the broken sword. 'And so you put yourself at Henry de Bowforde's service.'

'He asked for me. He uses me because I can fight, and because he knows we're loyal to Hal come what may. I'm fond of my half-brother. I fought at Verlamion alongside Henry's father, Duke Edgar. I was at his side when he was killed.'

Will recalled seeing the savagely torn body of the old Duke of Mells. 'You were fortunate to escape that day.'

'That's the truth.'

Will handed Jasper back the pieces of his second-best sword. 'There was a fault in the steel.'

Jasper looked ruefully at the blade, then searchingly at Will. 'I don't know who you are, but you're not what you seem.'

'Fare you well, Jasper,' Will said, meeting the other's eye. '*Slein an a!* – as we say in the Blessed Isle.'

Jasper grinned. 'So you do, Maceugh. *Slein an a!*'

The long, light evening sky finally faded to night. Will avoided the flaring lights down by the gate and bent his path to the shadows. A violet glow flickered at one of the slit windows that opened near the top of the south-eastern tower, and he recognized its deadly purple hue.

He shivered and stepped close to his door. There was a light burning inside, and low voices. Then he saw a number of pebbles of different sizes arranged on his doorstep, and his heart leapt. He tapped on the door lightly – one, one-two, one-two-three – and then stood back.

After a moment the reply came: one-two-three, one-two, one.

The bolt slid and a man stood framed in the doorway. Willow watched from the pool of golden candlelight beyond – Morann had returned.

'Did you find Gwydion?' Will asked as soon as the door was barred again.

Morann shrugged. He was newly arrived and road-dusty. 'The most I've had is that.' He pointed to the wreath of leaves that lay on the table. 'It's by Gort, but he does not tell good news. First he passes on Master Gwydion's apologies for sending no word direct. Master Gwydion has travelled far and wide, and is now as sure as he can be that the two battlestones you found near Arebury and Tysoe are not the stones that the Blood Stone points to. Neither of them will be the next one to draw men to battle.'

'Did he say anything about Maskull's meddlings with the Tysoe stone?'

Morann met his eye. 'Gort's message was long in reaching me, but it asked me to go at once into the Blessed Isle and keep close watch on Richard of Ebor's preparations.'

'For what reason?'

A strange light glinted in Morann's eye. 'Because timing is important when it comes to invasions.'

'Invasions . . .' Willow repeated, her voice falling away. 'You mean Duke Richard intends to bring an army back into the Realm?'

'Not if I can help it. My task is indeed to ask Friend Richard to return into the Realm – but I am to persuade him to come alone. Or at least, not in force.'

'What?' Will asked, incredulous. 'Richard won't do that!'

'He will if asked in the right way. He's to come with a small, unarmed entourage, no more. Master Gwydion believes that a great reconciliation might now be had.'

Willow shook her head. 'It's gone too far for that. The queen's ladies say she's determined to have Richard of Ebor's head. She can't do that while the Ebor forces are intact.'

Will cut in, 'Edward is with the earls and their army over in Callas. Gwydion must realize that if Richard returned, the earldom of Kennet and a dozen others would rise up in support of him. The burgesses of Trinovant have already declared as much. Ludford may be in the queen's hands, but there's Foderingham, the Castle of Sundials, Wedneslea, Sheriff Urton – all of these fortresses have yet to fall.'

'Still, I must do as Master Gwydion asks. My task is to persuade Friend Richard to land with no more than a thousand men and ride south on the queen's assurances of safety. Master Gwydion says he must be made to do this, or events will go astray from the true path.'

Willow threw up her hands. 'You'll never move the duke.'

'Master Gwydion says I must take the stump of the Blood Stone with me as an earnest, and say that with both the Blow Stone and the Blood Stone seeing to his protection he will be undefeatable.'

Will's inner warnings were sounding. 'Will Richard believe that? For I surely don't.'

Morann nodded abruptly. 'Master Gwydion thinks he will.

Friend Richard was at pains to take the Blow Stone with him when he departed into the Blessed Isle. He's had the stump installed under his bed these past months at Logh Elarnegh Castle after he had it brought away again from Derrih. He swears that's the reason he's been making some powerful good decisions of late. And indeed, that may be so.'

'You'd better prepare for failure, Morann,' Willow said, adamant.

'I have prepared for success. Twice I've visited An Blarna, and each time I pressed a different cheek upon the stone that Master Gwydion gave to Cormac. If that can't make me eloquent, I don't know what can!'

Will had wandered across the room. 'I still don't see how it would be a sound decision to walk naked into the lion's den. As you must have seen, every lord of the Realm except Sarum and Warrewyk and their close kin have pitched up here. They've come to strip Ebor of his properties and titles, and to place a sentence of death upon his head. He has spies. He must know what's afoot.'

Morann took up his satchel and slung it over his shoulder. 'The patterns of the world are complicated but I'd say that when Master Gwydion speaks, it's best to take good heed of his opinions.'

'You're leaving? Right away?' Will said, seeing Morann step towards the door. 'But there's much still to discuss.'

'I must. I'll go first to Ludford, then I'll take ship to Logh Elarnegh and speak the persuasions that Friend Richard must hear. Let's hope that I reach him in time.'

'They say the best-rested traveller goes furthest,' Willow said. 'And remember what Gwydion always says about more haste meaning less speed.'

'Yes, will you not sleep here tonight at least?'

'I thank you for your kindness, but I cannot afford to be seen here tonight. The court presently thinks I'm in Trinovant, and that's how I want it to stay.'

But Will put out a hand and stayed his friend, saying, 'Perhaps, after all, it would be better if you *were* to be seen here.'

Morann looked to him sharply. 'Why?'

'We might be able to kill two birds with one stone, and so win ourselves a few days' grace.'

He told Morann about Lord Dudlea's proposal, and how he had agreed to meet with him tomorrow to give his considered refusal.

'I hope you'll tell him you'll do as he asks,' Morann said, frowning. 'He's a dangerous man to cross, and no mistake.'

'I cannot agree to do as he asks. And his patience is by now worn through.'

'Then look to your safety, my friend.' Morann gestured towards the table, which held a basket of mushrooms that Willow had gathered at first light and a large jug. 'Dudlea's aura would curdle that milk. He'd think nothing of seizing a man's wife to make him do what he wishes.'

'I know what sort of man Dudlea is, and we're already looking to our safety as best we can. But what if I did tell him I'd agreed to his plan? What if I told him I'd persuaded you to go into the Blessed Isle to kill Duke Richard?'

Morann paused, thinking. 'You may tell him that if you want. Though it might make my reception at Logh Elarnegh less than warm if Richard's spies make report to that effect before I get there. Still, they say the best way to protect yourself in a nest of brigands is to make yourself useful to at least one of them, and I can see how in the end your suggestion might work to our advantage.'

'Then stay tonight, be seen with me tomorrow, and then continue on your errand.'

'Maybe I will at that.' Morann dropped his satchel on the chair. 'You're more persuasive than I, despite all my preparations. However, is there not a small hole in your plan? The moment Richard lands, or even if reliable news comes here that he's setting out, Lord Dudlea will consider his agreement with you reneged upon. In that case, he'd be bound to try to kill you.'

Will smiled a humourless smile. 'If I'm not much mistaken, he's going to try to do that anyway.'

Next morning, Will and Morann walked together in the gardens making sure they were seen by every eye in Corben. Then Morann took his leave, and as he mounted his horse he told Will to take heed of his inner feelings.

Willow had been down to get as close as she dared to the royal apartments, where she heard more from the queen's idle ladies-in-waiting, whose gossiping had forewarned them of Chlu's presence at Castle Corben. This time, though, they were talking excitedly about the queen's jewellery.

'And very strange some of it is too, by all accounts,' she told Will when she returned. 'Some of it was from "her wizard" they said, something that was meant to make up for a great diamond that he once took from her.'

Will's worries surged. 'The Star of Annuin! The diamond that Maskull was forced to return to the vault in the Realm Below. What could make up for losing that, even if she had no idea what it was?'

Willow nodded. 'Well, what he gave her was a pair of golden bracelets in the shape of fetters – cuffs of gold made for her wrists, each one, apparently, is set with a golden chain three links long.'

Will scratched his chin. 'Fetters? Perhaps it was meant to be a symbol of her relationship with the king.'

Willow looked unimpressed. 'Don't forget that the golden fetterlock is part of the livery badge of the Duke of Ebor.'

'True. Then do you think it was some kind of heraldic joke?'

'Maybe it's nothing at all, but the rumour is that these bracelets were very hard for Maskull to make. And they were something that the queen longed to have. Her lady of the chamber said they gave her feelings of great joy whenever she put them on. She said the queen would only put them on when she was alone, and then she would dance and laugh to herself.'

'I don't much like the sound of that.'

'Neither do I,' Willow said. 'And what's worse – she doesn't have them any more.'

CHAPTER TWENTY-NINE

THE NIGHT FLIER

The great lind that was the Corben Tree creaked and groaned, while underneath its spreading mass lay a span of darkness. Only thick, black tree roots crawled there, gnarled and sinister, like carved serpents. Not a blade of grass grew among them for, in times past, cloven hooves had danced this ground and warlocks had made it the scene of their murderous revels. It was certainly not a place of good aspect.

The prospect now, though less monstrous than in ancient times, was almost as unhappy to Will's eyes. There were flags flying from poles wrapped in coloured ribbon and the meadow below the Corben Tree was dressed and partitioned into lanes as at a royal tourney. Bench seats had been made ready in two great enclosures, and a royal dais set up under a great awning of cloth-of-gold. This lonely meadow had been turned into a place of splendid ceremony where all could be enacted just as if it was in the White Hall of Trinovant. But whereas spell and counterspell had always held fast around the king in Trinovant, here Will could feel a definite flow in favour of Maskull's sorcery.

A procession of earls and dukes began to gather between ranks of liveried men. Will and Willow waited in the enclosure that had been set aside for foreign emissaries. Beside them were seated the envoys of Cambray in their green and white robes and sporting the red dragon on their breasts. Next to them on the other side were the Weirds of Albanay, with their long braids, sombre plaids and swirlingly patterned silver brooches. To their left sat men and women of rank dressed in even stranger garb, ministers and merchants visiting Hal's court from kingdoms and principalities that lay in the far parts of the world.

At last the lords of the Realm emerged in procession from a great tent. They passed along the windbreaks where warm breezes fluttered sailcloth barriers that had been skilfully painted with faces and figures of the kings of old – all one hundred and fifty kings, from Brea to King Hal himself. The Lord Great Chamberlain, the Lord High Admiral, and the Earl Marshal of the Realm led the lords forward, each carrying high his mark of office. Dukes and marquesses followed, then earls, viscounts and barons, parading before an audience of gentlemen knights and esquires.

The breeze tugged at the coloured feathers that plumed two hundred lordly hats, but it barely moved their heavy ermine-trimmed cloaks. These nobles came in fine array to their seats, and there they waited, sweating in the heat, for their king and queen to arrive.

But the long wait went on. Those who next entered the enclosure were the gold-caped Elders of the Sightless Ones. Chokingly sweet incense burners fumed white before them, carried by pageboys who saw them to their places. Two gilded thrones stood ready beyond. They were set with cushions of gold and velvet, and between them was a smaller throne, its back made in the shape of a swan's neck and head.

The rumour was that the delay was caused by the queen herself. It seemed that she had been gone from the Castle of Corben for some days, for none had seen her, or her favourite horse. The breeze died. The air became humid, heavy and suffocating. When a shimmering haze played over the royal dais, Will's eyes were drawn to it. It awakened his talent, and a figure resolved itself there – a figure dressed in elegant black, lurking like a spider behind the king's throne.

Now began the Great Council of Peers. After the waiting, a chant from the Elders. A solemn moment followed, then a fanfare of silver trumpets. A mock combat was fought between twelve knights clad in bright armour and, when that was done, an anthem was sung by the Emasculate Fellows of the White Order, their reedy voices sounding to Will like those of sad, trapped creatures whose childhoods could never end. More sickly incense was burned at the four corners of the platform. At last the buzz of expectation was quelled by the raised rod of a sergeant-at-law who begged silence. Young pages carried four cushions forward. Each was set with its own symbol – one of the Great Hallows of Sovereignty: a sceptre, a sword, a chalice and a crown. Then came the king and queen: King Hal in a plain brown velvet coat with a sealed scroll in his hand. Next, Queen Mag, resplendent in crimson and gold and richly bejewelled with diamonds, rubies and pearls. Following on was the heir, a solemn little boy of six or seven now. Behind him came Duke Henry, who invited the Lord Great Chamberlain, the Earl Marshal of the Realm, the two Lord Constables and the other principal men of the king's government to follow their king in procession.

Maskull shifted himself, circled the thrones as the king approached. Hal was reluctant to mount the dais. Will saw how Maskull's form cast no shadow, but as he moved the smoke from the nearest censer curled strangely as if a lick of breeze had caught it. Hal forced one foot in front of the other and at the steps a footman took his elbow. Once upon the throne, the king's delicate, white fingers relinquished the scroll to his wife, who handed it to Duke Henry. She listened to Maskull's whisperings while oaths were affirmed, knights were knighted and other lesser matters transacted according to form. The Great Council of the Realm was now in session, and its age-old ritual had to be observed in strict sequence, for it was known that vestiges of old magic clung to ritual. But at last the time came for the day's deadly business to be carried through.

All who watched were brought to the highest pitch of excitement. The king's heralds, in tabards of red and blue quarters, blazoned with golden leopards and lilies, stepped forward again. They blew their silver trumpets. Then, in the dead quiet, the Chamberlain's voice barked out,

'Be it known that whereas Richard, lately styled "Duke of Ebor", along with several others . . .'

Will listened as the names of Richard's chief allies were read out in the curious way that lawyers used. Earls Sarum and Warrewyk came first, and then all the barons and knights who had sided with Duke Richard.

'. . . in the thirty-sixth year of the reign of our sovereign lord, they did assemble them at Ludford a great host, traitorously intending, imagining and conspiring the destruction of the king's royal person, our sovereign liege lord, Hal, the third of that name.

'And they, with the same host, with banners spread, mightily armed and defenced with all manner of arms, as guns, bows, arrows, spears, glaives, axes, and all other manner of articles apt or needful to give and cause mighty battle, they did array themselves in a field in the Earldom of Salop, and there by great and continued deliberation, traitorously levy war against our said sovereign lord and his true subjects there being in his service and assistance under a banner of our said sovereign lord, to the subversion of the Realm . . .'

When the Chamberlain had done, Duke Henry spoke briefly with the queen, then stepped forward. His voice was strained as he strove to be heard.

'My lords, it is the king's pleasure that the following order be understood by all:

'Whereas the traitor Richard of Ebor has rebelled against us, thus shall he and his heirs be lawfully attainted. Let all who oppose their king show themselves now or forever hold their peace!'

Not a single man in the crowd moved, nor was a word spoken.

'Then it is done!'

The spell Maskull had woven over the proceedings was broken. Will alone saw his dark figure waft across the platform and drift lightly down the aisle. He was leaving before the convocation had even finished, before the king had even risen. Now that his will had been done, there was no reason for him to linger.

Wind rustled the canopy of the Corben Tree, drowning everyone in sound. The oily stink of incense filled Will's nostrils. He saw the shadows under the tree moving; it seemed for a moment that a herd of swine were there watching what went on, but that was impossible. Suddenly, there was a hubbub at the back of the lords. Then a messenger came forward and spoke briefly with the Earl Marshal. The queen rose and hurried away with her son, King Hal and all their many attendants trailing in her wake.

A commotion began almost as soon as the members of the Great Council rose to their feet. Will saw Maskull turn about with raised arms and then he suddenly appeared in plain sight. His business now was with Lord Dudlea, who approached him and was struck down in a fit for his trouble. He gasped, rose quivering to his knees and tried to beg forgiveness, but Maskull strode away. Something was happening, something important, but its meaning was just beyond Will's power to grasp. Willow, seeing it, took his hand.

'What's happening?'

'I don't know,' he told her. Just then he saw Jasper in the crowd. With him was an older man, certainly his father, Owain, a man with white hair and beard and a round, red face now, but who must have looked much like Jasper in his younger days. The news, whatever it was, had reached them and so Will went towards them.

'Jasper!'

'Maceugh.'

'So much for the pronouncements of this Great Council of Peers,' Owain growled.

'What news?' Will asked.

'The Duke of Ebor,' Jasper's eyes sparked with excitement. 'He's landed on the northern coast, and with him has come a great army!'

Will stood rocklike as the crowd swirled around him. He wanted to make sense of these tidings, to foresee their consequences as Gwydion would have done. But then his arm was roughly seized. He tried to pull away, but Lord Dudlea's grip was tenacious. He was grey-faced with fear or anger or both. His nose was bleeding and he was trembling and the pupils of his eyes were shocked pin small. He held something in Will's face, something shining against his gloved hand. His voice hissed, 'Your delays have betrayed us, Maceugh! Now your life is worth no more than this.'

The noble threw the thing down, turned on his heel and left, and when Will picked up what had been cast away he saw that it was a silver farthing, the smallest coin of the Realm.

The deadlock of spell and counterspell that had been set about the court had at last been shaken loose. All the way back to the castle, Will heard a rising wind. It was roaring in the Corben Tree as the mystic boughs shed their leaves. He could feel instability growing almost palpably, as Gwydion's protective magic decayed. Everywhere around the court, the wizard's magic was unravelling.

'So much for Morann's errand,' Willow said. 'And so much for Master Gwydion's plan. It's a full armed invasion, after all!'

'Something's gone dreadfully wrong.' Will drew her on, still wondering what could have happened and what he should now do for the best. 'Quickly! We're no longer safe here!'

Fears about the Dragon Stone suddenly reared up in his mind. If Gwydion's binding magic was all that kept that stone safe in its cellar at Foderingham, what would happen now?

Willow gasped and stumbled at his side as if she had been shot by a crossbow bolt. Terror flooded through him and he grasped her close to him. 'What is it?'

'Nothing. Nothing. Keep going.'

They went on through the gate, mingling with a great crowd of servants. Most had been put under urgent orders to pack up and leave as quickly as they could. No sooner was Will inside the castle than he pulled Willow round a corner and towards a small storeroom.

Its door had a broken lock, so the room was unused. He looked both ways. 'Here! Inside the buttery. And close the door.'

'Look at me!' Willow cried once they were alone. 'My hair! It's coming out by the handful!'

Will stared. 'By the moon and stars!'

The dank little room was empty, except for some broken shelves. It was whitewashed yet half dark, for the only light came through two small vents high up on the wall. Will used his whittling knife to contrive a makeshift bolt that would hold the door shut so long as no one tried to force it. Willow blinked at him as he turned. 'Will – oh, your beard!'

Will seized her shoulders, searching her face. 'Your eyes are changing colour too. Not so quick that you'd notice it happening, but they're not the same colour they were this morning. And your skin – it's mottled.'

'It's the same with you. Your beard's thinner and the shape of your chin is changing. Oh, Will, what's happening to us? Is this Maskull's doing? Has he cast a spell on us?'

He lifted the russet sash that lay across his left shoulder and held it up to a shaft of light. The weave was finer, the wool faded almost to grey now, and the silver *delch* pin with its brown stone was smaller, its lustre gone. 'I shouldn't have waited so long. Our disguises are failing.'

'Then we must get out of here!'

'We can't! Not yet.' He quickly explained what Jarred had let slip. 'You see what that means, don't you? If we can catch the creature then we'll be able to ask it about Chlu.'

She stared back at him. 'Why are you worrying about the Dark Child now? Haven't we dangers enough?'

'It's the only way I can find out who I am, where I come from, who my real parents are. Don't you see?' He told her about the red fish, and repeated what Gwydion had said. 'I have to try, Willow. I may not get another chance.'

Willow touched his cheek. 'Whatever you do, I'm doing it with you. I've grown used to your new face – but it'll be good to have my old Will back again.'

They kissed, then hugged. 'Brave girl.'

She looked around at the bare room. 'We're changing fast. We ought to fetch a few things here while we still can.'

But their fears about raising suspicions proved unfounded. Of all the people who entered the castle court, not one turned to look at them. Their attention was directed at something else entirely, something so terrible it had reduced them to whispers.

'What is it?' Willow asked, craning her neck.

'Two statues of grey stone,' Will said. 'One is a woman, and the other's a boy.'

A crowd was gathered around them, and more were packing in to see. The statues were life-sized and carved in grotesque detail – Lady Dudlea and her son. Will could not take his eyes from the lady's face. Horror was frozen there and he realized that the boy must have been turned to stone even as his mother looked on.

'Maskull's creature!' Willow said, clutching him. 'They must have looked upon it!'

Will hurried her away, knowing that no cockatrice stare had done this, but Maskull himself. 'The plot to kill Duke Richard must have come from Maskull. And now Dudlea's had to pay for his failure.'

They dodged back into the storeroom and barred the door. For the rest of the afternoon they kept themselves hidden, watching one another as they slowly returned to their true selves. The noise and anxiety outside reminded Will of the days they had spent locked in the dark at Ludford, but this time the danger was greater. The news of the invasion had led the queen to issue an announcement. Every lord loyal to King Hal was to go immediately to his estate and gather his forces. There was uproar in the castle, with so many trying to leave at once. Carts rumbled through the yards outside. There was shouting and a great deal of hustle and bustle, but eventually the sounds died away, and as evening came there was an eerie quiet, broken only by the changing of the guards and the sound of birds cooing in the dovecote.

They waited in silence. Hunger began to gnaw at them. Though most of the earls and barons had departed, the kernel of the king's court remained, making it impossible to emerge. Then the moon sent a beam through a high vent in the wall, and a patch of silver began to creep across the stone floor. Once the castle doors were closed to traffic for the night, Will judged it safe to venture out. As he cracked the door ajar, the sweet smell of rot drifted in from the compost heaps in the garden beyond the wall. Will now looked sufficiently unlike the Maceugh to risk crossing the courtyard, though he never thought who he would claim to be if he was challenged.

He returned with a basket of food, two grubby travelling cloaks and some other necessaries. He had also found a sack, a cord and a spool of grey silk. When they had eaten bread and cheese he emptied out the sack and began to knot the silk into a net.

'The statues were gone,' he said.

'Both of them?'

'Yes. I suppose Dudlea must have taken them away with him.'

'Poor man.'

Will looked up. 'He threatens our lives, and you call him "poor man"?'

'But you saw what happened to his wife and child. Imagine how you'd feel if it had happened to you.'

'You're right. He is a poor man.'

As the darkness deepened, Will crept out again. First he checked to make sure of Maskull's whereabouts, and found that he was closeted with the queen. Then he went up onto the battlements and climbed perilously onto the tower's slate-shingled roof. He hung the net from the eaves so that it covered Maskull's window. When that was done he let down two long cords with which to spring the snare. It only remained for them to find a dark corner under the walls and wait.

Willow joined him and they huddled together in the shadows, taking it in turns to keep watch. Will studied the familiar star patterns that slowly wheeled above his head. He saw a barn owl swoop silently across the court. Bats flitted through the air after moths, and he heard the barking of dogs and a distant nightingale's call. Still no light appeared in Maskull's window, and no one entered the stone spiral that led up to the sorcerer's chamber. At last, as Will yawned and let his head loll forward, he heard the soft sound of wingbeats.

He nudged Willow gently, and pointed up to where a ghostly grey shape fluttered in over the castle wall. It disappeared for a moment but then came back again. In all, it flew three times about the tower before folding its wings and squatting as if by magic upon the sheer wall nearby.

Will saw the strange way it moved, climbing sideways with amazing agility across the featureless stone. Only when it had begun to poke its head in at the slit and the net snagged on its snout did Will pull the cords. Immediately, it was enveloped.

'Naaaaaw!' it screamed, and the sound echoed loudly through the castle court.

Will pulled again and the grey silken mesh that wound the ked up like a fly in a spider's web began to fall away from the window. He dashed out and tugged the cord one last time to dislodge the creature's grip. The whole dead weight of it plummeted down. He caught it heavily, as if it was a child falling from a window ledge, but this was no child. It was a creature with sharp teeth and wildly scratching claws, and it was frightened.

'Naaaw!'

'Come on, my little wriggler!' Will said, grabbing it by the back of the neck. He thrust it down into the sack that Willow held open. 'You're coming with us!'

The creature's pitiful screeches were muffled by the sack, and as they reached the buttery and Willow shut the door, he told the ked severely: 'You'd better be quiet, or I'll have to knock you on the head.'

When it showed no sign of settling down and one of its claws tore through the sack, he put it on the floor and laid some of his weight on top of it. 'No, you don't! I'll squeeze the breath out of you if you don't shut up. Quiet, I say! Or I'll sell you to the Sightless Ones.'

'Don't say that,' Willow told him. 'It's terrified enough.'

'It's more than terror,' Will said, holding tight to the struggling mass. 'There's something nasty gripping its heart, but if it doesn't shut up it'll bring the whole castle down on us.'

'Naaaaw,' the creature squawked, and Will bore down harder until the struggles slackened. After a moment he relaxed his grip a little.

'Listen, ked. You'd better keep still. If you do, I promise no harm will come to you.'

'Cannat breeeeathe . . .'

Will let go of its neck and it began to gurgle. Then it gave out a thin self-pitying whine.

'That's good,' Will said. 'You mustn't scream. No noise. We mean you no harm, but if you try to make a noise I'll stop you. Now – do you want me to let you out of the sack?'

'Yers,' the bundle croaked in a small voice.

'You promise? No more noise?'

'Little Ked keep quiet.'

'Good. That's . . . very good.'

Will loosened the sack enough for the ked to put its head out. It mewed plaintively, and Will saw its many needlelike teeth flash white in the moonlight.

Will did not let go of the sack. He said, 'What's your name?'

The ked stared and twitched, not knowing how to answer.

'Do you know who we are, Little Ked?' Willow asked.

Will glanced at her. He knew they had come to the crossroads, and that now there would be no going back. He said, 'Don't you remember me? I'm the one who let you go when your leg was caught in the iron trap.'

The ked flinched, but then its eyes widened and Will saw that it did know him.

'Saved Little Ked!'

'Even though you bit me, right here on my hand. Look.'

The ked blinked, and a shudder ran through it as if a fever gripped it. 'Sorry, sorry! Awwwwww! Awwww!'

The ked began to flap. Its threadbare wings, so skilled in the open air, were a useless encumbrance of skin here. Will made no move. His voice was firm. 'We don't mean to harm you, Little Ked, but if you make a fuss, we'll have to put you back in the sack. Do you understand?'

The ked's eyelids finally drooped. 'Yers.'

'Are you hungry?' Will asked after a moment's silence.

'Yers.'

'Perhaps you'd like a mushroom.'

There was silence, then: 'Mushroom?'

A look of concern crossed Willow's face. 'Will, should we? What if mushrooms don't agree with it?'

'Gwydion says they live in caverns under the ground. They eat morels and ceps that grow in great numbers down there. He once told me that the red hands use honeyed mushrooms as bait to catch them.'

Willow uncovered the basket and the ked's attention became fixed on it. Slowly it put its claw out. Then it took a large mushroom, very carefully peeled back the brown skin of the cap and began to chew the flesh.

'Good?'

'Good.'

'You're not still frightened of us, are you?'

The ked's eyes flicked from face to face. 'Yers.'

'Then you may have as many mushrooms as you like until you're not.'

The ked took another, then another. It broke off the stalks and bit into the heads with the side of its mouth. After the third, it tried a morel. 'Very good.'

'Now that we're friends,' Will said gently, 'maybe you'd like to tell us why you brought a bad man to us that night at the inn.'

The ked stopped chewing and the morel fell from its hand. It trembled again, and for a moment Will thought it might try to take flight. But it made no move to escape. Its eyes were fast on Will's face while its hand felt uncertainly for what was left of its meal.

'What's the matter? Why are you shivering?'

'Very frighty. Fog in head. Dust in throat. Need medicine soon.'

'Medicine?'

'Yers. Very soon!'

'Will, I told you some of those mushrooms might not agree with it,' Willow said, taking the basket away.

The ked made a grab for it, but then recoiled fearfully.

'Sorry, sorry!'

'Shhhhh . . . I'll soon make you feel better,' Will said gently. 'But first, why did you bring the bad man to me while I slept?'

The ked trembled again and moved away as Will's hand neared it 'Awww! Not coming for killing! Watching over. Only waking because Dark Child coming.'

Will flashed a meaningful glance at Willow.

'Shhhh . . . be easy,' she told the ked.

Will said, 'Who's the Dark Child? Why did he come to me?'

'Want find for killing! Little Ked tappy-tappy. Waking! For friend!'

Willow said, 'He was trying to warn us.'

'Yers. Warn us!'

The ked blinked and its small hands trembled. Will saw then that it gave trust as easily as a puppy and that, although Maskull had used it cruelly, he had not succeeded in entirely ruining its nature. It picked up a piece of mushroom and whimpered again, saying that it was very sorry it had bitten Will's hand.

Willow shook her head, anger simmering in her voice. 'My dad always used to say there's no such thing as a bad dog, only a bad owner.'

'You can say *that* again.'

A shiver passed through the creature and it began to tremble again. Then it began to fluster and flap. 'Must go.'

'Go where?'

'Need medicine!'

Willow put out a hand. 'What do you think it means?'

The ked's big eyes watched Willow reach out. 'Must have. Or die. Never go home.'

'Tell us about home,' Will said. 'Tell us how you came here and I'll give you better medicine than any you've had before.'

'Better medicine?'

'I promise.'

Will opened his mind and let the power of his talent flood out and the ked suffered Will to come close and place his big warm hands on its back and chest. Will felt the spells gripping its flesh, surging in agonizing waves over its delicate little ribs. They were too powerful for the ked to fight, but Will drained them. Then, holding the ked in his arms, he danced the sorcerer's magic off its heart.

As he removed the spell he remembered what Gwydion had told him about how Maskull's arrogance had so many times in the past led him to be magically careless. And so it proved with the ked, for Maskull had underestimated the reserve of innocent trust that the ked possessed. Nor had he ever imagined that his slave would be taken and his power over it challenged by kindness.

Will planted his feet and danced an incantation of cure until circles of white light haloed the ked and the purple shadows that befouled its aura began to lift. Then Will took the greenstone fish in one hand, knelt, laid both palms upon the swooning creature's head and slowly drew out the harm.

At last the ked fell down, limp and fragile. Will knew his breaking of the sorcerer's magic would alert Maskull. The sorcerer's own spells, exorcized so close by, must surely be felt by him. Yet for all the dangers, Will knew he had done what he should, and that was what mattered most.

'Good medicine . . .' the ked said, stirring at last. Then it began to tell how one day it had gone deeper into the Realm Below than ever before, and there in a luminous cavern in the ruined Land of Annuin, down in the forgotten city of Caer Sidhe, it had met with a lost wanderer. 'He very happy. He see me, say: "Friend!" Say "Now show the way! Up! Up!" And so we go out from Caer Sidhe. Up and up, up and up. Always by secret ways only I know. Sometimes in a dark cave, sometimes in starry bright. Sometimes wild mushroom, sometimes nothing. Long time we walk, then sometime come to place where water go like this.'

'An underground river?' Willow asked, seeing the way the ked moved its delicate hands.

'Yers, ugown river. Coming down from Realm of Light. This river end of Land of Annuin. Then some long time walking in tunnels and after starting the cool caves.' The ked blinked and looked to them helplessly. 'For me – this home!'

'But Maskull wouldn't let you stay?'

'I say show stranger way to Realm of Light – then he *catch* me. Tell me big sickness on me. Make me drink medicine!'

'How easily Maskull breaks faith,' Willow murmured. 'Even with those who've gone out of their way to help him.'

Will had listened in silence, and the more he had listened the angrier he had become, and the more he had pitied the ked. Here, perhaps, was a far descendant of the ancient fae who had left the Realm of Light so long ago. In some strange way, it reminded him of the noble creature who had drowned under the water wheel at Grendon Mill, and of the elfin retinue which he had seen accompanying the Green Man one night in Severed Neck Woods.

'There's a gaping void of human weakness that's powering Maskull's spells,' Will said grimly. 'Gwydion says Maskull has locked all the deceits and betrayals of five Ages into his heart and there he distils the foulness that turns everything he touches to filth!'

The ked went on to tell of its many torturesome days and nights, seeking out damp hidey-holes and cowering in shadows, or else flying in a strange and frightening world of boundless air. It told of the blinding, shrivelling sun it suffered by day and the terrible burden that Maskull's potion had laid upon it by night. It had been commanded to fly far across the Realm, and every three days to return and tell of the villages and towns it had passed over. The sorcerer had then checked them off in the pages of a great book, looking for any discrepancies. This, Will supposed, must be the king's book, the Great Book of the Realm that Gwydion had spoken of before.

'So *that* was how Maskull found the hidden village of Little Slaughter,' Willow marvelled.

'And how close he must have come to finding the Vale.'

But there was more, and Will now learned what he had hoped to learn, for the ked said, 'Dark Child also slave of sorcerer. Keep wrapped up in black. Make to obey him always.'

'But why does Maskull keep the Dark Child wrapped in black?' Will asked. 'And why does he want so much to murder me?'

But the ked said that it did not know the answer to that.

By the time it had finished telling its tale, it was sitting on Will's lap. He stroked the sparse grey fur of its head and let it cling securely to his chest. It looked up at him with big, sad eyes and trembled. And Will noticed the hollow way Willow looked at them then, with the glisten of a tear in her eye. He knew she was thinking of Bethe.

'Perhaps it would have been much better for all of us, Little Ked, if you'd not been so kindly to strangers, but how were you to know what a weak-hearted man you'd happened upon?' He gave Willow a smile. 'I think it's high time this Little Ked went home.'

'I think you're right,' Willow said, and now there were tears in both their eyes.

424

Will stroked the creature and comforted it, and as he did so he thought of what Gwydion had taught him about never talking thoughtlessly of 'good' and 'evil', and how the best way forward was often too hard for men to see with certainty. What always mattered most in the long run, he told himself, was to have a gentle aim and to keep a steady heart.

CHAPTER THIRTY

THE DUEL

They crossed the courtyard and mounted the stone stair up to the battlements. 'You need drink no more medicines, Little Ked,' he told the creature as he held its small hand in his. 'The sorcerer has lost his power over you. You'll feel no pain if you don't return to him. You're free again.'

'Good happiness now,' the ked said, opening its big, liquid eyes.

'Go home now! The ruined chapter house where you entered our world is no more than seven leagues to the south and there's still a good hour before sunrise. Fly home, and let no one see you.'

Will threw the creature into the air. It stretched its wings, dived, then rose, and was gone into the night.

When they had seen the last of it winging beyond the trees Willow whispered, 'We must go too. Maybe, if we can find a good horse . . .'

'No. Remember what Gwydion said: more haste, less speed. Now we're ourselves again Chlu will soon be on my trail. We'll leave him no easy track to follow but go softly on foot. If we travel east we'll reach the Mulart lign. I'm sure it's no more than half a dozen leagues from here. The stone I sensed at last full moon is standing on it, and though it's now three days before last quarter, we may be able it pick it up so long as the ground is kind—'

'Shhhh!' Her voice became a whisper. 'Look who Maskull has sent to do his bidding.'

His eyes followed where Willow pointed. On the far side of the courtyard, a figure slipped from the shadows and paused outside their quarters. A shaft of moonlight caught the movement. The figure's head was darkly swathed, but the jerky, animal movements were gone now, as if an invisible tether had been loosed. In its hand was a long dagger, and Will saw a glint of green flash from the blade.

He watched as Chlu hesitated, then turned away. Will thrilled with horror when the black-swathed figure swooped silently on the buttery where the ked's mental shackles had been broken just a little while before. Willow squeezed Will's arm silently, and they jumped blindly hand-in-hand into the garden yard beyond. They landed on top of a large compost heap. It was warm and moist under the surface and stank of rotting vegetation, but it was a silent place to come to earth. When they had rolled away, Will checked the moon-silvered parapets above.

Nothing.

They slipped through the gardens and fled. It was a fine feeling to run barefoot in the grass. After so long cooped up in the castle it felt like true freedom, and Will thrilled to know that a virtuous circle had been forged, that the gift of release he had made to the ked had come round so soon.

The moonlight waned as they ran, and was soon replaced by a pale summer dawn. Low mists clung to the river and Will took Willow's hand and hurried her across the place where hundreds of tents had stood only days before. The temporary village where he had fought with Jasper was now just a memory – only heaps of rubbish and old fire pits remained. Will's thoughts were in a whirl as he reminded himself of the invading army that was supposed to be marching south under the Duke of Ebor, and how the lords loyal to King Hal had been sent away to gather their strength. He wondered how strongly the lorc had sprung to life, and tried to estimate just how long they had to find the next stone.

Soon they were among the mists of Afon Water and stepping towards Stonelea Woods. The summer sun rose in the north-east. Cocks began to crow. Will kept the moon over his right shoulder and continued to follow the river. In the villages which they passed through folk were already going about their early morning chores. Most paid them friendly heed but little more, for their grey-brown wayfarer's cloaks showed them to be travellers passing through. Some folk asked what news there was. Others told what they had heard.

'Have a care!' a pedlar at a well warned them. 'The nobles are in a hurry to raise men. They'll not scruple to take an able young man like yourself off the road.'

'Is your own lord raising fighting men?' Will asked, feigning ignorance so as to learn more.

'Aye, all the lords are! Haven't you heard? A great invading army has landed in the west.'

Will thanked the pedlar for his advice and urged Willow on. She looked over her shoulder, still worried about Chlu. 'Surely he won't be able to track us across fords and along hard roads, will he?'

'Who knows? It's not our scent he's following, though after we fell into that compost heap he might easily be.'

'Then what shall we do to keep him off?'

'I don't know. It's dangerous to imagine too little of him. He found me at the Plough, and the only time he was not drawn to me was when I was in the Vale, or in disguise, and covered by one of Gwydion's spells.'

'But how does he do it?'

'He seems to feel my presence, and I light up like a stroke of lightning for him when I dance magic.'

'Then don't dance any!'

'I won't if I can help it. But he'll ask questions along the way, and he'll find answers, you can be sure of that.'

They came by a stream that wound among gentle slopes. Broad grazing meadows reached down to the water, and there were dozens of fresh molehills. Further up, older, drier molehills made bald patches in the grass. These had been crazed and cracked by a week of dry weather. Gwydion had once taught him how to read molehills, for the little velvet animals who made them felt very strongly the power that lay in the land.

'This way,' he said at last. 'I'm sure it's this way.'

The stream passed into the cool shade of a wood and then out again. There were forget-me-nevers where the stream joined a deeper one, and blue-bodied damsel flies danced over the water. They saw little pebbly beaches that fringed the river and muddy reaches where cattle came down to drink and where the bank was broken. Will felt the cool water lapping between his toes. He saw shoals of transparent fishlings darting and turning as one at his approach. He sang a ditty that he had learned as a child:

> *'Fishling fry,*
> *All of him is eye.*
> *He has naught for a body,*
> *But how fast does he fly!'*

He took Willow's hand in his. He felt suddenly strong and happy, and knew it was good for them to be themselves again.

'I wish Bethe was with us,' Willow said. 'She'll be all right, won't she?'

'She'll be the pride of the duchess herself. No child could be safer.'

'Except with her own mother.' Willow bit her lip. 'What if the duke's army gets beaten? You know what would happen then – the duke and his two eldest sons would be hunted down and killed at the queen's command, and that's if they lasted out the battle. Then Duchess Cicely would be captured and locked up forever in some guarded castle with her daughters . . . or sent to serve the White Order.'

'The duchess would never suffer herself to be locked up by the Sightless Ones.'

'She used to let them into her husband's castle at Foderingham.'

'But she doesn't like them. Nor does the duke. They have to play the game with the Fellowship, of course. All the lords do.' He turned and saw tears in Willow's eyes. 'Hey, don't cry . . .'

'I can't help it. Oh, where is she, Will? Where's my baby?'

He held her and hugged her tight. 'She's better off where she is. You know that. And if I know Duke Richard, he's far too wily for the queen. The duchess is no fool either – she'll stay in the Blessed Isle until there's news of the battle either way. I'm sure of that.'

She sniffed and dabbed at her eyes. 'Do you really think so?'

'I really think so.'

Will led her onward, cutting quickly across the land, following the flows just as Gwydion had taught him. He wanted to lay good words here and there, as he had seen Gwydion do so many times, but he knew he must keep their pace up and make their passing as unmarked as he could. When they finally stopped to eat breakfast, Will judged by the sun that it was already the middle of the morning. As he looked up he was assailed by a violent prickling in his skin, and so he began to scry the land around. He felt what he knew must be the Tanne lign, but it vanished within a few paces of the spot where he first found it.

They crossed the River Afon at the next suitable place, which was a ford at a village called Lawe. There they came upon a flock of honking geese.

'Beware the east road,' the gozzard told them as he saw them trying to choose the best way. 'Unless you have business in the town of Rucke, it's best left out of your plans.'

'Rucke, you say? The famous Rucke?'

'Ah, you've heard tell of the Towers, then?'

'That I have. But I thank you for the warning all the same.'

When they had gone on a way, Willow asked, 'What did you mean by the Towers?'

'You'll soon see.'

They went on further, following the river. It was partly to put Chlu off their trail, and partly for fear of the Towers that they went the longer way around. Yet as they passed by the walls and ditches of the town, they saw the Towers of Time.

'It's said there are a dozen needlewomen living there,' Will said. 'They've worked for two thousand years, making the tapestry called "The History of the World". Gwydion once told me about them. He said they were set to their task by King Gorboduc, who was the twenty-first king to reign in the Realm after the Age of Giants.'

'Do you mean the same women have been working there all that time?' Willow asked.

'I don't know about that, but Gwydion said they record all that happens in the Realm. He told me that if ever their stitching stopped, time would end, and all things would stand still forever.'

'Master Gwydion said that to you?'

'He did. He says that's why, whatever else may pass in the Realm, the town of Rucke is left to govern itself. It has a sheriff who makes the law, and no one from outside molests it.'

After that they followed the south bank of the Afon, giving as wide a berth as they could to the strange town. Will wondered about Gwydion, and what to do about him. How would they ever find him now? Or he them? Events were moving along too swiftly, and it was so long since they had heard from the wizard. Outlandish possibilities began to flit through Will's mind. Sight of the Towers of Rucke make him think of the far-famed Castle of Sundials – a fortress in the north that belonged to the Duke of Ebor, where many different machines of time were kept. Perhaps Gwydion was waiting there even now, poised to halt time and set everything to rights – but that was surely too much to wish for.

'I'd be very grateful,' he told Willow, 'if time did stop, at least for a little while.'

'How long for?' she asked.

'Just an hour. My feet hurt.'

'Don't be silly, how can time stop for an hour? An hour has to go by for that to happen.'

'Hmmm.'

'That's why if time ever stopped, there'd be no getting it started again.'

'I guess so.' Will hunted about distractedly – the power of the lorc rose at noon, and if he missed scrying for the lign then no better chance would come until midnight.

'Wait,' Willow said as they came to a great, dusty road that ran to the east of Rucke. 'Think about the verse: "He who seeks the flaxen thread, shall ravens find beside the road." I think this might be the road.'

Will rubbed his chin, and looked up and down it. It seemed ordinary enough. 'Why?'

'Could the bird in the verse have been translated "rook" instead of "raven"?'

Will tried to recall his lessons. 'The true word "bran" can mean either bird, depending on how you speak it. I think it can mean crow too. But I can't see any rooks. Can you?'

'No, but that sounds like "Rucke". It's possible, don't you think?'

Will looked back in the direction of the town, but then shook his head. 'But every battlestone we've found so far has been on a lign, and the most dangerous ones seem to be placed where two or even three ligns cross. There's no lign running through Rucke.'

'Are you sure?'

'Not completely. But look at the fields far over that way. Do you see what's growing in them?'

A patchwork of land stretched away eastward into the summer haze and many different crops grew there. Will meant the fields that had a pale blue sheen, a blue made by countless little flowers.

When Willow saw them, she said, 'Is that what I think it is? Flax?'

'It looks like it to me.'

They decided to press on again, and soon they came by the village of Elventoft. Will looked to north and south again and had another inkling about the way the land lay. Shifting power, and a sense of drifting to the south. A little further along the road they met a Wise Woman, whose back was bowed and whose stick was gnarled. They asked after the village that had planted the flax.

'By my warts!' she said. 'In Harleston they spin left-handed! It is sung of in these parts in a children's rhyme:

> *'Four-eyed folk weave the finest linen,*
> *The whitest linen there ever has been!*
> *For they use no flax to spin their linen,*
> *The softest linen that ever was seen!*
> *They pluck the locks from off their heads,*
> *And use white hair to make their threads,*
> *For the spreading over of kingly beds,*
> *Harleston linen, I ween!*

'The needlewomen of Rucke may make the history of the world, but it is stitched upon cloth woven in Harleston!'

'Thank you for your words, Wise Woman,' Will said. 'But before you go on I must ask a favour of you. If you should meet with another traveller coming along this road, one who enquires after us, what will you say to him?'

'I will tell him only to mind the crows, for they will peck his eyes out! Hurry on! Hurry on, my sweets, for it is near to the midday hour!' The Wise Woman laughed to herself again, and sang,

'Waxing, waning, fat full moon,
Stormy weather coming soon!
Make it wane, make it wax,
Use his hair instead of flax!'

The Sister of Elventoft's grating laugh made Will uneasy. He cut himself a switch from the nearest hazel and fashioned a wand from it, then he composed himself. At first the meadows yielded nothing to his probing. He felt no sense of what ran beneath the grass, but as the sun mounted higher towards noon his feet led him up a slight rise and the feelings he had hoped for began to tingle in his arms.

'I don't think it's just wishfulness on my part,' he said, walking a spiral. 'It's quite faint, but it seems to me this rise marks the Mulart lign. That's one of the three ligns that cross at Verlamion. Having touched the Doomstone I think I'd know that feeling anywhere, no matter how faint.'

'Which way should we go?' Willow asked, shading her eyes. 'North or south? Good sense says Duke Richard must have landed to the north and west of Corben.'

Will turned. 'When was good sense ever the best guide in matters touching the lorc? It controls men's wills. We ought to heed what's written on the stones first. It's south.'

'All the same . . .' He saw what was bothering her. Every step that took her further from their daughter was proving to be torturesome.

'We need to ask where Harleston village lies,' he said gently. 'I have an idea that we're now not so many leagues north of Eiton and the lign of the ash. It may be that the stone we seek lies at the crossing of Mulart and Indonen – if I can find that place.'

Judging by the sun, the lign led them a little south of southeast. They followed the road which wound along beside it, but now it seemed there was no one travelling except themselves. Will scanned the rolling lands anxiously. He had seen such things before, and an ominous feeling had begun to grow in the pit of his stomach. Even so, they pressed on and an hour or so later they saw an ox-cart coming in the other direction. They hailed the two carriers who sat beside one another, and asked what village they would come to next.

'Ravenstrop,' the elder of the two men called down.

They exchanged a meaningful glance. 'And beyond?'

The carrier eyed Will closely, but he was unwilling to call his oxen to a halt. 'Beyond lies Corde.'

'Do you mean Cordewan?'

'Arh. Corde's what the local folks call it. We've just come up past the cloister at Delamprey. The lands around are running with soldiers. There's big things going on down there, right enough. It's said the red hands have been fixing to receive the king for more than a week now, and there're strange noises come out of that cloister at night.'

The younger man gave a lewd smile. 'Them red hands at Delamprey has got women.'

'Women?' Willow repeated.

'Aye, bequines – you know, noblewomen who're lost to the world. Folks say the queen's sorcerer has been seen there working spells on them.'

Will tried not to show his dismay. He asked, 'Do you know of a village called Harleston that lies this way?'

'Hardingstones, did you say? They're down by Delamprey.'

'No. Harleston, I said. Harleston.'

'What business you got there?' the older man said, his eyes narrowing. 'Whatever it is, I'd turn around if I was you. There's trouble brewing down in them parts, and no mistake about it.'

'We have to go that way.'

'Then you're a bigger fool than you look.'

Will watched the cart rumble on, and called after it. 'At least tell us how far it is to Ravenstrop!'

'Two leagues, no more,' the younger man called back, then he pointed at Will's bare feet and grinned. 'Two leagues, but in shoes like yours you should do it in three.'

As soon as the cart was out of sight, Willow said, 'Well, at least we know we're going the right way.'

'This is exactly what happened after Gwydion took the battle-stone out of Aston Oddingley. Soldiers began gathering about us like wasps around a pot of honey. Before we could do anything about it the fight had already started.'

'What did he mean by "bequines"?' Willow asked, shading her eyes.

'When men of title die, inconvenient wives are sometimes left behind. They're often given into the care of the Fellowship and become bequines. It happened to Queen Kat, the king's mother. Jasper told me all about it.'

'That's horrible.' Willow looked up at the sky mistrustfully. 'But they said the red hands had been preparing royal lodgings for a week. How can that be?'

'Doubtless Maskull was looking ahead, beyond his Great Council. The royal victuallers will have been sent on to fix everything. But why Delamprey?'

'Now that they've eaten everyone in the district of Corben out of hearth and home, I expect the victuallers have to go a long way to find new supplies.'

'But Maskull is not the prime mover here. Don't forget what's really controlling events. If the king's soldiery is gathering at Delamprey the stone must be quite close.'

She tossed her head. 'A day's march anyway. But that's still a lot of ground.'

'Yes. It doesn't help us all that much.'

'Still, it seems strange that Maskull has sent the court to a cloister of the Fellowship,' Willow said glumly. 'He has no more regard for them than Master Gwydion does. Everything's strange about the way the stones work – no one can tell which of them will start trouble next, but the stones themselves must know, for their own verses foretell it.'

'The lorc warps men's fates so they are forced to fall in with its grand plan.'

'Was there never a way to control the lorc?'

'Gwydion said the fae left much of their knowledge with the First Men, but when the last of them died those secrets died also. Most of what the First Men did was revealed at Doward's Cave when King Cherin had his visions and the scribes wrote them down, but I don't think Cherin said anything about the stones.'

'Cherin – how long ago did he live?'

'Twelve hundred years ago. But Gwydion said the coming of the First Men into these parts of the world happened above twelve *thousand* years ago, and the fae went into the Realm Below a thousand years after that. He said the First Men dwelt peaceably here and lived according to the ways of the fae for thousands of years, and in those days there was more magic in the world.'

'But then, three and a half thousand years ago, the world changed,' Willow said. 'And the Age of Trees came to an end.'

Will looked at her. 'How do you know that?'

'Morann told me about the Ages.' She sighed. 'He said that when the Age of Trees ended, the first phantarch, who was called Celenost, went into the Far North with his deputy. Then the Age of Giants began, when there were no folk in the Isles at all. And that Age was a time of desolation that lasted a thousand years.'

As they walked, Will told her what Gwydion had said concerning the five Ages that had been, and of the Ogdoad of Nine who had arisen in the first Age when magic had been plentiful and the fae had clothed the land with trees. But then had come a great disaster and much magic had escaped the world. In the Age of Giants that followed, there had been only enough magic for an Ogdoad of Seven. And by the third Age, the Age of Iron, when the Isle was reconquered by the hero-king Brea, so much magic had drained from the world that there remained only enough for an Ogdoad of Five. In the fourth Age, the Age of Slavery and War, the Ogdoad had shrunk again to three, and now the world was in its Last Age, when all that had gone before could give no clue to what must come in future times . . .

As they walked, Will became aware of a strange sensation that came every now and then. It was hard to fathom its source, but it seemed almost like a distant stroke of black lightning that made him turn his head in its direction. Though whenever he did turn, he saw nothing in the sky. He rubbed his eyes, and looked instead at the tall cow parsley that nodded at the side of the road – its small creamy flowers, its leaves ferny and home to many small, resting flies. There was nothing to be seen that was out of the ordinary: a thickly overgrown ditch had been delved along their right, and blackberry bushes grew beyond, though the fruits were still green. A flurry of little buntings broke from cover and disappeared, chirruping, into the ripening wheatfield. Then the sun went behind a cloud. It took the fierce light off the road, but the day seemed no cooler. They hurried on, heedless now of their tiredness or of who might see them.

Will took out his hazel wand again. Scrying was not the same as casting magic, but even so he worried that the powers that stirred inside him while scrying might give some hint for Chlu to follow.

During most of the afternoon they traced the Mulart lign and all the while Will felt the strength rising in it like waves of pain increasing in an infected limb. That was against what he had expected, and could only mean that the waning that should have come between noon and midnight was being overwhelmed by a greater surge. There was as yet no sign of the Indonen lign.

They crossed a little brook and refreshed their feet in the cool water.

'Do you think the folk in Harleston really do have four eyes?' Willow asked uneasily. 'And do they spin linen from their own hair?'

He laughed. 'Who knows what's truth and what's fable in an old Sister's song?'

'The old one was right about stormy weather coming though.'

'Yes, the air's very *close*.'

'Do Wise Women have second sight?'

'Do pine cones?' he said. 'They foretell the weather too.'

She scoured the skies again, then ran her eyes along the horizon to where the haze was thickening and yellowing. 'When will the moon rise?'

'A little before midnight.' He followed her gaze to the north-west. She was right – the day was becoming unnaturally sticky and oppressive. It was not just a blight that came from his own feelings. He looked deep into the land and remembered what the Wortmaster had taught him. He noted how the vetches were patterned about in the verges of the meadow. Where before he had seen purple loosestrife and yellow toadflax and the white bells of wild carrot and pig nut, now they had begun to give way to the poisonous fool's parsley and hemlock. He looked back, checking that they were not straying from the lign, because to lose it now must cost them dear.

'We're coming to a place of poor aspect,' he said.

She looked around, unable to see what he meant. 'How many chimes before sunset?'

Will stretched out his hand and measured off the sun's path in the sky. 'About four. The sun will sink at the ninth chime this evening.'

Rooks cawed among the treetops, diving and clowning in the sky, irritated maybe by the sullen charge that hung in the air. As Will scried the green lane he looked up at the birds and saw they were mobbing a dove. But then he looked again and saw it was one of their own number which was pure white. The feeling in the ground heaved queasily like music that slides from one mode to another. He knew he had found the place he was looking for.

'This is Harleston,' he said. 'I'm sure of it.'

'Be careful.' Willow took his arm.

'With a battlestone so close I think that's good advice.' The

439

hazel in his hand twisted down powerfully. 'There's water near here too. Bigger than a pond. More like a small lake. This way.'

They came through long grass, past a spinney of yew trees and saw a stile set across a wooden fence. Will beat the stinging nettles away from it with his wand. When they entered the village they found it was no more than a few shabby hovels built around a long pond and the shacks of the linen weavers who lived there. Beyond it was the lake Will had felt. It was long and triangular, made generations ago by the damming of a stream. In the middle of its broadest part stood the Harle Stone.

'It's not even buried,' Willow said, looking unsmilingly at the pure white finger of stone that stuck up from the lake.

'Someone in the past tried to drown it,' he said distantly. 'They shouldn't have bothered. It was probably happy to be cut off by a moat. They don't like to be disturbed.'

'You make it sound like it's alive.'

'It might as well be. They harbour malice like a weakling's mind.'

Will wondered what violence he should expect from this battle-stone. It was the biggest one he had yet seen, almost twice the height of a man, though waist-slender from top to bottom. Its surface, he could see, was patterned with spirals, loops and whorls.

Willow tugged on his arm and whispered, 'Look what it's done to the folk who live here.'

The people they saw paid them no heed, but continued about their work. They were ungainly, awkward folk, tall and thin as reeds, with skin as pale as chalk and teeth that seemed yellow by contrast. Their hair was partly hidden under their wide-brimmed hats, but it was always silver-white, no matter what their age. They seemed to be all of one family.

There were dogs here too, half a dozen of them at least, hair-less, skinny creatures with long muzzles and mournful eyes. They trotted about but showed no interest in the new arrivals, which seemed most strange to Will. Perhaps they were mute, he thought, for they made no sound either.

When Will approached one of the young women, he could hardly contain his shock at seeing her face. The skin of her lips was an unnatural red, but what discomfited him most were her eyes: they were bright pink and each contained two pupils.

'Hey-ho,' Will said.

The girl twitched unhappily, half looking at him. She enquired softly what business he had in Harleston. The rest of them, mainly men, yet all dressed alike in unbleached smocks and wide-brimmed straw hats, hung back in the shade of their scutching shacks. They seemed like folk used to being left to themselves, and certainly unused to offering a welcome.

'Tell me,' Will said. 'How deep is your lake?'

The other screwed up her strange eyes to look at him. Her attention jinked about like a butterfly and hardly seemed able to settle. 'Not deep,' she muttered. 'It's our retting pond. It's where we steep the flax after harvest. What do you want?'

'Would the water come above my waist if I was to wade in?'

The girl seemed bewildered, flustered by the question. She bobbed her head like a bird and answered, 'You can't go in the water.'

'Why not?'

She twitched and turned away without answer.

'I asked you, why not? *Why can't I go in?*'

She gave a mew of a laugh. 'It's the law.'

With that she jerked up the bale of cloth she had been tying and carried it away.

'What do you make of that?' Willow asked, taking him by the arm again.

'They're an odd lot. Mild enough now, but I'm not sure what they'll do when I break their law.'

'What are you going to do?'

He looked at her for a long moment. 'You've caught the sun a bit,' he said at last.

'Will?'

'I'm going to do what I came to do.'

It pained him to see fear take all the beauty from her face, but it filled him with strength to see her nod at last.

Thunder sounded in the east and a cool wind rippled the fields. He looked up at the sky, then at the water. Midges danced over it as they always dance before a summer thunderstorm. But this was different. There was something unnatural stirring the air. When he looked up he saw that the sky had become slate grey and the stone was throwing out a brilliant reflection across the pond. It seemed to be whiter than it had been. It seemed to beckon.

He took a moment to put out of his mind a lingering fear of water. A scar had been left in him by the marish hag. He had almost drowned, then, and Gwydion had said that when a man came that close to death it always put an unseen wound in him, a wound that first had to be healed, but when that was done it could be turned into a powerful strength.

The rooks cawed and flapped overhead, and the wind began to ripple up small waves. It was strangely cold now, and Willow clasped her arms as she watched him kneel by a clump of windblown reeds and whisper to himself. After a while he rose and trod with great deliberation – and fully clothed – into the shallows.

'I'm with you, Will,' she said. But the wind took her words away.

Once over the shock of the water's touch he readied himself to face the task. He began chanting the spell that would allow him to come close to the stone. He could feel it drawing powerfully on the lorc now, pulling into itself the dark streams it needed before it could vomit out its harm.

Will knew at once that it was no guide stone. Its power ranked alongside that of the Dragon Stone. He saw its glowing, white finger pulse. Whatever power lay within was making acknowledgment. It understood that he had come, and it saw what he wanted.

'Hearken to me!' he called out in the true tongue. 'Your long slumber has ended! I am here!'

But his words sounded like thin vaunting, and when he took another step the water rose suddenly around his thighs. He drew out his hazel switch and held it before him like a charm, muttering the protective passes and cantrips that kept him in touch with the deadly stone. The end of the wand flexed powerfully as if it was being pulled down by an unseen hand. Then a scraping sound began to emanate from the stone, like fingernails drawn across slate. It shook Will's teeth in their sockets, but it did not break his concentration. A glance towards the village showed that those who had been working in the sheds had gone. They had fled, first to their homes, then out again and across the flax fields, their strange dogs running at their heels. Willow stood on the bank, a lone figure, watching.

He turned to look back, treading out the path of the lign, realizing that the stone meant to drive him onward, to duck his head under the water. He resisted too savagely, then remembered to relax, as Gwydion's teachings advised. He thought again about the mechanism of warped fate through which the stones worked their will. Against so ancient a power, a power that could make giants dance to its tune, only the strength of quiet certainty could be set. He must not lose faith in the stone's inevitable defeat, but neither must he fall prey to the great failing that was called vainglory. It was a path he had to feel for carefully. The redes of magic pointed the way forward, but his deeds were what counted. He must assert his will neatly at that magical point in time where all things happened – at the place where the future became the present, and the present became the past. That was what Gwydion meant when he spoke of 'the here and now'. Will knew that he must approach the battle as if his enemy's defeat had always been inevitable, yet without anticipating his own triumph. Only then would things fall properly into place and the true path be found.

Suddenly, he faltered at the enormousness of his burden.

Looked at from below it seemed an unclimbable peak. Seen all as one, an undoable task. But he drew a deep breath and took courage, because he knew that doubt could destroy him just as easily as arrogance. Any weakness could throw his destiny onto a track leading to disaster. In this endeavour he must stay alert and marshal all his powers. His chief task would be accomplished in the present – he must make sure that *his* preferred version of the future was the one that actually became real.

As the sky darkened further, the lign lit the water in bilious green. He followed the glow step by step, feeling out the way, stirring up stinking mud between his toes, fighting down the nausea conjured by the stone. But the water was cold and getting colder by the moment, as if some bitter current was refilling the pond with icewater. The moment he recognized the danger, goose-flesh covered him and he began to see his own breath. It steamed in what had moments ago been warm summer air.

Then he heard Willow screaming.

But he dared not turn to her. Not now. He was waist-deep and halfway out to the stone. He stared hard at it, feeling his progress impeded, his resolve once more under attack.

'*I must keep the balance . . .*' he murmured through his teeth.

But his steadiness was being violently shaken. As he went on, a whirlwind erupted from the top of the stone. A bolt of light-ning flashed bright somewhere behind him, the clap of thunder coming so close that it made his hair stand on end. The horror that lightning might strike his head – here, as he stood in the pond – flashed briefly in his mind, but still his pace did not waver.

All thoughts of his peril had to be cast aside. A maelstrom of vapours began to emerge from the stone – a grey cloud turning so swiftly that his eyes could not follow. Where it boiled, a scat-tering of hailstones formed. They fell around him, dropping like grains of corn at first, but soon their sound increased until it became a furious hiss against the water's surface. The hail turned the lake into a seething plain. The whirling column seemed to be sucking all the air above the lake in towards it. He could hardly breathe, or keep his feet, but he reached inside his shirt to draw out his fish talisman.

His hands were white, the pads of his fingers wrinkled like those of a drowned man.

How long have I been out here? he asked himself.

It seemed like an age.

With the talisman clenched in his fist he felt able to push on again towards the roaring stone. But now his hands and feet were growing numb and his legs would hardly move to his command. As he went forward he came into chest-deep water. The cold clasped his ribs like an iron band. What looked like apple blossom flew on the freezing wind. But it was not apple blossom, for it vanished without trace into the water wherever it hit. It's snow, he thought, and turned his face away as the storm hit.

A slush of ice quickly plastered the back of his head, sent his hair lashing wetly about his face and shoulders. He raised the talisman before him in both hands, whispering incantations to unlock his frozen muscles, to force the warm blood out into his numb arms and legs. The cold burned his nose and the rims of his ears. He was neck-deep in freezing water now. Almost weight-less. There was no longer any feeling in his feet as he propelled himself forward. His entire body began to shake uncontrollably. Then he saw the ice forming.

It was like nothing he had ever seen before – ice spreading across the water even as he watched. The top of the lake became glassy, thin panes floating around him. He beat the water as it began to thicken, trying to break it up, but it was no good. The stone was freezing the lake from where it stood and its effects had already reached to the shore. He saw the green light of the lign fade to blue and turn paler as the surface of the water froze around him. He stumbled, threshing against the stone's astonishing power, but as fast as he cracked the ice it froze again. Fear stole over him.

The ice began to harden. He danced magic for his life, treading out over and again the only spell of thawing that he knew. His knowledge was not deep, but he knew that magic repeated many times wanes in power. He was now in a pit of icy water, but the ice was closing on him again and he was beginning to lose the clarity of mind on which everything depended. He danced hard in the icy water, gestured and struck the poses of the spell, drawing power from the mud of the lakebed and the kind earth below. But the lign blocked his efforts. Snow filled the darkened air above him and mounted like a deadly white fur all around the ice-hole. His jaw locked, juddered, making the words of the spell slur and stutter. His knees and elbows touched the closing ice. Terror speared him through as he saw the water around his neck solidify like candlewax.

Large snowflakes stuck to his face, blotted out the world. When he closed his eyes he could not open them again – the cold had frozen the lids shut. That prompted a tremendous surge of fear. He broke off the spell to burst his arms upward and shatter the ice once more. And then he knew he was lost.

He cried out, but the ice only closed and closed. His arms felt like so much dead meat. All his strength had been frozen away. He had panicked. He had made the wrong moves. Without constantly danced magic, the ice-hole had been able to grip him. Too late, he acknowledged his mistake. As the ice crushed his ribs, he drew one last breath, to shout defiance at the thing that was killing him.

But then two hands were under his arms and hauling him up with strength enough to slide him forward out of the ice-hole and up into a drift of soft snow. Behind him the death pit slammed shut – solid, gone.

'Fight back!' Willow was screaming, raging at him. She had dashed across the ice to drag him clear, and now was shaking the life back into him. 'Get up and fight, Willand! Or I swear I'll take your talisman and do the job myself!'

And so he was roused. His eyes bled as he tore them open.

He looked at the dead fingers that grasped the leaping salmon. He forced himself to concentrate on it, to stand barefoot in the ankle-deep snow, shattering the ice from him where it had formed on his body. Willow had somehow resisted the stone's monstrous magic. Perhaps it had not thought her worthy of attention. That would be its undoing. He raised his arms and let forth a defiant burst of the true tongue, calling down all the powers of the air upon the white stone.

The warmth that came from within flooded him to blood heat. Feeling returned. Life went roaring through him again like the heat that Gwydion had taught him to summon while travelling the winter land. Love had done this – it was a force against which nothing could stand.

His body dripped and steamed. Water pooled on the ice. He became enwrapped in an aura of light and heat and gradually part of him became aware that the snow had stopped falling. The sky was clearing above, and the westering sun was throwing yellow beams across a small landscape of white drifts, beyond which a summer's day still prevailed across the Middle Shires. Yet here was the stone, still white and tall, silent and malevolent and unbroken. He gathered up all the strength left inside him, made blue fire and threw it. Once! Twice! Thrice! He ringed the stone as he had seen Gwydion do. He danced on the ice, kicking through the snow, chanting incantations that bound the stone ever tighter. In the end he had used the stone's own deadly defences against it, for the ice had become his floor and he could never have danced out magic this powerful in neck-deep water.

The first of his tasks done, he put his hands to his temples and took a deep breath. He knew he must fight the exhaustion and emptiness that threatened to undermine the calm he would need to seal the spells. The stone shone brilliantly, but while the blue rings sparked and flashed and complained, they held. They stayed tight on the stone's malice like the hoops around a barrel.

Will danced again, splashing through meltwater. Time dragged, then rushed on, then dragged again. When next he looked up, the sun was sinking fast towards the treetops, casting long shadows. Clouds raced overhead, spattering the land with brightness and shadow. At last, he sat down hard – the containing of the battlestone had been accomplished.

Willow touched him, almost waking him, or so it seemed. 'We must get off the ice,' she said.

'No. I must drain the stone,' he told her, stirring, unsure how long might have passed.

'But look at you. And look at the ice.' She hauled him up as the surface groaned under them. The snow had melted into pools. He slid and staggered to his knees. She supported him, led him back to the clump of reeds that marked the edge of the pond and he saw the snow banked there had collapsed into slush. Feeling no cold, he lay down in the mud and felt his body feed hungrily on the earth.

He knew what he must do. Willow was wrong – it must be done right away. But how? He felt spent, worn down on every edge, ready to rest, and ultimately to draw a reviving draught of power from the earth. But that would take time – he would need to recover a measure of strength in order to draw strength. By the time he had rebuilt his powers, the ice would have melted. He must go out to the stone now and engage it, ready or not. He must!

'There'll be a boat,' he said, looking around.

'Will . . . please.'

'There *must* be!' He heard the strain breaking in his own voice.

'I'll look. You stay here.' Willow ran towards the scutching shacks. Their roofs dripped under a melting burden.

Will opened his hand and studied the leaping salmon talisman. Its thong was still wrapped tight about his wrist. For a moment he could not take his eyes away from it. It seemed to be warning him to renew his fight before it was too late. He forced himself to his feet and began to walk back across the treacherous ice. The stone gleamed, brilliant as a diamond, proud and yet unbroken. The blue haloes of light encompassed it, but they had not humbled it.

He felt the ice begin to move beneath his feet.

'Will!'

Willow was waving madly, frantic to warn him.

'Leave me be,' he hissed, under his breath.

'Will! Will!'

'I must do it now!'

The ice was shaking underfoot, shaking and thundering. He looked up and saw that the noise was made by hooves. A horse was galloping towards him. The beats of its hooves sent up sprays of water, and on its back there sat a black-swathed figure. It leaned over and swept a flashing blade down towards him.

He caught a glint of green, threw himself down, then gritted his teeth at the pain. The strike slid him along the ice, pushing him to within a few paces of the stone. The horseman overshot his mark. He hauled back on his reins and threw his frightened mount into too sharp a turn. The horse skidded and fell in a flurry of water.

Will felt the wet ice crack and heave under the impact of the fall, but the masked figure rose up, long knife in hand. Chlu was moving like his old self again, all trace of Maskull's restraint had gone from him and he seemed strong and determined and ready to finish the job that he had begun.

Will's mind shrieked warnings. He backed towards the battle-stone, his eyes fast on his faceless adversary's green blade. Unarmed and out here on a surface of wet ice, it was impossible to run or to hide.

'Who are you?'

There was no reply.

'Tell me! You owe me that at least!'

The other made a lunge and swept the knife at Will again. It barely missed. Talking was useless – and it was impossible to read a man whose face was hidden. Dismay flooded him, while overhead the stone seemed to gloat.

'I know you're called the Dark Child,' he said, truly shaken by the other's purpose. He was still backing towards the stone. 'I know you lived in Little Slaughter. I know that Maskull took you from your home and then destroyed it. But why do you want to kill me when we could help each other?'

Another sweep of the long knife. Another miss. Will saw how the blade was patterned. Its green gleam stirred an insistent memory. Next time, if he could catch Chlu off balance, a push might bring him down. But Chlu seemed equally sharp-minded, and too aware of the dangers of the ice to overreach himself.

'I know what Maskull's done to you. Don't hide yourself away from me. Join with me, and I'll help you to be free again. Don't you see? I'll release you like I released the ked.'

'Aggggh!' This time, when Chlu ran at him, the hacks and slashes came in a frenzy. Dull blows rained on his upflung arms and back until he scrambled away. He was amazed he had avoided the attack unscathed. The horse whinnied piteously. He glanced to his right. It was still on its side, kicking and struggling to rise. Soon its vain attempts to lift itself must punch a hole in the ice and it would fall through.

Chlu was coming at him again. The next slash was too quick and though Will drew back the blade flashed across his head and the force of the blow was like a punch. Now he was backed almost against the stone. He feinted left, dodged right, twisted back to put the stone between them, but he had been slashed again and again.

Why aren't I bleeding? he thought. What's happening?

'If I'm to die I should know the reason!' he shouted.

Then Chlu spoke. 'It's you,' he said, his voice strangled. 'It's you – or me.'

'But you don't need to fight me!'

'Oh, but I do. *For, if I am to live, then you must die . . .*'

Chlu stabbed again. This time the knife rang off Will's breast-bone as if he had been miraculously armoured. The force of it pushed him to the left-hand side of the stone. Though he recalled what Gwydion had said about never going widdershins about any ancient stone, he was forced to step that way. But before he could complete the turn, Chlu stumbled, made another lunge and started to circle back again.

'Why are you the Dark Child?' Will demanded. 'Tell me what it means!'

But this time there was no reply. Will kept his distance, drawing his assailant on, hoping he could give Willow time enough to save herself. Whatever happened, she would escape, she would find Bethe.

Chlu made a feint, then chopped at him again. Will saw the stroke coming and thrust out a hand. He grabbed the blade blindly, but then felt it wrenched from his hand. A frenzy of stabs followed in a strength-sapping struggle. For a moment it seemed that he must be done for. *But where was the blood?* His water-sodden shirt shone grey-white under the stone's radiance. It was unslit, unruddied, untouched. His hand had not been sliced open at all.

His feet sloshed through the meltwater. For an unreal moment he and Chlu breathed heavily, watching one another. A tinge of green still glowed where the lign ran across the lakebed. Will wondered what spell of protection could have been put upon him, and who had done it. Whoever it was had cast the spell so perfectly that it left no trace. Surely such a thing was hardly possible . . .

He tried to gauge how thick the ice was now, how deep the water beneath. He put his hand out to steady himself against the stone. His wet palm burned. He tried to pull away, but found he could not. Then he saw for the first time the reason the stone was white. Its surface was covered in hoar frost. It was colder than anything Will had ever known, and his hand was stuck there.

He pulled again, but he had been trapped. The battlestone was taking its revenge. He grabbed his wrist and wrenched, Chlu was looking at the knife, studying it suspiciously. Will struggled. He gasped, pulling hard enough to rip the flesh from his hand. But it was no good. It was stuck fast.

Chlu cast the knife away, went to where the exhausted horse was sitting lamely on the ice. He drew a heavy mace from the saddle and advanced. The head of the mace was set with flanges; thongs hung from its shaft like a hawk's jesses. It was a deadly crushing weapon, designed to beat in a knight's sallet-helm, to crush the skull beneath.

'Now I have you,' the strained voice said exultantly. 'Now you'll die and I'll live forever!'

Chlu laughed, and he readied his killing blow, then time went awry again.

Strange connections formed in Will's mind: he thought of the diamond that Morann had once given as a gift to Breona, how the jewelmaster had cleaved a glittering gem from a smooth, round stone, how the stone had parted when struck a clever blow. He thought of the blow he himself had struck with a faulted sword to snap the blade. Cold meant brittle! Brittle! And a single blow could . . .

He ducked as the mace slewed at his head. Its full force rang against the edge of the battlestone. A crack appeared just above Will's hand. The top half tottered, then slid away, crashing down and through the ice near where Chlu stood. The ice under him fractured, tilted, so that he was thrown off balance. The haft of the mace slipped from his fingers. It fell as he fell, then disappeared into the green-lit water.

There was an eruption. Overhead a great, dark cloud of harm formed and surged out into the air, bursting the blue circles of light that had once contained its power. Will crouched down beside the stone while the air roared above. His hand still burned, was still locked to the frosted stone. But the talisman hung from his wrist. He clenched it now, tore it from the thong, gathered all his talent and punched as hard as he could into the stone.

The reaction was instant. He struggled to stem the rush of

harm, and a mighty grip closed, throttling the power of the stone. The flow slackened, was pinched off. Then the clouds above burst into countless motes that rained down all around. The roaring stopped. He dared to hope that the harm that had escaped into the air would not be able to coalesce and would disperse. As at Ludford and Verlamion, his attack seemed to have caused the bulk of the stone's malice to bleed harmlessly into the ground where it could not come together as it could when released into the air.

Willow did not falter. Regardless of the danger, she had dashed across the ice and now she flew at the Dark Child as he tried to regain his feet. She had not found a boat, but the scutching flail in her hand served her better. She hit the black-swathed head with the jointed rod and sent him sliding down onto the swilling water. Then, sliding to the edge of the hole that had been punched by the top half of the stone, she launched herself at Chlu and fought like a demon.

Her fingers tore at his eyes. She ripped away the bindings, revealing the face that Maskull had promised would turn all who looked upon it to stone.

And Willow *was* turned to stone.

Chlu howled and scrambled away. He made off, splashing and sliding towards the scutching shacks.

Will made one more effort to free himself, and tore his hand away. He ran to where Willow lay on her side. He seized her, swept her up.

'Willow!'

But he could see the ghastly look that was on her face. For the first time she seemed wholly fearful and for a moment Will supposed that the sight of Chlu's unmasked face had indeed cast the dread spell over her.

'Willow! Speak to me!'

Her eyes rolled, and she told him in a bewildered, faraway voice what she had seen: 'It was his face. His face!'

'What about it?'

'It was yours, Will.'

'Mine?'

'Will . . .' She put a hand to her mouth. 'His face was . . . *yours.*'

CHAPTER THIRTY-ONE

A SURFEIT AT DELAMPREY

They found Chlu's horse swimming for its life among the maze of melting floes into which the ice had now broken. Willow found a boat in one of the sheds and they led the anxious beast to shallow water, then they rowed out to read the verse that had appeared on the edges of the cloven Harle Stone.

The standing part of the stone was easy enough, but they had to wait until more of the ice had melted before Will could dive down to find the part that had fallen into the water. He read it with his fingers as the sun sank into a rosy western sky. Underwater, the green light of the lign still cast an eerie glow, fading too as night deepened, but it proved to be enough. Face by face, the message read:

> *Indiugh antar e faithche nai tahm,*
> *Cionna na brogana eth samghail a siubalag.*
> *Ferte inad sa menscailimen farsaing,*
> *Blaeg an cela ne chim a reasanscach.*

And when cross-read:

Indiugh cion ath afert blaeggan,
Antar a brog e inad celanne.
Faithchen samhaillen menscailim chimdhu,
Enaiu san tahm siubal la fairsing reasan.

Only when Will was sure of the words did he let Willow row him to shore. They went together into one of the weavers' hovels and made a fire in the hearth to dry their clothes. Despite his aches Will felt the strength slowly seeping back into him. He gleaned what food he could, and began to prepare a sparse supper.

'It seems the folk of Harleston made little profit from their labours,' he said, looking at the poor fare he had gathered.

'Do you think they'll come back?' Willow asked, glancing into the darkness.

'Not until they're sure we've gone. Perhaps never, now the battlestone's hold over them is broken.'

'It doesn't seem right eating their food, now we've destroyed their living.' She looked around the bleak, dirty place. 'What will they do if they can't make linen any more?'

'In the long run they'll be the better for their freedom. No battle will be fought here now. And the stump of the Harle Stone will bring a boon of some kind.'

'I wonder what will happen when the seamstresses of Rucke find there's no more fine linen to be had.'

'I guess we'll soon find out whether their stitching keeps time's wheel turning, or it's the other way about. Maybe they'll start to use linen of a coarser kind when the Harleston stuff runs out. And maybe that won't be such a bad thing.' He took out the long knife and turned it over in his hand. Its edge glinted green. 'This is what saved me. Chlu was using Morann's blade. It wouldn't cut my flesh because it was sharpened on the Whetstone of Tudwal. Morann told me about that himself.'

'What did he say?'

'That a blade sharpened on it would deal only a lethal blow,

456

or no blow at all. No matter how hard Chlu tried to kill me, Morann's blade would not allow it.'

She turned it over in her hand. 'How did Chlu come by it?'

'He must have taken it from Morann.'

Her eyes showed concern. 'So do you think Morann's been hurt?'

'I can't see him parting with so precious a thing as this willingly.'

'It seems he never reached Duke Richard, if the rumour of invasion is true.'

'Maybe. The lorc has been confounded in a small way once more, but it's surely not finished. Judging by what I read in the verse, the lorc's already redirecting its power towards the next strike. Listen to the plain reading.

> *'Soon, in a field of death,*
> *Barefoot statues shall walk.*
> *The graves shall yawn wide,*
> *And the plague-dead shall talk.'*

'Are you sure it says that?'

'I'm not as expert as Gwydion would have me be, but I think that's the gist of it.'

'Is it close enough?'

He sighed. 'I don't know. But it's the best I can do.'

For a while they puzzled through the reading together, aware that their time spent in disguise had left a ghost of ancient language with them, a ghost that helped them appreciate the true tongue a little more easily.

'What's the word for shoes? – *Broggh* – Goes like *giullogh* – But it's singular and placed after a negative signifier – A what? – That's the word here. It comes from *cione* – So then it would be *brogana* – But *samghan* – Statue? – Yes, it's more than one and when it owns something – so *eth samghail* – And in this place *a* shows intention so it's statues that have no shoes that are going

457

to do something – What are they going to do? – Well, that verb is *siubo* – Sheppa? – But it's spelt s-i-u-b-o. It means to walk, and the gerund is shown by this ending here, *-alag* – or is that the present subjunctive? By the moon and stars! You know, I think it might be the future tense, but only when it means not walking in any particular direction . . .'

At last Willow sat back. 'We can argue all night about what it says, but the real question is what does it *mean*?'

He shrugged. 'Shall we have a go at the cross-reading?'

It was even more difficult. But though the last vestiges of magical disguise had departed from them, Willow could still hear the far echoes of another tongue in her head, a mystical tongue it was and ancient, one spoken in Lerisay and the other isles that took the brunt of storms roaring and raging in from the Western Deeps. They were the isles where the Maceugh's wife had beach-combed as a little girl.

'So, what do we think?' Will said at length, drawing their guesses together.

Willow read it out,

> '*Soon shall there be no graves,*
> *In the dead place of the shoes.*
> *A field of statues yawns awake,*
> *Some say that death walks widely.*'

'That can't be right.'

They heard the horse whinny. Will put on a grubby weaver's cap of tight-fitting linen, the sort the Harleston men wore under their straw hats, and went outside. A profound darkness had fallen on the settlement. The night was mistily starlit and, though the ground underfoot was still wet with meltwater, the warmth of a summer night had returned. Overhead the star pattern called the Anvil dominated the south-eastern sky. Below it the lign, which an hour ago had been so bright, had now faded almost to nothing.

Willow joined him. 'What're you looking at?'

'He's skulking out there somewhere,' he said. 'But he won't come near us tonight, not if he knows what's good for him.'

'It's very strange. He came to kill you, but he's ended up helping you.'

'Ironies like that often happen where magic's involved. I'm sorry we let him get away. There's much he could have been made to tell.'

Willow touched his chin. 'I'm sorry, Will, but when I saw his face – your face, I mean – I couldn't hold on to him. Was it some kind of magical defence do you think? A trick to make me let go of him?'

'It must be. That night at the Plough I couldn't remember his face. And whenever Maskull sent him to walk abroad, it was with his face hidden. I want to know what kind of spell it is that drives him so hard to find me.'

'A powerful one. It has to be Maskull's doing.'

'But perhaps it's not a spell. There's no taint that I can taste.'

'Then why does Chlu want so much to kill you?'

'I meant to find that out . . .'

She lowered her head, too ready to take the blame. 'I'm sorry . . .'

'Oh, that wasn't your fault. You're the one that saved the day.' The horse stamped again and tried to pull away from the hitching post. 'Hush now. What's the matter with you, Dobbin?' he said gently, but she would not settle.

Willow's hand tugged her husband's arm. 'Shhhh! Did you hear . . . ?'

'What?'

'It sounded a long way off. I don't know what it was, but I've heard it before.'

As they listened, a thin cry trailed across the sky. It seemed at once alien and fearsomely familiar. The horse whinnied again and Will blew on the animal's muzzle and gentled her for a long time before she became calm again.

'Was it the Morrigain?' Willow asked. 'Is she abroad tonight, warning of deaths that are to come?'

'I don't think so,' he said, not wanting to worry her with his darkest thoughts. 'It's gone now. The best thing we can do is try to gather our strength for tomorrow.'

He walked a circle and checked the earth with his scrying sense. The stink of bad aspect had faded from the ground. He had a good feeling about the place now, and knew they would be safe tonight, though he wondered how long it would be before Chlu launched another attack.

When Willow went indoors, Will took his chance to assay the earth streams for a moment longer. He had felt the lorc directing its power urgently southward. Now that feeling was confirmed. Gwydion had made a mistake in leaving the stones undisturbed for so long. The four years of Maskull's exile had been a real opportunity, and Gwydion had squandered it.

You should have asked for my help, he told the wizard silently. I would have come. I would have found them all. But you chose caution. You hoped things would turn out all right on their own, and now the Doomstone has gathered its strength again.

But then an even more uncomfortable thought struck him, and he wondered if he had the courage to face it squarely.

'Then again, maybe I'm to blame,' he said. 'Maybe the magic that guides the fate of the world needed me to make an offer, rather than wait to be asked. Oh, where are you, Gwydion, when a man needs his most important questions answered?'

He went inside and barred the door.

Willow adjusted the sleeves of the shirt that hung next to the grate. The fire was dull red and ashy now, but a single rushlight was burning on the table nearby with a smoky flame that turned Willow's hair to gold.

'You're very beautiful,' he told her.

She touched the fish talisman that hung around his neck, looked up at him. She clutched her knees to her chest and warmed her toes, but when he leaned close she turned and kissed him, and they lay together and made love until the rushlight flame sputtered out.

460

'I love you,' she said in the darkness.

'And I love you too. And I always will.'

The next day he roused Willow before sunrise. The night had been untroubled, and there had been no sign of Chlu or the linen weavers. Out by the lake, a pair of mallard ducks had appeared, and there seemed no ill result caused by the harm that had escaped the Harle Stone.

Will made up a bundle of smoked ham and apples, took a water bottle from one of the weavers' sheds and paused to dance a spell of protection and cast words of thanks over the dwelling that had afforded them their rest. It was risky, but it felt right, and if that slight magic drew Chlu down on them, then so much the better.

He went out to sling their meagre pack behind the horse's saddle, and called Willow.

'You never do these up tight enough,' she chided as she checked the horse's girth strap.

'I don't like to hurt the beast.'

She rolled her eyes and tutted. 'I heard you whisper your bargain in the mare's ear –"You carry us without complaint and I'll not dig my heels in your ribs." Now what sort of a horseman says that, Willand?'

He grinned. 'A poor one.'

'So,' she said, putting hands on hips. 'Where shall we ride to?'

'Where we've been told we shouldn't.'

'You mean to Corde-whatever-it-is?'

'Cordewan.' He stroked the horse's neck solemnly. 'I think so.'

'Isn't that a bit too close?'

He shrugged. 'Why? Some battlestones are quite near one another, others stand far off.'

'But there's got to be a pattern to the way they're laid out, hasn't there?'

He looked hard at her, wondering why the same thought had never occurred to him. 'Fighting the lorc is certainly like fighting a many-headed monster, but if there is a pattern to its array, I can't see it. Still, I'll bet you a bag of gold to a buttercup that the next battlestone is buried at Delamprey.'

'Why? Because of the verse?'

He nodded. 'Partly. And partly what the carriers said – that Delamprey was near a place called Hardingstones. Listen to the verse: "Now in a field of death . . ." What's a field of death, do you suppose?'

She sighed. 'A battlefield?'

'Maybe. Or a cemetery. Then, "Barefoot statues shall walk, the graves shall yawn wide, and the plague-dead shall talk."'

She looked back blankly. 'I don't see the meaning of that at all. But it's a fair bet the battle will take place somewhere near Cordewan, if only because Maskull sent the king's victuallers to Delamprey, and all the nobility loyal to the king has been ordered to muster there.'

'I wonder why he chose Delamprey, when the Harle Stone was active. Do you think the lorc knew what would happen? Or Maskull – did *he* know?'

She shook her head. 'You're reading too much into it. Delamprey's near the Great North Road. Maybe they were planning to assemble and then march north to meet Duke Richard's army.' She rubbed her arms as if against a chill. 'I hope Morann's all right. Do you think the battle will come today?'

His eyes followed the skyline. 'The lorc is waxing. I remember how things felt on the day of Blow Heath. I think the battle will take place today, but it might come tomorrow or even the day after. I believe the reason Maskull went to Delamprey is because the battlestone's buried there.'

She blinked at the idea. 'Do you think he's found it?'

'He must have. You know that Foderingham is only seven or eight leagues to the north-east of here. One night, years ago, when I was lodging there but before you came, I had a dream that woke me up. I saw Death in the castle grounds as plain as day. I was scared. I thought he was searching for me. But I now know it was not Death I saw at all, it was Maskull – and what he was searching for was not me, but the Dragon Stone. He's like Gwydion. He doesn't have the talent in him to find the battle-stones by himself. He needs someone like me to help him.'

'Someone like you?' She looked at him suddenly, but said nothing more.

He stared at the shrunken, darkened stump that stood crookedly in the pond. The sun glinted on the jagged edge where the top half had been cloven free by Chlu. Gwydion had said long ago that the breaking of a battlestone by violence risked unforesee-able – but certainly terrible – consequences. Yet here was a second stone that had been cracked in two, and no great catastrophe had come to pass. Perhaps such harm as had escaped would come together and fall like poison rain over the next battle.

Fears welled up, and this time he chose to speak them aloud. 'When Gwydion and I first found the Dragon Stone, we took it to Foderingham,' he said. 'We followed the road that led by the town of Cordewan. We passed a meadow of grass along by the River Neane. There were many standing stones, hundreds of them, all grouped together, like so many people waiting for some-thing awful to happen. I had what Gwydion called a premoni-tion. It was an unpleasant feeling that came just as we passed by – a vision of the plague. I remember Gwydion remarking that I shivered, "as if someone had walked on my grave". Yes, those were his words. I asked him about the field and what was in it. He said they were tombstones, but unlike any tombstones that I might see elsewhere.'

'What do you think he meant by that?'

'When the Great Plague came to Cordewan in the olden days it killed many folk. When some saw the signs of the pestilence starting on their bodies they fled to the College of Delamprey. There a bargain was struck with the Sightless Ones. So great was their fear that they begged the red hands to use such sorcery as they commanded to turn them to stone and so preserve their lives.'

'They preferred to give themselves over to sorcery rather than die a natural death?' she asked, revolted by the idea.

'So Gwydion said. Then the red hands gave it out that those who were turned to stone must wait three times three dozen and one years, until a healer would come to bring them back to life. That's a hundred and nine years.'

'And how many years have passed since the Great Plague?'

'Let me reckon it back,' he said, counting the reigns of five kings off on his fingers, before looking up at her. 'It's . . . it's now a hundred and eleven years since the mortality came to Cordewan.'

'Then it doesn't fit,' she said. 'The Hardingstones should have been healed two years ago.'

'Not unless they've already been healed.'

'But that carrier said they were near Delamprey. He wouldn't have said that if they had gone two years ago.'

'Something's wrong. Or someone's been meddling. Maskull, or the red hands maybe.'

'Will?' she asked suddenly. 'Remind me what you made of the alternate reading of the verse.'

He thought for a moment, then began to stumble over the lines afresh,

'Soon shall there be no graves,
In the dead place of the shoes.
A field of statues yawns awake,
Some say that death walks widely.'

'"The dead place of the shoes",' Willow repeated. 'That doesn't sound right. Are you sure that's what it means?'

Will puzzled over it in silence for a while, then he said, 'Cordewan gets its name from its main trade, which is making shoes. A lot of cordwainers and leather tanners live there. Maybe the verse might be better this way,

'Soon no more the plague pits,
Shall hold the dead of Corde.
A field of statues shall awake,
And death shall walk abroad.'

She nodded approvingly. 'That sounds much better. It's a neater verse anyway. Though I don't know how much good will come of fathoming its meaning.'

'I really think we ought to head for Delamprey as fast as we can.'

She embraced him. 'We'd better take care not to be seen. We don't know where Chlu went, but he can't be far away. If the court have taken the straight road they must have arrived already. We're no longer in disguise, and there'll be plenty among Lord Strange's retinue who could remember us from Ludford before the castle fell.'

Will tied the strings of his weaver's cap and mounted up, wanting only to ride on and leave Harleston to those who lived in it. He leaned forward, ready to pull Willow up behind him, but she took her hand away from his and said, 'Do you think it'd be all right to fill our water flask from the pond?'

He nodded. 'We should. We have some thirsty work ahead.'

She bent to fill the flask, but then paused as if she had seen something in the mud by the pond's edge.

'What is it?' Will said, looking down from the horse.

'Oh, Will! Look! It's just like your talisman. Only it's . . . red.'

Will jumped down and took it from her, staring at it in amazement. 'By the moon and stars! It's the red fish, the token I found at Little Slaughter! The one I think Chlu stole from my belongings at Ludford just before you arrived. However did it come here?'

'He must have dropped it.'

'I don't believe it . . . Willow, something strange is happening here.' Will looked around and drew Morann's blade from his belt, suspecting a trap, but for all that he tried he could feel nothing of Chlu's presence.

'What's the meaning of it?' Willow asked sharply, disliking the red fish and reacting against the weirdness of the moment.

He studied the fish for a while longer, then brought his own talisman out of his shirt and compared them. Each was no bigger than his thumb. They were both graven with three triangles nested within one another. The two fish were identical in all respects except colour. 'It seems as if they were meant to fit together mouth to tail.'

He brought them together in that arrangement, but as he did so he felt a sudden pressure in his fingers. It was as if the two fish wanted to be connected. Then there was a sudden jolt and a flash of blinding light, and there in his hands was a real fish, a big, silver-grey salmon! It threshed and wriggled from his grasp, and leapt into the retting pond.

Will stared in awe as it swam quickly from the shallows and was gone.

Willow looked down at the water, dumbstruck. 'Oh, Will!'

'My talisman . . .' he said faintly. 'How am I going to break the next battlestone without my talisman?'

By the time they reached the River Neane they had still not recovered from the shock of the calamity, but Will knew there was nothing else for it but to go on. He saw men labouring and others foraging the land around. They were soldiers. Earthworks were being hastily thrown up on the far bank of the river and in the grounds of the old cloister of Delamprey. There was no doubt that this was a place being prepared for battle.

Will found a sandy mound smothered in burrows. It had been a thriving warren, but there were ferret tracks in the soil that spoke of a recent slaughter of coneys, killed to feed the army. Nearby stood a grove of ash trees. That was as near to Delamprey as Will dared go. He decided to leave the horse tethered in a glade and hope that it was close enough to the chapter house to have been already scavenged for game.

As for the battlestone, Will could feel nothing of its presence, except an eerie silence and perhaps the creeping sense of impending doom.

'I'll have to scry for it,' he said.

'You'll never get near. And if you did, how can you drain it without your talisman?'

'Maybe I can't, but I might be able to find out what Maskull's up to.'

'Be careful, Will.'

He smiled at her and cautiously opened his mind. Nothing. The absence of feeling was worrying. Even at this distance from the cloister he could see that a battle would have to take place here soon. As he passed a critical eye over the preparations, a persistent vision leapt at him – that of Maskull smugly believing he had chosen the time and place of battle. In reality, Will knew, the battlestone was doing the choosing.

Several thousand men were grimly going about the task of preparing the ground. They had secured both flanks and heaped up defences between. They had fortified the cloister itself too. It was old, little more than a royal manor house with a couple of large enclosed yards and a tall tower built of the local brownstone, though now an ornate iron weather vane surmounted it. Will recalled Gwydion's remarks, that it had indeed once been a royal house, but that over the centuries its lands had been granted away piecemeal to the Fellowship and eventually it had been taken over almost entirely by them. First they had made it into a cloister college. Now, from what Will could make out, it seemed to have become a sequestering hall, a place where the inconvenient womenfolk of lordly households could be sent to live if they incurred their masters' displeasure.

'You must go on from here alone,' Willow said, echoing his own thoughts. 'Two spies are better than one. I'll go over to the earthworks and see what I can find out about the king.'

They had already seen a regal-looking tent set up on the banks of the river, and far to the rear of the army. The queen had doubtless sent him there to wait, attended by two burly servants, while the battle was decided. Three horses were saddled and tethered nearby.

Will took a drink from the water flask, passed it to Willow and wiped his mouth on the back of his hand. 'We'll meet here again as soon after the noontide as we can. Or if we should miss one another, this is where I'll come back to.'

His mind had begun to flash with horrible visions – the carnage of Blow Heath, images of Willow cradling her father's bloody body after the clash at Verlamion. The stone's emanations were seeping into him, and his voice faltered, 'I hope we can stop this. All these men are looking to us . . .'

She gazed into his eyes. 'Save their lives, Will. They don't deserve to die.'

'They never do.'

He let out a long breath, and gave her Morann's blade. 'Look after this for Morann. It kills or it doesn't cut at all. I'll have no use for its peculiarities today.'

'I love you, Will.'

'And I love you.'

They held one another close for a long moment, then, when he was sure he could delay no longer, he kissed her and told her to be mindful of her safety and never stop believing she would see Bethe again. Then she set off through the bright sunshine. Once she had passed out of sight he forced a frosty calm to settle over his mind and tried to listen to his inner promptings, then he began to order his thoughts and started to work out a plan.

They had found the Dragon Stone at Nadderstone. It had drawn its power from the Indonen lign. The Blow Stone, too, had stood on only one lign – Caorthan – and the King's Stone battlestone on one lign, that called Eburos. The Harle Stone, too, had been on one lign, Mulart, the lign of the elder tree. The Plaguestone, however, had stood where two ligns crossed, Mulart and Bethe. And so had the Blood Stone – Bethe and Caorthan, and also the stones at Arebury and Tysoe – Indonen and Tanne, and Indonen and Caorthan, respectively. Lastly, the mighty

Verlamion Doomstone had stood upon three ligns – Caorthan, Celin and Mulart.

Will closed his eyes and tried to make sense of it all, but the names swam before his eyes and he could not picture the arrangement, or even see how such knowledge might help him. But then he thought of the ked, and the Great Book of the Realm of which the creature had spoken. And that made him think about the night when he had lain in sweating torment as his mind's eye had risen up and looked down over the lands around Ludford as if from above . . .

That was it!

Was there not a way of picturing the whole Realm, picturing it as if he was looking down on it from a great height? Making a plan that showed every coast, every hill and every river – every village, every road . . . *and every lign!*

What if such a picture could be drawn? Surely then every lign would be shown in its proper place. And the nine ligns that made up the lorc would be shown as straight lines, just as straight as they actually were. And so where these straight lines ran and crossed would show the places where the real battlestones lay. Find the underlying pattern and you could find every one of them!

The idea was exciting, and too important to let go. But how could such a picture of the ground be made? There was no art that could show the world in small size. There was no clue as to how such a thing might be accomplished – except perhaps by the use of magic.

'Oh, Gwydion,' he murmured. 'I have so much to tell you when next we meet.'

But he knew that before they could meet again the next battlestone would have to be thwarted. He would open his mind at noon to see if there was any hint of the lign. Whenever he had found the Indonen lign before, it had run broadly east and west, and since ligns always ran straight, it would have to run in the same direction here. But where exactly was it? Did it go through the place where the earthworks had been heaped up, and through the fields that the king's captains had sought to make a killing ground? That seemed likely. And if it was true, then the Indonen lign must also run through Delamprey's field of death. That meadow, with its strange tombstones, was now a soldiers' camp, filled with many hundreds of colourful tents. He peered across the field where the battle would have to take place. He tried to foresee how the royal forces would be drawn up, considering in turn each of the lords who might command the fight. The centre would almost certainly be led by Duke Henry, and the king's right by Duke Humphrey of Rockingham. But who would take charge of the king's left?

Will opened his mind cautiously again, but he could sense nothing. The battlestone was behaving stealthily, guarding itself. Even the power flowing in the lign had become hard to discern, like a fish moving in deep, murky water. He checked the sun. It was still rising higher in the south. This was still the forenoon – the best time for scrying would come soon. He undid the strings of his weaver's cap, and tried to look a little more like one of the archers loitering nearby. He began to follow the long grass by a water course that ran near the lign. As he made his way, he opened his mind wider to sense the strangeness of the tombstones. They were mute – unnaturally so, given the magic that tainted them.

He wondered again about Maskull, asking himself if the sorcerer had blanketed the ground with spells and spaes designed to deaden the lorc's emanations.

He went on a little way but no one approached, not even when he stopped in the shade of a big weeping willow. 'Where best to hide a tree?' he said to himself, then added, smiling, 'In a forest, of course . . .'

But which of the many stones was the culprit? There were hundreds of them, and hundreds of knights' battle tents set up among them, too. It was impossible even to approach. He was considering risking a foray into the camp when his skin began to tingle. He crouched down.

All his senses screamed that it was Duke Henry. He was riding at a gallop with half a dozen of his lieutenants, returning from the direction of the king's tent. Will felt a sudden anxiety for Willow, and his fears deepened as he saw Henry turn down the path.

Just as they drew abreast of Will's tree, the duke lifted his arm and reined in his horse. Will pulled back into the cool green shade and flattened himself against the willow's deeply riven bark. But not before he had seen what was in Duke Henry's raised hand. It was a piece of polished wood, half a span long, almost like a club, except that the narrow end was roughly broken off and the knobble at the top sparkled with a pale sheen.

Will knew it instantly – it was the top half of Gwydion's staff.

The shock made Will spin around and slide down between two tree roots. He crouched there among the moss for a moment, thinking hard. There could be only one explanation. Gwydion must have been taken. Or worse.

Will could feel the dread rising in him, the sweat beading his face as the duke dismounted and began to beat about in the stinging nettles twenty paces away.

'Look at it!' he heard Henry say. 'It's telling me there's danger here.'

Will put his head down and kept very still, his mind opened as he concentrated on the glow that haloed the staff. A large bumble bee threaded its way through the grass stalks near his head, distracting him and drowning out the talk. But then he caught, 'Did you see that?' and, 'It's gone out.' Will raised his head a fraction and saw Henry shake the staff and crack it against a tree trunk. Another of the duke's men spoke, then they all began to move away. Will could not hear what passed between them. A tense moment followed, before the duke remounted. He waved the staff around him briefly, and then they rode off.

Will's relief at not having been spotted drained guiltily into despair. The hopes he had cherished for so long had been dashed at a stroke. ' "It's hard to kill a wizard",' he quoted grimly.

'For once, try to be honest with yourself!' he hissed, being hard on himself. 'You knew all along that he'd been taken! You *knew* it! You even had confirmation when the disguises began to fall away. Yet you wilfully ignored it all.'

The despair that made him shiver stank like the black Charrel ooze that had tried to pull him down near Arebury, but once summoned, strength began to pool in him, and hope sprang up, a pure, shining stream of it, refreshing his spirit. 'Fortune favoureth he who doth himself encourage.' So said the rede.

'Well, if I did know all along, then it's served to cushion the bad news. And if Gwydion has been taken, then I'll just have to take him back. They'll soon find out they've bitten off more than they can chew!'

The truth of the rede coursed through his veins and a bold plan started to come together. More craven minds would have called it recklessness, but there was a rede that said, 'Desperate needs do desperate deeds require.' And so he dared freely.

He must not risk drawing Chlu down on himself here, but it seemed that the redes were pointing him towards what he must do next. He checked to left and right, came out from behind the willow's green protection and began to walk purposefully towards the cloister.

The buildings were grey and solemn, the shadows they cut from the summer sun cool. Hundreds of soldiers were moving hither and thither. He began to ask where Lord Dudlea might be found, and was quickly pointed to a cluster of tents that stood between the cloister and the river. Lord Dudlea's pavilion was striped blue and white, its canopy decorated in red and gold with a line of little red martlet birds. Dudlea was inside, and at Will's approach two guards sprang forward to bar his way.

'Stand!'

'My Lord of Dudlea!' Will called past the men. 'I bear a vital message!'

Dudlea looked up from his papers and rose from the table all in one motion. He wore leg armour, a padded arming doublet and a blue velvet hat with a feathered plume. On his breast, above his heart, was pinned the badge of the white swan. His eyes were darkly ringed, his face drawn like one beset with relentless cares. His suspicions were roused. Confronted by a common soldier speaking so brazenly to a man of rank, he expected some trick.

'Hold him!'

The guards gripped Will's arms expertly. He offered no resistance. 'My lord . . .'

'Who are you?' Dudlea demanded, pulling his dagger and putting its tip to the vein that pulsed in Will's neck.

'Only a messenger.'

'I won't ask you again.'

Pain knifed through his shoulder joints as the two guards did their duty. Though the agony contorted Will's face, he met Dudlea's eye steadily enough. 'My lord, the message I carry is *private.*' The pain came again. 'It concerns your family!'

Dudlea tried to hide his surprise. He seemed to Will suddenly to be like a condemned man who had been offered a miraculous reprieve but did not yet dare to believe it.

'Speak!'

Again the pain came. 'My lord, call them off! I bear you no grievance. I bring only hope with me.'

'Hope?' Dudlea's breath was sour in Will's face. 'What hope can there be for me and mine?'

'If you want to see them restored to you—' he glanced at the guards, '—we *must* speak privily.'

Dudlea's tormented eyes bored into him for a moment, then he signalled for Will's release. He was searched, and found to be weaponless, save for a short hazel switch which they took from his belt. When the guards left, Dudlea let the flap of the tent down to indicate that he wanted no interruptions. He had recovered his composure, but his dagger was still gripped tightly in his right hand.

'If this is some knavish trick—'

473

Will said in a low voice, 'Maskull put the spell on them. I tell you, it can be taken off again.'

Dudlea tensed, still not daring to believe. 'You can *reverse* it?'

'It's possible.' Will watched the fire that burned in Dudlea's mind. 'But first you must do something for me.'

'Who are you?'

'A man of magic.'

Dudlea's eyes sweated in their sockets. His knuckles were white on the handle of his dagger. 'What do you know about me?'

'More than you would like me to know.'

'What do you want?'

'Luckily for you, only a very small thing.'

That triggered Dudlea's anger. 'Before you get a penny I must have proof!'

'I don't want your silver. There is a rede that speaks of the faith that flees from the proof of powers—'

'I know naught concerning spells!' Dudlea's eyes cut away. He was trapped in a nightmare. 'Without proof, I dare not cross Maskull.'

A veil of fear was falling fast over Dudlea's mind. Will decided he must gamble. 'Show me where the Duke of Ebor's wizard is held. Show him to me, and you'll get your proof.'

Dudlea recoiled. 'The Old Crow? He's in the queen's care.'

'I must get to him, or nothing more is possible.' He risked pressing his advantage. 'My Lord Dudlea, since your plot to murder the Duke of Ebor went astray, your own life has been in danger.'

Dudlea took it like a hammer blow. 'You . . . you know about *that*?'

'That and more. Believe me when I tell you that the queen's sorcerer is wholly unforgiving. Maskull does not think you have suffered enough yet for having failed him.'

'He trusts me well enough. He's appointed me commander of the king's left in the coming fight.'

'He thinks you're too terrified to disobey. But he'll never restore your wife and son to you, whatever you do for him. Only I can do that.'

Dudlea stared at the table. His fear of the sorcerer contended visibly with his hopes. He threw back the flap of the tent and said, 'Follow me.'

As Dudlea took him across the path of the Indonen lign, Will felt all the hairs rise on his body. The lorc was running more strongly now, heading towards a mighty climax.

A hundred billmen were unloading poleaxes at the front of the cloister. Once Dudlea had rounded the corner of the tower he motioned Will into a gateway that led into the smaller of the cloister's two yards.

'What about the red hands?' Will said, alive now with warnings. 'They'll know we've broken their privacy if we pass the gate.'

'It has been defiled often enough of late. When Queen Mag demands the use of a sequestering hall, not even an Elder dare gainsay her.'

'But there are Fellows inside.'

'Yes. And fifty bequines, dwelling under the rule of an Elder of the Middle Shires. Their burden is daily suffering – perfect silence, the rigours of the flesh. You know what the Iron Rule means.'

'These bequines – they are not to be looked upon by outsiders.'

'Then don't look upon them! You wanted to be brought here.'

Dudlea was testing Will's reluctance to break the bounds of the cloister, using his fear to gauge the strength of his claims. Will saw that he must show no weakness. He shoved the gate open and entered.

The yard smelled of death, a slaughter yard where tithe beasts were brought twice yearly to be killed. The college's tall tower loomed over the yard. An acrid stink hung in the air, a smell that Will recognized. Blood channels were cut into the stone flagging. Iron flesh-hooks hung from beams above, and there were two great rendering cauldrons to boil up animal fat. Will heard the slow, muffled tolling of a handbell, but the yard was deserted.

As he passed the base of a slit window he saw what lay within the cloister. Ghostly figures moved in a line among the shadows. Their left hands were on the shoulders of those who went before, their right hands carried tapers. Each woman was draped in a shapeless robe of plain pale grey, cinched at the waist by an iron chain. Their heads were crudely shaved and they wore iron masks on which the semblance of a face had been painted. Ahead of them walked a senior Fellow, eerily steering his way along the familiar cloister. In his hand was a bell, and every five paces he would shake a double clang from it.

Dudlea pulled Will onward, beckoning him to move further along the wall. There, at the base of the tower, was a row of iron bars set into the ground. They covered a hole that afforded light and air to a noisome cellar below. When Will crept towards the hole the stink of ordure hit him. He saw a dismal scene. There, his hands chained around a slender stone pillar, stood Gwydion.

Will stifled a gasp and moved back. He knew he must not alert the wizard. It seemed that Gwydion must have spent many days in captivity, for he was dirty and dishevelled, bloodied and bruised. Yet his spirit seemed unbowed, and that made Will's heart leap for joy.

The wizard had been trapped. Will saw the delicate golden fetters that looped his wrists and the fine gold chain that secured him to the pillar. The chain was clasped by a small golden lock, and Will knew that for all their delicacy, these works must be of tremendous strength to prevent a wizard's magic.

Those fetters must be the gift and weapon about which Maskull boasted to the queen, Will thought. No wonder our disguises fell away. And no wonder all of Gwydion's holding magic has been decaying. How long has he been here?

He wanted to call out, to let Gwydion know that help was near at hand, but Dudlea grabbed his collar and pulled him aside, furiously signalling him to silence, for crunching down the gravel pathway outside was the queen's bodyguard.

Through a gap in the big wooden gates Will saw the glint of

their bright breastplates and helms. Above the wall he saw the tips of the fearsome poleaxes they carried. He felt himself being pulled down to his knees. Dudlea swept off his feathered hat and bowed low in an extravagant gesture as the queen came into view.

The queen did not deign to notice them. Out of the corner of his eye, Will saw the whiteness of her face, the pale skin of her neck revealed above a crimson gown. From a long chain depended a golden key that swung at her breast. She swept on, her armoured guard flanking her, heading into the darkness of the cloister. When she had passed from view, Will crept back to the foundations of the tower.

Dudlea hissed. 'You've seen the Old Crow! Now it's time for you to honour the bargain. Give me proof of your promises or I'll mark you as a liar and call Maskull down on your head!'

Will resisted as Dudlea tried to pull him away. 'If you love your wife and son, you'll give me a moment more here. One moment. That's all I ask.'

Will peered down through the bars and heard Queen Mag's men enter the dungeon. Locks were turned and bolts shot back. Beyond the open door there waited the queen's guard and two grovelling turnkeys.

The queen's voice was crisp. 'The last battle is almost upon us,' she said. 'There is little time remaining to you. Soon the war will be at an end, and you will have delivered my enemy to me. Ebor is yet a day or two away to the north. My spies tell me he has but a thousand men in his train.'

Will exulted over a part of the news, at least. That the duke had landed so lightly could only have meant that Morann had escaped his meeting with Chlu and reached the Blessed Isle. But there was now an added edge to the queen's words.

'You really are a most *meddlesome* fellow, Old Crow.'

'Lady, all is as I told you it would be,' Gwydion said. 'Friend Richard comes to you in good faith. Reach an agreement with him. This is the true path. Will you not receive him magnanimously?'

'Receive him?' She lifted a bloody rose to her nostrils and looked at her captive smilingly. 'I would much rather destroy him.'

'You said you would look for peace. You gave me your thrice-repeated word on it.'

'You were a fool to trust words.'

'They bind more than you know. I came to your summons. I knelt before you in open humility before all. I did everything that you asked of me. Why have you tricked me thus?'

'Oh, don't sicken me with your false humility.' The golden key glinted at her breast as she turned about. 'Your arts are laid threadbare. I simply tricked you before you were able to trick me. I saw that it was your habit to take the hands of those whom you greet, so I set a very simple trap for you. It was easy to let the fetters fall from my sleeves onto your wrists as you knelt.'

'Have no pride in that, for it was an artless betrayal of good faith.'

'Yes, well. Often the most artless plan is the best.'

'Lady, what has happened to you? You were not always so rotten-hearted.'

The amused smile fell from her lips so that her stare became unwavering and cold. 'How *dare* you speak to a queen thus? If it was my desire to have you taken to Trinovant and publicly gutted under the walls of the White Tower that is what would happen to you!'

Gwydion looked away. 'I think you would do well to examine the deep reasons for the anger that presently chokes you. Let us repair the rift between you and Ebor. Let us make peace again as you have promised. I beg you to release me, while there is still time.'

The queen watched him silently for a moment, peeling red rose petals now and letting them fall. Anger still seethed within her, but it was icily held in check. She slipped the secret she had been saving from its sheath. 'Time for what, I wonder? Time for Lord Warrewyk to arrive perhaps?'

'Lord Warrewyk?' Gwydion asked, looking up suddenly like one who has been caught unawares.

'Oh, do not pretend ignorance! Warrewyk is coming here to Delamprey with a great host, as well you know!'

Gwydion shook his head vigorously. 'If this is true, then we are both betrayed!'

The queen's laugh was dismissive. 'Not I. Do you imagine we have no spies? We've known for almost a week. Now what do you dare say to me concerning the keeping of good faith?'

'This was not planned by me. If it is true—'

'Warrewyk's army is real enough. And his design is clear. He brings with him his father and the Ebor whelp. They were to fall upon us, even as we supped with Ebor according to your formula.'

Up above in the yard, Will pulled away from the bars, shaken by what he had heard. He looked to Lord Dudlea who crouched beside him.

'Warrewyk?' he whispered, incredulous. 'Is it true?'

Dudlea stared at him. 'I was told of his landing yesterday.'

'And Edward? No! Never! He would not defy his father for anything.'

Dudlea's grimace was fierce. 'It's not defiance, but Ebor's own order! The Callas army came across the Narrow Seas a week ago. Ten thousand strong, voracious and swelling like a leaf-maggot during its march through Kennet and the City. Between twenty and thirty thousand troops left Trinovant two days ago to march north. What now of your wizard's integrity?'

Will was staggered. Once again the sly malice of the battle-stones was turning events upside down. He called to mind the huge royal army of sixty thousand that had once camped outside Ludford. That kind of strength might have deterred the fearsome Lord Warrewyk, but now the king's forces did not equal a third of that number. The fight would be far more equal, and so savagely hard-fought. Many men would die.

'You're coming with me!' Dudlea hissed, putting his dagger to Will's throat. 'I will have the proof you promised me, or I'll let a liar's blood flow.'

He gripped Dudlea's wrist, crushing it, turning the weapon

aside and making it fall. 'I'll give you a hundred proofs! A thousand! But first you will let me listen to what passes down below!'

Dudlea's eyes widened, first with pain, then with fear. Will let him go, approached the bars, and did not turn even when Dudlea picked up his dagger. Down in the gloom Gwydion's pleas were pitiful. As the last petal fell from the queen's blood-red rose, she made to leave. 'Let Warrewyk come. Let Ebor come. Let them all set their arms against me. They will not prevail. For I possess a secret weapon which none can withstand!'

'What weapon?' Gwydion called after her. 'Lady, what weapon?'

The queen turned on the stair. 'Oh, no, Old Crow. Not this time. Not this time!'

And then she was gone. The door slammed, echoing behind her, and the wizard fell to his knees, and sat alone in the silence.

CHAPTER THIRTY-TWO

THE SECRET WEAPON

Will allowed Lord Dudlea to hurry him from the foul cloister yard. He steeled himself for the coming fight and tried to ignore the ache that was growing across the crest of his head.

Once inside the tent, Lord Dudlea's manner changed. His anger fell away and he began to beg. 'Please help me! I am upon a bed of fire!'

'Gwydion will help you. I promise.'

'But you saw the wizard. He's a broken man. His powers are gone, and he'll soon be dead.'

The power rose up in Will and he said, 'Feed your hope and all will be well. Gwydion is not some banquet conjuror, he is an Ogdoad wizard. Do you know what that means?'

Dudlea pulled away, stabbed his dagger deep into the elmwood table. 'The queen will kill him whatever he is.'

'She cannot. Nor can Maskull. Don't you think they would have done so already if it were that simple?' He tried again to calm Dudlea's raging spirit. 'I tell you for the last time, if you would restore the flesh of your wife and son, then you must do exactly as I say.'

Dudlea was blowing hot and cold as the power in the lorc rose and fell. His strength seeped away again very suddenly. 'I will do *anything.*'

Will watched the man sink into his chair. He resisted the temptation to draw off by magic a measure of the pain that racked him. 'Do you not remember how the tide was turned at Ludford?'

'That was Lord Strange's doing,' Dudlea said, mastering himself with an effort. 'He betrayed Ebor. His treachery decided the day.'

'You see how he played a vital part in shaping the future that day? In the coming fight, you must do the same.'

Dudlea was aghast. 'That is too much!'

'Listen to me. You must, by your actions, bring about a future in which your wife and son live.'

'But – *how?*'

Will put a finger to his lips. 'Quietly, my lord. The moment draws nigh when you must marshal your troops. Do this – when the forces of the enemy charge at you, give way to them. Command your men-at-arms to admit the enemy over the ditch and barricade. Let the cavalry of the Earl of the Marches move freely to outflank the king's centre. This is the measure that will most speedily put an end to the fight.'

Dudlea's face was filled with fear. This was beyond anything he knew. 'Edward of Ebor will attack against our left? How do you know this?'

To meet the other's eye steadfastly Will closed his mind tightly shut. The stone's stifling emanations had made the pain in his head grow, oppressing him mightily. He said, 'It will happen as I predict. You may rest assured.'

'But you're asking me to betray my king in battle.' Lord Dudlea's voice grew hollow as the consequences of his task began to sink in.

'The king presently sits under guard in a tent by the river. He has been sent there by his wife. And you speak as if he is in full command of his—'

'Even so, I cannot do it!' Dudlea launched suddenly into the attack. 'Where's the proof you promised?'

'If proof you still crave then hear this!' Will thrust Dudlea back. 'You, who scruples now over fealty to a mad king, tried bare days ago to arrange a secret deal that would have sent the Maceugh, Lord of Eochaidhan, to murder Ebor in his bed – this much I do know of you.'

Lord Dudlea's eyes hardened. 'Such talk as that you might have had from any servant of mine for fivepence and a jug of ale!'

'Fivepence, aye, for that is all the loyalty you inspire, but could I have had it for this?' Will slammed a clipped silver farthing onto the table. 'You once said this was worth more than a man's life! It is the price of your own if you will not heed me.'

Dudlea stared at the coin, and knew it to be the one he had tossed disdainfully at the Maceugh. He was shaken, but still unmoved. 'You're quick with accusations, but you still have not offered me any proof.'

Will straightened. 'What would you have me do?'

Dudlea's eyes sweated in their sockets. 'Show me that you're a magician equal in power to Maskull. Show me the true strength of your art. Bring the dead to life!'

'You ask a very great deal.'

'Can you do it, or not? It is the only proof I will admit.'

'You don't *understand*.' Will's head ached. Pain laced his temples. He knew he must not reveal himself to Chlu yet, but what other way was there, except by the exercise of magic? He said wearily, 'You must have faith, my lord – belief is important. The spells that must be employed are driven by the faith of a loved one. This is their main ingredient. You must not take in vain the power that sustains hope, or they will fail.'

Dudlea grabbed him like a bitter enemy. 'If this is trickery—'

'Love is real! I have seen how well you love your wife and child. Have faith that you'll know them in the flesh again. Do it! Absolute faith, my lord. That is the key to the undoing of the dread spell that presently lies upon their stony hearts.'

Dudlea's fear-inspired fury rose again. He pulled his dagger from the table. 'These are lies! Stones cannot be brought to life! You are no magician! If you are, then save yourself from this!'

Will felt himself borne down. The knife bit into his flesh. He felt the sharp sting as it cut into his neck. Blood came. The blade trembled. And through it all, Lord Dudlea's face was a mask of torment. But then Dudlea's resolve slackened. He let the knife fall, and staggered from the tent, leaving the one he had meant to kill without a word.

Will lay there alone. He drew a ragged breath, clamped a hand on his neck. Relief flooded him, for when he pulled his hand away there was just a smear of red on his fingers. A shaving cut, little more.

When Dudlea's guards entered, they eyed him with gross fear. They seemed unable to decide whether they should detain him, but they stood back when he picked up his hazel switch from the table and made a sign over them.

Had he done enough to release the knot of mistrust in Dudlea's breast? he wondered. Perhaps he had done too much.

As he gathered his wits, a great misgiving assailed him. He had lied. He had promised Dudlea more than he had the power to give. And that, he knew, took matters to an entirely new brink of uncertainty. He saw it all so clearly now. In magic, *form mattered*. A break in trust disrupted the deep mechanisms that turned future into past. Lies interfered with the processes of fate and event, confounded the kindness that obliged things to turn out the way they should. Broken promises drew the world ever further away from the best of all possible worlds that Gwydion called the true path. Will had sold Dudlea onto the horns of a dilemma. To betray his king on the slenderest of promises, or to abandon his family.

'By the moon and stars, what have I done?' he asked himself. But then the pain in his head rose again and he gritted his teeth against it. 'It doesn't matter! None of it matters, so long as Dudlea does what he must!'

But he felt suddenly weak, unsure of the way forward. He needed help, but what help could there be?

'What's happening to me?' he asked. He found himself stumbling along the lign, shading his eyes, squinting. Overhead, the sky was a faultless blue that seemed close enough to reach up and touch. Noon was approaching. The emanations of the battle-stone were hammering in his head. The meadow began to slide beneath him as he walked. He stumbled and almost fell to his knees. His sight danced with motes, small lights that twinkled and died. And it seemed that the stones standing in the field of death rippled and shimmered like the air rising above a fire.

All along the lign labouring men were digging in the heat of the day, logging what trees remained, using hatchets to sharpen stakes, unloading a long procession of carts, filling baskets with earth, carrying sacks. Their mouths were mute and their eyes seemed to Will to be wholly blind, like those of men already fixed on death.

Squadrons of cavalry were marshalling here. And there, in the lanes formed by the tombstones, among the rows of lordly tents, were hard faces and muttered words; armour glinting as it was buckled on; the bright splash of battle colours as embroidered silk was unfurled to the breeze. Little time now remained.

He came to the ash copse where his horse was tethered. He delved deep into the undergrowth, into a darkness that smelled of summer, where flies buzzed and small white moths flitted in shafts of sunlight. Dry twigs cracked under him, small spiders fled. There, by a badger's set, he planted his feet and rested his forehead for a moment on the grey trunk of the tallest tree. He let his mind search out the ancient power that filled all the trees of the world. Then, he invited the power to come into him, and soon he felt the telltale tingle surging in his toes, the irresistible power that served his hopes. As his eyes closed and his mind opened fully, a thrill rushed through him, lighting his mind's eye with a brilliant pale glow. His ribs felt suddenly as if they would burst, as if the bear hug of the Green Man was upon him. He raised his arms, lifted them so that his whole body became like the five-armed Star of the Hallows of old. Its heart was his heart. His feet and hands and head were star-points, and all his body was wreathed in fiery glory.

There, borne up as if upon the air, came the vision of one shining in light, a stranger. Solemn. Undeniable. Glowing as the elfin host had once glowed, and strangely fearsome.

'Arthur,' she said.

'I am not he,' he replied, unsure, still haunted by the way he had lied and manipulated a man who was in torment.

'Are you not ready?'

'I am not fit to be a wizard!' he cried.

'Wizard? That is not your fate.'

'Then what am I?'

'You are Arthur. You are the true king.'

The figure approached closer and closer. He almost recognized her, but she was too bright for mortal eye to light upon. He threw up a hand in front of his face so that slowly she blurred and melted away.

Noon flashed by in sudden pain. He felt sick, as if something vile needed to be flushed from him. Joy and peace should be burning inside, pure and clean and timeless, yet something else was there now, something unwholesome. A nightmare stain.

When his eyes opened, he was lying in the sun-dappled glade, his horse's muzzle stretched close to his face, sniffing curiously at him. He stroked the animal's head, wondering for a moment where he was, but then he came back to himself, suddenly refreshed, it seemed, and blade sharp. It was done. He felt whole and ready for the fight. He had broken the battlestone's subtle attack, and all his doubts had crumbled. He was strong again. Filled with limitless power. Untouchable. A hero who had come into his own at last, except there was still a roaring pain in his head.

He knew he must ignore it, ride like the west wind to do what had to be done. He mounted up and galloped out of the clearing, going first by the hamlet of Hardingstones, through Cotton and Far Wooton, looking all the time for signs of Edward's approaching army. Edward was marching north. He must be coming along the line of the Wartling, the old Slaver road that ran from Trinovant into the Middle Shires.

He made for the village of Roade. It was close to the ancient highway, and a little beyond it he saw banners flying. He kicked the horse on towards the huge shimmering column of men, seeking out its head, knowing with certainty that his best chance lay in engaging the Earl of the Marches with well-chosen words.

But Edward greeted him with a roar.

'Keep that wizardling away from me at all costs!' he told his bodyguard as they closed off Will's approach.

But the order had been given with wry humour. Edward was pleased to be riding at the head of a powerful army, and the battlestone's emanations had stroked him into a blissful state. He seemed almost drunk at the prospect of a fight. Lords Warrewyk and Sarum flanked him, each as proud as a peacock. All three were fully armoured.

'Keep him off me, I say!' Edward cried, roistering, laughing at Will's efforts to reach him. 'The fellow believes I owe him money. He wishes to exact payment before I go to my grave! Ha ha ha!'

The joke made everyone laugh, all except Sarum and Warrewyk and the unsmiling guard whose weapon was menacingly drawn. He was not about to let anyone come within a sword's length of Edward without a direct order.

'Edged tools? This is no way to greet an old friend, Edward!'

'Friend, he says! Much good his friendship did us at Ludford! Oh, let the maggot through. He's harmless enough – though a little mad, I dare say.' He wafted a gauntleted hand and the riders parted.

Will steered his horse into the gap and came alongside the three earls. It made Will uneasy to see how the friend of his youth had changed. Seeing no other way to be his father's heir,

Edward had gone some way beyond the original. Here was the paladin, the brave warrior, the man Edward thought his father wanted him to be – perhaps even something close to the man Richard of Ebor wanted himself to be. And Edward's true self had been locked up within this greater, self-invented personality. The question immediately rose up in Will's mind: how would such a man be affected by the battlestone at the crucial moment?

Would *this* Edward change his mind once he was set on a course and sworn to it? Will doubted it, and so perhaps there was a way to use the warlike bravado that Edward had put on with his armour.

'Your face is white as dough,' Edward said, looking hard at him. 'Are you unwell?'

He took it how it was meant, as a joking slight against his courage. 'I'm no more scared of a fight than you! Or have you forgotten?'

'Well said!' Edward nodded using his father's best conciliatory gesture. 'But you've changed since those days. I suppose you've come on the orders of the Old Crow.'

'I seek you out on my own initiative.'

'If he's here to dissuade us, tell him to save his breath,' Lord Sarum said.

Edward shot him a glance. 'We're here as my father's avengers. We'll do now what we should have done long ago.'

The two earls made fierce, approving murmurs. But Will shook his head. 'I have not come to argue with your intent.'

'Then offer us marvels,' Lord Warrewyk said. 'That would make you welcome.'

Will's eyes flashed at him. 'Such marvels as you want, my lord, are not to be traded.'

'A pity!' Lord Sarum reached out and flipped the hazel wand from his belt. 'Are you still planning to fight alongside us with a wooden sword?'

Will caught the wand before it fell, but a ripple of amusement passed among the riders. Sarum had recalled the time before the battle at Verlamion when Will had brandished a stick of wood.

'I'll get this bumpkin into an iron suit yet!' Edward said.

'Fight for you? Not I, Edward.' Will thrust the hazel switch back into his belt. 'Not even with a wooden sword – unless the cause was greater than yours.'

Edward's face darkened. 'I know of no cause that's greater. Say what you've come to say and leave us, Willand. We have a stern task to accomplish this day, and we have no more time for your tomfoolery.'

'I came to tell you—' Will's words trailed off as another sharp pain creased him and passed, glittering, from temple to temple, '—that the battlestone is guarded by a powerful enemy. I cannot approach it. Today there will be no easy end to the fight. Therefore, beware!'

Edward's laugh was brassy and his bravado infectious to those around him. 'Is that all? Then you bring good news indeed, for we are ready to win a bloody set-to!'

Will wiped the sweat from his face. It seemed that the only way to ease the pain in his head now was to give in to it. He raised his hands ominously. 'Hearken to me, Edward! Lord Dudlea is to command the king's left. Attack him and he will receive you without reply.'

A moment passed while Edward stared back at him. The air was filled with the clatter of armour and the jangling of horse harness bells. 'Is this . . . a *prophecy*?'

Will felt the weird brightness suffuse him. It drove his actions. What harm would it do to give Edward the push he needed? Or, seen another way, what harm would inevitably follow if Edward was *not* given that push?

For a moment, Will struggled. But then he could no longer see why he was struggling, or what against. He had certainly done the right thing. This was the straightest means to a necessary end. And it was an end that justified all.

Wasn't it?

Wasn't it?

He shouted it out. 'Lord Dudlea will go over to you once battle is joined! He has promised this to me!'

Edward's glance was an eagle's. 'He gave you his word?'

'He did.'

A smile quickly grew across Edward's face. 'Then you are a friend indeed! And a finer fellow than ever I thought. But your eyes unsettle me, Will, for there is madness in them today.'

He felt such a surge of unease that his words came out as haughty. 'By my efforts I have brought you a victory! It remains only for you to ride out and take it!'

Will's aura burned with a strange, sallow glow. Something was wrong. Something important that could no longer be ignored. He felt the stone's power seeping into him like the wriggling of some loathsome worm climbing through all the chambers of his heart. But he clenched his thoughts against it, and it was stilled. A part of him wanted to blurt out the truth about Dudlea, to say how the deal had been left unsealed and hanging, that faith was the key here. But the urge vanished, for he knew that telling the truth would have undone all his hard work.

His mount lurched as loud bangs nearby surprised the horses. The sound was of arquebuses being touched off – tests to see if moisture had got into the sorcerer's powder they used. Will controlled the beast strictly, and called to Edward, 'There's a price to pay, Princeling of Ebor!'

Again, Edward's eyes narrowed. Nineteen, he was, and already riding into a third great test of arms. Had he fallen as fully under the battlestone's spell as the rest of them? It was impossible to know. 'Ask your price, Will, and let's be done with you!'

'It's this – once victory is yours you must issue the call for common quarter!'

Such an order would show the winning commander's mercy. It would prevent the battle, once won, turning into a bloodbath.

Edward grinned broadly. 'Two words? That's a small enough favour to ask.'

'Not so small to those whose lives they will save!' Will's horse tossed her head again and he reined her in severely. 'I must be away!'

Edward laughed, ignoring those around him who still showed their doubts. 'Let him go!'

'Look at his face! He's mad!' Lord Warrewyk objected. 'We'll not change our battle plans on the say-so of a barefoot beggar! And we should hold him, lest he betray us to the queen!'

But Lord Sarum stayed his son. 'That's the Crowmaster's apprentice. Let him take whatever word he will to the enemy. If news of common quarter is spread among the queen's people it will only help them to think better on surrender. I've seen this lad and his master work miracles upon Blow Heath, and I would rather he left us prophesying our victory than stayed to foredoom us with words of calamity.'

Edward gave neither earl much heed. He called out heartily, 'Fare you well, Willy Wag-staff. We are different, you and I. Yet I did love you almost as a brother once. And in all the world there are few whose word I would trust as readily as yours!'

Will turned his horse's head, whipped her hindquarters and dug his heels into her flanks so that she sprang away. He broke from the earls' column and rode ahead of Edward's proud army. The closer he came to the battlestone, the greater the shimmering glory that flowed in his veins. He felt as if he was outside himself. Invulnerable. All conquering. As if no one else in the world mattered.

He should have ridden back the way he had come, following the grain of the land. Instead, he bolted across open country, brazenly kicking the horse onward, not bothering to avoid woods that might conceal ambushing archers or squadrons of horsemen with orders to run down and kill enemy scouts.

Yet all the way back he felt the power massing in his flesh. A tremendous force was building underground and at the same time inside his skull. His head seemed ready to burst, so that he did not need to open his mind to feel the power of it. His one thought was to get back to Delamprey and save Gwydion. He would strike off the old man's fetters. How Willow would admire him then! How the world would fall at his feet! Today was going to be a glorious day. Nothing could stop him now. Nothing!

Will should have ridden more widely eastward around the king's army and the skirmishers which had been deployed to guard the southern approaches. He chose otherwise. He spurred his steed savagely, and burst straight across the lines, a lone horseman, looking for all the world – or so he imagined – like a royal messenger carrying the vital word that would save the day.

When at last he flung himself down from the saddle his mare was blown and heavily lathered. He pulled her into the ash spinney and began to tether her, but then the strap got in a knot and he threw the reins down and let the horse trot away as it would. He gave the secret whistle, waited to hear Willow's reply.

There was none.

His mind was spinning now. The afternoon was stealing on, and he felt the goading of a terrible impatience. He whistled again, but again there was no reply. At last he shouted out Willow's name angrily.

'Willow! *Willow, where are you!*'

Still no answer came. But was that surprising? He recalled the way the Verlamion Doomstone had turned Willow's mind. He began to think she must have fallen under the new battlestone's spell.

'*Willow! By the moon and stars!*'

He ground his teeth, staggered, felt his eyes pulse with anger, but then he caught himself up sharply. Were not his own thoughts sinking into error?

How could that be? After all his experience with battlestones, he knew how to deal with them!

'She's not as strong-minded as me,' he told the trees. 'The day that I fall under a battlestone's influence has yet to dawn!'

He felt hot, sweaty, confined. He needed to breathe, and ripped the breast of his shirt down to his navel, baring his chest to the sky. The shirt hung, cinched at his belt. One of the sleeves dangled like a tail. The horse would not let him approach. That was no longer important. He headed out of the spinney on foot, half-naked yet buoyed up on a tide of self-admiring thoughts. And now the promptings in his mind began to centre on Gwydion, and what tiresome failings he had. In truth, the wizard had begun to lose his powers long before the golden fetters had been put on him. He was old and fading.

'But I'm coming to save you anyway!' Will shouted, laughing at the breadth of his own charity.

His voice sounded harsh in his ears. He wished he had kept silent, for there were lines of men not far from the edge of the spinney and some of them had turned to look his way.

He ducked down in the long grass and began to laugh again. The grass here was luminously green, as if the stalks were filled with subterranean light. Little did those men out in the open realize that the man who would deliver them from pain and death was crouching in the grass nearby. That struck him as uproariously funny. He laughed until his belly ached and tears filled his eyes. Then, all at once, he put a finger to his lips and hushed himself. It was time to decide what to do. But thinking straight among all these whispering trees was like trying to listen to music in a high wind.

The battlestone seemed suddenly very close. It was beaming forth powerful waves. For a moment Will forgot what he was trying to do. There was a puddle of mud within reach and he crawled towards it. He smeared black lines on his face, mussed his hair like a wild man. Slowly a new plan had begun to hatch out. Why not lie low in the mud and watch the battle from the safety of the wood? He would become one with the earth without any need for dying.

Once he had thought of the idea, it seemed wholly excellent. So obvious. So clearly the wisest thing to do under the circumstances.

Except that he could not sit still. There was glory to be had!

Glory, and the small matter of a wizard to be redeemed. He would walk right up to the cloister and do that now!

First he collected dry branches from a dead tree and snapped them down into a bundle. He would carry them as if he had been sent by the Fellows to fetch ash twigs for their never-failing ritual fires. What was it the Wortmaster had taught him about the ash? He sang out the rhyme,

> *'The ash he be a goodly tree,*
> *Big black buds, one, two, three.*
> *Ashen handle – hoes and rakes,*
> *Always gives before he breaks!*

'Elm hub, oaken spoke, ashen rim,' he called out, repeating the words of the wheelwright's song. That ditty would serve as well as anything to keep the battlestone from finding its way into his mind. 'By the moon and stars, I'll be like the ash and spring back against whatever tries to break me!'

He strode out, carrying his bundle across the cloister's newly-made outworks, past the defensive mounds that the king's army had piled up. The lines were fully manned now; long swallowtail banners flew above them. A flash came from the barrier in the middle distance. Smoke obscured the king's standard, and a loud bang smote the air. Another bursting of sorcerer's powder, Will thought, delighting now in the brimstone taste of it. Some of the queen's soldiers carried arquebuses – cleverly wrought iron tubes that spurted flame and noise like fireworks. They cast stones that maimed or murdered. But the giant engines of death that also employed sorcerer's powder were more glamorous still – fearsome pipes of iron and brass that had been hauled into place on stout wooden frames and thick, iron-bound wheels. These wall-smashers had once belonged to Lord Warrewyk, but had been abandoned by him at Ludford.

A small voice in Will's head asked if Edward's attack could really succeed against these formidable weapons. But the question seemed meaningless. What did it matter how powerful the guns were? There would be no time for them to do their work. The battle would be over almost before it had begun. He would see to that!

He was almost at the cloister now. The strange feeling of immense strength surged in him as he entered the empty yard. The gate was unguarded, the Fellows, no doubt, hiding away like grubs from the sun's glare. There was a sour taste in his mouth. He spat. A nasty odour was here. Not sorcerer's powder, more like the reek of the sewer. And something like the sound of a tent flapping in the wind, though there *was* no wind.

A gang of men beyond the high wall were grunting and groaning as they went about some desperate business. They were in the adjoining yard, shouting, hauling hard on ropes. It sounded from the strain in their voices as if they were trying to drag some gigantic beast to a place that it did not want to go.

He felt the ground shake. There came the noise of large chains, of claws raking against cobbles, and a raucous hissing and spitting. Then came the clang of metal, furious shouts, and suddenly Will knew where he had smelled that boar's-sty stink before.

Aston Oddingley!

He had reached the main entrance of the College of Delamprey. Around every chapter house door were cut the letters:

Delamprey was no different. On the door was a great fist-shaped handle of tarnished bronze. As he kicked the door open, the fist unclenched and tried to take hold of him. He tore away from its grasp, then thrust an ash twig at it. It grabbed, then discarded it in disgust.

Will knew the Fellows were alerted, for a warning bell had begun to toll. Two men came groping into the dark corridor to discover who had broken the sanctuary threshold. Then two more Fellows appeared with a group of bequines who began to wail until they were hurried away from the intruder's profane gaze.

Will laughed, hooted at them in imitation of their dismal noise. 'Wooooo! Ha ha! Woooooooooo! Ha ha ha! Where's the sacred fire, ladies?'

But then he saw the way that must lead down into Gwydion's dungeon, and his heart leapt. Only four Fellows stood between him and the head of the stair. Blind to light, they nevertheless perceived him darkly through some dim sense. When the nearest Fellows drew cudgels from their robes, he yelled and roared like a lion, bearing down on their pathetic attempt to block his way.

'Who comes?' they demanded. 'Who comes?'

Suddenly, the cloying smell in the air made him gag, and the brightness coursing through his mind faltered. There is something wrong, he told himself. It's the stone . . . It's in me . . . I must . . . I must . . .

But then a bony hand grabbed at him and made him jump. He gritted his teeth, threw down his bundle of sticks and darted away from the clatter they made. The empty eye-sockets of the Fellows seemed to listen for him, but whatever had replaced their sense of sight could not find him fast enough.

'Who comes?' they cried again. 'Defiler! Defiler!'

As with the great chapter house of Verlamion, the stones of the cloister floor were carved with skulls and bones. Under them, Will knew, lay the remains of those who had lived and died in this dismal college over many centuries. Fear of death lay at the empty, white heart of the Fellowship. That was what Gwydion always said. Fear of death and the great entrapping lie that there was a way for mortal men to live forever.

He felt the idea inspire him. It seemed that he stood on the verge of a great insight, a vital discovery that could save all mankind. Glittering confidence welled up inside him once more, supreme self-belief, seemingly as elemental as the tide, yet groundless. He yelled, burst along the passageway, charged two of the Fellows aside, ran towards the stairhead. There he leapt a barrier of old bell-rope and, as he wrenched open the cellar door, he looked around.

Though the Fellows held out grasping hands, they no longer dared follow him. It was as if he had passed some limit beyond which they were forbidden to go.

Under his feet here, the stone flags were plain, the walls unadorned by any sign or symbol. This part of Delamprey still belonged to the king, and had not been dedicated to the Fellowship. Perhaps that was why the Fellows would go no further.

'Ha ha hahahahahaaa!'

He stuck out his tongue and made a gargoyle face at his pursuers. He laughed at them, taunted them. Then he threw a chair. Infuriated, one of the Fellows groped for the barrier, but then recoiled from its touch as if it had been on fire. Obedience was ground so deeply into them that they dared not cross. They're fools who should be baited! he thought. And what fine sport it is!

But that was not why he had come here. He remembered his reckless mission. It was not yet half done. On the cellar stair he saw one of the queen's turnkeys coming up to see what the disturbance was. The brute's neck was as thick as a bull's and he carried a long-handled war-hammer in his hand. But he found himself hurtling back down the way he had come after Will's foot crashed into his chest. He fell into a second man, and they lay collapsed together at the bottom of the steps.

They began to stir. Wild strength surged in Will's body. He walked down the stair and recovered the war-hammer. It was a formidable weapon, three feet long and with a square head that had a spike on the back meant to punch death holes in plate armour. As the men he had knocked senseless stirred and tried to get up, Will swung the hammer round his head, testing it, loving its feel and its weight, turning over the idea of driving its point through a couple of thick skulls.

But then he remembered an arsenal of far greater weapons that was at his disposal. He culled dangerous spells from the pages of his memory and danced magic over the men as they found their feet. His words raised their arms up, drew them through the air and violently pinioned them to the wall. As the raw, ragged magic pressed them hard against the stones, they endured rib-snapping pressure. They went pale in the face and their heads lolled. It was all they could do to breathe.

'Not as neat a job as Gwydion would have managed,' he announced exuberantly. 'But it'll have to do.'

Will took the ring of keys from a hook on the wall and unhurriedly opened Gwydion's cell.

'You are in peril, Willand . . .' Gwydion called through the door as Will began to slide back the five heavy bolts.

'Is it *ever* possible to catch a wizard unawares?' He threw back the heavy door and hurried over.

Gwydion took in the sight of him like a blow. 'A man's magic is his signature,' he warned grimly. 'And there is something very much amiss with yours, Willand. It was not wise to do as you have done.'

'Well, there's a fine way to greet your saviour!' he said. 'I'm here to redeem you!'

When the wizard fixed him with a hard gaze, he was suddenly aware that he must be presenting a less than heroic picture – filthy with half-dried mud and almost naked.

He inspected the golden chain and fetters. 'It looks to me like you're in quite a bind.'

'Chlu will have felt your magic too. And Maskull.'

He cocked his head and narrowed his eyes. 'Gwydion, do I look like a fool? Do I?' Then he hefted the hammer.

'What are you doing?'

'Hold still! I'm going to smash these fetters off.'

'You must not! They contain much harm drawn by Maskull from the Sparrowhawk Hill battlestone—'

'Yes, and Queen Mag has the key between her breasts. I know. I saw her. So this is the only way. Now hold still!'

'Willand—'

There was a black flash. Molten metal flew from the hammer head as he struck the gold chain open. Grainy smoke began to issue from the broken link. A piece of gold fell, wriggled down into the straw and vanished. Will stamped on it as if it was a venomous worm. Pain ripped through him. His foot became a misshapen claw, a hoof, a foot again. He danced the harm out of it. It was inelegant, but he twirled and twisted and danced the cloud of harm up and out through the vent, dispersing it as he had once seen Gwydion do.

'You see!' he said triumphantly. 'Anything you can do . . .'

Gwydion staggered back. The blow had released him from the pillar, but the fetters still held his wrists. '*What have you done?*'

Will stared hard at him. 'You're free, aren't you?'

'Free? I am powerless!' The wizard stared at his wrists. 'The harm you have released will turn the day against us.'

'Your gratitude overwhelms me!' Will seized his arm and dragged him towards the door. 'Come on, Gwydion! Where's your spirit?'

'That, I shall never tell you!'

Smoking hammer in hand, Will pulled the wizard past the struggling gaolers and up the stair. The Fellows moaned and threshed at the rope barrier as their unreachable quarry came into view. But now in their midst a gnarled Elder appeared and ordered his juniors in pursuit.

'In there!' Will cried, backing towards a second door. Once Gwydion was through, he propped it closed with the hammer, jamming the handle under the latch and kicking the part-melted head hard against a step.

'That'll hold up an army!'

'Where are you taking me?'

The stone spiral of the stair was like the inside of a seashell. It steepened and narrowed as they climbed. A beating began on the door below that echoed in the stifling, cramped space. They passed two small landings lit by small windows, and came at last to a worm-eaten door that opened out onto bright sunshine.

'A perfect view!'

The top of the tower seemed to Will to be much closer to the sun. It was hot up here, and smelled of half-melted tar. It was the perfect place to survey a field of war. The roof was splashed with the shadow of the great iron vane that surmounted it – a white heart and the letters A, A, E and F marking the directions of the four winds.

'What have you done with your talisman?' Gwydion demanded suddenly. He was staring down at Will's bare chest.

'That little fish? Oh, it's gone. You wouldn't believe me if I told you what happened to it.' He gave a brittle laugh.

'Try me!'

'It's no matter. No, no, really it's not, because you see I've found a far greater power,' he babbled. 'I've learned to believe in myself, Gwydion! Now I can move mountains! I could fly if I wanted to!'

Gwydion seized him. 'There's no need. The mountains, it seems, are already moving!'

Down below, the clash of arms had already begun. Will's lightning-fast eye took it all in at a glance. Ten thousand Callas men filled the meadows to the south, spreading out in battle array. More came on behind them. The sight was magnificent, and Will stared in delight as thousands of men, each of them as insignificant as an ant, went towards their doom.

From this height, Will could see the whole field, could sense exactly where the ligns lay. The battlestone was doing purposeful work. Whatever anyone might say, it was a glorious spectacle. Numberless men and horses, drawn here by an irresistible force, swirling into the fields around the cloister. Thousands of minds made murderous, filled with the battlestone's controlling emanations.

'Edward!' Will shouted out indignantly. 'Why doesn't he do as I told him? Attack the king's left! It's his only hope!'

But Lord Warrewyk was marshalling the attacking forces. A great shout went up, and there began a thundering of hooves. A mass advance had been ordered, and all three wings of the army started to move forward. As Will looked on, a volley of arrows was loosed against them, then the first cavalry assault was flung upon the king's centre. It was so fierce a charge that it almost succeeded. Axes and maces flashed over a sea of helms, but then the wave broke amid shrill cries and fell back under a forest of stabbing blades. Delight thrilled through Will's heart. In that charge alone two hundred men died, though Lord Warrewyk, struggling, bright armoured and in the middle of his fifty-strong bodyguard, escaped the slaughter.

Will congratulated himself on having managed everything so well. At last, he had begun to understand the true nature and magnificence of war. Despite Edward's treachery, the battle was turning out to be a worthy clash of arms. Edward and the others had been right all along. What higher station was there for a man than that of a warrior? What greater occupation could there be than warfare? And soon Will's chance would come to lay down his life for a great cause too.

Fortunately, he was well prepared. Earlier, in the glade, he had had the foresight to draw a great surfeit of earth power into himself. Now he felt drunk on it. The magic was fizzing in him. Potent. Ready. It was time to use it to turn the tide. But where to begin in the hurling of thunderbolts? He cast an eye at the enclosed yards below. Fellows! Those grey-faced fools would do for target practice! They were gathering in the nearer yard and—

But something else distracted his eye.

From up here he could see into the further yard, could see that it was occupied by a great cage. It was empty, and it exactly recalled the cage that he had seen at Clifton Grange.

He remembered the huge, red-and-gilt saddle that had been carried past him, the one that he had thought too big for any warhorse . . .

'By the moon and stars!' he shouted. 'I was right after all!'

'Willand, you are not yourself,' Gwydion insisted. 'Listen to me—'

But he would not listen. And nor could Gwydion make him stop. He dashed the cold sweat from his forehead, feeling wholly untouched by the futile emanations of the stone. This battle was different. This one was marvellous. It would turn out very well, because he was in perfect control of it. The Delamprey battle-stone was a tame crouching thing. He could feel its ineffectual fears snapping at his heels, as it pathetically tried to insinuate itself into his mind.

He punched the air, gesturing to where the stone lay, scornful of its efforts. His eyes ran along the thatches of the hamlet of Hardingstones and the strange cemetery that stood near it.

'Willand!' Gwydion stretched out his hands, looking strangely small and comical with his golden bracelets and the two absurd pieces of gold chain dangling from them. 'Willand, you must listen to me! You must not let the battlestone use you like this!'

But without magic to augment it, the wizard's voice carried none of its usual potency. Will cut him off, overrode all objections and stabbed a finger instead at the men streaming into battle below. 'Nothing of your protections now remains, Gwydion. If Maskull only realized what was happening out there, he'd send bolts of flame against Edward's army and destroy it! But if he does that now I'll counterspell him with green fire! I'll—'

The wizard grabbed his arms. 'You? Counterspell Maskull? You must not try that! You are not ready for it!'

'I'm ready for anything, the Lady has told me so!'

'*What lady?*'

'She told me! I am the true king! I am Arthur!' He pushed the frail old man aside.

'Beware, Willand! Maskull will destroy you!'

'My fear of that old conjuror has left me. His fires are burning low just like yours are. That's why he's not yet had the courage to show himself today.' He jumped up onto the battlements. 'It's time for me to bring this fight to its swiftest end!'

Gwydion seized his legs and pulled him down, but he lashed out. 'Get off me, old man!'

'Willand, you are filled with a strange light. You do not properly realize what is happening. Maskull attends the Delamprey stone as we speak. But he is not prompting it, he is working to *prevent* it from releasing all its harm over the battlefield.'

Will balked. The idea was absurd. 'What nonsense!'

'Maskull cares naught for this battle's outcome. He has fixed his desire upon a more terrible goal.' The wizard's eyes flickered as he strove to make Will understand. 'He means to work magic upon the stone even while it is in spate. His aim is to divert a great measure of its harm into a weapon of his own!'

He inclined his head, struck by the cleverness of the idea. 'You mean . . . like those bracelets?'

Gwydion raised his wrists. 'Exactly so! Only a hundred times more dangerous! During the time of my captivity I was forced to listen to Maskull's prideful harangues. I know well enough what is in his mind. During his years of wandering in the Realm Below he has dwelt much upon what went amiss for him at Verlamion. He believes his failure was due to magic that I worked on the Doomstone. Once he became aware that the harm in the stones could be manipulated he began to tamper with them. Our own work has revealed much to him, and latterly his attempts to tap a portion of the malice from the Sparrowhawk Hill stone have taken his art forward another step. This combat is nothing to him – merely that which will allow him to steal the Delamprey stone's power.'

'But he can't have succeeded!' Will pointed joyously into the middle distance. 'Even if you can't you feel the stone directly, you can still see that battle is already joined! Look there. The stone's power is going to be spent in the fighting!'

'Maskull requires the battle to be fought. He believes he can only divert significant harm while it is actually flowing from the stone – Willand, pay attention to what I tell you!'

But Will was not listening. He was watching the glorious fight unfold. It was happening just as he had supposed it would – Duke Henry of Mells was commanding the king's centre, and the Duke of Rockingham his right, while the banners of Lord Dudlea flew over the left.

Gwydion followed Will's insane stare. 'What did you offer Friend Dudlea, you fool?'

Will turned. 'How do you know I even spoke with him?'

'I see the stain of doubtful deeds in men's eyes. Answer me!'

'What's the matter? All I did was offer him his wife and his son back.'

'Is *that* all? And I suppose he demanded proof, for men like Dudlea take nothing on trust, and nor would you if you had lived his life.' Gwydion took Will's head in his hands and looked hard into his wild eyes. 'He who deals in magic must not make promises unless he knows for certain that he is going to be able to redeem them. If that rede applies to all men, then how much more to a Child of Destiny?'

Will tore away. 'I never said I'd transform the statues back myself. That's your job. Once we get those golden trinkets off your wrists—'

But the words failed on his lips.

A cloud had obscured the sun, and a dark pall seemed to have fallen across the battlefield. At the same time, a long drawn-out wail sounded in the distance. Will's eyes hunted excitedly for its source, though he already knew what it must be. There in the distance, no more than a black dot against the eastern sky, something was flying. It was bigger than a man. Much bigger. And it was approaching at great speed.

Gwydion seized him. 'What terror is come?'

Will broke the wizard's grip. With all his aimless prattling, he had forgotten about the queen's secret weapon! He saw its great red wings beating, its long neck and serrated tail snaking out behind and two talons drawn up close to its body. A rider sat astride it. When it reached the battlefield it wheeled and swooped down on Edward's cavalry. The sight of it threw all the horses into wild panic, driving the attacking knights into confusion.

'By the moon and stars!' Will cried, enraptured. 'I *knew* I hadn't imagined it all at Ludford!' He saw a sight that chilled a measure of the strange heat from his blood. In the saddle sat a fearsome knight, helmeted in polished steel and mailed in crimson scales. He dug long spurs into his beast's flanks and pulled hard on the reins to further infuriate his steed. Mad John Clifton cursed and roared, beating so violently at the dragon that Will thought that at any moment he would be thrown from its back.

Gwydion shaded his eyes, squinting into the distance, but he made no reply.

'*Willlaaaaand!*'

The cry came from below.

He dashed to the parapet and stared down. It was Willow, and she was banging on the closed gates of the slaughter yard. She had with her now a longbow and a quiver of green-flighted arrows. On the other side of the gates the yard had a dozen Fellows in it.

'Let me in!'

'There are red hands in the yard!' he shouted down. 'Go to the grove. Find the horse! I'll come for you when the day's won!'

But she threw up her hands and shrieked: 'Willaaaand!'

Just then a shower of stones rained over him, and he heard the groaning of a great weight of collapsing metal. A sense of danger thrilled through him and he dived aside. His first thought was that it must have been a great stone ball shot from one of the wall-smashing engines. Lumps of shattered masonry skittered around him as the twisted iron of the vane came crashing down. But then a huge, writhing shape loomed above. He threw up his arm against it, felt the blast of giant wingbeats. A red talon as big as he was reached into the tangle of debris to rake at him.

He was trapped among the rusted iron of the fallen weather vane – its ornaments were all that saved him. Gwydion was raging impotently at the monster, wrists fettered, dancing empty magic. It was amazing that so large a beast could have banked round and glided in upon them without being seen. Now Will realized what the ancient rede truly meant –'A man must be mad to ride a dragon.'

But insane or not, Mad John certainly knew how to control his fearsome steed. The creature's swoop had shattered the stair-house roof. Now two huge, muscular legs were trampling the fallen ironwork to pieces. Claws tore and kicked all around as the monster balanced on the draught of its outstretched wings. Its long, black tongue was like a lash as small, black eyes locked furiously on the defenceless figure of the wizard.

The viper neck carried a long-snouted head, brilliantly scaled and set with scarlet frills like the combs of a gigantic rooster. Its mouth was filled with a hundred backward-curving teeth. Will heard the roar and gurgle as it snapped at Gwydion, and when it screamed its voice tore at his ears.

The wizard had been backing towards the protection of the stair, but his escape was now cut off. Will dived to his left to where a handy piece of iron had been torn from the vane. He gripped it so tightly that it bit into his palm.

'Hyaaah! Hyaaah!' he cried, dodging past the deadly back-sweep of the wings. He used the bar as a mace, beating at the creature's hindquarters. Full blows were landed, but its hide was tougher than armour. Instead of turning to attack him, its threshing tail swept aside a jumble of iron that carried him off his feet. He was dumped hard against the battlements, but when the beast turned again, he had become its new quarry.

Now it was Will's turn to be trapped. There was blood in his left eye and when he brought his hand away from his face his fingers were wet. He was stuck in a corner, with a sheer drop on two sides and the third filled by snapping jaws.

'*Aillse, aillse nadir erchima archaste nie!*' he commanded in the true tongue, directing the full force of the drowsing spell into the beast's beetle-black eye. '*Musain! Nadir, codla samh agat! Deain ae!*'

But the beast's scaly eyelid did not droop as he had hoped. The magic had no effect. In desperation, he jabbed his rusty bar at the gnashing teeth. The piece of vane rang against them, breaking two, three. Baron John was laughing madly. He wheeled the spiked ball of a morning star around his head and brought it down on his steed's rump. The beast spat and shrieked. And then, just as it seemed that Will must be seized in that terrible, stinking maw, a thin, green shaft appeared in the beast's left cheek.

The creature shook its head in pain and broke off the attack. Will marvelled as it lowered its head and began to claw at the side of its face, snapping off the arrow that had pierced it just a hand-span below the left eye. But even as it plucked out the shaft, another arrow appeared, trembling, in the saddle bow, then a third sailed up past the rider tearing through the skin of the creature's wing. With an enraged shout, Baron John spurred his steed upward. The beast bore down with its great crimson wings. Its powerful legs thrust upward, and with a leap the creature was airborne again, winging away towards the battle.

Will flourished his iron rod at the creature and whooped in triumph. Then he leapt to the battlements and jumped up into one of the crannies to look for Willow.

She was nowhere to be seen.

Disappointment stabbed at him, formed heavily like a stone in his heart. He looked down from the dizzy height and felt the terrible constriction that had seized him. He threw his doubts off angrily, turned back. His eyes were fixed on the departing creature. He had seen the fear that had overcome Edward's cavalry. His horses had been thrown into wild confusion. If nothing was done the queen's secret weapon – this great dragon – might yet single-handedly turn the battle.

'You must not attack it!' Gwydion shouted.

'You said there were no more great dragons!' His angry accusation cut at the wizard.

But Gwydion took no hurt from it. His haggard face was alight with wonder. 'That was no dragon, great or otherwise! He has two legs, not four. And his eyes are black not golden.'

'Then what is he?'

'He is *nathirfang*! A Cambray red. And I had thought the last mountain wyvern long since departed from the world!'

'A wyvern? Why didn't you say? Look at the horses, they're terrified of it!'

'No horse would ever obey its rider in sight of a wyvern!'

Will tore his way angrily through the shattered ironwork. The reason his magic had failed was because he had not applied the true name of the beast. He gathered himself up and danced amid the rubble, drawing together the full store of power that his words and gestures would direct. He cast the spell then, a spell more powerful than any he had cast before. A bolt of bright, green fire formed in his palms. It burned hard, rushed in the wake of the wyvern, catching it hard under the wing, flashing like the sun on water. The blast felled it like a hunter's arrow loosed to bring down a fowl in flight. It gave a lurch, its wings crumpled, and it crashed to the ground on the far bank of the river, rolling over and over in a tumble of wings and tail.

Will, amazed at what he had done, looked at his hands as if they were someone else's. 'Yaaaah!'

'You shouldn't have done that!' Gwydion said. The golden fetterlocks jangled on his wrists.

Will thrust the wizard away. 'If not I, then who? Gwydion, do not lecture me when I have the power and you do not!'

He returned his gaze to the wrecked beast, saw that it lay in a heap, unmoving. The rider had been thrown clear. Baron John was crawling in the grass. Will wondered coldly if he had killed the wyvern, and whether he ought to send another bolt to incinerate it. One more bolt would be a mercy if it finished the beast's insane owner at the same time. But there was no chance to think further about Mad John, for Will's green ray had been noted, and now a spinning ball of purple fire came roaring up from the Hardingstones in answer.

'Look out!' Gwydion shouted.

Will turned towards the danger, but the wizard leapt up and hauled him down. Then the air boiled with violet fire as the bolt slammed into the south-west corner of the tower where he had been standing. It blasted another shower of masonry and dust over them, but the flame did not connect.

Gwydion coughed and muttered, 'What I meant to say was do *not* look out. What confusions the common parlance has in it these days!'

Will spat the dust from his mouth. 'I knew what you meant!'

'You have angered Maskull,' Gwydion warned as he crawled away. 'I said you would.'

'If I did, then I'm glad! Let him do his worst!' He jumped to his feet and waved a fist at the enemy from the battlement's edge.

'Get away from there, you fool!'

'Do you hear me, Maskull? Do your worst!'

'You will not say that when his next thunderbolt hits!'

'I don't mean to be here!' He grabbed the wizard by the golden chain that dangled from his cuff, and yanked. 'Come on! Follow me down. I have some hard questions to ask you. Questions you're not going to want to answer!'

Will flung himself into the narrow stairwell, thrusting his left shoulder forward in the rightward-turning hole. In that steep, dark descent he was unable to see where his feet were going, or to find enough room for his heels on the narrow treads. His fingers felt along the rough stone of the wall and his forehead scraped and bumped on the crumbling mortar overhead. He feared the sudden thrust of iron up into his belly as armed men rushed up at them, but then he realized that the banging he could hear below meant that the Fellows were still trying to open the door.

A sudden ripping of air made him flinch. There was a

tremendous whoosh as all his breath seemed to be sucked from him. Everything shook. Dust and pebbles fell as the stairwell lit purple. But it was the last thunderbolt to come from Maskull's hand. They had clattered down the tower one storey and had come to the tiny landing where an arrow-slit gave out onto the scene of battle. They paused, gasping for breath. Then Gwydion asked, 'Is the harm from the stone now in full spate?'

'It feels that way to me.'

'Then we have one less worry for the moment. We should make the most of our chance while Maskull is fully occupied.'

Will shoved his face into the arrow-slit, and what he saw made him gasp. He seized the wizard and pointed towards the Hardingstones. 'Look, there!'

'Alas! What terrors has Maskull awakened with his meddling? Those are the undead who once fled the plague! With all the magic whirling uncontrolled here, their transformation has been undone.'

And Will saw that the Delamprey tombstones were indeed changing shape, twisting, moving, groping towards life. They were rising up after their long slumbers. Hundreds of ghastly human forms, shaking off the solitude of the grave to wander at the rear of the king's lines.

At first, they went unregarded by the king's soldiers for there was deadlier work to the fore. Now that the wyvern had been downed, Edward's cavalry was brought under control again. Dense squadrons of knights had formed up, line upon line, their harnesses glittering in the sun, banners of every colour flying above them. They advanced at the trot towards the king's army, and Will knew this was the attack against the king's left that he had advised Edward to make.

Will was unable to do other than watch the fruits of his efforts ripen. He put a hand to his temple; his head had begun to ache unbearably again. His gaze passed along the king's left and settled on Lord Dudlea's colours. The shouts and thundering of hooves grew to a roar. And as the armies clashed he turned, blinking into the darkness of the stair and saw an ageless fire burning in Gwydion's face.

'I see you are returning to yourself at last. Do not turn away from the field,' the wizard told him. 'Watch, and discover what happens when two poorly promised lords face one another because a Child of Destiny has told them they must do so. Watch!'

And Will did watch, as thousands of horsemen charged in upon the king's left, as a desperate attack gathered like a gigantic wave bursting upon a rocky shore. Will could see that without Lord Dudlea's help the attack would founder, just as Lord Warrewyk's attack had foundered. The big guns would belch forth, the day would be carried in the king's favour, and Edward would die upon the field.

Yet to Will's astonishment, and even as the foremost of Edward's cavalry came to grips with their enemy, there was uproar to the rear of Lord Dudlea's men. The soldiers who held the king's left had seen an army of a different kind stealing upon them from behind. Men among the reserve swore that gravestones had come to life, and their fear had sent them fleeing in panic towards Dudlea's lines.

The movement soon came to the attention of their commander, who rode out with only his standard bearer as companion, to see for himself what was happening.

Gwydion hissed in Will's ear, 'Do you see? Lord Dudlea has got the proof he craved. The proof that you so unwisely promised that those turned to stone might live again.'

'But you told me those plaguestruck people would arise when three times three dozen and one years had passed – that's a hundred and nine years since the pestilence. That was two years ago!'

'But "three dozen and one" is thirty-seven. And three times that is one hundred and *eleven*,' Gwydion said grimly. '*You* are the one who has in the end summoned the Hardingstones back to life.'

Will cringed to think how he had made so simple an error,

and what had been its ghoulish consequence. The dancing dead had spread chaos and confusion across the field, wholly altering the outcome of the battle. He watched Lord Dudlea order his archers to fall back. No arrows were loosed at the onrushing enemy. Edward's horsemen mounted the earth bank unopposed. They wheeled. The centre of the king's army was outflanked at a stroke and came under a double blow as Lord Warrewyk's attack crashed into their wavering front.

After that, the resolve of the king's army broke. Thousands of terrified soldiers began to desert their lines. They threw down their weapons and ran for their lives. And, suddenly, the day that had seemed lost to Edward now belonged to him.

CHAPTER THIRTY-THREE

IN THE AFTERMATH

Down below, the beating on the tower door stopped. But there began in its place a wailing ghostly enough to chill Will's heart.

His face was pained as he turned away once more from the arrow-slit. The wizard pulled him into the light and slapped him hard across the face. 'It is time you woke up!'

He fell back on the stair, stunned by the unkind blow. Anger boiled up inside him. Things had turned out well, hadn't they? Far better than anyone had any right to expect! Far better than when Gwydion's efforts to carry a battlestone off into the north had caused the carnage on Blow Heath! Or when his foolish hesitations had led to the ruination of Ludford . . .

But the slap had been meant to help return Will to a proper understanding, and it did. The hubris went out of him and he fell to his knees. Gwydion raised him up again. The stone's grip was slackening now. Flashes of truth broke in on him, and he began to glimpse just how completely he had been taken over. He saw with dismay that he had not been the great prophet and hero of the hour, but a fool filled with false self-belief.

'What have I done?' he cried. 'Oh, Master Gwydion!'

'You let yourself be used,' the wizard told him gravely. 'In the end, things have gone as you said they would. What a pity you were not master of yourself and therefore able to force a more fortunate outcome.' Gwydion's grey eyes fixed once more on the field, where Edward's knights were riding down their broken enemy. 'As you should know by now, Willand, bloodlust is no more than left-over cowardice. In battles the rout is always the deadliest of times.'

Will jammed his face once more into the arrow-slit. 'But Edward promised he'd order common quarter once victory was won! I made him promise! Look!' And there, on the field below shouts were going up. 'You see? They *are* calling mercy!' he said. Pride strutted briefly in him again. 'Edward's been true to his word. I was right after all!'

'You could not have been wrong, for though you acted in igno-rance, still you are the Child of Destiny, and your presence forces the wheel of history to repeat itself. Yet, whatever the outcome today, I fear that we may have lost our fight in the long run. I have seen enough to know that Maskull's dread spark has fallen upon dry tinder here. Soon there will be a blaze hot enough to consume all that we know and love!'

'It sounds to me as if some of the harm that poured from the broken link of your fetters has entered you and poisoned your thoughts, Gwydion. Can't you see that we've achieved our aim? The day has seen less blood than any of us might have hoped when we awoke this morning!'

'The day is not yet ended.'

Gwydion leapt down the remaining turns of the stair. When he reached the bottom he wrenched the war-hammer away from the door and opened it. Outside, half a dozen Fellows were grov-elling on the floor, their mouths open, their hands pressed to their bellies. They were wailing in agony. Then Will saw the redness on their gowns, and the dark, spreading pool under the nearest of them. A figure dressed in tall boots and a suit of black hide came forward and stood over the body, a bloodied poleaxe in his hand. It was Chlu.

Gwydion threw the war-hammer to Will. 'Beware, Willand! A deep urge to harm you drives him. Be ready to defend yourself.'

Will nodded. Chlu's murderously implacable nature was already clear to him. There was a foul desire in those too-familiar eyes, the more hideous for Will because it was like looking at himself in a weird's mirror, being forced to recognize the beast that dwelt within.

Chlu took stock warily. As ever, he moved deliberately on Will.

'Begone, Dark Child!' Gwydion commanded, stepping between them. '*Eoist liomma* – apprentice of a loathsome master! *Deain huir!*'

But the fetters were still upon the wizard's wrists and the power of magic no longer swelled the true tongue in his mouth. Chlu's eyes, though, never wavered. He thrust Gwydion aside and snarled at Will. 'You must die!'

When Will hefted the war-hammer, the iron felt heavy and dead in his hand. He whirled it in figures of eight before him, preparing a counterstrike for the moment when Chlu lunged. But there were footsteps beyond the cloister yard, and through the broken windows there could be glimpsed soldiers, dozens of them. They were wearing blue-and-white quartered colours – Edward's men! Will saw them running, weapons in hand, and he had no doubt what their mission was. They had been sent here under special orders, sent to hunt down men of rank. Two or three had come to the very threshold of sanctuary, but they quailed before it, suddenly assailed by superstitious terror, and afraid to cross.

Still Chlu sought a way past the whirling war-hammer. He jabbed and jabbed again, but dared not step closer for fear the wizard would slip past him and attack his exposed back. But Gwydion had other ideas.

'Bring the king here!' he shouted, guilefully feigning an Elder's voice. 'The king's enemies are nigh! Hide the king away! Hide him, I say! Give him sanctuary in our House!'

The soldiers outside became suddenly like wolves scenting

prey. Those who had entered the yard now approached the great oaken door. One began to jab at the brazen fist with a helm-axe. Their leader drew his dagger and kicked the never-locked door fully open.

The sanctuary bell began to toll. At the sound of it, muffled screams issued from the chamber where the bequines had been hidden.

Chlu lunged, lunged again, but as he swung a second time he clattered the blade of his poleaxe off the low wooden beam above his head. Will caught him off balance, forced him back.

'Fly, Dark Child!' Gwydion hissed. He held up his arms and the golden bands on his wrists flashed with a baleful light. 'Go while you may!'

Chlu hesitated. His garb was strange, unlike the plain-weave of a common man's clothing – enemy soldiers would see a ransom to be had from taking him. He thrust the poleaxe furiously at Will, enraged to have come so close to his prey once again only to be forced to quit the fight. He let out a shout of such grotesque torment that the cry went through Will like a knife, but then he threw down his weapon, backed away, and finally he ran.

Will started after him, but Gwydion pulled him back. 'Let him go, Willand! There will be time enough to fight with Chlu another day.'

Will turned, an echo of the madness still boiling his blood, and took a rough hold on the wizard. *'Who is he, Gwydion? You must tell me! I have to know!'*

'I shall tell you once the battle is over. That much I lay my word to!'

He opened his fists, suddenly ashamed to have laid angry hands on so stalwart a friend, but his penance did not last long, for a peal of screams came from one of the inner chambers. Will spun, recognizing the voice.

'Willow!'

He broke away and ran down the cloister, leaping over the

writing bodies that lay scattered in his path. But which of the chambers had the scream come from?

He stared around wildly. '*Willow?*'

When the scream came again, it was muffled, more distant, but it seemed to come from the stair. He ran up it, burst in through the nearest door, and found that it opened onto a gallery that overlooked a lower room. Down below a bald-headed bequine was being held down in a chair by two others wearing iron masks. They were binding her wrists in leather thongs while her feet lashed out at anything that came near. Her struggles were weakening, and when she turned her head and screamed out again, Will knew who it was. Like the bequines, she had been forced to wear a grey sackcloth robe, torn and in disarray now, and Will knew that once a bequine's robe had been accepted there was no return to the world.

Will's stunned eye took it all in in a moment. Blonde locks lay on the floor all around, freshly shorn from Willow's head, and a third bequine was picking them up and stuffing them into a bag. His wife's quiver of green-flighted arrows had also been scattered across the floor and her unstrung bow thrown into the corner. A large, robed Fellow stood guard nearby and a wizened Elder stood over the chair with the shears; then to Will's horror he saw they were not shears but a far crueller instrument.

'No!' Willow shouted 'Please, no! Not my eyes!'

The Elder leaned forward. There was no time to run back down the stair. Will jumped from the gallery rail. He crashed down onto the guard and brought him down like a dead weight. In the same movement the iron hook was spun out of the Elder's hand.

When Will got to his feet, the Elder dropped to his knees and began to wail piteously. His empty sockets were painted with unblinking eyes that stared at Will. The bequines flung themselves down as Will cut the lashings and swept his wife up from the blinding chair.

'They came out from the yard and took me!' she cried, white-faced and terrified. 'Oh, Will, they were going to cut my eyes out!'

But already a new emergency had overtaken them. Edward's soldiers had found the gallery, and more now burst into the room. Will was driven back against the wall at blade-point. Magical power tingled in his spine as one of the men took Willow by the throat and another demanded to know where the king might be hidden.

'You will not find King Hal here,' Gwydion told them from the doorway. 'He sits some way distant, in a tent by the river-bank, awaiting the outcome of the battle.'

The soldier sneered, pushed a mailed hand in Gwydion's face. 'And who might you be?'

'Have a care!' Will growled. 'Do you not know the Duke of Ebor's wizard?'

The man stepped back, turning on his men angrily. 'You heard him! To the river! Do you want to catch a king or not?'

'What about these?' a lone voice asked.

'Since you've shown yourself willing, you can take them out and hold them in the yard!'

The three young troopers left to watch over them did not dare to touch the Elder or his bequines, but they seemed to have fewer scruples where wizards were concerned, and so Will, Willow and Gwydion were shoved out, first into the cloister walk and then into the yard, where they were put under an order of silence and made to face the wall, hands on heads.

'You must do as you see fit,' Gwydion murmured, until the prod of a spear haft to his ribs shut him up.

'I think we must do as they say, at least until they calm down,' Will said, thinking he had understood Gwydion's wisdom well enough. The magical power that stirred in his belly tempted him to act, for with its aid he could easily overcome Edward's three young troopers and work an escape, but now the battlestone had released him from its seductive grip and the shame of his recent actions hung over him. He decided he should refuse the power. To attempt magic now might compound the disaster, and for Willow and the now-defenceless Gwydion, there was greater safety here than outside – at least until the call for common quarter was generally heeded.

So it was that the battle of Delamprey was wholly done with. All around, Edward's victors ran amok, turning over the sequestering hall, looking for fugitive noblemen. Others tried to find hidden gold, though the Delamprey bullion had long since been carted off to the chapter house in Cordewan. When, some time later, the three captives were led out of the yard, they saw that the ground had been trampled and the bodies of men lay scattered upon it like leaves in autumn. But there were far fewer dead than had befouled the field of Blow Heath.

By now the chaos of battle had already begun to resolve itself after its usual fashion. Thousands of the common soldiery of the king's army had been disarmed and were sitting bound in sullen groups, watched over by knots of cavalrymen. But still Will could feel the stain of cold blood in this place, and he knew at once that there had been some hideous additional slaughter.

'Oh!' Willow cried, turning away with pursed lips from the sudden horrific sight.

A score of heads lay on the grass – eyes open, mouths agape. And a bloody piece of beech-trunk stood in pride of place in the grassy sward, weltered in gore.

Will recognized many of the ghastly faces from the king's court – maybe two dozen knights and nobles had been deliberately butchered here, including the Duke of Rockingham, the Earl of Shroppesburgh, Lords Bowmonde and Egremonde . . . broken swords and strapless spurs attested a grand public degradation.

Two carts were filled with naked bodies, their flesh the colour of finest Fellowship wax. They were headless, and all had their wrists roped together behind their backs. Nor was it over yet.

Disgust turned to rage in Will's heart.

'*Villains!*' he shouted at the sky. '*Murderers!* Where is Edward of Ebor? Take me to the Earl of the Marches!'

He struggled with the guards, then saw a head of unruly red-gold hair bowed near to the block. It was Jasper, and Lord Dudlea was next behind him. They were kneeling captives, stripped to their loins, heads bowed.

'So, it's you, is it?' Dudlea called out in miserable disgust. 'You unconscionable liar.'

Nearby, another nobleman strutted, helmless but in full armour and surrounded by lesser knights and men-at-arms, the latter all in red surcoats bearing the white badge of the bear and butchered tree on their breasts.

'What is this bloody mess, my lord?' Will roared at Lord Warrewyk, pointing at the block. Warrewyk's guards seized him. His hands shook, overtaken by wrath, they itched to blast forth the power that remained in him. 'Edward promised me common quarter! *He promised!*'

'And common quarter was called.' Lord Warrewyk's voice cut like a shard of obsidian. He poked the point of his sabaton at the nearest head that lolled forlornly on the grass. 'But as you see, none of these fine fellows were commoners.'

There was laughter at that. Will struggled against the guards until Willow feared he would be hurt, or the magic that was in him would burst forth uncontrolled. 'You have betrayed me! You have betrayed Edward! And you have destroyed the cause of peace!'

Lord Warrewyk's tight smile snapped into anger and he lifted his sword so that the point of it was in Will's face. 'If there have been scores settled among men of noble birth what business is that of yours?'

'And all this wading in blood settles it, does it, my lord? *Well? Does it?*'

'Willand, be easy now!' Gwydion's voice was a growl of

reprimand as he stepped between them. 'Perhaps you will tell me this, Friend Warrewyk: do you propose to sully this ground with more blood? *Royal* blood perhaps?'

'Royal blood?' The earl turned, put a mailed hand to his chin as if perplexed. 'Howso? The king is once more among his true friends. But if you mean the she-wolf who calls herself queen, she is gone. Fled, along with her paramour, her sorcerer and the treacherous Hogshead whom I dearly wished to bring here and see relieved of his troublesome burden.'

Warrewyk's followers laughed again, but Gwydion took the news impassively. 'So the queen has escaped . . .'

'She and her friends will be hunted down in due course, you may be sure of that.'

'Hunted down? Oh . . . will she?' Gwydion's words mocked Warrewyk with scant belief.

'You have your victory, my lord!' Willow said. 'If you have any honour, tell these men to unhand us so we may go from here!'

'What's this?' Warrewyk stepped close, studying the upstart, cheek and chin. 'Her hair has been cut off, yet still it seems to me that this woman was a companion of Lord Morann's once. Yes, it was she who gave us good warning of the queen's forces while we marched up to Ludford.'

'I won't deny that I once saved your neck,' Willow said staunchly. 'Though I'd never do it a second time!'

Warrewyk pursed his lips in amusement, full of himself and playing up before a dozen admirers. 'You know, it's always good policy to repay favours, be they for good or ill.'

'May your own neck find a sharp blade at the next battle's end, my lord,' she spat.

'Oh, curses upon me now, is it?' He looked around, his dignity teetering in the balance now, but then he gave a deliberately magnanimous smile. 'Still, I say this shrew deserves her reward. Let her go. Let them all go. Stand up, Dudlea! And the others too, for you are summarily pardoned! And know that you owe your worthless lives to a serving woman!'

Warrewyk's men laughed at that. Warrewyk himself gestured to his men that Dudlea and Jasper and two other minor noblemen were to be untied and driven off – until one of his knights spoke privately to him and he bethought himself.

'Wait!'

Warrewyk pulled off his mailed glove and examined a bloodied knuckle, saying to Will, 'Before you go – I'm told you're a healer. Perhaps you would care to test your skills on a very nasty little cut.' Then he stooped down and lifted up Humphrey of Rockingham's head so that it dripped red.

Will turned away, tight-lipped. Willow and Gwydion followed him, even though he kept walking until the laughter of Lord Warrewyk and his raucous followers had long ceased to ring.

They headed across the part of the field in which the dead lay thickest. An acre of grass was heaped with the slain. Despite the heat of the day a pale mist was rising from them as hundreds of bodies gave up the ghost.

Gwydion's eyes hardened as he scoured the killing ground. 'Maskull has gone,' he murmured. 'Perhaps, after that attack on the wyvern, he supposed I was no longer bound by these fetters. Whatever the case, he has decided it is unwise to be drawn into a fight now. We may suppose he has already taken all that he wanted from the day.'

Will stopped and stared, and tears rolled down his cheeks. 'Again,' he said, looking around him forlornly. 'It's happened again. And again there was no reason for it.'

He buried his face in his hands. Willow did not yet know the full truth of what had happened. How could she? She did not know he had failed to resist the battlestone, that it had found his weakness and he had let it master him at a crucial time. He had done nothing to end the fight. That had been Maskull's doing. He had drawn off a portion of the stone's harm and captured it in a weapon to be held against some dread moment when it could be decisively visited upon the world.

Will closed his eyes. The sight of so much defaced flesh had grown so wearisome that he could feel little comfort, even in Willow's touch.

Gwydion's remarks were bitter and doom laden. 'Today we have passed the point of no return. All virtuous circles have turned vicious. A better receipt for disaster would be hard to imagine – the king is taken, yet the queen has escaped. She will go into the North and gather her strength, while he will become the pawn of a new gang. This killing of nobles – the revenges sought by their kin – that is what will fuel the war now. We cannot stop it, Willand. Not until, like a wildfire, it has exhausted itself through lack of human kindling.'

'That's enough, Master Gwydion!' Willow cried. 'I don't know whether it's those golden bracelets that're making you talk like a fool, but if you must say things like that, then go and say them in a place where Will can't hear you!'

But the wizard faced her angrily. 'The fault is mine! I delayed overlong! I groped in the dark! I did not dare to make the first move! And now all is lost!'

'All is *not* lost!'

Gwydion turned away from them like a broken man. 'I am done for, Willand. My powers of healing have deserted me. You must work alone among the wounded of the field of Delamprey. You must try to make some little amends for my great failure.'

Gwydion walked through the despoiled camp of the king's army, and there he searched out the tent that contained the spent battle-stone. It was not hard to discover, for it was painted with mystical staves, and a multitude of blue butterflies had already settled on it.

As for Will, he tended the wounded, doing what he could. Willow saw many bodies, stripped and floating in the shallows of the Neane. Some were soldiers who had been ridden down for the sake of their jackets and kettle hats, and whose ragged throats now stained the green waters red. Many more of the mutilated dead wore the marks of the plague upon them. Willow knew they had fled into the river and drowned while trying to return home to Cordewan more than a century out of their time.

Dusk was deepening when Will, bloodied and filled with pain, joined his wife and Gwydion in the black tent. He was shown the inscription that was incised in a sharp-edged plinth of reddish ironstone – the stump was all that remained of the Delamprey battlestone. This time, the words were in no language that Gwydion knew.

The wizard's voice was hopeless. 'Maskull's spells have done this. He knows my powers well enough. He has locked it tight, and made it impossible for us to follow the lorc further by means of the verses.'

Will picked up an abandoned stool and sat down heavily on it. 'Don't say that.'

'I *do* say it, for it is the truth! And I will go further: if we should find the next stone, the leaping salmon talisman will no longer be our great advantage!'

The recrimination hurt. 'I'm sorry about that,' Will said, and in a voice that was flat from fatigue he began to tell what had happened at Harleston lake, saying how the green fish had fused with the red and become real. But Gwydion seemed hardly to be listening, and before Will had finished the wizard let out a long howl of despair.

'The prospect is bleaker than ever it was before! So much has conspired against us that Maskull must now prevail! When he duelled with me at the Giant's Ring his words were more than mere boasts. I am indeed too weak! And too craven to resist him! This is the way the Last Age must end!'

Willow gave him a look that was as dark as thunder and said, 'All I want to know is where's my Bethe.'

The wizard's sigh dismissed Willow's cares, but then he stirred himself to make an answer. 'Edward, Lord of the Marches, came here a little while ago to claim this stump which he calls his victory monument. He says the Lady Cicely is waiting at the port of Dundelgan. She will stay there until news of the outcome of the battle reaches her. Because of Ebor's victory, you may now hope that Bethe will come across with her.'

'Hope?' Will said. 'We'll do more than that. Are the duke and duchess intending to meet here?'

'That is not Richard's plan. Edward says his father must continue south with all speed. He will meet the victors of Delamprey Field at some convenient place between here and Trinovant. They desire to enter the city together and in triumph, with Richard and the king riding side by side. It is in Richard's mind to try himself against the Stone of Scions. He wishes to ask questions of Magog and Gogmagog.'

'Who?' Willow asked.

'Magog and Gogmagog are the guardians of the throne,' Will said bluntly. 'They—'

But Gwydion interrupted him. 'It is the Stone of Scions that is the true guardian of the throne. It lies within the base of the throne in the White Hall in Trinovant. It was fetched into the Realm from Albanay, but before that it dwelt in the Blessed Isle, at Tara, and was the stone upon which the High Kings there were crowned. In ancient times it was brought out of the city of Falias by one of the Ogdoad whose name was Morfesa. He claimed it was made by the fae, and it may be so, for no king may sit the throne of the Realm for long without its approval.'

'And the other two?' Willow said. 'Magog and Gogmagog?'

Gwydion nodded. 'When King Brea captured the Isle of Albion, they were the last of the giants that he overcame. They became Brea's loyal servants, and were seen for many years fetching and carrying about the palace of White Hall. When they died two great oaken statues were carved in their likenesses and much magic placed upon their heads. They stand in their niches behind the throne and will cry out against any man who attempts to sit upon it without the mandate of Sovereignty . . .'

He stumbled over his words as if overtaken by a sudden bout of dizziness, and then tried to stand. 'I must go ahead and prepare the ground in Trinovant against the day of Duke Richard's arrival . . .'

'It looks to me,' Willow said, 'that Master Gwydion is in no fit state to go anywhere just now.'

The wizard rattled the hateful fetters, and said through gritted teeth, 'My powers have been drawn, yet I must try to salvage what advantages I can. Some small delays may yet be strewn in the road to hamper Maskull's progress.'

Will, wearied by his effort but more so by the wizard's bleakness, felt his spirits flickering and fading. But he had promised all his strength, and so he steeled himself for another effort. 'We shall fight on with you.' He took Willow's hand. 'We'll travel with you, Master Gwydion, at least until Duke Richard's retinue arrives. By the time we have our daughter back, we'll know what else we should do.'

But the wizard gazed back, lost in his own decaying vision. 'Better, I think, that you return home to the Vale where you belong. If the Realm is now to fall into ruin you may as well wait for the end in the peace of your own home. You will have a year – two maybe, if you are lucky – before Maskull's fireball finally falls on you. You saw what happened in Little Slaughter. The end, when it came, arrived at once and was painless. Knowing the end is coming, but not precisely when – that may sound like unendurable torture, but it is not so very different from the burden that is shouldered by all mortal men. You will not have quite so long to enjoy the delights of this life as you thought, and of course you will miss the satisfactions of seeing your beautiful child grow up, but—'

'Now that's more than enough of that kind of talk!' Willow said, breaking in on him. 'You can certainly tell it plain when you choose. But there's nothing very brave or clever about spreading gloom and despondency, Master Gwydion, no matter how heavy your heart may feel at present.'

The wizard held his head in his hands. 'I do not regret it, for what I have said is only the truth.'

She shook her head, her patience spent. 'Well, if that's all we have to look forward to, we might as well fight on. That's what I say. And in the meantime, I'll remind you that you've a promise to keep. Will told me you'd give up all you knew about the Dark Child once the battle was done, and now it is done. So you'd better be quick and say how you've fathomed so much about that villain so fast. We ought to know why he hungers to kill my Willand, for I don't think we've seen the last of him, and I expect there's nothing worse than being murdered over something without ever knowing the reason for it.'

She meant for her commonsensical remarks to buck the wizard up, but Gwydion's head sank down and he would say nothing. Willow suddenly stood up and, touching Will's arm meaningfully, said, 'I need to get some air.'

He followed her outside, and they went a little way from the tent. 'What is it?'

'The fetters are bleeding,' she murmured.

'Bleeding?'

'They're bleeding harm. Dripping their poison into him. He's trying to fight it, but he's failing. Can't you see it? You said you cut him loose from the pillar, though he begged you not to for fear of what might happen. Some of that cloud of viciousness has got inside him. It's doing him down.'

Will swallowed, suppressed the urge to turn. 'You're right.'

'So what shall we do?'

He thought for a moment, then said, 'They'll have to come off. And right away.'

'But how? Isn't that even more dangerous?'

'Maybe.'

'Surely if they contain a measure of harm drawn out of one of the stones—'

He met her concern steadily. 'I know what I can do. I'm going to use the stump.'

'*What?*'

'You go back in there and keep him talking. When I come in you must take a firm hold of him. But watch out. Despite appearances, he's strong. Even with those fetters weakening him, he'll fight like a lion.'

'Will, are you sure?'

'Just do as I ask.'

He walked away, and began quietly to prepare himself for the coming fight. He found his place on a slight rise where the earth patterns spiralled, and there he stood, feet planted, and began to drink in the power. He drew on it too greedily at first. The power quivered in his legs, squeezing like cramp in his calf muscles, rose up, threatening to buckle his knees. He was like a thirst-maddened man – bolting it, then coughing it back. But soon he felt the spangling cool thrill running freely in his bones. It flooded his breast and flowed up into his head and hands until, once again, he became the white star, enrayed and encircled in light. Time stuttered, passed swiftly, froze crystal solid. He felt the whole world in him and nothing stood between his infinitely reaching spirit and what lay beyond. Then, quite suddenly, the flow ceased and he was Will again. Awed. Amazed. Renewed. And the stain he had felt on his heart before seemed to have gone.

When he entered the tent, his mind was focused. He approached the stump, laid both hands on it and began to blow, spending a portion of the power he had just drawn.

His breath blew hotter, and had Gwydion been himself he would instantly have been aware that a plot was being hatched against him. But he did not stir while Willow talked. She was asking about Bethe, then about the Vale and what she should tell her neighbours about their absence. But then the wizard did look up from her chatter.

'What are you doing?'

Will's body shielded the stump. He made no reply, nor could he, for his task was tricky. When setting his mind against a live battlestone his every effort was opposed, but here his will was accepted and he needed to find a different kind of balance. It was like pushing against something that did not push back but drew him eagerly on.

He took heart from that, and the fact that the stump's top had already begun to glow easily. Red became yellow, and yellow white. Then the glow melted in on itself and became liquid, like the wax in the top of a burning candle.

Gwydion jumped up, took him by the arm. He cried out, '*What meddling is this?*'

'Trust me, Gwydion!'

'*O miec a cheait!*' The wizard flinched away from the mounting heat, but Willow had stepped behind him. She threw her arms around his chest and locked her hands together over his breastbone, hugging him tight. Her grip did not falter. Will laid a quelling mark on his forehead, seized his arms strongly, suppressed his struggles. 'I'm taking these off before they destroy you!'

'You must not break them!'

'I have no need to break them. They'll drop away of their own accord.'

'But they are filled with harm! It must not be allowed to escape! It must not!'

'It won't.' He took Gwydion by the wrists and pulled his hands towards the bubbling, white pool of molten ironstone.

'But you have not the power to contain it – agggh!'

It was too late. Willow hung on until Will's mind was hardened, set firm on its course. Every hair on his body rose up as he pronounced the spells that directed his powers. Then he plunged Gwydion's splayed hands into the spitting furnace, and watched the wizard's fingers catch fire.

'*Cher mhac maer ane t-athair thu!*' Gwydion screamed, struggled, kicked out. His face lit with ghastly brilliance as he watched his fingers burn down. Black bones charred away in the blast, yet the gold dripped from his wrists like melted butter until the fetters fell away into the ironstone pool and vanished.

The furnace light dimmed. The stump writhed, shrank down to a grey cinder. As Will withdrew Gwydion's hands, he saw that the bracelets were gone, but the flesh was unscathed. There had been no seething out of harm, no explosion of malice. Not the faintest hint of the black smoke that had issued from the broken chain in the dungeon was seen, nor did the spell break back against them.

Gwydion's harrowed amazement as he examined his unhurt hands was a joy for Will to witness. 'But – the *price?*'

'There is none to pay here. Remember the residue of kindness that exists in every spent battlestone? I hoped it would be enough to contain the bale that Maskull put into those bracelets.'

Gwydion rolled his eyes. 'You *hoped?*'

'What else was I to do? You yourself said that all was lost otherwise.'

'It was the bracelets making me speak that way!'

'But you did say that I should listen to my inner voice. Of course, this stump will no longer grant boons, but that's a price worth the paying, don't you think?'

Gwydion's eyes rolled and he slumped down, exhausted by his experience. 'I hope Edward doesn't blame you for destroying his precious victory stone.'

'He will.'

Willow was puffing and wiping her sleeve across her brow. 'I think our friend's customary humour is coming back to him.' She poked the wizard's shoulder. 'Now, Master Gwydion, "One good turn deserveth another." Isn't that what wizards say? We must know the reason why Chlu wears a semblance of Willand's face. Did Maskull shape him so with a spell? And if he did, what's been the purpose of it?'

When Gwydion hesitated once more, Will's levity deserted him. 'I was once led to believe that Maskull was my father, and though you assured me it wasn't so, still I don't know why he said, "I made you, I can just as easily unmake you."'

'Then perhaps the time has come for you to know.' Gwydion

hunched, seeming incomplete without his staff to lean on. 'Listen, then, and learn, and come at last – if I may re-use an ancient formula – to a true understanding. During my captivity much was revealed to me that was hidden before, and this knowledge has served to make matters all the clearer. Since there is no longer any doubt in my mind, there is no longer any cause to withhold from you the three secrets that have lain heavy on my heart. The first is that Chlu's name is spelled thus in the old tongue of the west: L-l-y-w. This is his true name, Will, and you must never pronounce that name in a spell, no matter what the temptation. If you do you will be destroyed yourself.'

He blinked with surprise. 'But that makes no sense. Surely—'

Gwydion brooked no objection. 'What I tell you has been prophesied. The second secret is this – though Chlu has acted somewhat as Maskull's agent, his form and features are not the result of any imposed enchantment. When you look at Chlu you are looking at his true appearance, for you see . . . Chlu is your own twin brother.'

'My *brother*? But how can that be?'

'Chlu is everything that you are not. Even when you were boys this was so. Through Loremaster Morann, I kept a discreet watch on you both. Whereas you were drawn to the accomplishment of noble tasks, he was most easily drawn into mischief. Whereas you were conscientious and cared for the comfort of your friends, he was selfish and took pleasure in cruelty. And now that you are men, you feel the urge to know Chlu and to love him as a brother, whereas he wants only to have done with you, to destroy you if he can. His desire to seek you out is strong, and this urge has been used by Maskull for his own ends. But there is a deeper link between Chlu and the betrayer.'

'That's what we can't understand,' Willow said. 'Why Maskull wants so much to find Will.'

'It may be answered in part by the third secret. It was

Loremaster Morann and I who first brought Will to the Vale. Will knows nothing of this, though he has asked many times where I found him. I can now tell how it was.

'Back in the spring of the twentieth year of the reign of King Hal, when Cuckootide fell upon a full moon, I was riding in pursuit of Maskull. I stopped at a place not so many leagues from here. At that time, I had lately inflicted a setback on him, and it seemed to me that if I could only confront him in a suitable place – and on a magically important day – then, and only then, might I be able to confine him and so bring our conflict to an end.

'But tracking his movements has always proved difficult. On the day in question, three days before the magical moment, I lost him. Darkness began to fall, and I was considering where I might lay my head for the night, when I passed through a wooded glade in which I smelled once again a strong whiff of sorcery. "By his magic, so shall ye know him," thus runs the well-known rede, and so I knew straight away that the taint was Maskull's, and that he was active in his mischief. There was no doubt of its source, but there was in the magic a hint of the workings of a far more ancient power.

'Thus was I drawn forward, in the direction of a certain tower which was known to me. I thought Maskull must have found it and turned it into his secret workshop. My best hope was to surprise him there and, if I could, bring to naught whatever scheme he had put in hand to turn the destiny of the world to his advantage. But as I drew nigh, I felt the ground begin to tremble beneath my feet and the boughs above me start to shake.

'My first feeling was that it was a quaking of the earth – these happenings come from time to time when one of the halls of the fae falls in on itself down in the Realm Below. But here the telltale signs of Maskull's magic told me the cause was otherwise. The power that had made the earth quake had another source, for there suddenly appeared from the highest part of the tower a spinning, violet ray of enormous strength. The magic was powerful and carefully conducted, yet its style echoed that of the fae.

'This was the last thing I had expected, for the fae never much figured in Maskull's preferences, nor did he care to study their arts. I pressed on quietly through the undergrowth, following along deer paths, and pausing in the shadows of great beech trees. The smooth, grey trunks of those trees seemed to me to be moving like the legs of giant beasts as I crept among them, for the ray was sweeping ever faster overhead. Still, I pushed myself onward, and I was about to emerge onto the grassy sward at the foot of the tower when the door burst into flame, and Maskull fled out through a ring of fire and into the woods, running as if his very life depended upon it.

'You may imagine my surprise at this but, as soon as I turned my eyes skyward, that fast-spinning light burst screaming into the air, and a great cloud lifted the top from the tower. The concussion threw me down and put my own lights out. A wave of pain passed through my flesh, and it was an agony unlike any that I had felt before.

'As I lay there, pieces of stone fell like rain through the trees. I do not know how long I lay on the ground. At first, I thought that Maskull had divined my coming and prepared a blast to receive me. Then I thought he might have accidentally set light to some great store of sorcerer's powder. It would not have been the first time his experiments had gone awry, though in the devising of weapons he knows no peer. But neither of these explanations was the true cause, for I had felt an undeniable accompaniment of fae magic colouring the blast. That marked it as an event unparalleled in latter days. I knew then that Maskull's tests and trials in the tower must have had an even more sinister goal.'

Will stirred. He heard the persuasive power growing once more in the wizard's voice, and knew that something important must soon be told, though Gwydion remained reluctant to tell it.

'You're going to say, after all, that in some way Maskull *is* my father,' he said stonily. 'Aren't you?'

The wizard's face was unreadable. 'Willand, you must not think that, though perhaps you will decide the truth is even worse.'

'Worse?' Willow cried. 'What does it matter where Will's from? He's as fine a man as any who lives!'

He held up a hand. 'I do not doubt that you think so, nor even that it may be so, but you asked for the truth, and so you must hear me out. When I came to my senses, I approached the foundations of that broken tower. A night mist had settled over the eerie twilight, making the scene ghostly. Gradually, I became aware of a sound – two infants crying, or so it seemed to my ringing ears. They bawled out lustily, and so I hurried into the tower and climbed to a place just below the shattered top. There I found, naked and abandoned, two babies. The first was a boy-child, and the second also, and as alike as twins. They were lying upon a stone, a table carved from a single block, much like one of the altar-stones of the Sightless Ones. A great swirling slab of green and red marble whereon were set two small tokens—'

Will threw back his head and muttered, 'They were the fish. Two leaping salmon.'

Willow grasped Will's hand, and said, 'Go on, Master Gwydion.'

'As I watched, one child moved towards the red fish, and the other towards the green, and each took up the fish that was nearest to him and clasped it to his breast. But other than this there was no sign. I wondered what I should do. I was in a quandary, for there was no way to know where these newborn babes might belong, or what should be done with them.

'One thing alone was certain: these babes must not be left to Maskull's untender mercies. Being naked and motherless they seemed to me to want for proper care and indeed to be already quite hungry. It angered me greatly to see how they had been left to die by Maskull when he ran to save his own skin. Therefore I danced a protection over them, and as I danced, I tried to foresee the purpose for which two infants might have been brought here, to discover what part they were meant to play in Maskull's foul magical ambitions. It was clear to me that Maskull had already moved, in spirit at least, into the strange future that he wished then, and wishes still, to foist upon the world.

'Eventually I began to recall to mind certain of the prophecies of the Black Book, those several indeed that concerned the Child of Destiny and the third coming of the king. Once the spells of protection were cast, I determined on a plan. I knew I must move swiftly, before Maskull could recover his boldness and return to the tower. I took the babes, one in each arm, and I plunged into the woods. All that night, I moved across the moonwashed darks and deeps of the forest until I came at last to a place that I delighted in, and there I urgently summoned Loremaster Morann to meet me.'

Gwydion sighed. 'The rest, Willand, you already know. For we rode many a league that night before we parted. Then Morann took one of the children off to Little Slaughter and I took the other down into the Vale.'

Will's heart beat like a drum. He swallowed drily. What he had heard needed much thought. It still did not explain everything he wanted to know, but Mother Brig's words had already begun to make more sense.

> *Will the dark,*
> *Will the light,*
> *Will his brother left or right?*
> *Will take cover,*
> *Will take fright,*
> *Will his brother stand and fight?*

He met Gwydion's eye. 'You could have told me a lot sooner.'
'Could I? When every weft thread in the great tapestry of fate

touches every warp? Should I without huge reason adjust the destiny of a Willand – or an Arthur – when I am yet unsure? But . . . were I in your place, I have no doubt that I would see things differently. My question to you is this: has what I have just told you made you care for me any the less?'

Will drew a deep breath and looked up with a tear in his eye. 'I've said I'll stick with you, Master Gwydion, and I will.'

'That goes for both of us,' Willow said.

Gwydion stood up, his face still grave. 'Your choices please me more than I can say. From now on, we must be venturesome without being foolhardy. My staff is broken and there is now a greater enemy that threatens to overbear us, for I have lately learned of a dark arithmetic concerning the operation of the battlestones, and this more than anything has afflicted me with woes. It may be that the loss of your leaping salmon came only just in the nick of time, for I now know that even the harm that we send up into the middle airs has grim consequences for the world, no matter how or when it is done. We have seen what happens when a battlestone delivers forth its harm unhampered, but our plight is worse than ever we thought, for that harm which we have succeeded in drawing out gradually and dispersing continues in the air like a poisonous smoke, settling harm on everyone in tiny quantities, *but also bringing down the very future that Maskull so desires*. The path to his future, it seems, is paved just as easily by countless tiny acts of ill grace as it is by one grand calamity. Therefore, we must find a new solution. Those who have died so far in the battles of this war have died for us, my friends. Our chance of a future has cost them their lives. Let us not betray their memory.'

Willow burst into tears. Will hugged her to him and thought of Bethe. Then he clasped the wizard's hand in his own. 'I pledge you this much, Master Gwydion, that together we shall bring this great fight to its final conclusion very soon. And we shall not fail!'

When they stepped outside they found that the sun had set. Stars spangled the great, misty dome of the sky, and the butterflies that had covered the black tent were gone.

AUTHOR'S NOTE

Nowhere in *The Giants' Dance* is mention made of Britain or Ireland or any other familiar country, for these are places in our world. But the world in which Will lived is not wholly imaginary and a correspondence does exist between places and events in Will's world and those in our own.

'The Tews' in Oxfordshire would be the right place to go to find traces of the Vale. The Cotswolds, hills not far to the east, have a couple of villages with 'Slaughter' in their name, and by them runs the Roman road that has become in part the A429, but was once the mighty Foss Way.

Visitors to Moreton-in-Marsh will be able to find a 'Four-shire Stone' nearby. And where the upper parts of the River Cherwell run there are villages called Eydon and Adstone, and between them at Canons Ashby there was once a priory.

Modern-day stone hunters have three villages with Tysoe in their name to choose from. If they were to set out from Stratford-upon-Avon and travel a dozen miles due west, then trend north of east through the wilds of Worcestershire (where there are villages that bear such curious names as Flyford Flavell, North Piddle and Upton Snodsbury), they would eventually arrive at the Worcester and Birmingham Canal and, not far from Junction 6 of the M5 motorway, they would find Oddingley.

The meandering cart ride that Will and Gwydion take with the Aston Oddingley stone goes north, in our terms, through modern Droitwich. There is a River Saltwarpe there, and the elms mentioned were perhaps those that gave the name to Elmbridge before they vanished.

There are hills near Clent, a Hagley Wood, and near it, Wychbury Hill. Fiveways is a junction on the A451 north of Kidderminster. From Stourbridge, modern road travellers might skirt the great West Midlands conurbation going north along the A491, A449 and finally peeling off north-westerly along the A41. Across Shropshire our travellers would go – Gwydion's aim was 'the city of Caistre on the Gut of Dee' – but before they could reach Cheshire their car engine would likely overheat at a place called Loggerheads, not far to the east of Market Drayton . . . In our world a famous battle was fought there, at a place forever after remembered as Blore Heath.

From there to Wenlock Edge is a journey south of thirty miles, and thence to the favourite town of Ludlow perhaps a dozen more.

The next stage of Will's story takes him to where 'three waters join', the Findon Brook, the Sow and the Afon, names perhaps half familiar to the students of Warwick University, whose campus is sited only a mile or two from a similar confluence.

There was once a famous tree, in what is now Coventry's Broadgate, which gave its name to that fine city. And although it has long since been torn down, there was once a Coventry Castle too. Later, that city became justly famous for its big cats, but they were never pards of the kind that Will would have recognized.

When Will and Willow flee from Castle Corben they pass by the Towers of Time at a place called Rucke, which was situated along the valley of the River Afon. It may be left to the reader to make whatever connections they want here, but if there was a Mulart lign in our world it would pass a mile or so to the east of Yelvertoft, a mile or so to the west of Ravensthorpe, and directly through a Northamptonshire village called Harelstone, close by the estate of Althorpe, where Princess Diana now lies buried.

Where the Mulart lign crosses with Indonen, the lign of the ash tree, we find in our world the Abbey of Delapre which has survived into our era in a much altered form as the Northamptonshire Record Office. It was around this spot that the Wars of the Roses were brought to a new pitch of fury in July, 1459 when Cardinal Coppini, an inept papal legate, excommunicated Henry VI and a battle royal ensued. The Hardingstones of Will's world (which were also mentioned in *The Language of Stones*) are commemorated in our world by a Northampton suburb.

APPENDIX I

THE OGDOAD

The Ogdoad came together during the first Age, the Age of Trees. There were nine guardians, but as magic left the world, so the Ages declined. Thus, at the ending of each Age, the Phantarch and the foremost of his deputies departed into the Far North, leaving the lesser deputy to become the new Phantarch.

Age of Trees	CELENOST (Phantarch)
	Brynach (his deputy)
Age of Giants	MAGLIN
	Urias
Age of Iron	ESRAS
	Morfesa
Age of Slavery and War	SEMIAS
Age of Dispute	Gwydion and Maskull

APPENDIX II

THE LORC

There were nine ligns spoken of in the Black Book, but they are unequal. The weakest flow is in Heligan, whereas Eburos, the strongest, has almost twice its flow. This list shows the ligns in order of their power and shows the trees with which they are associated.

1. Eburos   Yew
2. Mulart   Elder
3. Bethe   Birch
4. Indonen   Ash
5. Caorthan   Rowan
6. Tanne   Oak
7. Celin   Holly
8. Collen   Hazel
9. Heligan   Willow

All battlestones stand on at least one lign. The ligns, which are always straight, cross at 24 points around the Realm. There is always a stone where the ligns cross, but not all stones standing on the lorc are battlestones.

APPENDIX III

THE LORC IN OUR WORLD

The places in Will's world where the stones of the lorc are sited all have, of course, equivalent places in our world. Those who want to find these places and perhaps plot them on a map should start by looking for the places where the main battles of the Wars of the Roses were fought.

A further clue to how the ligns of the lorc connect these places is given by the device that appears on the side of Will's fish talisman – three triangles drawn within one another.

Readers with access to the Internet (or perhaps a GPS receiver) and Ordnance Survey maps might like to have slightly more detailed information. The approximate OS grid references given below show to within half a mile where the stones of the lorc would stand if we were in Will's world.

Of these grid references, the first points to the Giant's Ring, the next eighteen point to all the major battlestones, and the final eighteen to the lesser guidestones.

SP3030

TQ2693, SO4364, TL1307, SO9444, SP7261, SE3418,
SK3803, SP5755, SE4840, SO5074, SP9672, SP4951,

SP4192, SK9813, SP6669, SO9156, NU0423, NY9562,
SP1635, SJ9755, TQ1698, SP5522, SJ6793, SS9280,
SE5448, SK2194, TL0576, SP2941, ST3198, ND1546,
NJ2658, TL2402, SP5332, NU0207, NY9241, SO4675

If you type these map references into an Internet OS grid map webpage, such as the ones found at:

www.streetmap.co.uk

or

www.ordnancesurvey.co.uk/oswebsite/getamap

you will see the approximate location. Try it, you might find you're living on top of a battlestone.

DATE DUE

AUG 0 2 2005	
AUG 1 7 2005	
SEP 0 3 2005	
SEP 1 5 2005	
OCT 0 4 2005	
DEC 1 9 2011	
JAN 1 2 2012	
MAY 0 9 2012	